ELLA'S SECRET FAMILY RECIPES

ELLA'S SECRET FAMILY RECIPES

KAY BELL

CAMPANILE
PUBLISHING

Published by Campanile Publishing
www.twlawless.com

Cover design by Greg Vasey: vaseydesign.com.au

Cover photograph by Simon Woodcock: www.manwithacamera.com.au

Text design and production by Golden Orb Creative: www.goldenorbcreative.com

National Library of Australia Cataloguing-in-Publication entry:

Bell, Kay, author

Ella's secret family recipes / Kay Bell

ISBN 9780994265135 (paperback)

ISBN 9780994265128 (ebook)

Cookbooks—Fiction
Cooking —Fiction
Families—History—Fiction

A823.4

To my husband Tom,
to Irene, Effie and Alex, and
to all the women from whom I descend

Prelude

I am just about to cook Sunday lunch for five of my relatives. You might think that there's nothing strange about that, except that I don't cook. Oh, and did I mention that the relatives who are coming for lunch are all dead?

Although we locked eyes for only a moment, it was enough.

Another Hollywood party crowded with the same actors wearing their latest faces, boozing and schmoozing with a smattering of indifferent industry players. Surrounded by the uber-rich and uber-beautiful, he made straight for me, his gaze deviating neither left nor right. He was the hottest new talent and I was the woman in red, and red was definitely my colour.

'So you're the infamous writer Kat Bower.' His smile was disarming. 'I'm a huge fan, you know. I follow your blog.'

'Is that so?' Cool and self-assured, I returned his smile.

'I've heard so many good things about you, but the best surprise of all is finally meeting you in person.' Eyes still fixed on mine: I felt my knees buckling.

'Oh yes? How's that?'

'Intelligent and attractive. A rare combination.'

Just as I was searching for something witty to reinforce his already glowing opinion of me, his phone began to chime Kinderkull's first hit, *Scream Till You're Heard*. It was, coincidentally, exactly the same ringtone as I had on my phone. 'Wow, you like Kinderkull too. Isn't Daley just the best singer? They're my favourite thrash metal band of all time.' I was gushing. I was thinking obscure thrash metal bands were a less obvious choice for someone as smooth as him, when he glanced at the screen and winced.

'Will you excuse me for just one moment?' He lowered his doe eyes seductively. 'I'd better answer this.'

As he moved away, I noticed his feet seemed mired to the ground and the cuffs of his pants were melting into his boots. I smiled. And then the phone began again, Daley's unmistakable voice: *...full of evil jesters spinning round my head...* His phone kept ringing. With every note, bits of him evaporated like liquid nitrogen in the midday sun. And there! Once more: *send them all away, cos I'd rather be dead...* Lord, would it never cease? I knew that if it didn't stop soon, he would be lost to me forever.

'Shut that thing up!' I yelled in frustration. 'Won't someone puh-leese answer the phone? Paul? Answer the bloody phone!' I had been ripped away from sleep, torn from my magnificent dream.

Eyes still closed tight against the first rays of daybreak, I thought if I could just keep them shut and ignore the phone, I might be able to return to my dream. *The day doesn't start—can't start—until you open your eyes, right?* Burrowing in, I felt for the warm lump that was Paul. I patted up and down his side of the bed, but felt nothing more than the tepid shadow of his body. Minus bedclothes and exposed to the cold air, it was quickly losing heat. He was already up. Which was probably why the song had finally stopped. *Never mind, he'd have called out if it was for you.* I pulled up the bedclothes in anticipation of Paul's swift return. Now, what had I been dreaming about?

I remembered. I was the woman in red—celebrated, idolised and very expensive—the woman I had always expected to become. The man of my dreams started out as my husband Paul, but then morphed into the handsome stranger. In my dream he was the perfect man—sensual, forceful, romantic. Still dozy, I was desperate to get back into that dream. But Paul was talking. His bass-baritone hacked through the dawn air like a machete. *That's it, I've lost it!* While I couldn't distinguish Paul's words, I could make out the urgency in his voice. I could hear his footsteps approaching, still talking as he advanced. *Oh God, no one phones before 8 a.m. unless...* There was no good way to end this sentence.

'Yes,' said Paul. 'She's right here.'

I wrested my eyes open. In the demilight, I guess Paul could be mistaken for a movie star. Except for the glasses. And the receding hairline. And the greying cowlick that stuck out at a right-angle.

'It's Chris,' Paul mouthed.

I groaned inwardly, or perhaps it was outwardly, since Paul frowned, silently shaking his head. I was about to ask what Chris wanted, when Paul thrust the receiver at me.

'Hi, Chris,' I croaked in my usual desultory manner.

'Hi, Kat.' Chris's voice seemed even more strangulated than mine, as if he was battling with his words.

'What's wrong? Are you okay?' Chris was always okay, always in control—wasn't he? After my dad's death he'd made himself the rock on which the family stood. Over the phone, I heard him draw breath. It seemed that the rock was in the midst of a landslide.

'I'm afraid I have some bad news.' He gulped another breath. 'Mama's in the hospital, Kat. Georgie went past last night to take her some groceries and found her lying in a pool of blood in the hallway.'

'What? Is Mama all right?'

'No, I'm afraid she's not,' he again fumbled for words. 'She had a head injury and she's got a lot of bruising. Kat, she's had a massive stroke. She's in a coma and she's not expected to make it. I think you should get here as soon as you can.'

The words slammed into me like a truck. Mama may have been old but to me she was eternal—there at the beginning, there at every milestone and still there now. I had never really considered her mortality until this moment. Now suddenly there we were: Mama's knocking at the door and death is definitely at home. As unambiguous as Chris's words were, part of me still struggled to comprehend them. Mama was in another world, shut off from this one. *In a coma.* I shook my head, trying to clear the cobwebs.

'Why didn't you tell me last night?'

'We didn't want to worry you, Kat. Our night was ruined. We didn't want to ruin yours.'

'But, she was my mother… No, I mean she *is*…she is my mother too, Chris.'

Mama was still alive and, no matter what Chris believed, doctors sometimes made mistakes, didn't they? A rush of outrageous ideas and mismatched words flooded my mind. I had to be clear. The only finality was death and, since Mama wasn't dead, nothing was final.

'You should have called me. You should have called me last night.'

'And what would you have done? What could you have done? No point in you losing a night's sleep, too. Anyhow,' which was Chris's way of ending an uncomfortable topic of conversation, 'anyhow, could you come over as soon as you can?'

'Yes, of course. Straight away. Do they know what happened?'

'We'll talk when you get here.'

My mind spiralled into a maelstrom of half-formed thoughts swirling around fully-formed fears. In my zeal to circumvent Chris's one-upmanship, I hadn't insisted that he provide me with details. I had even neglected to ask him how badly she had been injured. I should have been crying, but I wasn't. I kept drifting back to the horrible reality that Chris hadn't answered my question. Why wouldn't he tell me what had happened?

I handed the phone to Paul, who was trying to embrace me as I lay staring at the ceiling. I could have sworn it was receding into the roof space, even as I watched.

'You left your phone in the kitchen. It scared the shit out of me when it rang. I wish you'd change the ringtone—' he stopped mid-sentence. 'Are you okay, love?'

In a blur.

'Kat? Are you okay?'

'Huh?' I gazed up at his earnest face, so full of love and concern. It became apparent to me that Chris must have broken the news to Paul first. 'Yes. Yes, I think so.'

'Well, when do you want to go?'

'Soon, I guess.' I sat up and swung my legs out of bed.

'You'll feel better after a bath,' said Paul, wrapping his arms around my waist. 'I'll cook us some bacon and eggs.'

I hardly heard a word. 'I'm sure you're right.' I stood up and trudged into the bathroom. If what Chris said was true, the pale face reflected back in the mirror would soon be that of an orphan. I was alone in the world, father already gone and mother lying insensible in a hospital bed. Once she was gone, there was nothing standing between Chris and me and our own mortality. I chased away the thought. It was far too early to worry about that.

I thought of Mama as I washed my hair, so much like hers that even strangers commented. Her startling cornflower-blue eyes, her cheekbones—what was hers was mine. I thought of her as I dried my feet, exactly the same shape and size as hers. Since I was exactly like Mama on the outside, perhaps it was in our inner worlds that we differed. *Oh, I hope so!* I prayed that Daddy, who had contributed nothing to my appearance, had at least provided me with my humanity, my soul, my intellect, my essence. I squeezed my eyes shut and looked again at the image in the mirror. *Long after Mama dies, her memory will be etched all over my face.*

The smell of the bacon wafted through the house. *Thank God for Paul!* Without him I would have probably starved to death. I ringed my eyes with black liner and painted my lips with a new plumping lipstick I had bought on a whim the night before. All the make-up in the world couldn't hide the little-girl fear in my eyes. And yet there wasn't a tear for Mama.

2

By the time we arrived at Chris's house, I had already played out every possible scenario in my head. Chris's words echoed in my imagination, growing by the moment until they assumed their own personality. Badly bruised? Bleeding? Blessed with a fruitful imagination, my mind went to places that sane me would normally never visit. Mama had collapsed after being attacked by an intruder. She became disoriented after taking an overdose of pills, in a bid to end a challenging life. Logic asserted that neither scenario was even remotely likely. In the former case, the police would have surely contacted me. The latter seemed even more fantastic, since Mama never took anything stronger than iron tablets and therefore all she would have risked was a bad case of constipation.

I hardly saw the landscape flash by as we drove the almost three hours that separated us from Mama and Chris. Deep in my own world, it seemed that barely any time had elapsed at all by the time we arrived. I had accepted that Mama had lived her life and I could endure whatever happened now. Paul pulled up outside the house and, although it was already past midday, the curtains were still drawn. Georgia answered the door after the first ding of the doorbell. The dong was still hanging in the air as she rushed us over the threshold, kissing me and then Paul on each cheek. I wondered for a moment if she had been loitering about the door in anticipation of our arrival, when I noticed the bag of rubbish dangling from her right hand.

'You got here faster than I thought. I was just about to put this in the bin, but Chris is in the kitchen. Go right in.'

Paul and I exchanged a quick glance.

'Be nice!' he hissed.

'Since when have I ever been anything else?' I replied sweetly as he rolled his eyes.

Chris was sitting at the table, head in hands. He looked up at us as we approached, eyes rimmed red. I was jolted by disbelief, quickly followed by distress, at his overt grief. Chris never fell apart. Not ever.

Not even when our father had died, a decade ago. Yet here he was, blubbering like a child when I couldn't even summon a single tear.

'I'm so sorry,' I stammered. Chris looked as if he needed a hug so I embraced him as best as I could, given that he was still seated and I was hovering over him.

'You caught me at a bad moment.' He dabbed his eyes as manfully as he could.

Georgia came back into the kitchen and began to make coffee.

'Oh no,' I began, 'I don't like Greek coffee.'

'But it's tradition,' Georgia returned. 'Mama was Greek, after all.'

I flinched at the *was*, but let it pass. 'Yes, but Chris and I are only half Greek. So can I please have normal coffee instead?' Paul was throwing daggers in my direction as Georgia spun on her heel.

'Mama was Greek. Let's honour her traditions. For once!'

Was again? Last I'd heard Mama was still alive, although Georgia had already consigned her to history. I didn't need tears or ritual to honour my mother. How dared Georgia! I yearned to claim Mama as mine and Chris's alone, and point out that Mama was not and never had been Georgia's. The two of them had formed an uneasy alliance over the almost three decades since Georgia had entered our lives. They'd worked out a détente cordiale of sorts. Having married the son—the golden child—Georgia should have never expected a warm welcome. Words had formed in my brain and were tickling the tip of my tongue, when Paul pulled out a chair and pushed me into it.

'Well then.' I returned Georgia's sneer with my own. 'If it's all the same to you, I'll have tea.'

Paul nodded agreement and Georgia put the Greek coffee away with a shrug of her shoulders. She plopped a teabag into each cup and poured boiling water over them. She then positioned the cups on two saucers and set them on the table with a clatter.

'Thank you for coming,' said Chris as Paul stirred sugar into his tea and looked for the milk.

'Yes, thank you,' echoed Georgia.

The cup almost slipped from my grasp. What in the world did they mean by that? *Thank you for coming?* They were talking to me as if I were a mere guest. Had I stepped into an alternate reality in which I had forfeited my mother's kinship?

There are some people in this world who have the knack of making strangers feel like family. We all know them and some of us have the good fortune of claiming them as relatives. They open their hearts and homes, they are *take-us-as-we-are* people who don't hang onto a misplaced word or strain at a dropped crumb. But not Chris and Georgia. They could alienate with a smile. Chris and Georgia were all politeness and petty ritual. The right thing done and said at the right time, whether it was genuine or not. Only a couple so attuned to one another could use a simple expression of gratitude to render me a stranger in my brother's home.

Georgia was clueless as to Mama's true opinion of her. I sniggered as a solitary thought flashed to mind. A long time ago, Mama had given Georgia the nickname *Fantasia*, in recognition of her grand delusions, and Mama used it as code whenever she talked about her. Yet here was Georgia, sitting opposite me, sipping water as if it were French champagne and looking smug and self-satisfied. If the table hadn't been so wide, I could have knocked the smirk off her face once and for all.

'Err, she's my mother too,' I commented, exchanging knowing glances with Paul.

'Of course.'

A moment's silence to drive home the point.

'We've spoken all around Mama, but you haven't told us anything of substance. What happened to her? At the risk of upsetting you again I need to know. Exactly how bad is she?' I ventured. My questions apparently threw Chris off once more. Georgia tossed me a look of disapproval that I caught in mid-air and was about to return to her, when Paul stepped in once more.

'We've both been worried sick since we left home. When can we see her?'

I was not usually short of words, so I pondered why Paul had taken the liberty of speaking for me.

Georgia looked at her weeping husband, and the shadow of disappointment passed over her face. 'She's really not well. We only came home for a nap and a wash. We're headed back to the hospital soon. You can follow us in your car. You might not want to stay at the hospital as long as we do.'

And there it was. Love and devotion measured by minutes. It was Georgia's right jab. So fast that it would take an expert eye to spot it. She and Chris, the dutiful children, who never left Mama's bedside first. Georgia had it fixed in her mind that I was a second-rate daughter. As I saw things, all I had done was to make a life for my husband and myself a few hours down the road. I had hardly left the country! Since Georgia and Chris weren't volunteering any information, it was time to broach the thorny subject of Mama's injuries. I drew a deep breath and braced myself for a moral pounding.

'So what happened?'

'Well, Mama hasn't been all that well lately, so I've been buying her groceries and taking them to her...' I knew from painful experience that everything Georgia said had a subtext. My mind had learned to perform a simultaneous translation. I heard her say: *See how thoughtful and self-sacrificing I can be? Unlike you, Kat...* It was her version of a left jab, but it fell short of its mark.

'Oh? That's odd, she didn't mention anything to me.' I could deliver the same back at her: *Is that so, Georgia? Well, Mama and I have a great relationship. We talk to each other all the time. We just don't tell you about it.* A right undercut from me.

'Well, she wouldn't, you being so far away. She wouldn't have wanted to worry you.' *You're never around, Kat, and even if you were, you couldn't handle this.* A left hook by Georgia and another smirk. 'When Mama didn't answer the doorbell, I opened with my key and there she was! Face down in the hall.'

Chris moaned again. 'Georgia called me and I left work straight away. Oh, Mama!' He dabbed his eyes.

The time it had taken to drive over had allowed things to settle in my mind. I was about to point out that, at near eighty years of age, Mama's chances of suffering a stroke, or worse, at any moment were probably pretty good. I decided that telling him would probably be no comfort for Chris at that moment.

'Yes, but what happened? What caused all of this? Was she attacked?'

'Oh no, nothing like that. The doctor thought the injuries were probably a result of her fall.'

'It was horrible,' continued Georgia, shuddering. 'She looked awful.'

'So what was with the cloak-and-dagger? Why didn't you just say so over the phone?'

'Cloak-and-dagger? Are you serious? I don't know how you got that idea. Chris was just too distressed to tell you.'

Roundhouse to the head. In her own way, Georgia had just accused me of paranoia. It all boiled down to Chris's discomfit versus my rights as a daughter. Apparently, it was no contest—Chris's emotions came first. It was her knockout blow.

'That's it? Do you have any idea how many scenes I played out in my head, wondering how it happened and why you couldn't tell me? Thanks a bunch.'

Georgia could get stuffed for all I cared. My mind drifted to my nephew and niece.

'Do Ethan and Poppy know?'

'We caught Ethan at home between shifts at the hospital about an hour ago. He said that he'd already spoken to the neurologist and it sounded like Mama had an aneurism. He said the neurologist thought her chance of recovery was pretty slim.'

'Well, I guess he'd know.'

'We told Poppy at home this morning. They'll probably come over later tonight. Ethan just has to organise for someone to take his shift.'

Ethan and Poppy were the cement that bound me to Chris and Georgia. Ethan was the golden child's golden boy, although that epithet weighed heavily around his neck. Ethan had achieved every Greek mother's ambition. He was a fledgling doctor headed up the charts with a bullet. Poppy was my godchild as well as my niece. She was, well, Poppy.

'We'll leave for the hospital in a half hour. In the meantime,' Georgia said, collecting cups and saucers, 'you'll probably want to freshen up. I thought you might want to stay, so I've made up the spare room. It'll save you hours of driving up and back over the next few days.'

'That's very kind, but we wouldn't want to be a bother. We can stay at a hotel.'

'It's no bother, really.'

I grumbled something approximating agreement. Paul led me away in the direction of the spare room. In actuality it was Ethan's old room, kept almost exactly as it had been when he lived there as a child, right down to his dressing gown and down-at-heel slippers. The only substitution was that of a double bed for Ethan's old single. Georgia knocked on the door moments later with a bundle of towels and another pillow. Clutching the pillow, I threw myself down on the bed with a sigh.

'Do you think you could cut them a little slack?' Paul was unusually terse. 'Can't you see Chris is in pain?'

'And what about me? She's my mother, too.'

'Yes, I know. We all know. What I can't work out is whether you keep saying it to remind us or yourself of that fact.'

Huh! If I hadn't been lying face up I could have sworn that Paul had just stuck a knife in my back. What was wrong with all of them? I was a loving daughter. I was a devoted daughter. Why couldn't any of them see that?

'It's all right for you. You and Fiona have a great relationship. You know nothing about each other really, hardly ever talk, and yet it all seems to work fine. It's the same with your dad. Greek families aren't like that, even when they are only part Greek. Our roots are so tightly bound together it's impossible to tease them out.'

'Is that so? When was the last time you saw your mother?' Paul asked.

'I saw her on her birthday.'

'No, we were on holidays at the beach on her birthday.'

'Well, we must have seen her at Christmas.'

'Nup, we spent last Christmas with my sister.'

So it had been a while. 'But I call her all the time.'

'Okay. So when was the last time you two spoke?'

My brow furrowed as I struggled to remember. That couldn't be a good sign.

'Exactly!' exclaimed Paul. 'Too long ago to remember.'

'You know how difficult she can be. It's not like speaking to a normal person.'

'Yes, but she's the same Mama with Chris and Georgia,' he reasoned. 'She doesn't just save up all the good stuff for you. You have to admit that they've been good to her over the years.'

The hurt I had been carrying around was starting to chafe my shoulders and I longed to put it down. Paul must have noticed it and he lay down next to me.

'Now get yourself ready and let's go visit Mama.'

3

I have a longstanding, pathological hatred of hospitals. The only things I dislike more than hospitals are funerals, and it is unfortunate that the two are so frequently inextricably connected. For that matter, I don't much like doctors—Ethan excepted, of course—and, as far as I'm concerned, nurses, with their thick-gauge needles and arm-numbing tourniquets, are little more than their sadistic minions. So it seemed absolutely right that we should be met at the door of intensive care by the worst of the worst—a middle-aged unit manager with a seen-it-all, heard-it-all, done-it-all mien and a nurse's sense of humour.

It is a shame that they're not called hospital matrons any longer, for the woman standing in front of us, hands on hips, pen stuck in her greying hair, was nothing if not matronly. She spent the next few seconds eyeing the four of us up and down repeatedly.

'And you are?' she asked, barely parting her lips wide enough to mouth the words. She had the air of someone who had passed a sleepless night and was desperate to go home to bed. Apparently we were the only impediment to her doing so.

'We're Ella's family.'

She reminded me of someone. Perhaps it was the Marquis De Sade's lesser-known and much crueller sister. In my mind I dubbed her accordingly. Matron De Sade sniffed as if she could read my thoughts.

'See the sign?' She tapped the glass adjacent to the door. 'No more than two visitors at a time. Discuss between yourselves which of you will wait, and ring the doorbell again once you've decided.'

She was about to close the door in our expectant faces when I volunteered that no discussion was necessary, and Paul and I were going first. After all, Chris and Georgia had already visited Mama once today.

Matron De Sade humphed and snorted her impatience as Paul and I followed her to Mama's cubicle. What confronted us was unexpected. I had never seen Mama look so tiny, or the tubes emanating from every orifice look so large. A fresh-faced nurse was perched at an oversized pulpit alongside her. Mama was mottled head to toe with bruises of all shades of claret and black, but she was hardly the apparition of death that had occupied my imagination. She was still recognisably Mama. Mouth gaping, she looked asleep for all the world.

'Hi, I'm Mandy,' the girl introduced herself, her cheerfulness a glaring contrast to Matron De Sade's sourness. 'I'm caring for Ella today.'

'Kat and Paul.' Short and to the point. 'I'm Ella's daughter.'

'Well,' said Mandy studying the notes in front of her, 'Ella's a little better this afternoon. Her blood pressure's good and she's breathing on her own now. She's just got some oxygen going in through her nose and a drip in her arm.'

I felt vaguely confused. According to Chris and Georgia, Mama was just moments away from passing through heaven's gates without a return ticket.

'That's good, isn't it?'

'Yes, that's good. Her doctor should be on his rounds soon and he can tell you more. In the meantime, I have to check her obs again now.'

Paul and I traded looks and he motioned towards the door.

'It's perfectly all right for you to stay. I'll find you a chair once I'm done.'

With her easy manner and bright smile, Mandy forced me to revisit my opinion of nurses. Watching her fuss over Mama, I had to concede I might have been a little hasty to judge.

I had just settled into my chair and was conducting a meaningful, if one-sided, conversation with Mama when Ethan arrived with his parents in his wake. They had evaded Matron De Sade by using the staff access, but no sooner had they entered than she fixed all five of us in her birdlike stare, and made a beeline for Mama's cubicle. I was sure she must have felt breaches of protocol in much the same way that Darth Vader sensed disruptions in the force.

Ethan smiled at Matron De Sade as she approached, tugging at the stethoscope around his neck. It was little more than a grin, but it was evidently enough to disarm her.

'Oh, it's you, Ethan. I didn't recognise you.'

'Gillian, how are you?' Ethan had switched on his voice of authority. Matron De Sade had a given name as well as a softer side. Who'd have thought it?

'Fine, thank you,' she returned. 'You have a patient in this ward?'

'Not really. Ella is my grandmother. These are my parents and this is my aunt and my uncle.' Ethan must have anticipated Gillian's next words, and added, 'They're not staying very long. You won't even know they're here.'

Gillian snorted. 'You know the rules.' She checked her watch. 'Anyway, it's the end of my shift and I'm off home.' That said, Gillian flatfooted across the ward to her office and disappeared. Mandy smiled again and left her station to find more chairs.

'Gillian's a bitch,' said Ethan superfluously when Mandy was out of earshot. 'She made my life hell when I was an intern here. I can't wait to be a consultant and pay it all back to her.'

'Make sure you don't hold back the interest,' I added.

We sat around as Mama lay comatose. We watched Mandy take her observations and turn Mama from time to time, all the while waiting for the neurologist to arrive and impart his wisdom to us. We exchanged few words, hanging on each of Mama's breaths as if it might be her last, but the jagged line kept rolling across the monitor, regular and steady, and her oxygen saturation remained at ninety-seven per cent. Ethan left us for a while 'to do some paperwork', returning an hour later with a cardboard tray of coffees. As I surveyed Mama's impassive, furrowed face I could have sworn I detected a grimace. A flash and then it was gone. I glanced around to see if it had registered with anyone else, but no one appeared to have noticed it except me. Perhaps I had imagined it.

It was early evening by the time Mama's neurologist appeared. He blew in on a gust and blew out almost as quickly. What I understood from his visit was this: it was early days, she had made some improvement, it was too soon to know if and how far she might recover, and they would be starting a barrage of tests tomorrow if they thought her strong enough to take them. Oh, and by the way, we didn't want her resuscitated, did we? In the event she suffered another stroke, it would be far more humane to let her go. Especially at her age.

I was thunderstruck. I wanted to say that Mama was right there in front of him and for all he knew she might even be able to hear him. What did her age have to do with things? She might have been eighty but she was still our mother. Besides, there were so many centenarians these days that to reach and surpass Mama's age had almost become humdrum.

I half expected her to sit up and tell him as much herself, but she remained disappointingly silent. While I might have been able to accept her death, I don't know that I was really ready to make a decision to end her life. Was Chris? Ethan had moved just outside the cubicle, only barely within hearing distance—a tacit admission that the decision had to be ours alone. I looked over at Chris, who was studying his hands. After a while, Chris ventured that we hadn't really discussed it and couldn't give him an answer right away.

'Yes, but I'm sure your mother wouldn't want to live this way,' the neurologist added. 'What quality of life could she possibly have?'

'We need to talk it over,' Chris repeated.

'Well, don't take too long over it. You wouldn't want her to suffer unnecessarily.'

No matter how hard he tried, we wouldn't let him pressure us into making an instant decision. Even the vet had given Paul and me time to reflect when old Flossie the Labrador, named in honour of Paul's grandmother because she had the same knowing eyes, had to be put down. Surely human life was sacrosanct?

Now that the neurologist had been and gone, and with Mandy handing over to an older and far less tolerant nurse for the night, we decided it was time to call it a day. We each kissed Mama in turn and the last of all was me. Mama, who always scented herself with *Soir de Paris*. As I bent towards her I felt her faintly medicinal breath caress my face. Although her cheek was still warm and velvet soft, she no longer smelled of lipstick and powder.

I looked at Mama again, lying there oblivious to the discussion that had taken place around her, ignorant of our presence, unaware of the sunny day that was fading to night outside her window, insensible to everything. Then again, I had to admit to myself, perhaps there were worse things than dying.

4

The next morning dawned grey and desolate. Georgia and Chris had decided that, given Mama's improved state, they might as well go to work, leaving Paul and me to our own devices. Paul was ready to drive home at a moment's notice, but I convinced him that we should stay one more day and that I should go to the hospital alone. So, both of us grateful for the solitude, I set off to see Mama.

I detoured along the way for an enormous cafe latte, so hot that even through the thick, ribbed cardboard it burned my fingers as I held it. I discovered that the very thought of facing Matron De Sade again chased away my pain, so I held a mental picture of her until I made it past the nurses' station and safely into Mama's cubicle, fingers reddened but undamaged. Matron De Sade was nowhere to be seen and I was glad to find smiling Mandy by Mama's bedside.

There were things I needed to tell Mama that I could never say to her face when she was conscious. Laundry that needed airing before she died. So once Mandy had finished checking Mama over, I asked her if it would be all right if Mama and I had a private moment.

'Yes, of course. I'll be right outside. Call me if you need me.'

Mandy closed the door behind her as she left. Even though I was assured that I couldn't be overheard, I was all too aware that Mama and I were surrounded by glass. The face could not betray the words. Whatever I had to say, I would say with a smile.

'Mama,' I began, 'it's Kat. We need to talk. Well actually, I need to talk and you need to listen.'

It seemed a bit foolish, but I knew this needed to be done. This could be my only opportunity to say what I should have said to Mama long ago. She lay there impassively, oxygen lines disappearing up her nostrils, mouth still gaping open, hanging on my every word.

'We haven't always gotten along, you and I. I know I can be difficult and sometimes it was probably my fault.' I paused. It was all a bit disingenuous, since it really wasn't my fault at all. If I was going to do this, I needed to be honest about it.

'Actually Mama, that's wrong. I wasn't to blame. You were.'

I glanced back at Mandy who was having an animated conversation with one of the other nurses. I checked my expression. Still pleasant. I took a deep breath.

'Do you remember you taught me how to pray when I was a little girl? Remember how you told me that those prayers would keep me safe, and God could make everything better?' I said, hoping that Mama would come out of her coma just long enough to nod. I took her continued silence to mean acceptance.

'Well, I learned those lessons well, Mama. I prayed every single night before bed.'

I searched her face for a silent acknowledgement, but found none.

'You know what I prayed for every night when I was small? I prayed for you, Mama.'

I hesitated for a moment and took a sip of my coffee. It scorched my lips. I grimaced with pain as I continued.

'I prayed that you could be like everyone else's mother. I prayed that you wouldn't talk to people who weren't there. I prayed for God to make you better so you'd only see what the rest of us saw. What a waste of breath that was.'

I had opened up the cage, but had no idea how I was going to get the tiger back into it again. I had to let it all out now but however it was received, there was consolation in the thought that only Mama's body was present. Her mind was, well, elsewhere.

'Why did you have to be so crazy, Mama? Why did you have to hear things that no one else could hear, see things that just weren't there? Do you know you made life hell for Dad and me?

And Chris? 'Well Chris was on your side, he was always prepared to make excuses for you. The truth is, we all made excuses for you. Once, just once, I wanted you to be just like everyone else. Why couldn't you be normal?' I found my voice rising with emotion and so I stopped. Mandy still chatting. Mama still lying there.

'No one ever broke into our house, Mama. No one ever left you messages. That was you, just you, no one else.' I paused and gathered my thoughts.

'Oh, and one more thing—you know why I haven't given you that grandchild you've been longing for? Because of you.' The act of confession was proving intoxicating, and I knew I should have left it at that, but I couldn't. 'In fact, I probably owe everything that's wrong in my life to one cause—being brought up by a crazy woman like you.'

I stopped talking just as the tears began to form in the corners of my eyes. They weren't tears for her but for me. Tears for the tiny child who had to reason like an adult, because her mother couldn't. There was one final point to be made and I would be done.

'So you can go ahead and die with a clear conscience now, Mama, I've set the record straight. I can't forgive you just yet, but one day, who knows… Wherever it is that you end up, I hope you have the peace you never found here.'

I sat back in my chair, exhausted. Mandy was gazing into the room, although I was confident that I had delivered my message definitively and discreetly. I motioned to her that it was all right to return to the room, I was done. Paul and I were going home and Mama could get better or not, that was her journey, no longer mine. My face must have momentarily betrayed my thoughts. I glimpsed Mandy giving me the once over.

'Are you all right?' she asked.

'Yes, fine, thank you. It's all been a bit of a strain.' It was a half-truth and I could see that Mandy knew it.

'Since Mama seems to be stable now, we'll be going home for a while. As it might be the last time I see you, I just wanted to thank you for all that you've done for Mama. You've been great.'

'That's okay. Ella's been the model patient,' said Mandy. 'And by the way, thanks for the feedback. You see, I've only just graduated and she was my first patient. Could you tell?'

'Only in that you've been very kind and thoughtful. I guess experience knocks that out of you.'

'Oh,' Mandy responded. 'I hope not.'

I tossed Mandy a smile I hoped she would interpret as worldly-wise and enigmatic, and then departed with my cup of coffee, now finally cool enough to drink. I was leaving Mandy to her innocent delusions and Mama with the stark reality of how our lives had been. In a few hours' time I expected to be home.

5

Paul had already stripped the bed and packed up the car by the time I returned from the hospital. He had diplomatically taken my Kinderkull CD out of the car and placed it in my bag. While we shared many tastes, thrash metal music was not one of them. He called it my futile attempt to hold onto a misspent youth.

'Well?' he asked. 'How did it go with Mama?'

'Okay, I suppose. I got a few things off my chest and I gave Mama a chance to get a few things off hers. She didn't say much. In fact she didn't say anything. I had all the grievances, while she had none. See, honey, I told you I was the perfect child,' I smirked.

'Sure you were.'

We had just sat down for a cup of tea when my phone rang. *Scream, scream, scream to be heard…* Paul writhed in his seat. The display read *Simeon,* which was my phone's way of telling me that the caller was in fact my friend Simone. She called to ask after Mama's health.

I was almost as ambivalent about predictive text as I was about smartphones—I could see the benefits but I could never quite get the best out of it. I was of the opinion that the likelihood of my phone correctly anticipating the word I was tapping out on the screen was roughly equal to its intelligence. I would correct the errors one day, when nothing else was happening in the world, but until then, answering calls could continue with an element of risk and just a modicum of surprise. Since I found them quite amusing, I let the phone tell me Georgia was Geocentric and Christopher was Christmas.

Paul and I had driven barely a block when the telephone announced that Geocentric was on the line. I grappled with the thought of ignoring it but in the end, a barrowload of guilt and Paul's threat that he would toss the phone out the window if I didn't silence it, won me over.

'Hi Georgia,' I said, switching the phone onto speaker so that Paul could share her insight.

'Where are you?' she asked.

'Fine, thanks for asking,' I responded curtly. 'We've only just left your house.'

'Oh good, you haven't gone far. Can you meet me at Mama's?'

'What for?'

'I've been going through some of Mama's things and I just want to make sure you didn't want any of this stuff.'

'What? Why? I thought you were at work.'

'Well, I knew there'd be spoiled food in her fridge, so I left work early to sort it out.'

'You can safely assume that we don't want any rotten food, Georgia.'

'Yes, but there's more. Other things that shouldn't remain in an empty house.'

I looked at Paul. He rolled his eyes and began indicating a left turn.

'We'll be there in a few minutes.'

***

Georgia had left the front door ajar. She had filled the hall with two separate mounds of green plastic bags, separated by a narrow passageway, along which we crabwalked. Guided by the sound of banging cupboard doors we made our way to Mama's bedroom.

'What are you doing?' I asked. Georgia was sitting on the floor with Mama's clothes strewn all about her.

'Georgia? What are you doing?' I repeated.

'Oh hi, Kat. I told you I came by to clean out the fridge. Then I began to realise that that even if Mama gets better, she'll probably never be able to live here again. So I thought I'd start sorting things out.'

'Without telling me? Why? There'll be plenty of time for all that later. For mercy's sake, Georgia, Mama's not dead yet.'

'Yes, but she can never live here alone again,' she said. 'And since you're so far away, we'll have to take care of this house as well as our own. We can't leave Mama's valuables here to be stolen.'

I looked about us. Mama's house was filled with furniture too new to be classified as antique and too old to be valuable and I told Georgia as much. Everything else was so well hidden that I had often thought we'd probably need to demolish the house to locate Mama's buried treasure.

'Well, we shouldn't leave her jewellery in an empty house.'

The truth. Finally.

'Oh, I see.' Georgia glared but remained silent. I continued. 'Exactly what did you propose to do with Mama's jewellery?'

'I was going to take it home. For safekeeping.'

Safekeeping? Georgia had no idea where Mama hid it. So that's why she phoned me. *She's called me in to find it for her.*

'Didn't Mama tell you that she kept her jewellery in a safe deposit box at the bank? Surely you knew?' I lied. 'I don't know where Mama keeps the key but I have a copy at home. I didn't think to bring it with us.' Georgia looked crestfallen as Paul flashed a wink at me behind her back. 'So, I'll help you put back Mama's clothes. Or you can get along home and we'll finish tidying this mess and lock up.'

'Chris is coming around soon to help. Maybe we should wait until he gets here.'

I watched all hope of returning home early dissipate into thin air.

'Good idea,' I lied again. 'Let's do that, shall we?'

I was fighting out of a corner. I hoped I had said enough to put her off the scent, although, quite frankly, Georgia didn't look convinced. I wondered if Chris knew what she was up to and if he'd okayed his wife's scavenger hunt. He and I had always agreed that I was going to inherit Mama's jewellery. If it found its way into Georgia's house, I doubted it would ever find its way out again.

Paul helped Georgia carry the bags of trash outside while I checked the second pile that Georgia had deemed worthy to donate to charity. Along with a load of Mama's knick-knacks were my old books, which I had always intended to take home with me but just hadn't got around to. I could feel the swell of rage rising with every bag I opened. By the time Chris arrived, there was a veritable tsunami of fury within me.

'Did you know about this?' I demanded before he had landed both feet inside the door.

'What?' he blinked at Georgia and then at me.

'All this?' I waved my arm around.

'I knew Georgia wanted to come over and clean up, if that's what you mean.'

Oh, I'll say she wanted to clean up. 'That's not really what I meant, Chris. Did you agree to Georgia making the decision as to which of Mama's things to donate, which to throw out and which she should keep?'

Chris glanced at Georgia quizzically. 'Yes, of course.'

I knew he'd lied to cover his wife. He was pathetic.

'Well then. I have a thing or two to say,' I began. The tidal wave was about to meet the shore.

'First, and most importantly, MAMA IS NOT DEAD!' I paused for dramatic effect as the first breaker hit.

'If and when she does die, it is up to you and me, Chris—just you and me—to go through Mama's things and decide what goes where. In case you haven't heard, Mama has only one son and one daughter. SHE IS NOT GEORGIA'S MOTHER.'

It was said. Chris and I rarely crossed swords and from the look on his face I could tell that neither of us had relished the experience, but enough was enough. I desperately wanted to go home, but I knew that Georgia would return to pick over the bones the moment I left. Paul and I would have to wait until they left and then I was having new locks fitted.

Georgia turned a curious shade of plum as Chris measured his words.

'I can see you're angry, Kat, but I'm sure Georgia was just trying to be helpful. She may not be Mama's biological daughter but she is the mother of Mama's grandchildren, after all.'

I had wondered how long it would take for Chris to bring Ethan and Poppy out of his arsenal. *Oh yes, you are a master debater, Chris.* Georgia had given Mama grandchildren and I hadn't. How dare he patronise me! *He wants to rumble, I can match him word for word. I was the mistress of psychological doubletalk.*

'Clearly I've touched a raw nerve, Chris, I can see that. But Georgia can be most helpful by going home right now and leaving me to sort out what's what,' I said.

Chris's phone began to chime *Girls Just Wanna Have Fun* as I spoke. I doubted it was his choice of ringtone.

'Yes, hello?' I marvelled at how smoothly he exchanged condescending for courteous without missing a solitary beat. 'Oh, okay. We'll come now.'

'Was that the hospital?' I guessed. 'Is she…is she gone?'

Chris was too stunned to speak. Georgia's eyes darted from her husband to me and back again. I could have sworn she looked elated.

'No,' he stammered. 'She's out of her coma. Mama's just woken up.'

6

A single thought kept churning around in my mind—our altercation that morning must have been Mama's wakeup call. It couldn't have been such a bad thing, could it?

'What exactly did you say to your mother?' asked Paul once we were in our car and far away from Chris and Georgia.

'Oh, you know. The usual mother–daughter discussion. I called her a crazy paranoid schizophrenic and she said nothing. I guess my words must have resonated with her on some level.'

'That, or she's woken up just to exercise her right of reply,' said Paul.

'Do you think so?' If she had I could be in trouble.

'She won't remember a thing. Anyway, you couldn't have said anything that bad.'

I blessed Paul's naiveté.

Gnawing guilt was gathering in my bowels like a storm. In the hospital elevator it was a distant rumble. Approaching the corridor outside ICU, the clouds were gathering and by the time I made it to Mama's ward, it became a full-on cataclysm. Only in the washroom would I be able to find relief. So while the others made their way to Mama's bedside, I was dashing to the toilet on the other side of the hall. When I returned, I found Georgia stroking Mama's hand as Chris looked on. Paul had saved me a spot adjacent to Mama's head. Mama's eyes followed me as I assumed my position.

'How are you feeling today?' asked Georgia, enunciating every syllable. She had tossed the words out directionless, but I was sure they weren't meant for me.

Mama did not reply. She tried to pull her hand away, which Georgia clung to leech-like until it became a farcical tug-of-war. She turned her head towards me and grunted.

'Mama?' I whispered.

Mama finally worked her hand free and caressed my face before Georgia could dive across and reclaim it. She grunted again softly and I realised that she was alert but had not yet regained her speech.

I wiped away a tear that spilled out of her right eye, carefully avoiding the bruises that surrounded it, softened by this display of emotion.

'Oh, Mama,' I murmured. 'It's all right now.'

The nurse that had replaced Mandy for the afternoon commented that Mama was paralysed on that side and her eye was likely to water from time to time. Perhaps I had read way too much into it.

'She's had a left-sided stroke which has affected her speech,' the nurse continued matter-of-factly. She glanced at the notes in Mama's file. 'And she has right-sided hemiplegia.'

'Left-sided? Right-sided?' repeated Georgia.

'Yes. Damage to the left side of the brain affects the right side of the body and vice versa. She may recover her speech and sensation. Or it may be gone forever,' she said.

Mama sighed as the nurse spoke and then fell silent. As Georgia searched for conversation to fill the void, Mama's grunts became louder and more insistent, and always directed at me.

'What, Mama? What is it?' asked Chris.

Mama rolled her eyes in frustration.

'Perhaps she could write?' Paul suggested.

'But Mama's right-handed,' said Georgia.

'She could still try. Would you mind...' he turned to the nurse.

The nurse hunted down a spare clipboard, attached a piece of paper to it and propped it on a pillow under Mama's left hand. She tried to place a pencil between her fingers, but it slipped repeatedly from her grasp. Try as she might, Mama couldn't grip the pencil. Eventually, she slid down the bed in frustrated resignation. She stayed in that position, her eyes fixed on me, until she fell asleep.

'Is she...' Chris began, 'is she?'

'Back in a coma? Oh no,' said Mama's nurse. 'She's just exhausted. All the emotion. Just having you all here takes it out of them. She's been napping and waking since she came out of the coma.'

Poppy and Ethan arrived barely a minute after Mama dozed off. Although there was now three times the permitted number of visitors in Mama's cubicle, Matron De Sade remained seated in her office. She had been monitoring our comings and goings like a hawk, but had evidently decided that discretion was the better option. Ethan remarked that he almost wished she would take us on, just so that he could have the pleasure of returning Matron De Sade to her rightful place.

We took advantage of Mama's snooze to have a bite to eat and to mull over what had just happened. Paul and I descended the stairs to the cafeteria separately from the others, who had taken the elevator.

'I think you can be pretty sure that whatever you said to her has had an effect. She's busting to say something to you.'

'Hmm. Seems so.'

We caught up with the rest of the family seated at a table meant for four. In the time it had taken us to descend, they had fashioned a lazy Susan out of a tray and filled it with things to eat and drink. I thought I heard Georgia moan as we approached but, in her world, my status as her daughter's godmother made it impossible for her to exclude me.

I glanced around as we took chairs from a neighbouring table and sat down. All eyes rested on my godchild. Straight men and lesbians wanted to possess her, and gays and women wanted to be her. Poppy glowed in ochre, long blonde hair snaking down her back in a tight ponytail. She was sweetly ignorant that she had caught everyone's attention.

'You could snare yourself a nice doctor here,' I quipped, looking about.

'Hey, Kat,' she responded, lifting up her glorious green eyes.

Poppy was as exquisite as she was scatty. It always amazed me that Chris and Georgia had managed to produce two such very different but equally beautiful offspring.

'She'd never see him,' observed Ethan. 'Her husband, I mean. If he was a doctor.'

'Who cares, as long as he's rich,' said Georgia, as Ethan grimaced and Poppy blushed. Ethan used that as his cue to gobble the remainder of his sandwich and drift off to work, leaving the five of us scratching awkwardly for small talk. It took little time before Poppy also made a vague excuse before leaving Paul and me alone with her parents. To their credit, Chris and Georgia waited while we finished our meal in silence.

Mama was awake again when the four of us returned. The clipboard had been cast aside and was tangled up in her blanket. She was sipping water through a plastic straw. I wiped the dribble that escaped from the side of her mouth and her eyes softened. We sat around her silently until Georgia breached the peace by vocalising her thoughts on Mama's return to the world.

'It's a shame we don't have the room for Mama at our house,' said Georgia. 'Otherwise she could live with us.'

'She could have Ethan's old room,' I suggested. Ethan had long moved on, although Georgia had not.

'That would have worked if the house was on a single level. It could be dangerous for her,' she said. As the nurse slipped outside, she added, 'Now that Mama's awake, I think we should ask her about her jewellery, don't you, Kat?'

The woman had a mind like a steel trap. 'Why don't we do that?' I agreed.

'Mama,' Georgia shouted at her in an effort to make herself easily understood. 'I was going to take your jewellery out of the house and put it in mine for safekeeping.'

'Yes,' I interjected serenely. The juxtaposition was flawless. 'But then I explained to Georgia that you had already moved it all to the bank.'

Mama glared at Georgia and gesticulated. She was pointing to the wedding ring still on her finger and then at me.

'Not your ring, Mama,' she said. 'Everything else.'

Mama screeched and moaned at Georgia. She was stabbing the air furiously with her left index finger in my direction.

'I don't understand what you're trying to say,' she continued. 'Are you saying that Kat's taken your jewels?'

Mama shook her head. She groaned in frustration as the nurse returned to the cubicle.

'What's happening here? Could you please be quiet? Ella's clearly distressed and I'm sorry, but you'll all have to go.'

At this, Mama shook her head frantically and motioned once more to her ring and then to me. Georgia shrugged her shoulders dismissively and picked up her handbag. The rest of us watched as Mama repeated the motion.

'Mama, do you want Kat to have your jewellery?' asked Chris as Georgia glared.

Mama nodded and settled back into the bed. Her face creased into a lopsided smile.

'Well then, that's that,' he said. As Georgia opened her mouth to protest, Chris added, 'Enough!'

I raised an eyebrow in Paul's direction, delighting in the fact that he was wrong. Chris could find his balls even without a map and a flashlight. We kissed Mama goodbye and made preparations to leave as the nurse hurried us along. I straightened Mama's sheets, untangled the clipboard and put it on her bedside table. As I placed it down I noticed a childish scribble, faint and poorly formed but still legible. I unclipped the sheet of paper, folded it and placed it in my pocket as Mama watched me, nodding gently. When we were back in our car, simply the two of us, I unfolded the paper and read it. There were just three words running in a jagged line across the page. The three words read:

Sorry Kat Book.

7

Paul and I decided to postpone our return home for another couple of days until we knew exactly how Mama was going to fare. I was prepared to bear Georgia and Chris's hospitality a little longer and they were prepared to bear the burden of offering it. That was the price of family.

One of the perks of being a freelance writer married to a freelance IT consultant was that we could be anywhere we needed to be at a moment's notice. No kids, one dog. We were married but we kept our own, separate identities. I maintained that it was a joint decision to liberate ourselves in that way, although Paul did not agree entirely.

If it were up to Paul, first of all, we would share the same surname. That proved to be quite contentious, but if he'd only given it enough consideration, I'm sure he would have understood. Paul's surname had been the reason why I had considered refusing his marriage proposal. Honestly, I didn't think Paul Cage was too bad a combination, but Kat Cage was nothing short of abysmal. I told him that if he insisted that I change my name to his, it would be a deal breaker. He begrudgingly acquiesced to me retaining Bower.

Second in Paul's grand plan would have been a houseful of babies. 'Paul' and 'motherly' may have belonged in the same sentence, but as far as I was concerned the pitter-patter of little paws was more than sufficient to satisfy any maternal yearnings. Our dog had become our *ersatz-child*. Therefore, a simple message to my friend Simone to please keep feeding Boz Scraggs was all we needed to change our plans. I couldn't have done that with a baby and not have had a social worker involved.

We weren't tied to the nine to five, and we were the envy of all our married-with-children, tied-to-the-desk friends. It could and it should have given us the jetsetting lifestyle we had imagined when we abandoned our regular careers, but truthfully? Sadly it didn't. Although our jobs sounded far more alluring than the income they generated, we still had the advantage of being able to work equally well from anywhere in the world. We just didn't have the money to go anywhere very glamorous. One day, all that was going to change.

It wasn't as if I wasn't grateful for everything we had—our situation wasn't breadline and by most measures we were pretty comfortable. Food—plenty, bills—paid, debts—covered. It was only poverty relative to our friends' prosperity. It wasn't a result of our indolence, and neither were we trying to make it a living example of our political opinions, it was just that we weren't very good at asking people for money. In short, Paul and I were suckers. Simone said it was a reflection of the fact that we didn't value ourselves enough, so we never set our prices high enough. I told her that I couldn't speak for Paul, but magazine and newspaper publishers were, in my experience, very wealthy people who didn't get that way by paying their writers well. She said everything was negotiable.

While Simone and I debated this and so many other things at length, I watched from below as she leapt up the rungs of success. Sometimes, it felt like I held the ladder still for her but I was happy to do it. I genuinely missed her company right now. Georgia was hostile. Chris was emotional. Paul was my friend and husband, always was, always would be, but Simone had nothing invested in sweetening the bitter truth. I needed some good, unadulterated advice right about now. I pored over the piece of paper until late into the night, after Paul had gone to bed and was well on his way to puffing himself into deep sleep. I stared at it until the words transfigured themselves into weird shapes, but the meaning behind them continued to escape me.

I understood what Mama meant when she wrote *sorry*, but I wasn't sure whether my name was associated with that word or the word *book*. What book did she mean? What book did she want me to have? Or to write? Did Mama's message of regret signify that she had heard and understood everything I had said the day before at the hospital? Simone had insight born of forced introspection. She was a gay, Jewish lawyer who always demanded a bit more than her clients could afford and always got paid. But I got the benefit of her opinion for free.

There were three of us in my tight little company: Simone, Nicole and Kat. Nothing and no one separated us. Nicole was the late bloomer, the child-woman who clung to her parents long after the rest of us had moved on to a world of shoddy furniture and cheap housing, shared with indifferent housemates with bad habits. I recalled watching TV once, as one of my early housemates (male) picked the scabs off his knees and deposited them into his mouth, as if they were salted peanuts. It was at that moment that I understood the wisdom of staying home, where the pillowcases and sheets came in sets, and always found their way into a washing machine well before they turned grey. And where no one ever farted publicly and then rated their farts by decibels multiplied by the length of time taken for the odour to infiltrate the far end of the room. This was the life that Paul saved me from a long, long time ago, and the one Nicole had avoided altogether simply by having the good sense to stay put.

I was lying in bed, cosy after an early morning game we called Dawnbusters, in which Paul thrust his erect penis in my direction while I pretended to snore, in an effort to claw back a few more minutes of sleep. Clearly, he found me equally as arousing in black negligee and make-up as I was in tatty PJ's, with foul bed-breath and duster-head tossed in for good measure, buzz-sawing into his left ear. As punishment for waking me up with his boner—in the event that I complied—he got to sleep on the wet patch afterwards. Meanwhile, desperate for coffee, I listened for the signs of life in the kitchen that signalled the start of Chris and Georgia Bower's day. Morning began at last with the clatter of last night's dishes being put away.

With my brother and sister-in-law finally afoot, I made coffee for Paul and me in the French press, while Georgia cooked Greek coffee on the stove. After trading desultory good mornings, we exchanged only silence punctuated by the chinking of crockery and the fizzing of the Greek coffee as it reached the boil. Chris and Georgia were old school. Greek coffee and a rusk for breakfast. That's it. While Georgia remained rake thin on this regime, Chris ate his real breakfast a half-hour after getting to work and then complained about his slow metabolism.

Paul got up when the ping of the microwave announced that the milk for our cafe lattes had reached optimal warmth. He was cheerful and teasing, sure signs of a man who had got a bit before breakfast. Fortunately, Chris and Georgia were too self-absorbed to care.

I was too tired from having gone to bed too late and having been woken up too early, to participate in Paul's shenanigans.

'What are we doing today?' asked Paul brightly as I stared daggers at him.

I poured his coffee and slammed the cup down, repeated seconds later with my own. What did he mean *we*? By saying *we*, he could easily be misinterpreted as including everyone present. *Families don't have to hunt in packs, Paul.* A quick pop into the hospital to see Mama and we could claim a day full of city delights as our own. I was holding onto this thought when the phone rang and then I found myself holding my breath. If calls before eight always signalled bad news, what, then, did calls before seven signify? Chris moved faster than he had in the last thirty years, and answered before the second ring.

'Yes, this is he,' he said as we all scrutinised his face for clues. He followed this up immediately with, 'Oh. When? Yes. I understand. Thank you. Of course. Right away. Goodbye,' each spaced a few seconds apart.

He hung up and crumpled into his chair. Even without asking what the call had been about, his appearance betrayed him and we all knew. I, strangely, had expected to sense a disturbance in the fabric of the universe when Mama died, but I had felt nothing out of the ordinary. Chris's words, although rendered utterly redundant by his mien, verified all our fears.

'Mama's dead. She had another stroke early this morning and this time there was nothing they could do. They rang to say she's only just passed away.'

Chris sat with his head in his hands, sobs rippling across his body. Georgia sat down next to him, patting his back and saying, 'It's better for her, don't you see? She's had a good life.'

My eyes shifted to Paul, who was studying me in the way a scientist might observe his test-subject.

'You okay, babe?'

'Yes. Ah ha.'

The strange thing was, I still didn't feel even close to crying. Paul led me by the hand back into our bedroom, opened my bag and lay out clothes for me to wear. He had never done that before. The normal me would have judged him crazy for doing that, but this me ignored the clash of colours and fabrics, and obediently dressed myself in his choices.

Suddenly the piece of paper Mama had written out for me attained the importance of a priceless relic and I was frantic to find it. Where had I put it after my nocturnal analysis? Not in my bag. Not on the bedside table. Not on the floor. Then I remembered. I dug it out of my jeans pocket, smoothed it out and pressed it flat between the pages of Ethan's old bible. The last message from my mother was a cryptic *Sorry Kat Book*. There'd be no more greeting cards with Mama's spider-web writing wishing her beloved daughter a happy anything. This solitary piece of paper would have to last me a lifetime.

And yet there were still no tears.

8

Georgia drove us all one last time to the hospital in her car. Of the four of us, she was the only one who repeatedly declared herself brokenhearted that Mama had died, and yet she was also the only one who had the presence of mind to be able to drive. Chris was inconsolable in fits and bursts. He seesawed from gut-wrenching sobbing to quiet reminiscing while I sat soberly and silently, which Paul claimed was a sure sign that something was very wrong. Paul probably could have driven us, except that he was preoccupied that moment with monitoring my every reaction.

Mama was lying in her bed just as we had left her the night before. She might have been in a coma, except all the tubes had been removed and the screens and alarms disconnected. There was no nurse at her bedside. Chris took her hand and held it to his lips in silent prayer. Georgia kissed her forehead, but I stayed by her feet.

'God rest her soul,' I said, crossing myself in the Orthodox manner, exactly as she had taught me to do some three-plus decades ago. I knew she'd be cold and I didn't want to kiss her. I wanted to hold onto the memory of a warm, living being, not this hideous shell, still battered and bruised from the misery of her final days.

'Life was pretty hard on Mama,' I said to no one in particular as Chris began to weep again. With a sweep of his hand, Paul made it clear to me that he'd had enough and he needed to leave.

'We'll make our own way home, Chris. We'll see you later on.'

I took one last look at Mama, knowing I probably wouldn't have another chance.

'Let's go,' I said to Paul. 'Bye bye, Mama.'

I blew her a kiss and waved. I wanted to tell her I loved her as it seemed the right thing to say in a moment such as this, but the words stuck fast in my throat. We never did have that chat about our stance on resuscitation, Chris and I, and I was very glad we hadn't. This way the decision had been taken away from us. Chris would have undoubtedly viewed whatever decision we would have made as the wrong one. I could offer him no fitting words of consolation, so we said nothing and left him to his mourning. We wandered about the city for a while, before taking a cab back to Chris and Georgia's. My head was cleared of the clutter that accompanied my own grief, and I was prepared for what I knew lay ahead.

When we got back to the house, we were surprised to find that not only had they had beaten us back by a good hour and a half but Georgia was already baking a tray of aniseed rusks.

'You're back in the nick of time. I've made some of Mama's *paximadia*,' she said, and sensing my confusion she added, 'Aniseed rusks, Kat. Chris is with the undertaker in the living room, and I was just about to make coffee.'

Things were moving much faster than I had anticipated. I was considering asking Georgia if I could make myself tea instead, but thought better of it. Georgia had already begun making Greek coffee in what seemed to me to be commercial quantities.

'We'll have *Greek* coffee,' Paul said resolutely as I opened my mouth to protest.

'Any chance of milk and sugar?' I added, fully knowing the answer would be no.

Georgia had pulled out her biggest long-handled pot from the cupboard together with an enormous jar of Greek coffee, ground so fine that it resembled topsoil. To my unrefined palate, it also tasted like topsoil. She heaped teaspoon after teaspoon of the powder on top of cold water and set the *briki* on the stovetop to boil. No sugar, in deference to the tradition of serving bitter coffee during mourning. As the froth rose up the sides, she lifted the *briki* from the flame and poured the contents into demitasse cups. She divided the treasured foam, the *kaimaki*, which had formed over the liquid, equally between them.

I watched Georgia perform the coffee ritual in silence, wondering how I would drink it without gagging.

'Why don't you go inside? I'll bring the coffee in a minute.'

We left Georgia stacking the cups and saucers onto a tray, and joined Chris.

'Oh, hello,' said Chris as we entered. He wore sunglasses to mask his red-rimmed eyes. 'I've called in Mr Manolis to organise Mama's funeral. She would have wanted a traditional Greek funeral.'

'Yes,' I acknowledged, 'and regrettably neither Chris nor I is a traditional Greek. We're only half-Greek really. So, you see, the both of us together would make up a whole traditional Greek. But not each of us individually.'

Georgia entered just in time to catch my babbling and looked at me as if I had completely lost my mind. Good Greek wife that she was, she distributed the cups and sat down next to her husband. I looked at the brown sludge that had settled in my cup and wondered how I was going to get to the bottom of it. My salvation came in the form of rusks she had already baked, sitting on a nearby plate and which, dunked and eaten, might mask the taste. Georgia had withheld some of the sugar so they weren't particularly sweet, but they packed enough aniseed–sesame flavour to make pretty much anything palatable.

I was still struggling with the first gritty sip when Chris spoke again.

'The service will be at the Church of the Assumption at nine-thirty on Thursday.'

'Isn't that a bit too early?' Georgia remarked.

I took another bite of my coffee-soaked rusk and stared down Georgia. She lowered her eyes and fiddled with her napkin.

'The perfect time,' Mr Manolis interjected. 'Let's see. Funeral—one hour; burial—one hour, then it's lunch for everyone starting midday and all over by mid-afternoon.'

Mr Manolis's pragmatic approach, coupled with the reality of it all being over by mid-afternoon Thursday, was more than Chris could bear. Georgia's face projected a blend of disappointment and humiliation as he raised his sunglasses to wipe his eyes. I was certain that any Spartan woman worth her salt would have pushed him over the nearest cliff right about then. Once he had regained his composure, Chris and I signed a mountain of papers ensuring that Mama would be properly dispatched according to tradition and end up as fertiliser for roses at the Greener Pastures Cemetery, or some such. I celebrated the act by holding my breath and taking my final sip of coffee. All gone. Thank God!

Mr Manolis tugged at his goatee and stood up. I was sure he was a hit with the Greek widows, all five feet, four inches of him. To me, he appeared half car salesman, half cultural attaché. It was clear he took himself and his job very seriously. From his sober black pinstriped suit to his impeccably groomed white pompadour he screamed *mourning*. In the proper Greek manner, of course.

'I will leave you this booklet on the traditions surrounding Greek funerals,' he said. 'Make certain you all read it.'

He handed it to Georgia who put it down immediately, muttering, 'I don't need it. I already know.'

Of course she did. Trust Georgia to have embraced the Greek art of mourning so completely and so literally.

Later that evening, Paul announced the funeral details for me on Facebook. Not that I expected any of our friends to come, and that was fine with me. It was going to be an arduous time and I needed the support, even from a distance and even via the internet. I wouldn't wish a traditional Greek funeral on anybody. In an effort to embrace my enemy, I opened Mr Manolis's book and began to read.

'Honey,' I said to Paul as we lay in bed. 'You have no idea how well Greeks do death.'

'What do you mean?'

'It's a bit like a dance routine. You get one foot out of line and the whole thing collapses. It's so ritualised it's ridiculous, what with the nightly coffin-side prayers, the special words you have to say to one another, the foods you must serve to the mourners and the other foods you must not. And, best of all, it's all done with the dead person watching it happen from an open casket.'

'Aren't you glad you're Greek?'

'Half-Greek. And I spent the whole of my life nurturing my non-Greek, thank you very much. I like the way normal people do death. A quick funeral service followed by cremation, then a booze-up at the wake, where there's plenty to drink but hardly anything to eat. After which, the relatives trade blows over the will. Now that's how to bury the dead.'

'No, it's not,' Paul disagreed. 'It's better to get it all out. Make it incredibly special and pay the dead their dues. It helps with the healing.'

'Yeah, I guess that's right, provided you really care about the deceased. They should market it as "cathartic bereavement". Get social workers onto it and they'll make a fortune.'

Paul didn't laugh.

'Even now you're very down on your mother,' he said.

'No, I'm not. We made amends and she's dead. Book closed.'

'Face facts, Kat. You are half your mother. By the looks of you, you're way more, besides. You can't make the Greek in you go away by pretending it was never there.'

'I don't want it to go away. I just don't connect with my inner-Greek. Chris did, but I didn't. He was the perfect son. He became an accountant, married a Greek girl, worked hard in a job he still loathes, bought a house, had two gorgeous children and took care of his mama until she died. He is just as angry with her as I am. He just shows it in a different way. He's also older than me by nearly a decade, don't forget. His perspective is a bit different.'

'And you? Remember when we had our DNA tested to find out where our ancestors came from and whose chromosomes we each inherited?'

'Yes,' I said hesitantly.

'Well, you never even bothered to find out the results. What a waste of money that was.'

'But I know where I come from. Greek, Greek, Greek, Greek, Greek on Mama's side. English, English, English, English, English on Dad's. *Finito.*'

'Ugh. You're impossible.'

'Yup, I am. I inherited that from my mother.'

Overnight, I developed a hint of remorse over our argument. I woke up early, ready to make amends, but Paul was already up and I could hear him talking to Chris in the kitchen. Paul's computer was sitting on a tower of old chemistry books, piled on top of Ethan's desk. Paul kept himself perennially logged on and I could swear I saw his computer blink at me. He was right: he had spent all that money having both of us tested as a special anniversary present and I had never looked at the results. To me it was like having your cholesterol tested—if you never did it then you could never have high cholesterol.

I logged myself on and went straight to my emails. Somewhere among my hundred and sixty-four unread emails was one from *AncestorFinder DNA*. It took a few minutes to locate it, but there it was, complete with its web link, *where you can discover exactly what you are made of!* If only it were that simple!

Here goes nothing! I clicked on the link and in a matter of seconds I was directed to my own personal page. *Welcome, Kat Bower,* it said, right next to a dancing double helix. I clicked on the drop-down menu and simultaneously sucked half the air in the room into my lungs and held it there. *My autosomal DNA—Where do I come from?* I hoped it would prove more enlightening than my mother's advice on that same subject. One more click, and there it was.

What the...? I steadied myself on the desk. This had to be a mistake. I logged out and repeated steps one to five. The same result again. As if to drive it home, this time a little map of the world was replicated under the bar graph that declared my results. The country of my ancestors' origin glowed red. I looked at it again in a struggle to comprehend exactly what I was reading.

You are one hundred per cent Middle Eastern Jewish (plus or minus 0.01 error).

9

It took me a good ten minutes to recover from the initial shock. Me? Middle Eastern? Jewish? How the hell did they figure that out? I was an amalgam of Mama and Dad, wasn't I? And as far as I was aware, neither of them was remotely Middle Eastern or Jewish. Or maybe they were because, maybe, I was adopted. Maybe I wasn't related to Mama and Dad at all! I felt relief for the moment it took to turn that thought over in my mind, but a quick glance in the mirror dispelled the theory. No doubt about it, I was one hundred per cent mother on the outside and, with a bit of luck, one hundred per cent father on the inside. Plus or minus an error of 0.01 per cent.

It was true that I had always loved bagels and lox, Joan Rivers and Jackie Mason, even as a little girl. Perhaps it was no coincidence that my very first boyfriend had been Jewish—although that ended badly because I wasn't. Who knew? If only ancestral DNA testing had been around twenty-three years ago, I might have been Mrs Kat Hertzel. Were these all signs? Maybe Mama was adopted? Dad was way too HP Sauce and Branston Pickle to have ever been anything but British.

Just then Paul returned.

'Oh,' he said. 'You're up.'

'Yes and you're going to be very proud of me.'

'And how so?'

'I've been on the internet. I went on *AncestorFinder*...'

'Well, good for you.' It was clear that, for Paul at least, it was still a sore point.

'Don't be like that. Please?'

'Well?'

'You'll never guess. Not in a million years.' I turned the computer around so Paul could read it from where he stood. I watched his mouth fall open while he read.

'I know,' I said, anticipating his reaction.

'Well, that explains a lot,' he said. 'Ever known the Middle East to be at peace? You were born fighting with yourself.'

'I think they probably got it wrong,' I remarked. 'Mixed my sample up with someone else's.'

'I think they did too. Never mind, let's put it away for now. There's a lot to be done today and Chris could do with a little of your detachment.'

I wasn't sure if Paul was taking a swipe at me, but I nodded anyway. Today was not the day for working out exactly who I was. Or for fighting with Paul.

That afternoon, I received flowers from Simone and Nicole. Along with the bouquets Chris and Georgia had already received, their house adopted the appearance of a high-end florist. It was a florist with an open door and a café attached, as a steady stream of Mama's friends, their friends and our combined relatives dropped in to pass on their condolences. Ethan and Poppy had freed themselves of all commitment until Thursday, although for Poppy, I never worked out quite what those commitments were.

I lent a hand making the coffee and serving the mourners *Metaxa* brandy and Cypriot *Comandaria* wine in tiny thimble-shaped glasses. Georgia's face was etched with exhaustion and she complained of not having had time to prepare the boiled wheat for Mama's funeral.

'Can't we buy it?' I asked.

'No. Besides, I've got everything I need to make it. I just haven't had a break long enough to start.'

'I could do it for you,' I offered. It never occurred to me that she'd ever agree to me messing up her kitchen.

'I wouldn't normally ask, and I know you hate to cook, but I'd be grateful if you would. The recipe's on the counter. I got the recipe out of a book when I was at Mama's. Weird thing was, she had a family recipe book with nothing in it at all. Except for the rusks and the boiled wheat recipe, that is.'

I frowned.

'Mama often made things from her recipe book, as I recall. She had to scale down the proportions of course. No one makes cakes calling for a dozen eggs and serving tens of people these days.'

'Well, that must be another book. These were the only recipes in the one I saw. Every other page was completely blank.'

'Okay,' I said doubtfully. 'I'll give it a go. No promises.'

'It's simple. You can't stuff it up.'

It was so busy that I forgot precisely why we were there and Chris forgot to cry. By the time Thursday rolled by, I had to practise looking suitably sad, and even Chris's capacity to grieve had begun to wane. One more day to be endured and we could all continue our lives. Home to Boz Scraggs the Wonderdog, who could find you no matter where you were. Back to blogging about my life as a freelance writer.

The disruption to our lives had been complete. Privacy was non-existent, and even our meals were taken whenever someone had the foresight to go and buy something hot, salty and fast. By mid-afternoon Wednesday, I suggested Chris hide his car once he got home with our lunch of hamburgers and fries, and that we lock the door. We were finally seated together around the table, so hungry and tired that even Poppy inhaled her mini burger in two mouthfuls.

'The Greek guy called you this morning,' said Poppy between bites. 'We need to take him an outfit for Granny Ella to wear.'

Georgia flashed a look at me and quickly volunteered to go. 'I thought Mama would be going to a nursing home to convalesce, so I packed a lot of her clothes up already. I guess I really should go.'

Last I remembered, Mama's clothes were strewn around her bed-room and Georgia was sitting in the middle, scratching about like a hen.

'No, Georgia, your place is in your home,' I countered. 'I'll go with Paul. We'll be back before you notice we've gone.'

'But you won't know where to find Mama's clothes…'

'I think I can work it out.'

Grateful for us to be alone, Paul was the first to speak.

'I'll drive back home straight after the funeral but I think you may have to stay here and keep an eye on things.'

'You don't trust them either?'

'I think Chris's as honest as the day is long. Georgia, well, I'm not so sure.'

'We have to find Mama's valuables before Georgia has a chance to get to them,' I added. 'You know, the more time I spend with her the less I like that woman. I almost feel sorry for Chris and the kids.'

'Your brother's glued to his choices. You know he hates change and he's going to stick by her, no matter what.'

'I know.' I paused for a moment. 'Maybe we should call a lock-smith while we're down there? That way she won't be able to come and go as she pleases.'

'Your choice, Kat, but it mightn't be a bad idea.'

Paul stayed in the car while I went into Mama's house to find an outfit to bury her in. The house had Georgia's tag written all over it. It was clear that she'd been back without us and this time she had taken an industrial waste bin. The drawers in the kitchen had been pulled out and left on the floor.

'No, Georgia,' I muttered to myself, 'Mama didn't keep her jewellery there.'

She had turned her attention next to the linen press and Mama's bedroom. I thought about calling the police and reporting a break-in, but everything was intact. I found an outfit for Mama and I was searching for undergarments when the locksmith arrived. When he was done, I locked up the house, secure in the knowledge that the only way for Georgia to do anything now was in my presence. As Paul and I were about to leave, I thought I would take a second look at the things Georgia had thrown into the bin. I rescued the dress Mama had worn to my wedding and three boxes filled with photographs.

As I moved a carton filled with Mama's collection of potpourri holders, I noticed a tatty, leather-covered writing book wedged into the corner of the bin. I tugged at it and the pile of rubbish resting against it moved. It came free in my hand. The book was stuffed with some additional loose pages, all held together by criss-crossing red ribbon tied in a bow. On top of the book, secured by the ribbon, were an old iron key and a page torn from an old schoolbook. On the page, Mama had written:

For Kat. A Book of our Family Recipes.

Georgia had tossed it away without heeding what was written on the page. Or possibly because of what was written there. I was infuriated by her contemptuousness of me almost as much as I was by her disrespect of Mama. Yes, my relationship with my mother had always been tumultuous, but this book, as old and tattered as it was, was part of her legacy. And it was destined for me.

I lifted the book to my lips without thinking through my actions. It was far from being a holy book and really didn't deserve such reverence, but, like Mama, it was beautiful and flawed. What happened next was nothing short of bizarre. As I turned the book over in my hands and loosened the knot that bound it, I heard a chorus of voices—all female, all chattering at once. It was gentle and strangely melodic, but so unexpected that I dropped the book. The babble stopped as it fell to the ground. A distant radio perhaps? Or an echo of Mama's ghosts? I spun around. There was no one and nothing except an ocean of silence. I picked up the book, placed it in a plastic bag and took it with me. I tossed it together with a bag of Mama's clothes into the back of the car and said nothing to Paul. We drove back to Chris's in uncommon silence.

10

I was so angry with Georgia that I could barely look at her. The sight of her sashaying around the kitchen with her huge jaw and her perfectly coiffed helmet of hair was enough to set me off.

'Oh you're back,' she flung across the kitchen, as she poured another kettleful of water on another pot of tea. 'You were away longer than I expected. Did you find what you were looking for?'

'Oh yes—that and a bit more. But don't you worry, we've already taken Mama's clothes to the undertaker. He sent you his regards.'

If revenge was best cold, I told myself, mine would be glacial.

'Is that tea?' asked Paul.

'Yes. It's Earl Grey,' she said. We hated Earl Grey tea and she knew it.

'Fine. I'll have a cup,' I said. 'You've made it for us so often that I'm developing the taste for it.'

Paul looked at me incredulously. To me, it tasted as if someone had washed the teacup in soapy water but had forgotten to rinse it. To Georgia, it sounded regal and therefore exclusive, no matter the taste. Therefore she had to serve it in her best Royal Albert.

'More visitors?' I asked.

'No, this pot's just for us,' she replied, pouring me my cup. 'Chris is in the living room.'

I took myself and my cup of Earl Grey to the living room.

'Back already?' said Chris.

'Yes. And we've delivered the clothes so you don't have to worry about it.'

'Thanks,' he said. 'Is everything all right?' Georgia entered on cue with her tea tray.

'Why shouldn't it be?'

'You look out of sorts.'

How was I going to put it? Your bitch of a wife threw out Mama's cookbook, which Mama had specified was to be given to me! Too straightforward. Better get Georgia's eyesight checked. Want to see what landed on the rubbish pile? Too sardonic.

'You must be under so much stress, Georgia,' I began.

'Yes. It's been a very difficult time,' she replied.

'And you've had so much to do, what with the funeral preparations and with cleaning out Mama's house. Whenever did you find the time to go back there and get rid of so many things?'

Chris looked confused. 'But Georgia hasn't been there for days.'

'Oh? Well someone's been there. We would have called the police, but we figured that Georgia might have popped by on the way to her meeting with the caterer yesterday.'

Georgia looked uncomfortable.

'I thought we'd agreed to only go there together,' I added for good measure. 'But never you mind. We didn't know who might have had Mama's keys, so we went ahead and changed the locks. That way there can be no more mistakes.'

'Mistakes?' asked Chris.

'Yes. Like the one Georgia made when she put this on the rubbish pile.' I pulled Mama's book out of the plastic bag.

'But it's just an old book,' protested Georgia. 'The key doesn't seem to match any of the locks and I thumbed through the book before I threw it away. The pages are all blank. Anyway, it'd be no use to you. You can't cook.'

'Yes, but it's Mama's old book with my name on it. And, by the way, I can cook—I simply choose not to.'

'We can't keep everything, Kat,' Chris began.

'Shut up, Chris. Just stop it. How can you defend the indefensible?'

Chris looked crestfallen. 'But she's my wife.'

'And I've been in your life for forty-three years, Chris. We've shared an awful lot during that time. I can understand that you want to support your wife, but sometimes you need to stand back and call her for what she is.' I drew a blank from him. 'No? Nothing? Okay then, we're outta here. See you at the funeral, Chris. You can lose my number after that.'

It hadn't gone quite the way I'd envisaged. Maybe the book was empty but it didn't matter to me. It was a keepsake and it was mine.

'And don't even think of breaking back into the house and changing the locks unless you get yourself a very good lawyer first, 'cause I've got one of the best.'

Paul and I stayed in a hotel for the night.

Mama's funeral proved to be a tense affair all round. Georgia and Chris sat on one end of the pew, we sat at the other, and Ethan and Poppy sat between us, creating a conduit through which we could trade messages.

'Do you have an order of service?' asked Georgia via Ethan and Poppy.

'Yes,' I replied, aware that it wasn't the messengers I wanted to shoot.

Then a few seconds later: 'Do you have enough tissues?'

'Don't need them,' I hissed back.

When I noticed Georgia's head incline towards Poppy's once more I whispered, 'Tell your mother to shut up. Please.'

Ethan's eyes had rolled so often that he was in danger of looking like a fairground clown. Were we being silly? Perhaps, but Georgia had created the gulf and Chris and I weren't inclined to bridge it. Georgia, meanwhile, leapt to her feet for the gospel reading, tugging at her black, pencil-skirted shift dress that hugged her twig thighs and skimmed her knees. I had to concede that she looked impeccable in sheer black tights and high-heeled pumps. Her gold bangles clinked as she crossed herself.

Chris's and Georgia's eyes were hidden by sunglasses, making it impossible to tell whether the tears she was dabbing at were real or imaginary. If only I'd thought of that, it would have been less obvious that I had absolutely no use for a handkerchief. As horrifying as the thought was, with her red-ringed mouth, she had the air of a dominatrix and a thought flashed. Maybe that was what Chris found so alluring about her. A dreadful thought to have smack bang in the middle of the Gospel according to St John.

At the conclusion of the service, we lined up so that the mourners could pay their respects. Georgia babbled away with them in Greek, where I could only nod and look suitably sober. Mama was born of dust and to dust she would return. I had been rapt in my own thoughts and hadn't noticed Simone and Nicole until they were right in front of me.

'I'm so sorry,' said Simone.

'Thanks, but it's not your fault,' I replied. Simone was taken aback. 'Sorry,' I added. 'Bad humour.'

'It's been hard?'

'Hard? Oh yes, you might say that. You have to save me!'

'Are you okay?' asked Nicole. 'What's wrong?'

'The family is driving me nuts. I need to come home.'

'That's their job. Don't you know everybody's family drives them nuts? You'll be home soon.'

'We're leaving tomorrow, but that's still a whole day away.'

'Call us the moment you get home. We'll go out for coffee and therapy.'

'Fabulous.' Our twenty-second discourse had disrupted the line. The rest of the mourners were hopping from foot to foot, eager to draw the formalities to a close so they could get to the food in the hall next door. With Georgia glancing at her watch and staring daggers at me, Simone and Nicole kissed me on both cheeks and were gone.

We endured the burial, the six of us, the priest, old Mr Manolis and his two assistants. The throng had melted away, and only a few stragglers had made it to the graveside. I figured that the rest were probably already drinking and eating at our expense. Paul had followed the hearse to the cemetery, and, having gone out with Chris and Georgia, I happily accepted a ride back in our own car. Like vision from a merry-go-round, the day was swirling around me, all bright lights and dim faces.

We returned about forty minutes later to the church hall for the wake. Mr Manolis had disappeared after the burial and he had left his son in his stead, moustachioed heir to a growing empire engendered by bereavement and sorrow. He wore the same sombre expression as his father, the same black pinstriped suit, the same tired pompadour, except that his was shiny black like his shoes.

'Your loss,' he stammered. 'We are very sorry for your loss.'

I was having a momentary out of body experience and ran a quick check. Telephone? Jacket pocket. Handbag? Over my shoulder. So what exactly had I misplaced? I frowned. His delivery had confused me. *He's talking about Mama, you fool.*

'Thank you,' I replied. How could I have forgotten her on the very day of her funeral? As Daley from Kinderkull would have sung, *The veil was torn and I could see you, all bloody spectre that you are. My heart is stone so I can't feel you. You too should die a death of scorn.* Such insightful lyrics lost on everyone but me and a handful of devoted fans.

By day's end I felt little beyond the burning of the soles of my feet where the pantihose had rubbed them raw. My legs ached and my neck hurt where a small but muscle-bound septuagenarian Greek widow had practically yanked it off my shoulders in her eagerness to plant me a kiss. I tried to find a quiet corner with Paul, hoping we could melt into the wall, but even there they found us. Having already embraced us once, I wondered what the mourners thought was gained through repetition.

'I can't take too much more of this,' I muttered to Paul.

'Almost done,' he replied. 'I don't know about you but I have a bad case of stub-rub.'

'You have what?'

'Stub-rub. My face is red-raw from kissing Greek men with stubble. There, I bet you never thought you'd hear me say that.'

'Stub-rub? Never heard of it.'

'That's because I made it up while I was waiting for the kissing to stop.'

Paul was right; my cheeks were burning courtesy of the same affliction. Then Poppy drew me aside as the last of the mourners were leaving.

'I can feel pimples developing where their lips have been,' she said. 'I need to wash my face.'

'Yes,' I agreed. 'I just don't get the whole thing. I'm not into kissing strangers and open displays of grief. If Chris is buried this way and I survive him, I am definitely not going to be part of the line-up. Just so you know not to ask me.'

I rummaged through my bag for my medicated wipes.

'In the meantime, use one of these.'

Poppy took the packet and scampered away towards the toilet. I threw my bag over my shoulder with a sigh. Just as Mr Manolis had predicted, it was all done and dusted by a little before three.

'Are you too tired to drive home?' I asked Paul hopefully.

'I'm fine. Do you want to leave straight away?'

'Yes please. Only I left a few things behind at Chris's last night, so we'll need to go past and collect them.'

'No we won't.'

'Oh? Why's that?'

'Because I borrowed his keys and packed everything into the car after you left in the hearse,' said Paul. 'And before you ask, yes, I remembered.'

'What?'

'Your book. The one Mama left you.'

Paul looked so proud of himself, just like Boz had when he did his first doggy-doo in the yard. He was so unbearably endearing that I wanted to crush him in a bear hug, even though he was half a head taller than me and twice as strong.

'And that's why I love you.'

'Me too. Let's say goodbye to the others and get out of here. We can come back next weekend to clear out Mama's house, after things have had a chance to settle. Okay?' he said.

'Okay.'

I air-kissed Chris and Georgia and we brushed cheeks without either of them pretending to reciprocate. Ethan gave me the hug I craved. Paul and I were headed home just after three, Mama was safe in her grave and I still hadn't shed a tear.

11

I called Simone and Nicole early Friday morning and we agreed to meet for lunch. Paul asked me to remember to give his best to Intimidatrix, his nickname for Simone, and Fickle Spice, his equally cruel but infinitely more tasteful nickname for Nicole. Simone turned up, as always, a few minutes early. Having arrived at the café even earlier, I took the high moral ground and waved at her as she entered.

'You're punctual,' she said.

'I know how much you hate to be kept waiting. Nicole's not here yet.'

'I really didn't expect her to be. She lives in her own time. I'd hate to employ her,' she observed. 'Have you ordered yet?'

I shook my head. 'I thought I'd wait.'

'I think I'll order. God knows when she'll get here and I'm starving.' Simone waved down the nearest waitress. 'I'll have the Thai beef salad and a double espresso.'

'Anything for you?' asked the waitress, turning to me.

'Not yet. We're waiting for another friend.'

The waitress made a honking noise like an aborted snort, and turned back to Simone. Anticipating her next question, Simone added, 'I'd like my meal straight away. With my coffee.'

The waitress snorted again, leaving me to wonder if she was suffering from an illness and if so, whether it was communicable.

'Thanks for feeding Boz,' I said.

'Don't mention it. How are you coping?'

'So-so. Chris and I have had a falling out, no thanks to Georgia.'

'That woman's a fucking bitch. Always has been, always will be. Chris made his choice and has to live with the consequences. Just because you happen to be related doesn't mean you have to be friends,' said Simone as her salad arrived without her coffee. The waitress pretended not to notice her raised eyebrow, and placed a bottle of water and three glasses on the table instead.

'He's not just some random cosmic coincidence; he's my only brother. It would be nice for us to get along.'

'Please don't tell me you think we get to choose our family before we're born because we have something to work out,' she said, lowering her fork. 'Hey, you! Wake up and smell the fucking roses! You don't need Chris's approval. You're never going to get it, so why waste your time?'

'It's not about his approval, it's just nice to be part of a close family.'

'It's all about Chris's approval. You *are* part of a close family—you, me and, if she ever turns up, Nicole.'

Just as she finished speaking, Nicole approached, baby on her hip, hair wild and bags hanging off both arms.

'What were you two saying about me?' she asked, adding in the same breath, 'Not my fault. He overslept.'

'See? This is what happens when you become a mother at forty,' Simone sniffed.

'You want a cuddle?' Nicole offered, thrusting her baby forward.

'No!' we replied in unison.

'Well one of you had better hold him while I set this stuff down.' She shoved Bailey across the table like a sack of groceries. I glanced at Simone, who was suddenly busy retrieving messages from her phone. I took Bailey into my arms and sat him on the edge of the table while he kicked me in the stomach. I swear I saw him grin as he did it.

'So how are you?' asked Nicole, pulling jars, spoons and toys out of a clown bag.

'Okay, I suppose. It's been a difficult week and to top it off, Chris and I have had a fight.' I commented as Bailey yanked a wisp of my hair and simultaneously clawed my face with his fingernails. The kid was malevolent.

'Of course it has. Losing your mother is awful. I can't imagine how I'd cope without mine. But as for Chris, that's no loss. You don't need his approval,' she responded, taking Bailey from my hands and shoving a spoonful of puree in his mouth.

'You too? But I'm not seeking… Oh, I give up.'

Nicole did everything according to an inventory. She was born with a bucket list of things to do, places to go and experiences to have. It was just that she got to most things later than everyone else, so, by the time she reached the next milestone, she was always better prepared than everyone else. *Graduated at thirty-two—tick. Left home at thirty-five—tick. Married at thirty-nine—tick. Baby at forty—tick.* And now she had asked me about Mama—*another tick.* I always sensed that for Nicole it was all about the destination and never the journey. Which was the reason for Paul assigning her the nickname.

Nicole continued spooning pumpkin into Bailey as he flapped his arms in excitement. *She's morphed into a mother bird,* I thought. I wouldn't be flummoxed at all if she regurgitated a worm and fed it to him.

'It's true,' she continued. 'You've turned Chris into an authority figure.'

'Oh Lord! Okay! I promise to mend my ways.'

'Now you're doing the same to us.'

The waitress returned to frown at our indecision and eventually to take our order. We watched Nicole order a Caesar salad without dressing and anchovies, and with a poached egg and croutons on the side. Simone reminded the waitress about the coffee as she grimaced.

'Why don't you just order breakfast and a bowl of lettuce?' Simone asked Nicole. From anyone else the comment would have been perceived as bitchy, but from Simone it was sassy. She had perfected angry lesbian chic. Swearing tossed in gratis, for effect.

'This way Bailey gets to eat the yolk and I have the white. It's a win–win. Besides, I don't need all that oil. I'm trying to lose the baby weight for his christening next month. To which you're all invited and expected to come. No excuses.'

'I won't be there. I don't do baby things since I fainted at my nephew's bris. I only do bat and bar mitzvahs,' Simone commented. 'By the age of thirteen, most kids start to develop a personality.'

'Do you see a problem here, Simone?' said Nicole twisting her face by way of emphasis. 'He's never going to have a bar mitzvah. It's a christening, not a circumcision. It's this or nothing.'

'You could come with us, Simone,' I offered. 'Paul's a great distraction.'

'Yes, that's exactly what I was thinking myself. If ever I am out of my mind with boredom, Paul can step in as entertainment. Sorry, Kat, somehow I've never thought of him that way.'

Nicknames aside, Paul could be very funny if he turned his mind to it. I opened my mouth and was about to say as much when Nicole interjected.

'I need to ask you for a tiny, teeny favour, Kat. I'm absolutely desperate, or else I wouldn't be asking.'

'Go on.'

'Do you think you could make some finger food for the christening party? I've already organised the sandwiches but I really need something hot. As I recall, you're very good at making fabulous morsels.'

'Me?" I said incredulously. 'Wherever did you get that idea? You know I don't cook.'

'Yes but you *can* cook. I can't ask Simone. She doesn't own any pans.'

'That's right,' said Simone. 'No pots, no pans, not even a kitchen. Just a sink and a microwave. For heating up something when I can't buy anything already hot.'

'Well?'

I turned it over in my mind. I hated being put on the spot, but Nicole had her best puppy dog face on. It seemed mean not to agree, especially after she had gone so far out of her way to come to Mama's funeral.

'If Simone can come to a christening, I guess I could make something fabulous.'

Simone stopped mid-bite. 'No, no, no! Not fair, Kat. The kid was her choice. Why should I suffer?'

'The kid has a name. Or he will do, after the christening. In the meantime, you'd better get used to the idea of being there with us. You'll enjoy it. I promise.'

'I won't and that's one you'll both owe me.'

Our meals arrived at the same time as Simone's coffee.

'At last!' she exclaimed as she downed it in a series of gulps and stood up to leave.

'Before you go, there's one more thing I need to tell you both,' I said, fishing out a piece of paper from my pocket and smoothing it out.

'What's this then?' asked Simone.

'Read it.'

I watched as Simone and then Nicole read the piece of paper together.

'What?' said Nicole. 'That can't be right, can it?

'I don't know,' I replied.

'One hundred per cent Middle Eastern Jew? What the fuck?' exclaimed Simone.

'Plus or minus 0.01 per cent.'

'But aren't you half Greek?'

'I don't know,' I repeated.

'That would make you more Jewish than me,' Simone observed. 'My family is Ashkenazi. According to this, it looks like you're descended directly from the lost Greek tribe of Israel.'

'Apparently so.'

'You realise, of course, that being Jewish isn't a club you can join. It's a state of being. You're born Jewish and no matter what else you become, that's what defines you. From the day I was conceived I was Jewish above all else. And so now I'm a Jewish lawyer and a Jewish lesbian.'

'I didn't ask for this, Simone. It's in my biology.'

'Take it from a Jew. I say this with the greatest of respect. No matter what your DNA says, you're not Jewish.'

'It appears you might well be wrong about that.'

'Believe me, Kat. Not Jewish.'

My lips parted in protest as Simone raised her hands to her ears.

'If you keep persisting with this shit, I'll be compelled to go away for a very long time. This is bullshit.'

'But…' I began.

'Shut up, Kat. Not Jewish,' she pronounced as she flounced out.

12

By the time I got home, Paul was out visiting a client. Chris had left me a message asking me to call him back, but as far as I was concerned he could whistle for it. I sat down to blog the day away. I wrote the same sentence three different ways and deleted it, initially substituting each word with another and then erasing the whole lot.

I thought about my day, my lunch with Simone and Nicole, but still nothing. Not enough to blog about if I didn't want to bore everyone to tears. I put some pithy comments on a couple of writer's threads. And then nothing. *Nada. Niente.* I was drying up. *A writer without a single word? That's me all washed up. Finished.* I turned on the television and flicked through the channels. I settled on the home shopping network. Animated chatter without any appreciable content of interest to me, it was great as background noise.

Since I was now traversing the Gobi of the blogosphere, I decided that my time might be better spent working out what I would cook for Bailey's christening. What did I know about finger food? Certainly even less than I knew about blogging. Perhaps because the notion of cooking held infinite fascination for me, I owned a shelf full of cookbooks. A similar notion motivated me to own a shelf full of cleaning products that I knew I would probably never use.

Mama had been an indifferent housekeeper but an excellent cook. Since her death I had picked up and put down her book a dozen times. I doubted Mama would have made such a big deal if the book had been empty, as Georgia thought. She probably said it out of spite, hoping I wouldn't bother with it, and by doing so, lose a bit more of Mama's essence. Perhaps this was the right time to open up her cookbook and see what she had to say on the topic of finger food.

I ran my finger along the ridges of the grosgrain ribbon and untied it carefully. The iron key swung free but did not fall, since it was secured to the book by a second, finer ribbon. The key had left a brown stain where it had pressed for a very long time against the cover. It seemed an odd thing to attach to a book. I presumed it was intended to serve as a bookmark of sorts. I turned the book over in my hands. The hide had been buffed smooth by many fingers, but the spine was still solid, if a little nibbled at either end. It smelled of rust and dust and old leather. I drew in a deep breath and let the yellowed pages fall open.

'Ekaterini, my love.'

I twirled about. I could have sworn I'd heard Mama's voice calling my name and I listened out for it again. Nothing. Over the noise of the television I heard, with a mixture of relief and disappointment, Chris's voice. He was talking through the answer phone. Odd that I hadn't heard the phone ring or the sound of Memo-man's voice (as Paul had named the electronic announcer). I crossed the room and picked up the receiver.

'Hi, Chris.'

'Oh, you're home.'

'Yes.'

'I left a message but you never called me back.'

'No.'

I could have made up an excuse about being very busy, but that would have been a lie.

'Well, I phoned because I needed to tell you that Mama's lawyer has been in touch with us. She named you and me as her executors. We need to get together with him and talk things through.'

'You and me?' I said. 'Just you and me. Not Georgia, right? She's not an executor.'

'No.'

'And does she know that? I mean, does she understand that?'

'Yes.'

'And do you understand that too, Chris?'

'Oh come on, Kat…'

'No, Chris, you come on. I'm sick of her meddling in things that have nothing to do with her. I don't want to make this any harder than it needs to be, but you need to stand up to her and set some boundaries.'

'She's my wife…'

'And I'm your sister. Look, let's not fight over this. You keep the hound in check and I'll be my usual agreeable self. But if she gets off the leash even once, it's battle-stations. Got it?'

'I don't appreciate you calling my wife a bitch.'

'Is that what I did? Listen, Chris, it's not negotiable.'

'Okay. I'll try, but you know how she is.'

'Oh, grow a backbone! You placated Mama your whole life and now you're doing the same thing with Georgia. You'd better try harder.'

'That's how you see it, fine. Anyhow,' he said, while I cringed. 'Anyhow, there's a meeting set up for Friday week. Can you make it?'

'Message me the details and I'll be there.'

'I'll do it now. Look, I know Georgia can be difficult sometimes. I'm sorry you left here so angry.'

'Yeah?'

'Yes.'

'Okay, Chris, I appreciate that,' I said, letting him off the hook. 'I'll see you later. Give Ethan and Poppy my love.'

'I will. Are we okay?'

I thought about how to answer him. *No, we're not okay.* We hadn't been okay since 1985.

'Sure we are,' I said. 'Bye, Chris.'

'Good. Bye, Kat.'

I put the phone down. *Now, where was I? That's right, Mama's book.* A few moments later, my phone announced that it had received Chris's message with a bloodcurdling scream from Daley. It was attention-grabbing and occasionally embarrassing, but it always made me smile. Paul had threatened many times to toss it out the window if I didn't change it, but I wasn't inclined to give up Kinderkull quite yet.

I ignored Daley and picked up the recipe book once again. This time I opened it purposefully on the first page. There was something written there in Greek. I had never learned how to read the language, and Mama had never bothered to teach us. Yet as I stared at it, the words began to make as much sense to me as if they had been written in English. The first part was written by my grandmother to Mama:

For Elleni, My mother's recipe book.

The message was suitably direct and devoid of sentiment. Beneath that Mama had added:

Ekaterini, This book is my treasure. Mama Ella.

My finger traced the outline of her writing. As I did so, I perceived my name being called aloud. *Get a grip, Kat. There's no one here but you.* There it was again.

'*Kat.*'

'Yes?' I replied. It was my name, as clear as day and loud as a bell. I couldn't exactly pretend I hadn't heard anything.

'Oh good, you can hear me. Don't be afraid, my darling. It's me. It's Mama.'

'Mama?' Of course it was. I was hallucinating. Not content to just drive herself mad, she was now having a crack at me. *Don't be afraid?* What was she saying? Obviously I had every right to be afraid. Dead people don't talk. Or at least they never used to talk to me.

'Not now, Mama,' I said, rolling my eyes and gathering what was left of my fast departing wits about me. I took the crucifix Mama had mounted on the wall as a talisman when we first moved in and thrust it around me. If it worked on vampires then possibly, just possibly, it might work on lingering ghosts.

'I have to work out some finger food for Bailey's christening.'

'Then I suggest you stop doing that and look at page twenty-one.'

Great, I had a phantasm with handy recipe hints and an attitude. After one last thrust, I put the crucifix on my lap. Cautious not to unsettle the spirits, I flipped through the book with its strange writing in various hands and inks, exactly as I had been instructed. Just as before, the writing instantly made sense to me, even though I knew I had never learned to read the script in which it was written. The page was headed *Fotini's Cheese and Meat Bourekia.*

'Fotini?' I said aloud. I had never heard anyone speak of a Fotini in the family.

From somewhere—nowhere—a voice replied, '*Merhaba*'.

My heart was thumping in my ears and, for a moment, the floor below me pitched and rolled.

'I'm going to be sick!' I exclaimed. 'Oh God! Oh God! Oh God!' I repeated.

'No, don't call on God,' the disembodied voice replied.

'I need a drink!' I slammed the book shut. With shaking hands and still holding fast to the crucifix, I poured myself a very, very, very long brandy and took a sip. I looked about the room. I walked over and turned off the television. Contrary to every scary movie I had ever watched, the room was bathed in magnificent sunshine and everything was serene.

'Mama?' I called. 'Are you there?'

Silence. Steeling myself, I determined to return to Mama's book and try once more. Ghosts and other non-existent visitors were a figment of Mama's imagination, but not mine. Courtesy of Mama, I was all too grounded in reality. If the strange magic was somehow in the book, I would soon discover it, although what exactly I was going to do after that, I hadn't considered.

I picked up the book and sat down with it resting on my lap on top of the crucifix. As if in a state of suspended animation, I opened it. Not a word. I turned the pages gently, furtively, one at a time, not looking at the contents, until I had counted off ten. Since the numbering was on both sides, I figured that the next page was sure to be twenty-one.

I looked down. There was the recipe again. I held my breath and silently read the title: *Fotini's Cheese and Meat Bourekia*. Outside, the traffic hummed. Inside, absolute peace and quiet. Relieved, I exhaled. *See, there's nothing here.* There was nothing to see, nothing to hear. Nothing, that was, until I started to examine the recipe once more.

Fotini returned as soon as I began to read. At first she came as a whisper, a voice-shadow that drifted in on the breeze. Had I been alone in a forest, I would have certainly mistaken her murmur for the wind.

Ignore her! Concentrate on the recipe!

But I wasn't in a forest and she wasn't the howling wind. I was sitting on my own chair in my own kitchen. I tried to push Fotini away, but she wouldn't move. It wasn't my own voice I heard as I read *'Take one oka of lamb cut up very finely…'* It was her gentle intonation, the sadness in her tone, the unfamiliarity of her accent. It wasn't any use. I had to face the grim reality that one of two things was happening: either this was real and I had somehow stumbled upon a conduit to the spectral otherworld, or—and this was the more probable—I was going mad. I had choices—embrace it or ignore it. Or I could close the book and never open it again.

My thoughts turned to Mama. She was not much beyond eighty when she died. I was now a bit over half that age. Daddy often said that Mama changed after she had given birth to me. I never asked him what he meant by that, because I assumed that I already knew. We all knew. Her madness came and went with the seasons. Sometimes Mama could be perfectly sane for weeks at a time and then it would arrive in a rush: the voices, the things lost or missing, the fractured logic, the lost looks. Perhaps I, too, had reached the witching hour, that moment in the lives of the women of my family when all sense departs.

I put down and re-opened the book several times at random. No matter where I opened it, I heard the voice of a woman, but not always the same woman. What I found strangest of all was that, while the thought of disembodied spirits scared me witless, none of the voices actually frightened me. They were softly resonant and, although the only one I recognised was Mama's, they seemed oddly familiar, like reconnecting with a school friend after an absence of decades. I was aware that they didn't always speak English, yet I understood each one of them perfectly. It was only when I flipped through the pages that all the voices seemed to cry out at once and the kitchen turned into the Tower of Babel.

I shut the book and tied it with the ribbon. What would I do next? What would I tell Paul? My mind kept churning like a front-load washer. There was absolutely no clarity in my thoughts, but the one I kept tripping over was the notion that none of this was real. What if I'd imagined the lot? I had the single, solitary fear my entire life that I would become Mama in my mind as well as in my appearance. I couldn't say anything to Paul, not yet anyway. I knew he would support me and he would try to understand, even though I didn't understand it myself. No, not Paul. I would speak to Ethan— he'd know what was happening to me and what I could do about it. *Speak to Ethan first and then what?* What if my problem wasn't medical? It dawned on me. I had no Plan B.

13

I sent Ethan a message, hoping that he would get back to me before I could consider the full significance of what had just happened. I expected to have the mystery fully explained before I returned to Chris's. Paul had been busier that week than he had been for the last six months, so I had been intending to go to the meeting alone. Now I wasn't so certain that solitude was such a good idea. With nothing to distract me, I fixated on what had just occurred. I began a chant of *I am not my mother, I am sane,* interspersed with *Please call me, Ethan!* I was so sure that the power of the spirit world would intercede and compel Ethan to call me that I found myself compulsively checking the phone every few minutes in case I'd missed a call. It was something I hadn't done since I broke up with my last boyfriend fifteen years earlier. I knew from bitter experience how well that tactic worked, but I was powerless to stop myself. If obsession went hand in hand with psychosis, then I was already a self-diagnosed basket case.

In the meantime, I prepared myself for the worst. *Kat Bower, you are as crazy as a nervous dog in a thunderstorm. Dead people cannot talk to the living.* Intellectually I knew that to be true, even if somewhere inside of me I felt it wasn't. Feelings meant nothing. After over forty years of studying Mama, who had been convinced beyond reason that she was visited by people invisible to the rest of us, I would try anything to stop this even if it meant therapy, hypnosis and the use of heavy-duty drugs. I had heard of people who wore silver-foil hats to stop the voices entering their heads, and the thought crossed my mind ever-so-briefly before I blew it away.

I stole a glance at the book lying on the table, inert in its well-worn splendour, and I itched to open it again. What if, just what if, I wasn't crazy at all and the book really was some kind of conduit directly to my ancestors? A love connection between the generations? Was it the key to a back door someone had forgotten to lock? What would it say about the futility of life and the finality of death then? What sort of Sartre-ian dialogue would that engender? That kind of thinking would either get me a Nobel Prize or admission to a psych ward.

I was so deep in my own thoughts that I jumped when the phone finally rang.

'Hello?' I was ashamed at my disappointment when I realised the caller was Paul and not Ethan.

'Are you okay?' he said.

'Why do you ask? Don't I sound okay?'

'Not really. You sound edgy. Is it that time of month again?'

'What? No!' I yelled, validating Paul's point. *How dare he assume I was premenstrual!* 'Not that you deserve an answer but, actually, it's about halfway!'

'Oh, okay. I just rang to let you know that I'm going to be a couple of hours late. I'll try to finish up as soon as I can and get home sooner, though.'

'That would be good,' I replied. 'Sorry about being snappy before. I spoke to Chris, and he and I are seeing Mama's lawyer next week.'

'Is that all? Don't let him shake you up. Let's talk about it when I get home,' he said, adding, 'I love you.'

'Love you too.'

I wanted to tell Paul what had happened but I couldn't. The right words just didn't come to mind and, besides, it seemed wrong to burden him while he was working. There was probably no good time to tell my husband I had finally lost my mind. It could wait. But the moment I hung up from Paul, my phone stalking resumed. So much for spectral intervention!

At three I had my third coffee and made my second call to Ethan. I had rehearsed the message I was going to leave. I had written it down, so I would get it exactly right. It would be adequate to elicit an immediate reply, but insufficient to get me committed. Sadly, my strategy was abandoned the second he answered the phone.

'Hello?'

'Oh hi, Ethan? It's Kat.'

'I was just about to call you.'

'Oh, sorry. I guess I got in first. It's just that I was nearly out of battery…' I lied.

'You seem anxious. Is everything okay?'

Et tu, Ethan? Here was I thinking that I sounded very together. Clearly, I wore my stress on my sleeve.

'Yes, everything's fine,' I lied again. 'No. No, it's not.' If I wanted help I had to confess it now. 'You know how Mama used to think her family visited her?'

'Olanzapine would have stopped that.'

'Well then, maybe you need to get me some,' I said. 'Mama spoke to me today. She came through loud and clear. But it wasn't just Mama—a woman named Fotini spoke to me, too. It was real, Ethan, or at least it was real to me. I guess I had what you guys call an auditory hallucination.'

He fell silent.

'Ethan?'

'It's probably nothing. You've been under a lot of stress lately, Kat. But just in case it's something else, do yourself a favour and see a neurologist.'

'And what if they say I'm fine but it doesn't go away?'

'Then we try something else.'

Nothing Ethan said assured me in the slightest, but I really had no alternative but to take his advice. I had sworn off diagnosis-by-computer after an ugly incident four years ago involving parasites, explosive diarrhoea and three courses of antibiotics imported from Mexico. That almost had a very bad ending, but I had two whole hours before Paul would be home and an imagination that just wouldn't quit. So if medical sites were off-limits, maybe I could do better tapping into the collective intelligence.

My exomorphic experience (my own expression) had the effect of returning my writing-rhythm, my blog-beat, as I liked to call it. I had turned a corner and was hoping that my readers, who numbered in the very low hundreds—or more accurately, high dozens—would veer along with me. My blog had been such a modest success that I figured there was nothing to lose. My fingers developed their own spirit, flying across the keyboard, my vigour renewed.

Losing a Parent and Finding them in an Unexpected Place, I wrote. Today, Mama and I had a conversation, even though she's been dead a week. I don't mean a one-sided, stream-of-consciousness monologue, I mean a real dialogue. Now that's bizarre…

Apparently, among my followers there were a few who spoke to dead people on a regular basis. And now, thanks to a very bad idea and an impulsive nature, I was counted among that select number. I had no sooner posted my blog than the helpful responses began flowing in. *They're not messages from beyond the grave, they're alien love poems. Open yourself up to them and enter a realm of anal probing and midnight cornfield abductions. Or else you could block the messages by making a hat out of a lead apron. Or tin foil,* they wrote.

Hell no! I thought.

Then my phone rang. I had already changed my ringtone to one of Kinderkull's lesser-known but more appropriate songs *Dead but Not Gone.* The call was from an undisclosed number.

'Hello,' I said.

'What the fuck have you written?'

'Hi, Simone. I thought we weren't speaking.'

'We weren't but I'm over it. As long as you know you're not Jewish, right?'

'Right.'

'So what the fuck is this shit I just read about your mother? Have you completely lost your mind?'

'You read my blog?'

'How the fuck else do you think I find out what's happening with you when I'm too pissed off to talk to you?'

'Thanks. I think.'

'Well?'

'Well that's the burning question, isn't it? You tell me. Have I?'

'Of course you haven't. It's just grief. Get a grip.'

'But I really heard her, Simone.'

'Okay. So, you think you heard your mother speaking to you. It happens. I'm sending you the name of a good shrink. He's helped dozens of my clients. He usually helps to prove they are crazy but he's actually pretty good. Do the world a favour and go see him.'

Ethan and Simone had to be right. Dead people don't talk to the living. I regretted in an instant trumpeting my hallucinations to the universe for everyone to read, so I borrowed the phrase popularised by starlets around the world as an excuse for everything from alcoholism to shoplifting: *Sorry guys, it wasn't me. I was just researching a character.*

In one afternoon I had flip-flopped between scepticism and conviction, finally settling on an agreement to do myself and the world a favour by getting professional help. And I left it at that.

Paul was unusually frisky when he came home so I decided to keep my day to myself. We spent what was left of the afternoon playing adult games in the bedroom, the hallway and the kitchen until I began to think about extraterrestrial abductions again. Paul was so preoccupied with sex that a thought entered my mind: whether the man who had just put the contents of our refrigerator to novel use was an alien substitute for my husband. I kept that thought unspoken. This was definitely not fodder for the blogosphere.

I figured I could ignore Simone's psychiatrist for a few weeks while I nutted out what I was going to do. Ethan pulled some strings and Dr Tricky the neurologist was able to fit me in the following day. His receptionist said it was a last-minute cancellation, and if I couldn't come tomorrow at two-fifteen, I'd be waiting another three months. The thought of three months of Mama's vocalisations in my head was intolerable. I was ready for anything short of a lobotomy, although if he suggested it I might even agree to that as well.

After seeing Dr Tricky, I discovered I had an innate talent for remaining upright while standing on one foot with my eyes shut and repeatedly touching the tip of my nose. After the MRI scans I discovered that, whatever had happened to me that day, I couldn't blame it on anything sinister in my brain. I was normal. *Praise the Lord.* Which meant only one of two things. Either Mama and Fotini were real or I was absolutely, undeniably, certifiably crazy.

14

Even though I knew it would mean a very long day for me, I decided not to call up and stay with Chris, but to go straight home after seeing Dr Tricky; Paul and I would make a separate daytrip to the lawyer the following Friday. By the time Friday arrived, Paul decided he'd had enough of my family and would stay at home instead.

'Whatever happens, don't lose your cool,' were his parting words to me. A quick kiss and a stroke of my cheek and I was backing down the driveway, Kinderkull blaring through the speakers so loudly that I could see Paul shaking his head, hands clamped over his ears, as he walked back inside.

Paul hardly ever read my blogs. He especially never read any that I asked him to read as a draft before I posted them, so I made sure I gave him a fabricated version of my latest one three times. He didn't know anything about the book incident. I could count on Ethan's discretion, and so I hadn't mentioned the visit to the neurologist to Paul either. I simply told him that I'd gone to see a gynaecologist. That way, I was certain not to get any questions. I also hadn't had the courage to open Mama's book again, although, truth be told, even lying there inert on the desk, it was piquing my curiosity once more. I swore off ever blogging about it again, no matter what happened in the future. I would never have believed there were so many mad people in cyberspace, each with an opinion more outrageous than the last.

I arrived at the offices of Clark, Lawless and Clark ten minutes early. I had hoped that Chris would have the good sense and enough respect for me to come alone, but I wasn't really surprised to find both Chris and Georgia already seated there.

I was curt but polite with them and quickly found a seat in the corner. Since I never bought junky gossip magazines, I savoured the opportunity of reading someone—anyone—else's. I was that infuriating person who reads a magazine over another person's shoulder or from the chair opposite. I preferred my trash fresh, but even a few months stale it was still palatable. And so now, in October, I read about the undying love of a Hollywood power couple in April, who I knew to have separated in May and divorced by August. Mr Clark, I presumed, was running late and I devoured three full issues from cover to cover before his assistant finally showed us into his office.

The man behind the desk stood as we entered. He was tall and crumpled, as if he had spent far too much time sitting in the same position, and that position was far too low for his great stature. He bent forward to shake our hands.

'Sorry to have kept you waiting,' he said to no one in particular, adding, 'I don't think we've met before,' directed straight at me. 'I'm Tim Lawless.'

'Kat. Kat Bower. A pleasure,' I tittered as we shook hands.

He caught my titter and returned it with a chuckle of his own. 'And before you say anything, I know. You'd think a name such as mine would be an impediment in my profession.'

'Oh really?' I replied with a grin. 'I hadn't realised.' I was going to be as charming and dizzy as possible. *Just wrap him in a bow and give him to me. Beware, Georgia—I'll soon have Mr Lawless eating out of the palm of my hand.* 'It's only that I was expecting to see Mr Clark. I guess I had a two in three chance of being right. So when you said you were Tim Lawless, well, it came as a bit of a surprise.'

Georgia tossed me a look somewhere between humiliation and disdain. I crossed my legs in Tim Lawless's direction, glad to have chosen the tight skirt and heels over the harem pants and ballet flats. I caught him looking at my calves, and he cleared his throat.

'Thank you all for coming here today,' he began. 'I wanted to talk to you as executors about the bequests in Mrs Bower's will.'

'Tim?' I interrupted sweetly. 'I may call you Tim?'

'But of course.'

'Before we go any further, Tim, I just need a little guidance.' I said. 'If I am not mistaken, you called us here because you wanted to speak to the executors, right?'

'That's right,' he replied. His eyes settled back on my legs.

'That being the case, I was wondering, shouldn't we exclude Georgia at this point?'

'Well,' he responded, 'Georgia is your brother's wife. I have no problem with her being present, if he wants her here.'

'Oh yes, of course,' I paused as he shuffled papers. 'But just so that we're clear, am I your client?'

'Your mother's estate is my client.'

'And Chris and I are administering Mama's estate. Just the two of us.'

'Correct.'

'Thanks for clearing that up for me,' I continued, emboldened. 'Chris and I are close, but there are things that, as brother and sister, we sometimes disagree about. Always have, always will, and, to me, that's healthy.' Chris and Georgia exchanged nervous glances, as I carried on. 'I'm thinking of the best interests of the estate here. From time to time, Chris and I may not see things exactly alike as far as the estate is concerned, too. Because of that, I'd prefer all of our discussions to be in private, so we both feel free to make the best decisions. For the sake of the estate. It's nothing personal, you understand, but I'd rather Georgia waited outside.'

Yes, it was a cheap shot. Did I really care if Georgia was present? Probably not, if I could be assured she would keep her opinions to herself and allow us to make the decisions. *Chris needs to put that woman on a leash!* I had seen Georgia angry before, but now she was livid. I had already warned Chris that she wouldn't be welcome and, as far as I was concerned, Georgia had chosen to tag along at her own peril. In the space of seconds, she turned more shades of red than are found on a paint chart.

'Georgia,' I said in my best impersonation of a newsreader, 'would you be a sweetheart and wait for Chris outside, please?'

She looked at Chris to save her but he avoided her gaze and simply nodded his agreement. As she stood up to leave, I called out a cheery 'Thank you!'

Tim waited for the door to close before he brought out Mama's will. 'I wanted you both here because you may find your mother's will a little surprising.'

That sounded ominous to me. 'Oh? How so?'

'Well,' he began, 'your mother saw me last year to tidy up her affairs. She was concerned to divide her estate equally, so that everyone could be taken care of.'

'That sounds fair to me,' I returned. To my consternation, Tim ignored me.

'She told me that since Chris had two children and as you were over forty and you hadn't had any children, it seemed unfair to her that the estate simply be divided into halves. So instead of that, her will has the effect of giving you both and each of her grandchildren living at the time of her death, an equal share of her estate. If you'd had a child, Kat, your child would have received a share too, but as it stands, the four of you get an equal share.'

'So we get a quarter each?' Truthfully, I was a little disappointed, but I wasn't showing Chris any of it. 'That seems fair.'

'I'm glad you think so, Kat.' Chris looked relieved. 'When Mama told me about her plans, I was worried you might have thought you were being cut out.'

'I love Ethan and Poppy as if they were my own, Chris, you know that.' That much was true. 'I wouldn't begrudge them anything, but I don't want Georgia to claim it as some kind of victory.'

I raised my eyebrow as he mumbled something about Georgia *not being like that.* He looked undeniably sheepish as Tim Lawless pushed a stack of papers in our direction, embellished with pink stickers protruding at right angles, which directed us where to sign and where to initial. We quickly agreed that we should each choose a keepsake of Mama (Georgia included) and everything else of value would be auctioned off and the proceeds divided. I figured Paul wouldn't want anything and I already had Mama's jewellery and my keepsake so, after Chris gave me his word to keep Georgia away from Mama's house, I handed him the key.

'One last visit?' he suggested. 'Wouldn't you like some time alone to say goodbye to our old home?'

'No need. I've seen enough of it already. I'm going back to my old home right now.' As I stood up to leave, my phone rang. *In this place there is no winner, only the vanquished, the sad and the sinner...*

'I'm so sorry,' I mumbled, rejecting the call. 'I thought it was off.'

'Interesting choice of music,' said Tim. 'You certainly can't ignore that.'

'No.' I smiled weakly. 'You'll let me know if you need me?'

'Yes of course.'

I said my goodbyes, we all shook hands and I departed the offices, hardly daring to look left or right. To my relief, Georgia wasn't anywhere to be seen.

I climbed into my car, turned the ignition on and the music up. As I rounded the corner, I spotted Georgia sitting on a bench, head in hands. I thought about stopping but what would be the point? She didn't deserve words of comfort and I had mutely allowed her to ride roughshod over us all for long enough. She and Chris needed to reinforce some boundaries for her—a novel thought, but I couldn't be swayed by sympathy any more. From the moment she'd stamped on Chris's foot during their Greek wedding ceremony twenty-eight years ago, it was all about taking the ascendancy. I got that she was still a teenager and Chris barely twenty-one when they had wed, but everyone else had grown up around them, while Georgia had remained ever the child bride, petulant and difficult. It was time to bring her childhood to an end, and if Chris wouldn't do it, I would.

Fuelled by Kinderkull's driving beat and confrontational lyrics, I made it home in record time, stretching but not completely shattering the speed limit. I turned off the music a block before home, and let the car glide up the driveway. For a moment, I sat in complete silence. I had done all I needed to. No more Mama. No more Mama's house. And if I wanted it that way, no more Georgia or Chris.

Paul was home when I arrived and he had just made coffee. Our home welcomed me with a hug—it was warm with the fragrance of freshly ground coffee beans and the scent of something heavenly. I sucked in the aroma and allowed Paul to fuss over me.

'I didn't hear you drive up,' he said. 'Whatever happened to the God-awful music?'

'I thought I'd do you and the neighbours a good turn,' I laughed.

'You look exhausted,' he remarked. 'How did it go?'

'So-so. I got Georgia ejected from the meeting. That was the good bit.' I paused. 'But the bad bit was that we only got left a quarter share of the estate.'

'And does that worry you?'

'I know it shouldn't. I mean, I love the kids and all, but yes, I guess it does. It would have been nice not to be bothered about money ever again.'

'Don't kid yourself, everyone bothers about money. The more they have, the worse it gets. So why don't you relax while I'll get you a cup of coffee.'

How typical of Paul to cosset over me like a mother hen. He was the gayest straight man I'd ever met. I had to admit, I was pretty tired and a little annoyed. I kicked off my high heels and rubbed the soreness out of my feet. Meanwhile, Paul returned with coffee and a plate piled high with shortbreads.

'Here, try one,' he offered, adding by way of explanation, 'I was bored without you.'

I took a bite of his wonderful confection. It was at once buttery and crumbly, succulent and sweet—a fabulous sugary explosion. A sip of coffee and together, they hit the mark. I began to feel better about the money, about Georgia and about Mama's legacy.

'Wow!' I exclaimed. 'Wherever did you get them?'

'I made them.' Paul beamed at me proudly as Boz circled around, tail whipping furiously, waiting to lap up any crumbs.

'And that's exactly why I married you, you wonderful man!' I kissed him square on the mouth. He saw the opportunity to fondle my breast and took it. 'Sex later,' I laughed, smacking my lips and groaning. 'These are too good. More of these first.'

I devoured another and was thinking about eating one more, when it occurred to me. 'These taste faintly familiar? Have you made them before?'

'I haven't,' Paul replied. 'But Mama might have. It's her recipe.' He indicated Mama's book on the coffee table.

I stopped mid-bite, shortbread in my fingers, hovering over the plate. A morsel stuck in my throat and I began to choke. *Mama's recipe?* I spluttered into my sleeve and took another sip of coffee.

'Did you get the recipe from Mama's book?' I resumed nonchalantly.

'Yes,' he replied. I must have looked aghast. 'What?' he said.

'Nothing. I'm just glad you found it useful.' I finished my shortbread. 'So, what did you think of it?'

'It's surprising,' he replied. 'I had been thinking of baking something sweet for you when I opened the book, but the recipes seemed to be written in Greek or something.'

'Anything else?'

'Like what?'

I don't know, voices perhaps? The odd ghost or two? 'Did you notice anything unusual about the book?'

'Not really. The rusty old key's a bit of a puzzle and I couldn't make sense of a lot of it,' he responded. 'Strange thing though…'

'What's that?'

'I was about to give up on the idea when, there it was, a short-bread recipe written in English. And another thing…'

'Yes?'

'I was sure I put the book back here in the bookcase when I finished with it, but when I went back into the kitchen, there it was on the table.' Paul shook his head. 'I must have left it there. I guess I'm getting old.'

'Happens to me all the time. Forty-five is not old, Paul. You probably thought about it and then forgot to put it away. You just have too much on your mind.'

Paul snorted at me and disappeared into the kitchen. I picked up the book and returned it to the shelf. 'Now, Mama,' I said, hoping Paul was out of earshot. 'Behave!'

By the following morning I had put enough clear air between myself and what had happened the last time I had opened Mama's book to feel audacious enough to repeat the performance. I had always lived by the adage that only a fool does the same thing over and over again and expects a different result—until now. Was I really a fool? I used Paul to justify my repeated venture into the well-known. If he was able to follow Mama's recipe without any ill-effects, perhaps I could too. I was happy enough to assume that it had been situational stress and emotion that had triggered my previous hallucination.

Paul had left home early. He was going to be away for a few hours, training some people to use software he had devised for them. I had the opportunity and no excuses. I checked my vital signs. Breathing? Check. Vision? Good. Distractions? None. I felt calm and composed. I took Mama's book off the shelf with the sole intention of copying the recipe for cheese and meat pies, in anticipation of making them later for Nicole. It was going to be a ram-raid, in and out quickly and cleanly. No time wasting, flipping of pages or browsing. And absolutely no ghosts.

My hands shook as I laid the book on the table and untied the ribbon. *Come on, Kat. You're being totally ridiculous. It's just a book.* I closed my eyes and let the covers fall apart. When I opened my eyes again, I was only a teeny bit surprised to find the pages had separated at exactly the right place. *Fotini's Cheese and Meat Bourekia.* Silence. So far so good. I began to read.

'Merhaba,' said the disembodied voice. Oh dear Lord, not again! But this time, I wasn't going to be put off. You come onto my turf and into my mind, you had better expect to answer some questions.

'Hello?' I said doubtfully. 'Who are you?'

'My name is Fotini,' replied the voice. 'The recipe you're about to read was handed down to you by me.'

'Who are you exactly? What are you? And why can I hear you?'

'I am an ancestor. You are the daughter of my great-great-great-great-great-granddaughter, more or less. I may have missed or added a generation along the way.'

'Okay.' A little imprecise, but I got the picture. 'And so why are you talking to me?'

'Why? Because I have something I need to tell you and something you should hear.'

'Right. And how is it you're able to talk to me? I mean, you must be dead.' Oh Lord, I hoped I wasn't telling her something she didn't already know. 'I mean, you know you're dead, don't you?'

If a phantasm could roll her eyes, I got the impression that was exactly what Fotini was doing. 'Of course I know I'm dead. I've been dead for nearly two hundred years.'

I figured at that rate, what she had to tell me had to be mind-blowing.

'I don't know how I am able to talk to you,' she continued. 'I just am. Just as I was able to talk to your mother. I am what I am.'

'Can you understand that this is pretty scary stuff? I didn't conjure you up somehow, did I? I don't know if I'm ready for this!'

'You didn't do a thing. I don't know how this happens any more than you do. If you weren't ready then you wouldn't be able to hear me. And before you become frantic, I probably should warn you that in time you may be able to see me as well.'

So this was just the thin edge of the wedge, the foot in the door, and there was likely worse to come. I opened my mouth to protest when she added, 'Some can, some cannot. I don't know how or why, I just know that your mother could see us, but your grandmother never could.'

'Us? Us? What do you mean, "us"?' I asked, a combination of dread and frustration rising in my throat. If she'd been born a man five generations later, my sixth great-grandmother (give or take) would have made a wonderful door-to-door salesman. 'Who are "us", and I'd like you to be precise with your answer, please. I like to know exactly what I can expect. No springing things on me without proper notice.'

'Well,' she replied, 'life is a mystery, don't you know? Sometimes it's better not to know at the beginning where your path will lead you.'

'What crap,' I said in the full expectation that the connotations of my remark wouldn't be lost in translation. 'You can do better than that.'

'Well, you don't have to keep reading this book.' Her speech drifted from prosaic to hyperbole without missing a single beat. 'There are many, many generations of women in your family, almost as many as there are hairs in your head. Do you think that what you know and who you are, are just the result of your upbringing? You want things to be exact and according to your script? Well, life isn't like that. I don't know who you'll meet if you continue, so I can't answer your question precisely. All I can ask is for you to trust yourself and me, and whichever of the others decide to join us on the way.'

I hesitated. There would be time for psychoanalysis (hers and mine) later. I was happy to assume for the moment that Fotini was real. She certainly sounded and felt real enough.

'Well, Fotini, I'm sufficiently certain of who and what I am to take you up on that. Let's see what you and the others have to offer. But I warn you, the minute you or any of the others sprout horns and start poking me in the ribs with a pitchfork, the book goes straight onto the fire. So play nice. Agreed?'

'I think I understand what you are trying to say. I can assure you that you are not in any danger. Shall I proceed?'

'Please.'

'I was born a long, long time ago near the Greek town of Nauplion.'

'Okay, that's nice. So when do you get to the bourekia recipe?'

'The recipe? Is that what this is about? If you just wanted my recipes, you could have read them yourself.'

'Well, that was exactly what I was trying to do. Until you showed up, that is.'

'Ah yes, and here's me thinking that you were after enlightenment. If it's a recipe you want, then that's what you'll get. Take one *oka* of beef chopped very finely…'

'Great. I had to dream up a hallucination with attitude,' I said as Fotini droned on. But she had misunderstood me. I was open to the possibility that what she had to say could be something I might want to hear. If it proved to be boring I could switch her off simply by shutting the book.

'Stop! Stop!' I waved my hands about. 'Please stop… I'm sorry. We can get to the recipe later. Of course I want to learn more about you.'

'All right. But I am not just something you dreamed up, Miss Know-Everything. As I was saying, I was born near Nauplion...' If she was starting with the beginning, this was clearly going to take a long time. I settled myself into a comfy chair as she continued. 'I don't know exactly when, because no one kept records of anything in those days. Oh, and I had better tell you from the outset that Fotini wasn't the name I was given when I was born. My real name is Fatima. *Merhaba, Kat.*'

16

FATIMA

I was born in Greece at a time when much of the world was Ottoman, from Budapest in the west to Baghdad in the east. Even south of us, in North Africa, everything was the realm of Turkic people, just like us. Perhaps, on reflection, they weren't at all like us.

I supposed I was born sometime during the latter half of the eighteenth century, but there had been so much upheaval that no one knew exactly, not even my mother. All my mother knew for certain was that I was born during a winter not long after Abdulhamid the First had succeeded his brother Mustafa as sultan of our glorious empire. I was the third child in a family of eight children who survived childhood and six who did not. My father, Hassan, considered himself blessed, since I was the eldest of only two daughters.

My earliest memory was of my mother, Yasmina, either pregnant or nursing, and the two became interchangeable in my mind. When I was born, we were neither the richest nor the poorest of families, and, courtesy of our herd of sheep and goats, there was always an abundance of food on the table and warm clothes in the winter. When Yasmina wasn't bringing up children or attending to the needs of her husband and sons, she wove carpets. Not fine ones from silk, with threads so sleek that they felt like the fur of a cat. No, she wove robust ones made of wool that she had spun and dyed herself. She told me that her mother had woven carpets and her mother's mother before her, and the clack of the loom was so familiar and soothing to me as a child that, whenever I could not sleep, she would set to work. Because of that, and since Yasmina never seemed to have enough milk to feed me, I believed myself suckled by our goats and raised beside that loom.

I was the second generation of my family to be born in the. According to my mother, my father's father had come to Greece as part of the Ottoman army. He was a foot soldier, an infantryman, who had stood against the Venetians in Nauplion, part of an army of one hundred thousand against a Venetian force of eighty and a handful of mercenaries. I don't believe he ever saw combat. He soon settled himself in Greece, acquired a wife and insinuated himself into a *dunam* of land.

Although my mother was very certain of her own roots and the purity of her family's Turkic blood, she doubted that her husband shared her pedigree, and frequently muttered behind his back. I remember her calling him a filthy Syrian once when she was washing clothes, believing herself to be unobserved. She put so much energy into rubbing the cloth against the washing stone that I feared she would soon wear it out. I realised in a heartbeat that I'd heard something not meant for my ears. I didn't dare breathe for fear she might hear me. As she turned her back, I darted towards a tree, but she must have caught my outline from the corner of her eye. The next thing I knew, she had grabbed my arm and thrown me to the ground.

'You are a wicked child, *Safir*,' Yasmina yelled at me, slapping me with open palms. '*Kötü!* With your sapphire eyes, always snooping around and watching me.'

I lifted my arms to protect my face and rolled myself, as best I could, into a ball as the blows hailed down on me. That was her way. When I was good, she called me Fatima, my real name. Whenever the caught me playing with the cat instead of doing my chores, or doing something—anything—she didn't like, she called me Safir, on account of the colour of my eyes. I realised, as I grew older, that she was just passing along the same treatment she received at the hands of my father. They were both capricious in their punishment and I felt the wrath of both from time to time. As I grew older I learned how to remain invisible in my father's presence and I became adept at avoiding the barb of my mother's tongue and the sting of her callused hands.

Yasmina had never learned to read and I never went to school. Girls were not educated then and even boys had the most rudimentary of lessons—just enough to ensure that they could not be cheated in business. It was not a time of invention and enlightenment. Far from it. Everything was in decline. Instead of writing and reckoning, little by little and blow by blow, my mother taught me to weave, to keep house and to cook. Even before I was twelve, I had surpassed her in all three, which only had the effect of making Yasmina even angrier.

'We will need to find her a husband soon,' she told my father and my brothers. 'Those sapphire eyes will get us all into trouble and she's better off with one of the old men of the village.' I looked at my family in horror and my sapphire eyes clouded with tears. I resolved for my own preservation to stay as far away from her as I dared.

But it wasn't always possible to get away from Yasmina, and when I was forced to remain at home, I would cook. You see, for Yasmina everything was a chore, so when I cooked, she was free to pursue other delights, such as gossiping with the neighbour. What did I cook? Everything and anything, although I was reputed for the excellence of my pastry goods. I felt no joy in cooking but I had a sense of freedom, not least because my mother stayed far away from the oven and the grate. There was as much of art to it as there was to weaving, and for me that was hard work.

We were blessed with an abundance of fresh produce that I could use any way I wanted, as long as it tasted good and filled my father's and brothers' bellies. Besides our animals, we owned groves of olive, almond and fig trees, as well as an enormous plot filled with grapevines, broad beans, wheat and barley, depending on the season. It was poor, rocky land but, for all that, we had made it productive. Whenever I could, I disappeared into the groves, eating summer grapes or autumn figs until I was sick of the very sight of them. I was quick to learn and very easy to distract. During one escape, I noticed that others were planting mulberry bushes besides their usual crops, as food for the silk worms they were rearing. I thought that was clever, since silk rugs fetched a premium at market and the effort couldn't possibly be that much greater than weaving wool. Too afraid to suggest it to my father for fear it might speed up his search for a husband, I consigned that fact to memory.

We were surrounded by other farmers, Muslim and Greek, some wealthy, others poor, all of them trying to keep their families, pay their taxes and obey the law. I distinctly remember my father's dispute with a neighbouring Greek, whom my father believed to have stolen a portion of his land. So adamant was my father that he decided to have the matter determined in court. In those days, the word of a Muslim man was paramount and a non-Muslim could not bear witness against a Muslim. While Old Michalis protested that the land in question, an isolated strip of land between our fields and the road into town, historically belonged to his family, the *Kadi* swiftly dispatched the case in my father's favour. They found Old Michalis that evening swinging from a limb of his tallest fig tree, on the very grove that my father had just taken ownership of. I have always suspected that Old Michalis was probably right, and that we had acquired most, if not all, of our landholding by increments, one sliver at a time, but I was wise enough to keep those suspicions to myself.

A family of Greek peasants helped us to cultivate the land and harvest our crops, in exchange for which they received just enough to feed themselves and pay their taxes. They were known by the name of Hatzifrangoulis. I saw them occasionally working in the fields but I never looked at them and they never spoke to me. As a child, they seemed as foreign to me as a Scotsman in a kilt, even though we had grown up alongside each other, eaten the same food and drunk from the same spring. I didn't speak Greek, although I knew enough words to know if I was being talked about. Old man Hatzifrangoulis spoke fluent Turkish. I knew that as I had overheard him talking to my father from time to time.

'*Efendi,*' he would say, 'we must begin the harvest on Thursday,' or, 'this animal is hurt,' or 'you remember my son Ilias?' Meanwhile, I was undetectable, always hidden from view, listening to everything but saying nothing.

Life stumbled along in this fashion for another month or so. It was just before the beginning of summer that I learned that

I was soon to be betrothed to Timur Copkun, the son of the old man my mother had spoken about. Yasmina told me I should be glad that I was destined to marry the son and not the old man, but betrothal was betrothal, and to my twelve-year-old eyes, the son, at twenty-five, seemed only a little younger than the father. Besides which, he was ugly, with his hooked nose and swarthy skin. The bargaining happened without any consultation or input from me; a bride price was negotiated and paid, and the contract settled. I was betrothed to a man I knew by sight but had never even spoken to. That was the way things were done. In a few years, as soon as I left my childhood, I would marry Timur Copkun, who was nothing short of repulsive to me. My fate in this regard was sealed. I would be expected to lie beside him in his bed and bear him children, in exchange for which my father had received dowry. In another place and another time there might have been a name for such a transaction.

17

Fatima interrupted her story for a moment, and I wondered why. Surely ghosts didn't tire that easily. When she resumed speaking it was just to inform me that Paul was about to come home. Evidently ghosts were also clairvoyant.

'I think it would be better if you closed the book now,' she said. 'Whenever you're ready to resume, all you need to do is...'

'Yes, I know, open the book at the recipe.'

'Such impatience,' she replied. 'I don't know where you got that from. Certainly not from me.' I felt her smile and had a sudden urge to see her face. 'You might see me when the time is right. Meanwhile, you'll have to quench your curiosity by looking in the mirror and wondering.'

I began to miss her the moment I closed the book and had to resist the desire to reopen it immediately. She was unexpectedly engaging and her tale tugged at my heart, but I had to be honest: the whole idea that the dead could talk to the living seemed preposterous. Correction: it *was* undoubtedly ridiculous. Fatima's story had sounded real enough and yet I knew logically that its origin had to be wholly inside my mind. But there was a way I could know for certain.

I pulled out my notebook and began to type. There had to be a reason why I was a writer and why this was happening to me and to nobody else. Both Paul and Georgia had opened the book and heard nothing. I would record Fatima's story precisely as she told it, and later on I could check the facts. If her story were true, told to me just as she had experienced it, then I could also expect it to be factually accurate. I knew nothing of Greek history or the Turkish language myself, so I couldn't compose a realistic story by myself. If the facts didn't check out, then the inevitable conclusion would be that I had made the whole thing up. *Treat it just as you would an interview with any other source, Kat.* It was going to be simple.

Paul walked in just as I was returning the book to the shelf.

'Miss me?' He kissed me on the lips.

'Can't you tell?'

'Mmm. How about we go out for lunch?'

'Just give me a while to finish this up, and I'm all yours.' I returned to my desk and hammered on the keys while Paul sat adjacent. 'A bit of fresh air might do me good.'

Paul often sat watching me type but he never checked the screen for content. Fortunately, what I did bored him and I reciprocated in kind. We each had a healthy respect for the money the other made, but there remained an unspoken mystery about how exactly we had earned it. I stopped reading my articles aloud to Paul the first time I caught him stifling a yawn and he never told me about the software he was designing. If he ever happened to catch an article of mine in a magazine he was reading, he would always tell me how proud he was and how well it was written. Since I never used his software, I was at a disadvantage but he never grumbled about my disinterest. He was both my anchor and my rock.

I wound up the last few words of Fatima's story and decided to stop writing for the day. It had been an emotional morning.

'Done!' I said and logged off.

We drove into town in silence. All the while I thought about Fatima. I was still a child at twelve—I had only barely outgrown my Barbies. The thought that I could have been engaged and contemplating a loveless marriage was unfathomable.

'You're unusually quiet,' Paul remarked.

'Tough morning.'

'What do you feel like eating?' he asked, taking his hand off the steering wheel to stroke my cheek.

'Anything, really.'

'Would you mind if we had Turkish?' I had a chuckle, which unfortunately sounded like a snigger.

'What?' he exclaimed. 'I feel like a kebab. It's strange, but I've been craving one all morning. I don't know why.'

I giggled. 'It's just a coincidence.' *Should I tell him?* He wasn't just my husband; Paul was my best friend and I never wanted to jeopardise that. But surely, of everyone in the world, he would understand. I just wasn't sure that he was ready to hear about Fatima, so I bit my tongue and said nothing. Instead, we stopped in front of the Turkish café, went in and ordered kebabs.

After a short wait, during which Paul read the paper and I stared into space, a surly, swarthy young man with a hooked nose brought out two kebabs swaddled in paper, rolling back and forwards on a single platter. I wondered if all of reality was sending me a single message.

'Your name wouldn't happen to be Timur?' I asked him as Paul shot me a quizzical glance.

'No. Why do you ask?' His accent was thick with the sound of the Bosphorus. He slammed the platter down in front of us with feigned attitude.

'Oh, nothing. Just a hunch.'

He retreated to the kitchen, still staring back at me suspiciously.

'What was that about? You'll get us both killed,' Paul commented. 'I just watched him carve up the doner kebab. That man can certainly handle a knife.'

He lifted a kebab, peeled back the paper and sank his teeth into it. I resolved to tell Paul that very moment. We were, after all, in a public place and his response would have to be measured. *Here goes nothing!*

'Darling,' I began as Paul bit into the fragrant kebab again. 'You think I'm a fairly well balanced person, don't you?'

'Why do you ask?'

'Oh, no reason, really. Have I ever seemed odd to you?'

'When haven't you been odd?'

'No, really.'

'Okay, this is all leading somewhere, and I never get your hints, so you might as well just say whatever it is you're trying to tell me.' He swallowed, wiped his mouth and frowned. 'Come on.'

'Well,' I said, returning my kebab to the platter untouched, 'I opened up Mama's cookbook today. When you were out.'

'And?'

'And it spoke to me.' There it was. Paul put down his kebab alongside mine.

'What do you mean, it spoke to you?'

'I was looking for a recipe for bourekia—you know, Turkish pies—and suddenly I could hear my whatever-great-grandmother Fatima talking to me.'

'Oh yes. And what did she say to you?'

'She began telling me about her life. In Greece.'

'She's dead, I presume?' he asked. I nodded. 'She did this instead of giving you the recipe?'

'Instead of the recipe.'

'So, and correct me if I misheard you, Granny Fatima came back from the grave to tell you the story of her life. So, how did she look? Well, I hope.'

'I don't know. I couldn't see her,' I admitted. 'Am I crazy?'

'Sounds like it.'

'I mean, these things don't happen to sane people, do they?'

'Not usually. I'm no psychiatrist, but I think hearing voices is generally not considered a sign of sanity.'

'Hmm. I thought so. But you must have felt something, too. After all, you craved a kebab today. That's got to be more than a coincidence?'

'I do eat kebabs occasionally. You can't really compare a food craving to a full blown psychotic experience.'

'Is that what it was?' I pondered. 'I guess you're right.'

'So, what are you going to do about it?' he asked, picking up his kebab again.

'I don't know. See someone, I guess.'

'Maybe you should take the book to a priest or a mufti or whatever, and have it blessed. I mean, you do that kind of thing?'

'You know I'm a lapsed Christian. Although that mightn't be such a bad idea.'

'Well,' he said taking another bite, 'whatever you do don't be too hard on yourself. You've been under a lot of stress lately. Stress can do weird things to people.'

I began to chew on my first mouthful. 'The thing is, I don't know that I really want her to go away. You'll think this odd, but I really, really like her. I want to know what happened to her, Paul.'

'Kat,' he responded, 'you know I love you above everyone and everything. You're the love of my life. But I'm not like your dad. I don't know if I could cope if you turned into your mother.'

'I hope—no—I *believe* that will never occur. This is different from Mama. I'm aware of what's happening to me and I know it may not be real. She never was. And it's not like I hear voices all the time. It only ever happens when I open the book.'

'Well, I guess it's your life and your choice what you do about it. You were obviously worried enough to tell me. I personally think you need help, but in the end that's up to you.'

'Thanks, Paul. I love you too—more than you know. I'm going to make you a promise. If this gets out of hand, I give you the right to institutionalise me. I'll get some help too, I swear, but I feel like I'm invested in Fatima's story now, and it's going to be hard to shut the book and walk away. What if *this* is my novel? What if *this* is what I was destined to write?'

'I don't want to have to put you away, Kat. Not ever. I want you safe and well. If anything places your health in doubt, then I'll destroy it, whatever it is. That includes Mama's book. Are we clear?'

'Clear.' I nodded. I believed Paul when he said he would destroy anything to preserve my sanity and our marriage. One thing was sure and for certain: I was going to have to hide that book.

18

Paul worked from home for the next three days and by the morning of the fourth, I found myself willing him to leave, just so that Fatima and I could continue where we had left off. I even considered giving him a fake message and sending him off on a wild goose chase, to gain a little solitude. I only barely hid my pleasure when, that afternoon, one of his major clients called. Their complete computer catastrophe meant that Paul would have to work away from home for the next two or three days, rebuilding their entire system. If happiness had a name it would have been called *schadenfreude*. And I was absolutely fine with that.

I'm doing research for my first novel, I blogged. Moving into the big league. Next stop, twenty thousand words.

The moment I heard Paul's car reversing down the driveway, I was on my feet to retrieve Mama's cookbook from the box in which I had hidden it. This was going to be my dirty little secret. I carried the book to the kitchen. After all, rituals had to have their temples and the kitchen was a fitting place to read a cookbook, ghost or no ghost. I sat at the table and opened the book carefully.

'*Merhaba*, Fatima,' I said.

'*Merhaba*, Kat.'

'I'm sorry I wasn't able to get back to you sooner…'

I heard a gentle laugh—more of a titter, really. 'Do you actually think I can discern time? Generations can pass in the blink of an eye.'

'Is that what happens after we die? I mean, we do go on, don't we?' I ventured.

'I can't tell you that. All I know is time is not ordered as it is where you are—it is meaningless here. I wouldn't know if I saw you or your daughter today, or yesterday, last year or twenty years from now.'

'I have no daughter, Fatima. In fact, I don't have any children.'

'Oh, is that so?' she said. 'I am so sorry.'

'No need to be. My choice.' I sensed that she seemed puzzled by my last remark.

She paused before asking, 'Shall I continue?'

'Please.' I leaned back in my chair and listened to Fatima's gentle voice rising and falling with the undulations of her life.

19

For the first time in my life, I saw my future stretched out as far as the horizon, and it had an ugly face and a hooked nose. My father was very happy with the deal he had struck with Timur and his father, and that summer he allowed my mother the privilege of beginning the task of assembling my trousseau, a thing she had previously been forbidden to do. My mother had been collecting pieces of linen and putting them away for me for a long time, in spite of my father and without his knowledge. Whenever she embroidered a tablecloth or wove a rug for a customer, she bought extra material and made one for me as well. You might have thought that this was uncharacteristic kindness on her part, and so it might seem, until you realise that she was only doing it to ensure that one day I would have everything I needed to leave home and start my own family somewhere else.

I imagine you are a little surprised by my resignation to my fate. Although the law might have said that women could own land and they could decide for themselves who they would marry, the reality was different. I personally knew of no girls who had married against their fathers' wishes, or whose lands were given to them by their fathers and not taken away by their husbands on their wedding day.

From the moment of my betrothal, my life changed. My mother now ruled me with a fist of iron, and my every waking moment was taken up with sewing and embroidery, making lace and weaving carpets. Long gone were the games, the walks to the groves, the late summer afternoons watching the Hatzifrangoulis children tapping the almond trees with sticks and collecting the fallen nuts in straw baskets. Every morning I woke without hope until I felt my chest, knowing that the moment I sprouted breasts, preparations for my wedding would begin in earnest.

But even on the darkest day, clouds can part for a moment and let the sun stream through. And so it happened to me. I had never before experienced how life could change in an instant, and how easily a catastrophe can be replaced with something quite unexpected that spins your life completely around.

My father took my brothers to the mosque for prayers every Friday, but my mother never went, preferring to pray at home. That autumn morning, after they had gone, my mother placed my baby sister on her hip and, without saying another word to me, she left. I watched as she disappeared down the cobbled street that ran alongside our home and away from the fields. The opportunity was too great and I left as well a minute or two later, running as quickly as I could in the opposite direction. I only stopped when I reached the almond grove.

The almond trees were already stark as skeletons, and the harvest had been and gone without me witnessing the joy of its abundance. The adjoining fig trees were by contrast full of leaves and heavy with ripening fruit. I had grown thin and pale from a season spent mostly indoors, without my usual access to the summer crops, and I yearned to taste the first figs. Sadly, the only ripe ones were at the top of the tree and there was only one way I could get to them—I would have to climb up. I tucked my skirt into my pantaloons and began to ascend.

I had been taught from my earliest childhood never to look up from beneath a fig tree, in case a branch above was weeping and the gummy sap ended up in my eyes. That very thing had happened to a distant relative of my grandmother, and he had lived his whole life blinded in one eye. *Kara Saleh!* Poor, stupid, unlucky Saleh! I had heard of his wasted youth so often that I came to call all foolish boys Saleh, in his honour. So frightened was I of sap-blindness that I did not look ahead to where I was climbing, I just felt for the next knobbly limb that seemed thick enough to support my weight and dragged myself up to it. By the time I had finally reached the ripest figs and looked down, I was surprised to find that I had climbed all the way to the tree's crown and the ground was now a good eight metres below me.

I can't quite remember what happened after that, whether I became dizzy from the heights I had climbed or whether the branch, not quite as thick as an old lady's wrist but just as

gnarled, gave way. I felt myself tumble from my perch, somer-
sault once, perhaps twice, and land in the soft ground under the
tree with an excruciating thud. I recollect lying there thinking
how lucky I was that the Hatzifrangoulis kept the soil beneath
the trees moist under a bed of rotting leaves and straw, and it was
only when I tried to move that the agony returned. The slightest
effort sucked the air from my lungs and made me whimper. I
don't know how long I lay there, or when and why the world disappeared, but I woke up in a strange place, stretched out on a
pallet, alongside a disinterested nanny goat.

In the gloom, I made out a woman's figure and that of a boy,
whom I immediately recognised as one of the Hatzifrangoulis
children. As soon as I moved, the pain caused me to cry out.
The woman turned to look at me and said something to the boy
in Greek, which I couldn't quite make out. The boy crossed the
room.

'Are you awake, Madam Fatima?' said the boy. He was tiny in
stature, but from his composure I guessed he was at least my age
and most probably older.

'Yes,' I replied. 'Where am I?'

'You are in our house, Madam Fatima. We found you lying
under a tree this morning.'

'Yes, I remember that I fell. It hurts when I move.'

'I know. My father has already gone to tell the effendi.'

'No, but he mustn't! Please, I will get into awful trouble. You
must help me go home.'

'I can't. You've hurt yourself. You have to lie still until Baba
returns.'

'What is your name, boy?' I asked.

'Ilias Hatzifrangoulis, Madam Fatima,' he replied, blushing.

'Well, Ilias Hatzifrangoulis, as our servant it is your duty to
help me go home.'

'I'm afraid I cannot. You have broken bones and you must lie
still for now. When my father returns, we will see what can be
done.'

I tried to move again but the pain overcame me and I fell
silent once more. Time barely trickled along, as it does when

awaiting something much feared or much anticipated, but eventually Hatzifrangoulis returned alone. I awoke when the door opened and the afternoon sun struck my face. Ilias Hatzifrangoulis sat on a milking stool in the corner but the woman had gone. They exchanged words in Greek, and I knew they spoke about my father. After a while, the man approached.

'I have spoken to your father and explained how we found you. Your father has asked me to bring you home as soon as you are well enough to travel.'

'Was he very angry?' I asked.

'He was angry enough. I've seen the broken branch and it is a miracle you weren't killed. What were you doing?'

'I was hungry.' I felt as foolish as Saleh. 'How long will it take before I can go home?'

'Your leg is broken and you have bruised your ribs very badly, Madam Fatima. I have splinted your leg as well as I can, but I am used to animals, not children.'

'Aren't they coming to get me?' No matter the answer, I was already filled with dread.

'Not yet. You can stay here for a few days and then we'll see.' He motioned to Ilias. 'The boy will give you some food and my wife can help you with anything else you need. She doesn't speak Turkish, so it's best to tell the boy.'

Ilias brought me some dense bread, a plate of broad beans and a bowl of the much longed-for figs topped with honeyed yoghurt. He watched me in silence as, with some difficulty, I managed to devour the lot. After that, he brought me water to drink and a basin to wash myself.

'Do you want to pee, Madam Fatima?' I had wanted to pee for ages, but I hadn't the courage to ask. I lowered my eyes and nodded. 'I will get my mother,' he said.

Nobody had helped me in such things since my earliest childhood and I cannot explain to you the humiliation of becoming a burden to another person, even at the age of twelve. Somehow, the kind woman was able to manoeuvre me, splint, bruised ribs and all, so that I could use the pan. She whisked it away and disappeared even as I called out words of thanks. When Ilias

returned I asked him to just call me Fatima, since I considered
that I had neither earned nor did I merit the honorific with which
he and his family had endowed me. He sat by me until the light
began to fade.

'Shall I tell you a story, Fatima?'

'Yes, please do.'

'This is a story that happened a very long time ago. Even
before our great-great-grandfathers were born. Once there was
a boy, a Greek boy, who was invited into the court of the pasha.'

'Why was he invited?' I asked.

'Perhaps if you are patient you will find out. You see, the pasha
was a lover of beautiful things. He owned the finest jewels, married the most attractive wives and his clothing was made of the
best silks. The Greek boy had the voice of an angel, and one day,
when the pasha's favourite wife was passing in her wagon she
heard him singing. So beautiful was the sound of his voice and
so entranced was his wife that she went home and immediately
told the pasha. The pasha sent one of his guards to fetch the boy,
so he could hear him too, and be entertained.'

'And what happened then?'

'The pasha's wife had the boy washed and dressed him in
the most superb clothes. She sent him to sing to the pasha. But
when he came before the pasha, he would not open his mouth.
The pasha ordered the boy to sing, but he would not. He threatened to kill the boy but still he remained mute. Finally, in his
rage, the pasha sent his guards to bring the boy's family to him,
so that he might watch them suffer as punishment for his obsti-
nacy. When the boy saw his family there, tears welled in his
eyes. When his mother beheld her son, she cared nothing for herself, but begged him to do whatever the pasha asked, so that he
might be safe. The boy brokered a deal with the pasha that his
family would be returned safely to their home, in exchange for
which he would sing for the pasha. But the pasha was a cruel
man who never kept his word and he ordered that the family be
killed the moment they left his palace. When one of the servants
told the boy the fate intended for his family, instead of singing
for the pasha, the boy took a knife from the table and cut out

his own tongue. In doing this he condemned himself to his own death. And so the pasha never heard the boy's beautiful voice. You see, even a man with all that wealth wasn't rich enough to buy a peasant boy's soul.'

'That's it? But it's a horrible story!'

'Do you think so?' said Ilias. 'Unfortunately many horrible things are true. I think it's a good story, you see, because ultimately the boy won. Do you want to hear another?'

'Absolutely not,' I replied, squirming under my sheepskin.

'Good night then, Fatima.'

'Good night, Ilias.'

I was so exhausted that I slept in spite of the story, there, right next to the nanny goat. Ilias was occupied the following few days with work and other things, so I saw little of him, and one of his many siblings was sent to sit with me instead. All in all, I stayed with the Hatzifrangoulis family for another week and a half before my father came to fetch me.

I could see anger etched on my father's face from the moment he arrived. It followed the creases of his brow, ran along his cheeks to the droop of his ever-scowling mouth. He had brought along two of my brothers, who helped lift me onto the back of the cart. I didn't have time to say goodbye to anyone, although I caught sight of Ilias watching the cart as we passed the field. We drove home in silence.

At home, my mother was furious. I later learned that, courtesy of my injury, my father had discovered her absence that day and had beaten her. She had tried to explain how she had visited a neighbour, but he reprimanded her once for missing her prayers and a second time for leaving home without his permission. He told her she was shameless and worse than an infidel. My mother satisfied her rage on me in a never-ending tirade of humiliation that continued for as long as I was in her presence.

While my physical injuries eventually healed, I was not without many scars that remained for a lifetime. A legacy of my broken leg was a limp that continued long after the bone had knitted together again. Although Hatzifrangoulis was a good farmer, he made a very poor doctor. His splint meant that I was left with one leg a finger's width shorter than the other. After a year or so, when it became apparent that I would never regain full use of my leg again, I was given the epithet of *kara*, meaning unfortunate, so the children of the village soon replaced Saleh's name with mine when they spoke of bad fortune and stupidity. I never again heard my mother call me Fatima. She called me Safir almost exclusively, and, to prove a point, she often called me Saleh to my face.

My only friend throughout what was left of my childhood was Ilias Hatzifrangoulis. Although I was constantly under my mother's control, when she did go out with my father's permission, she foolishly believed my leg to be sufficient impediment to any plans I might have had of escape. I had taught myself to scurry around quickly, and I had learned how to cut across the fields so as to avoid, as much as possible, the prying eyes of neighbours. From Ilias I never heard a single rebuke, even when he took it upon himself to assume the arduous task of teaching me how to read and write.

I mentioned to you before that I was a quick student, and I often wonder if I had been born a man instead of a woman, or at a different time, what heights I might have climbed. Instead of scaling fig trees and making myself a cripple, I might have scaled knowledge and made myself a great scholar. I drank in the lessons Ilias taught, smuggled books and manuscripts home, and was soon reasonably fluent in Greek, which I could read easily and write a little.

But I have forgotten to tell you what became of my betrothal. My father was so adamant that news of my injury be kept from Timur for as long as possible, that I was kept in the house day and night until after the Eid. I'm certain he was worried that Timur would never accept a wife with a limp and that he might be called upon to repay the money Timur had given him. My injuries were all but completely healed by then, so the harness was loosened just enough for me to be able to help my mother take our rugs to Nauplion, despite my limp. That same day, Timur's mother just happened to be travelling on the same road. I was unloading the cart when the eagle-eyed woman spotted me from afar. Although knowledge of my accident had not yet circulated beyond our immediate neighbourhood, she soon learned from this one and that one that I had suffered a misfortune and was lucky to have survived.

'Yasmina!' She was tripping over her skirts in her eagerness and calling out loudly enough for everyone to hear. 'Yasmina! When were you going to tell my son that your daughter is a cripple?'

I watched a grimace replace the fatigue on my mother's face. 'Oh, it's you,' she replied. 'There was nothing to tell him. She isn't a cripple. She had a fall, that's all, but she is healing very well. Your son has nothing to concern himself about.'

'You should have told us anyway, even if it was nothing. Why do I have to learn this awful news from the mouths of strangers?'

My mother sighed. 'Busybodies surround us all the time. Not everything they say is true.' I could see from her manner that Timur's mother disbelieved mine. She scrutinised me from a distance for a while, and apparently saw no further purpose in speaking to us. She turned her back without another word and scampered off in the direction of her house.

That evening, after our return, Timur's father came to our house and demanded that I parade in front of him like a brood mare, so he could reconsider my ability to become his daughter-in-law. My father told him that I would not, that the bargain had already been made and that, short of my death, Timur would have to accept me, no matter what injury I suffered thereafter. Even though I hid behind a wall, I glimpsed the old man's face swell in anger. I heard him threaten that he would bring the matter before the court, saying that I was no longer any use to them, and asking that his money should be returned. My father laughed at this.

'Take me to court?' he chuckled. 'Have you lost your mind? Have you forgotten what became of Old Michalis when he tried to take me to court?' His response was sodden with irony.

'I remember it well but, you see, I am not a stupid old Greek. You may have had the *kadi* in your pocket, Hassan, but I have Allah on my side.'

'How dare you insult me!' My father's disposition turned from mockery to irritation in an instant. 'I am just as faithful as you are and I have no need of a *kadi* in my pocket, as you say, when I have the power of the law on my side. So get out of my house and never speak of this to me again. I tell you, Fatima will be brought to you as your son's bride when she is of age. Exactly as we bargained. What you and your son do with her after that is your concern.'

I expected them to come to blows but instead, Timur's father cleared his throat and spat. 'And I tell you I will not have a cripple as my son's wife. I release you from the betrothal. Keep the money, may it bring you no happiness. This is my final word on the subject—you had better teach your sons to have eyes in the back of their heads and to always look behind them.' Then, as an afterthought, he added. 'And your daughters, too.' And with that said, he left and we never saw him again.

I became a hopeful nobody from that moment on. What do I mean by that? The fog that had clouded my future disappeared that day along with Timur's father, but the reality was that I had no standing in my father's house. Just a few days earlier, I had been contemplating a marriage I did not want, but for my father, my marriage would have signalled the end of his obligation to feed, clothe and house me. That day, I became a girl without prospects, and what was worse, I was branded by my limp. My father considered me nothing more than a burden he would now have to carry for life. He had never been an engaging man at the best of times but from that moment on, he looked straight through me as if I wasn't there. He told my mother to keep me out of his sight at all times. In order to reinforce his words when she passed them along to me, my mother added a series of slaps to my face.

I had experienced the cruelty of my family from time to time, but I had never understood the random cruelty of children until then. I am ashamed to admit that I include myself in that number. If I am honest, I have to admit that I had been just as horrible to Saleh as they now were to me. Even the younger Hatzifrangou-lis children sniggered when I passed, and no one bothered to call me Madam Fatima any longer. Not that I cared about that. My response to their scorn was that I rarely left the house. When I did, I tried to make sure that my path still crossed that of Ilias Hatzifrangoulis. He had remained a friend and I never heard an ill word pass his lips about anybody, ever. I admired that most of all.

Although he was two years older than me, Ilias was a good head and a half shorter than I was, and still childish in features. He was not particularly handsome by all usual measures; his ears were far too big for his head and his nose a little too pronounced. Then one day—it seemed to happen overnight—Ilias sprang from a boy into a young man. He approached his sixteenth birthday still a sapling but by the time he reached it, he had become a tree. In the space of a few weeks, he began to tower over me and his chin was darkened by hair. His face made more sense and it grew into its features. Although I had also grown taller, my changes were not as obvious. I was still horribly thin and, truthfully, more than a little boyish. And of course, I was still burdened with the limp.

We stayed friends in the years that followed, most often from a distance, passing notes when words could not be exchanged. I am a little ashamed to admit that, once my sister was betrothed at barely ten years old and her place in the family was elevated above mine, he became my only friend. He was a friend I hardly ever saw, and my isolation was complete. I had nothing but the stories in my head with which to entertain myself, to end the dreariness of my own existence and to keep myself from madness.

You can only imagine, then, how painful it was for me when I reached the age of nineteen, and I noticed a shift in the way Ilias spoke and acted on the rare occasion that I was around. He appeared more aloof to me, as if he harboured a painful secret, but worst of all was that I suspected he was avoiding me. I had watched one day as he changed his path just to avoid intersecting with mine, believing himself undetected. I guessed that he must have formed an attachment elsewhere. I knew that it was inevitable that our friendship would end the day he married, if not before. I had no prospects, so my companionship was guaranteed for as long as I could conceal it from my mother, but no wife would stand for a husband with a Turkish woman for a friend. I understood that, but it was still agonising for me to accept it.

When we met, I acted as if nothing at all had changed between us, and I continued this way for as long as I could endure the difficult silences and contrived conversation. Little by little, I came to the realisation that I needed to know the truth, no matter how unpleasant that might be. My suffering ended the day I spotted him alone in the barley field, and determined to finally clear the air. I needed certainty about the end of our friendship. I couldn't allow our companionship to be the stream which gushes in winter, becomes a trickle by mid-summer and by autumn has stopped flowing altogether.

'*Yiasou*, Ilias,' I called out, confident that it was too late for him to avoid me.

'*Yiasou*, Fatima. How are you?'

'I am much the same as always. And you? What news do you have?'

'Nothing. No news.' He was staring at his feet and fidgeting. 'You just caught me. I was just about to go home.'

'Oh? You didn't look as if you were just about to go. That is, not until the moment you saw me.' I knew this was my opportunity. I had to summon up the courage to say how I felt. 'We've been friends a long time, Ilias. Friends tell each other the truth, don't they?'

'Yes. Sometimes.'

'No. Always. You have been avoiding me, and I know it. I want you to tell me why.'

Ilias did not respond and I controlled the impulse to fill the silence with chatter. When he finally spoke his response was surprising. 'Is it that obvious? Yes, it's true. I have avoided you and I ask for your forgiveness.'

'But why?' I pleaded.

'Why?' He paused to choose his words. 'Because of you. You say we are friends. I say we are more than friends, but you are Turkish and I am Greek. I am Christian and you are Muslim.

All the time I think. I worry. I imagine things that cannot be. You have driven me mad.'

'Me?' I was incredulous. Of all the explanations I had prepared myself for, this was not one.

'You. You bewitched me with your eyes when I was a child.' He struck his chest with the palm of his hand. 'Your eyes pierced me here, and these past seven years have changed nothing. You come and then you go, no matter what your parents say. You laugh and then you cry at my stories. You learn my lessons and then you challenge me about everything. And a single thought enters my mind and grows until I can think of nothing else. I want to marry you, Fatima. I would marry you tomorrow but I know I cannot. I have no fortune and we are not supposed to be. It is impossible.'

'Have you told anyone this? Does anyone know?'

'Who would I tell?'

'But I am a cripple, Ilias. You couldn't possibly feel that way about me.'

'I don't see a cripple. I see the most beautiful woman in the world. If there was a way… If there was a way, we would marry this minute and begin our life together now.'

It was madness, but I was convinced that none of my family would care if I lived or died, so surely my marriage to Ilias would simply discharge my father's obligation to provide for me until death.

After a minute of thought I heard myself say, 'There could be a way if you are daring enough. Me a Muslim and you a Christian? That is not insurmountable for me. Many Turkish men have taken Greek wives, so what if I do the reverse. I would be prepared to join your religion to marry you. But what of your father? Surely he wouldn't want a daughter with a limp.'

'My father has never said a bad word against you. But the villagers are a different thing altogether. If we were to do this, we could never stay here.'

'If we were to do this we would have to go far away. You would do that for me?' We both knew that escape required more than mere sentiment. 'I know where my father keeps bags filled

with *akce*. He never spends any money if he can avoid it. As I figure it, since he kept my bride price and he has profited for years
from the rugs that I have woven, some of that money is mine. I
could take just enough to help us on our way, but not so much
that he would discover its loss. At least not straight away.'

'I would never take another man's money. If we do this, I pledge
to repay whatever you take as my debt.' The boy I had once called
my servant had grown up to be proud and self-sufficient.

'Yes. It is agreed.'

When my life had seemed doomed to interminable unhappi-
ness, it had spun around once again. At a time when marriages
were brokered by men and alliances created on the basis of status and silver, I can admit to you that ours was an unlikely love
match. But only the innocent and the foolish believe success to
be the inevitable conclusion of their dreams, and we were neither.
We plotted our future, the two of us, as if it were one of Ilias's
convoluted tales, planning our escape with precision and keeping it a secret for fear of discovery. My mother was consumed
by her own misery, and my father and my brothers too occupied
with commerce, to worry about anything as insignificant as me.
I was free to make plans and to execute them as long as, from a
distance, everything appeared normal to them.

Aside from being the eldest, Ilias was also his mother's favourite. I thought she knew nothing of our relationship because she
said nothing. She may have been taciturn but she observed everything, and we ought to have credited her with more insight. When
she learned of it, instead of opposing our plan, she suggested that
we leave the Morea as soon as we married and that we live our
life on her ancestral island. Her island was so close to Turkey that,
at night, you could see the fires illuminating the jagged archipel-
ago opposite. She said nothing to her husband and arranged our
passage to Chios on a fishing boat. That signalled the beginning
of the rest of my life.

First, Ilias and his mother took me to the priest to be baptised.
It was Ilias's mother who initially suggested I be given the name
of Fotini, after the saint, the woman of the well who travelled
all the way to Rome. And by baptism with water, I left Fatima,

whose life had been filled with darkness, pain and tragedy, far behind. I was ready for Fotini's journey to begin in a matter of days.

I returned home after my baptism, hair greasy from the *myr-rod*, the holy oil with which I had been anointed, and terrified that my mother might notice the silver baptismal medallion hanging around my neck. I shouldn't have worried. That night, I stayed awake and when all were asleep, I got up and dragged a cedar box filled with a rug and linen from the stable where it was hidden, to the shack in Old Michalis's orchard. Ilias, his mother and I made the journey to Nauplion by cart a week later. Ilias and I were married there at dusk in a church no bigger than a pigpen, witnessed only by his mother and the priest's wife. The priest blessed us and guided us to the harbour by moon-light, by which time my mother was no doubt wondering where I had gone. Together, Ilias and I stepped onto a boat that would take us to an island neither of us knew, for a future we could not have imagined. I carried a bundle of clothes and a bag filled with my father's silver coins and Ilias brought my box, which we had filled with every possession we had in the world. It was to be the beginning of our new life.

20

It took over a week for us to reach the little harbour at Chora on the island of Chios. Fortunately, the first three days of the journey had been calm and we made good progress, but by the fourth day, the *borias* had begun to blow a gale, making it impossible for the caïque to tack north. We stayed in Mykonos for a day and a half before the northerly wind subsided enough for us to resume our journey.

I cannot tell you the relief I felt when I caught sight of the village we were about to call our home. Ilias's great-aunt still lived in Thimiana with her family, but please don't think for a minute that they were happy to see us. We were as strange to them as if we had come from China and probably far more menacing. We were interlopers, and it wasn't because I was Turkish. It was simply that they were worried that Ilias had come to reclaim his family's land and that, as a consequence, they would be dispossessed.

Ilias had the notion that with our remaining money we would secure a small plot of land, and on this we were agreed. Once he had convinced his family that our purpose wasn't to acquire their land, they agreed to help him negotiate the purchase. Ilias planned to plant mastic trees and crops to feed ourselves, and then sell the prized mastic resin at market. I thought we'd be better off filling the plot with mulberry trees and, with a loom and some silk worms, we could weave our way out of poverty. Somewhere between the two, we reached a compromise.

Ilias made me a loom and his cousin agreed to let us have a clip of wool on the understanding that we would share the profits equally when I sold the rugs. That winter we both spun wool and wove in shifts, so that when one of us was sleeping, the other worked. In spring, we planted mulberries, mastic and olives, a couple of almond trees and a single fig.

Shortly before our second Christmas, Anastassi was born, just in time to watch us spinning the thread we had unravelled a few months earlier from our first silk cocoons. Did you know that the moth is helpless and dies after it lays its eggs? The acrid, putrid smell of the boiling cocoons seared my nose at first, but it later become as familiar and as welcome to me as the summer jasmine. Knot by knot, the rug took shape, soft as my son's breath and almost as precious. When it was finished, Ilias sold it to a Greek merchant for a good sum of money. It was destined to adorn the floor of one of the mansions that line the road from Thimiana to Chora.

I am not meaning to be boastful, but my reputation as a maker of the finest rugs spread along the length of that road, and then hitched a ride on the merchant ships, as far as the ears of the pasha himself. My skills were greatly sought after. And so it went on from season to season—a cycle of hatching silk worms' eggs, spinning, weaving and selling, the bearing of children—all done to the beat of my own heart.

I heard little about my family after I left the Morea, only passing word from Ilias's mother from time to time when she remembered to write. Quite frankly, I wasted little time thinking of them and I couldn't have cared in the slightest if they had all disappeared from the face of the earth. In time, Ilias grew grey and weary, but his back remained straight as a shotgun barrel. Together with our sons, he made certain that we had enough of everything we needed, but not so much that it made us insensible to the world in which we lived. One thing never changed, no matter how hard I worked and no matter what I did. Ilias's family never stopped calling me *Turkala*, the Turk. Despite their name-calling no one ever said a word against me when I baked my pittes stuffed with cheese and spinach, or my bourekia or even my *susamli simit*.

When you are so far away from home, what you eat becomes the thread that connects you with your origins. Perhaps that sounds strange to you, but that's how it felt to me. In marrying Ilias, I had become Greek but my heritage remained in the food that comforted my family. And so, you see, we often trade names along the journey—daughter, cripple, Turk, Muslim, Christian, wife. What does it all matter?

We were getting old when the first stirrings of war reached our island. Our boys had grown tall and upright like their father and, apart from Mikes who was still an infant, they were about to make their mark on the world. Because of them, my life made sense and I greeted each morning with purpose. But as had happened so many times in my life, my path was about to take another turn.

We had heard about a revolutionary fire that had begun in the Morea the preceding spring. The Turks told of horrible crimes the Greeks had perpetrated against them, of slaughter by scythe and slingshot, the only weapons available to most Greeks. When the Maniot Greeks had decided to rise up against the Ottomans we thought ourselves far enough away not to feel the heat. We were wrong.

One night, when I was scurrying home from the fields in the diminishing daylight, a man in pantaloons appeared before me, brandishing an Islamic dagger, laughing at me and calling me Safir. I might have been frightened of him had he not had an otherworldly quality about him, not quite real, a shadow of a man I once knew. I told Ilias of my vision, and he admonished me for having an overactive imagination. You know of course that Muslims do not believe in ghosts, but even Christian that I had become, I was convinced this was a *jinn* in the form of my father. News eventually dribbled along to us that my father had died of a fever and that two of my brothers has joined Hursid Pasha's soldiers in an effort to quell the Greek uprising. I thought that this, perhaps, accounted for the apparition.

Ilias's family informed us that they were surrounded by war, but they kept largely to themselves, and had so far survived the battles that flared up around them. But the revolution was not destined to stay on the mainland. Before too long, the fire spread to the islands, and village by village, the Greeks took on the Ottomans. We had seen the coming and going of Greek ships since the preceding summer, and Ilias spoke of things he had heard in hushed voices.

When one of the Greek leaders, Tompazis, came from the neighbouring island to speak to the elders of our village, Ilias was counted among them. He told me that revolution did not suit our purpose, and he wanted nothing to do with it. Nobody in Chora wanted war to disrupt their lives, by which they meant their ability to make vast sums of money. Since the Ottomans recognised Chios as a prosperous island, they left it mostly alone. We were opposed to war then, and the revolutionaries came and left, and life limped along for a while. But not all Chiots were united under the same purpose.

We never expected the flames to reach Chios quite as quickly or as suddenly as they did. One moment, our little world was calm, Easter was approaching and it hadn't been long since we had sown our barley. The next, word got around that revolutionaries from Samos had arrived along with a fleet of ships and Greek troops numbering a few thousand. Those who had been silent before, when the elders had thrown the revolutionaries off the island, finally found their voices. A patriotic blaze tore along the road that led to Thimiana, and many of the men of our village rushed to join others in the battle against the Turks. In turn, the pasha sent Turkish troops numbering many tens of thousands. I was grateful that my sons were too young to take up arms and Ilias too old, but there was no mistaking the fact that war had found us. It had ignited everywhere and in its intensity, it threatened to overcome us and ruin us all.

It was Good Friday when the slaughter began. We were told of the sultan's order that all Greek infants aged up to three, males over twelve and women over forty years old were to be killed. Females from three to forty and boys between three and twelve years old would be captured as slaves. Only those who accepted Islam would be spared. In many ways, my life appeared to have come full circle. Ilias hinted that I should assume my name of Fatima once more, but I saw his relief when I refused. Fatima had been washed away more than twenty years ago. I told him I would rather die as the mother and wife I had become, than live on as the cripple I once was.

Once the news of the massacre of the congregation of the Church of the Virgin Mary reached town, the people of Chora began to evacuate to the villages. They abandoned their beautiful mansions, their stone houses and their modest shacks, and passed Thimiana on their way to claim sanctuary at the monastery of St Minas. They told tales as they went, of the bounty offered by the pasha to buy Greek tongues and ears for ever-increasing sums of money. Ilias told me to take the children and seek refuge there myself, but I didn't want to leave him. On Easter Sunday, after he had begged me a third time, I agreed to go. Our four eldest boys were to stay behind with their father. Mikes would come with me.

Ilias made me a promise. 'If I hear of anything bad coming in this direction, I swear to take the boys and head for the hills. I know how to find shepherd huts in the mountains. If you need us, you'll find the boys and me in the *Provata*, feasting on bandit's lamb.'

'Knowing you, I'll be able to track you down just from the scent of that lamb.'

He smiled at me. 'A Turk could pass right by us and see, hear and smell nothing. Don't worry about us—we will be fine. Just take care of yourself and Mikes.'

You cannot know the heartbreak I felt saying goodbye. How do you leave everything you value most, not knowing what might become of them or of yourself? I held each one of them in my arms until I thought my heart would shatter and stared at their faces so that I would not forget them either in this world or the next. Then I took Mikes's hand and together we walked to Neochori, barely two kilometres away, and from there we climbed the hill path that led to the old monastery. When we arrived, we found that two, maybe three thousand townsfolk had preceded us. They crowded into the church and prayed for a miracle.

The monks had opened all the doors to the church, but it was simply not large enough to accommodate everyone and the throng spilled out into the courtyard, almost to the gate. We threaded our way through the multitude, until, exhausted and sore, I searched for a place to sit down and rest for a moment. An old monk took pity on me when he saw me hobble past carrying sleeping Mikes in my arms.

'Come, stay in my cell for a while,' he said, leaving us alone and partly closing the door.

I must have fallen asleep for a bit, but I woke up with Mikes's howls and the cries of the townsfolk in my ears, and the stink of death in my nose. I peered through the crack between the door and the jamb, and then slowly pulled the door towards me until it was only barely ajar. That way, I hoped we might not be spotted.

You cannot imagine the awfulness of what I saw that day. Fifteen thousand Ottoman soldiers had stormed the monastery, armed to the teeth with weapons. They were slaughtering everyone in sight—men, children, women—the lot of them. It was nothing short of an orgy of killing. The soldiers slashed at the people with swords, swinging at random, hacking at arms, heads, anything. They shot them with muskets and set them alight with torches, even where they stood, and not a single one of the townsfolk had any way of defending themselves.

Soldiers will never tell you of the awful stench that accompanies such a slaughter, but I will. It is worse than anything you have ever experienced and your own fear magnifies the odour a hundredfold. The sticky-sweet scent of blood is the least of it. Combine that with the smell of excrement, of urine and vomit, and mix in a measure of burning hair and you might just about have it. That is a recipe you will never find in a book.

My thoughts drifted to the unanswered prayers of thousands of people. I am a little ashamed that for the briefest moment in the midst of the maddening chaos, I contemplated crying out in Turkish and declaring myself a Muslim woman, and thereby claiming for Mikes and me the sultan's mercy that had been promised. But who would hear me? A raging soldier wouldn't have the presence of mind to distinguish one from another, a Greek from a Turk, a Christian from a Muslim. It was clothing that distinguished one from the other and I was dressed like a Greek. Even if it had been possible for a soldier to hear me, I would have to live the rest of my life with the knowledge that I had disavowed everything I had become. And what of Ilias and my sons? Had they left for the *Provata*, as he had promised to do? I wondered what had happened to those left behind in the village. In my mind, death was preferable to life without my boys.

I hid Mikes as well as I could behind the straw pallet the monk used as his bed, told him to be silent, and awaited my fate. After what seemed like hours, the crack of the pistols and thud of sword on flesh tapered off and then stopped completely. All that was left was the crackling fire and the stench of burning flesh. Just as I began to imagine that we were saved, the door, which I had purposely left only barely open, creaked. It swayed a little and then a bit more, until it finally swung entirely open.

My eyes hardly had time to adjust to the daylight that streamed into the lightless cell when they fixed on a sight far worse than anything imaginable. A group of soldiers, heads wrapped in bloody turbans, pantaloons soaked in gore, swords dangling in their filthy hands, pushed their way into the cell.

'What is this? How can she have escaped?' One guffawed and spat at me.

I said nothing and prepared myself for the worst. Suddenly one of the other soldiers, his face covered in grime and soot, caught his breath and began to yowl like a wounded dog.

'Safir! I recognise you! Your eyes betray you!'

I stared at the soldier's face until it began to make sense. His features were those of my mother, a little debased and slightly more masculine. Yusif was still a tiny child when I had last seen him, hardly older than my Mikes. The soldiers exchanged quizzical glances. One commented to Yusif that if I was a Muslim, then I should be taken away and not harmed.

'This woman was my sister, but she ran away many years ago. She robbed my father and disgraced my family,' Yusif replied. Something must have caught his eye as he spoke, and he darted forward abruptly. In a single, fluid motion, he reached out and pulled the pallet aside, revealing Mikes. 'And this?' he asked, pointing to the cowering child. 'What is this?'

'He has a name. He is Mikes. He is your nephew,' I said.

'My nephew? I claim him in part satisfaction of your debt. He is now my slave,' Yusif replied with a sneer, pulling Mikes towards him and stroking his hair. 'So, what about you,' he continued. 'What are you now?'

'I am Fotini Hatzifrangoulis.'

At this, Yusif howled with laughter. 'No, Safir. You are Fatima the cripple, as I remember it.'

'You're wrong, I am not. I'm Fotini Hatzifrangoulis. I am a wife and a mother.'

'Is that so? Well, well, well. Fotini Hatzifrangoulis... Now that's a Christian name, isn't it? Do you understand what you're saying?'

'Yes.'

'And you understand that you are guilty of an unforgivable insult against your family as well as your faith?'

If I had had a knife I might have done as did the Greek boy in Ilias's story but, instead, all I said to Yusif was, 'I am Fotini Hatzifrangoulis.' They were to be my last words.

'There is no God but He!' was Yusif's reply before he put his sabre to my throat.

21

Fotini finally fell silent. I sensed the need to say something, to acknowledge her suffering in some way. I scratched around for some words of comfort, but there were none. I couldn't say that I understood, because I didn't. There was simply zero I could say to her. I felt tears forming (which was strange to me because I hadn't cried since childhood). I held them back, sniffed up the mucus dribbling from my nose and reached for a tissue.

'Why are you weeping?' Fotini said. 'If it's for me, then you needn't waste your tears.'

'I'm not actually crying, but what if I were? Why shouldn't I be emotional? After everything you endured?'

'Ah, yes. Well, that's it precisely. Life is a mystery.'

'Oh no, don't play that card with me. And death?'

'No. You mustn't ask me. Death is even more a mystery.'

It seemed we had reached a philosophical impasse. Dealing with ghosts or spirits, or figments of one's imagination (whichever of these categories she fell into), was evidently tricky. 'So what happened to your sons? Were they killed too?'

'What do you think? You're here, aren't you?'

'So they survived. Or at least one of them did.' I paused. 'I'm so sorry your brother did this to you.'

'My brother did nothing. It was my fate. We all have our fate decided a long time before we're born.'

'Do we? So nothing I do or say makes any difference to what happens to me? That's absurd.'

'Perhaps.'

I wiped my eyes, sick of her enigmatic replies. 'What you're saying is that we are destined from birth to live a certain life? And our death? I've heard philosophies like that before and I'm not sure that I agree. I'd hate to think that everything's already mapped out for me and I can't do anything to change my fate. I'd prefer to think it's all random.'

'Then I have no answer for you. I can give you my recipes and the wisdom of my story but that's all.'

'You just said that your suffering was predetermined. I was destined to have a crazy woman for a mother and a bitch for a sister-in-law. No free will at all.'

'I said it was my fate. You, Kat, think in absolutes. Good, bad, my fault, your fault. And why do you say your mother was crazy?'

'Well, she heard voices and saw people who weren't there.'

'Like you?'

No, not like me. I've never seen anyone who wasn't there. I've never even seen you.'

'But you hear my voice, don't you? If you want to see the best of me, just take a look in the mirror. You inherited my eyes. And my stubbornness. You want to know what you inherited from your mother?'

I snapped the book shut. I wasn't about to argue semantics with an auditory hallucination. I opened up my computer and wrote down the rest of Fotini's story exactly as she had told it. After I had finished that, I began fact-checking. Imperfect or not, I tested everything she had said against the internet. After that, just to be sure, I got online and chatted theology for a while with an imam from Bangladesh. Or at least that was what he told me he was, and I believed him. I thought things were going pretty well, right up to the point that I asked him for his view on ghosts and mental illness, and the conversation ended abruptly.

Paul came home that night for the first time in three days and he was bleary-eyed and short-tempered. I poured him a glass of wine and rubbed his feet and when he asked what I'd been doing, I answered vaguely. I guessed it probably wasn't the best time for me to tell him what I had been up to, or the story that Fotini had recounted. By nine he was asleep on the sofa. The following day, I made good on my promise to Paul and had an appointment scheduled with a psychologist.

The woman I was about to see was a friend of Simone's, who frequently gave forensic evidence on behalf of some of her more disturbed clients. Apparently she was an expert in the field of post-traumatic stress disorder, with particular emphasis on treating the children of troubled parents. Even though I had clearly left my childhood far behind me, I counted myself among that number. All good thus far.

Lena Edelbaum practised psychology out of the front sitting room of a tumbledown house she shared with her husband Lenny and their three, mostly adult, children. It just so happened that Lenny was a practising psychiatrist, another expert witness of Simone's, so together Lena and Lenny ran a one-stop psycho-shop. It was the ultimate symphony of marital and professional harmony, crammed into an unruly, overstuffed facade of peeling paint and wilting hydrangeas.

I waited for her in a small anteroom crowded with mismatched chairs and old sofas. A rolled-up rug stood propped in one corner, waiting to be unfurled. A web that tied the rug to the cornice suggested it had been waiting for quite some while. There was an enormous aquarium in another corner, full of angelfish and goldfish and a noisy filter that belched a stream of bubbles every few seconds. Whoever had said that fish were calming knew nothing about the stress that attaches to the thought that you are about to give a total stranger the password to your brain. While the fish swam in lazy circles around their tank, I was only just succeeding in stopping my heart from leaping out of my mouth and fluttering all over the floor.

I picked up one of the magazines from the coffee table, flipped through it and tossed it aside. I didn't care which yummy mummy wore their baby bump best, or where the best celebrity-lookalike shoes could be bought for next to nix. I simply wouldn't be distracted. I watched a series of framed Rorschach inkblots loop the room and disappear down a corridor, and decided they all looked like various bits of genitalia. I was still wondering what Lena Edelbaum would make of that when the door slid open—actually, it rattled across its rail and stuck halfway—and Mrs Edelbaum appeared in person, hair neatly curled into a greying blonde helmet. She was an attractive, fifty-something woman, cloaked in a soft, motherly wrapping.

'Kat Bower?' Unnecessary, since I was the only one there, not counting the fish.

'Yes. That's me.' I leapt to my feet.

'Why don't you follow me?' I couldn't think of a single reason not to.

She led me down a labyrinthine corridor to her office and opened the door. Inside was a continuation of outside, only more so. She cleared a pile of books from the chair so I could sit and moved them over to the chaise longue. Three walls were floor to ceiling bookcases so filled with books that, to fit them all in, they had to be turned around and stacked on each shelf in individual piles. It was jammed with everything psychological from the nineteenth century and beyond—Freud, Jung, PTSD and the Overactive Adrenal Gland, and so on and so forth. A phrenology skull sat on her desk and I fixated on that for a while, somewhere between cautious and secretive.

'So, tell me something about yourself.'

Just as I opened my mouth to respond, the telephone rang. She lifted her hand to stop me and said, 'Sorry, I have to answer that.'

'Yes, of course,' I replied, already feeling a little neglected.

'Hello, Dr Edelbaum's rooms. Yes it's me, Lena. No, Lenny's with a patient. Oh. Uh huh. Uh huh. No! I'm so sorry! Yes, of course, Roger, I'll tell him. Tuesday at three. Uh huh. And how is your wife? No! Really? Is she still in hospital? Really? Well be sure to send her my regards when you see her. All right then. Bye bye, Roger. Yes of course. No I won't forget to tell him. Bye bye now.' She hung up and turned to me. 'Where were we…'

'We weren't. You asked me…'

'Oh yes, of course. So, tell me something about yourself.'

'I'm not sure what to say. I'm happily married, no kids, forty-something and a writer.'

'That's nice. What do you write?'

'Oh, magazine articles, social commentary, all kinds of things. I blog mostly. The latest project I'm working on is a novel.'

'Really. So why have you come to see me?'

'Well, I wanted to get some perspective on something—on my novel—that I'm writing about, and, well, I was hoping that you could help me.' I had gone in with the full intention of telling Mrs Edelbaum the truth, but this seemed so much more convenient. Depersonalised somehow. Much cleaner this way.

'Is that so?'

'Yes. You see, my character—my protagonist really—hears voices.'

'She hears voices.'

'Yes.'

'All the time?'

'No, not all the time.'

'When does she hear the voices? I mean, what sets it off?'

'When she opens her dead mother's recipe book, she hears the voices of her ancestors talking to her.'

'And what do they say? What do they tell you—sorry, I mean tell her—to do?'

'Nothing really. They just tell her about their lives. They don't tell her to do anything. It's not like the voices tell her to kill people or do anything bad like that. They have names, identities. She doesn't go around wearing an aluminium foil hat and talking about the radio waves in her head.' I had said way too much. I feared I was in danger of being discovered and then committed to an asylum.

'Hmm. Would you say that you're generally a straightforward person?'

'A what? I don't quite grasp…'

'Open, honest…'

'Yes, I think so.'

'How would you rate yourself?'

'Pretty truthful. Only lies under extreme pressure.'

'And do you feel as if you're under pressure now?'

'Right this minute? Maybe.'

'So how would you rate what you just told me, if one is a complete fabrication and five is the absolute truth?'

'A five.' The substance was true even if the subject was a fiction.

'You know, Kat, this can only work if you are prepared for us to be totally frank with each other.'

'I know.'

'Okay then. So you've come here to research a book you're writing and the heroine hears voices.' She paused and stared me down. 'I have a confession to make. I read your blog.'

'I'm very flattered.'

'No, I read it in preparation for meeting you today. Unless I'm mistaken, a few weeks ago you blogged about hearing voices. Yourself.'

'That's right.' I wasn't missing a beat. 'And did you also read the bit where I blogged that I wasn't talking about myself, but about my character?'

'You see, I have a dilemma here. If you're asking me to help you research your book, I'm sorry, I don't think I can help you. If you want to consult me professionally, then that's all right. So it's up to you.'

As I was composing the correct response in my mind, the telephone rang again. Mrs Edelbaum's hand shot up again as she told me once more that she was sorry but she had to answer that.

'Hello, Dr Edelbaum's rooms. Yes, it's Lena. No, he's with a patient. Oh. Yes. Uh huh. With me this time? Let's see. I can fit you in at six-fifteen next Wednesday. That's good? Okay then, I'll see you Wednesday. Yes. Six-fifteen. Bye bye now.' She hung up and turned back to me. 'Where were we... Oh yes. So what have you decided?'

'Can I be frank with you?'

'Of course.'

'That whole answering-the-telephone-thing while you're meant to be focusing on me is getting old and very annoying. I'll tell you what, why don't you use the money you made from this session to buy yourself an answering machine. Or better yet, employ a receptionist. I think I'm done here.' I stood up to leave.

'I hear what you're saying. But before you go, Kat, I have to confess that Simone spoke to me about you. It wasn't malicious, but she called me as a very concerned friend, that's all. Now you can say whatever you want, you can leave now and never come back, but she told me about your recent episode. She also told me that your relationship with your mother was problematic and that your mother died recently.'

I was taken aback. Clearly, Simone had discovered a loophole to friend–friend confidentiality.

'So, Kat, what are your earliest memories of your mother?'

I hesitated for a moment. A series of intercuts replayed in my mind, random episodes without obvious association—the sweetness of Mama's scent, my infant face buried in the gentle curve of her neck just above the collarbone, the sound of sobbing. Then Mama in the kitchen, wrestling butter and sugar together in an enormous bowl while I perch on a chair, distracted.

'You must watch me, Katy,' she said to me. 'This is how you learn.' She was angry now. 'See what I'm doing? If you don't watch, how will you know how to cook for your family?'

'What else do you remember?' Lena's simple question opened a floodgate.

'I remember Mama saying that there was someone outside my window.'

I was overwhelmed by the immediacy of my memories as they played once more in my mind. I slid back into my seat and told her what I remembered with such clarity that it frightened me.

Mama came into my bedroom the minute Daddy left for night shift. She eased the blades of the blind a crack and peered out.

'Stay in bed and don't say a word!'

'Mama? Mama, don't go. Please! Mama…'

She moved towards the bedroom door. 'Stay in bed! Be quiet!'

'No, don't go, Mama!'

She left without another word as I caught the sob in my throat before it could escape. I swallowed it down, hard. Shivering, I pulled the blanket over my head and, for the briefest moment, I was safe in the stifling darkness. I heard Mama lock my door, as she did every night when Daddy left, followed by my brother's and then the others, one by one, the slap of her footsteps as she progressed down the hall. Loud clacks growing more distant as each of the tumblers turned and then, silence. After an interminable stillness, unable to breathe, I ventured out from under the covers, ears still straining for the sounds of an intruder. I fell asleep like that, and woke again to the clicking of locks, this time as Mama unlocked the doors in the early morning just before Daddy's return.

For a while I drifted in and out of sleep, conscious of Daddy's voice and the chinking of plates in the kitchen. Then the silence returned, punctuated by hushing, as Chris and I prepared for school.

Daddy was always awake by the time we got home. I knew that thunderclouds were gathering over the house with a single look. I scampered to my room. For a while, comfort came in the guise of storybook characters, drowning out Mama's and Daddy's voices. Soon enough though, their animated conversation became louder and more insistent and finally turned into scalding argument. I sucked in a lungful of air and held it in. When the bedroom door opened in sync with the jarring of shattered glass, I released my breath with a squeal.

Chris shut the door behind him and said that if we were really good then Mama and Daddy would stop fighting. As reinforcement, he clamped his hand tight over my mouth. Filthy from school and playing football in the garden with the kids next door, he smelt of sweat and dirt and his stench singed my nose until I thought I might vomit. Chris's grip tightened as I grunted my disapproval and struggled against him.

'Be quiet,' he hissed, 'and I'll let you go.'

I nodded. He slowly loosened his grip, and I pushed myself free of him and spat on the floor. Mama's voice resonated now from the other side of the wall.

'But it's true,' she said, 'my mother visited me here last night.'

'No, Ella, she didn't.'

'Why do you say that? I tell you she did,' Mama insisted, her voice rising a semitone with each word. 'You were at work. How could you know?'

'I know, Ella. Your mother could not have possibly visited you.'

'No one believes me. You think I'm lying to you.' She was in anguish.

'I don't think you're lying.'

'Well, how can that be? Please,' she begged, 'she was here.'

I could hear the tap-tap of Daddy's shoes as he paced back and forth, measuring his response.

'Ella, your mother couldn't have visited you last night.'

'Why?' she moaned, crumpling to her knees with a thud.

'Why? Because she's been dead for thirty-two years.'

Then I stopped talking.

Lena Edelbaum drew in breath so abruptly that she sounded as if she was imitating a vacuum cleaner. 'That was most illuminating. How did that feel?'

'Okay, I guess,' I replied, my fingers travelling the length of the seat cushion under my thighs, feeling for a thread to pull. 'So you already know that I converse with some of my female ancestors. Some of my dead, female ancestors. But it only happens when I open my mother's recipe book. I hear them but I can't see them, at least not yet.'

'And does that worry you?'

'Yes, of course. At first it frightened the curl right out of my hair. But now, I'm getting used to it. The thing is, what scares me most is that my mother heard and saw things that weren't there. What I need to know is if I'm normal. Or am I becoming her?'

'Do you think you're like your mother?'

'No, not at all. She was needy and pathetic. Mama was a crazy lady who made life hell for us all.'

'And how do you see yourself?'

How did I see myself? I thought about her question. How was I different from Mama? Let me count the ways. I was self-sufficient and decisive. I was married because I loved my husband, and not because I needed Paul to save me. Or to complete me. I told Mrs Edelbaum all of this and a whole lot more. A few minutes later, her hand shot up again and she proclaimed the session ended. I made another appointment, but as I left I had the strong sense that I was no wiser now than I had been before I walked in. I got more insight listening to Kinderkull's latest album. *Two reflections in a mirror, which is watching, which is me? Free to smash it and escape it, it's just fear that stops my flee.*

After the third session, Lena introduced me to Lenny. By the end of my consultation with Dr Edelbaum, I left with an outrageous bill and a prescription for an antipsychotic drug in my hand. I never saw either of them ever again.

Things moved pretty fast in the week that followed. Ethan called me to ask me how I was and to tell me that Chris had been in hospital having his gall bladder taken out. Chris was home now and doing fine. As soon as her father was home, Poppy had hopped on a plane to Paris on a whim and, by week's end, was already being invited to parties by Europe's prosperous and prominent. I could see how that would happen. The fact that neither Chris nor Georgia had called me to let me know any of this stung a little. It seemed the only contact we had these days was through the lawyer. I guess I should have been pleased—it kept emotion out of the equation and, in the circumstances, worked out well for us all. It was obvious to me that they had no intention of apologising for Georgia's appalling behaviour or of extending an olive branch. As I saw things, it was up to them to make the first move.

I also caught up with Simone who, naturally, asked me about Lena and Lenny Edelbaum. I told her that things were progressing nicely thanks *(I really can't go into too much detail, you understand)* and trusted that doctor–patient confidentiality would take care of everything else.

By the middle of the week, my fact-checking was complete and I was ready to tell Paul about Fotini. It had been hard keeping her story a secret from him and I resisted the almost daily urge to blurt out how my umpteenth-great-grandmother had had this amazing life and what a courageous woman she had been.

I kept it to myself until one evening when I ventured, 'Paul darling, I'd really like it if you'd read a story that I've written and tell me what you think.'

He was slumped on the couch in front of the TV scratching Boz Scraggs's belly and watching nothing much in particular.

'Okay,' he replied. 'I'll read it later.'

'No, Paul, I'd like you to read it now.'

'What's it about?'

'Oh, nothing.'

'If it's nothing, then what's the urgency?'

'I've started writing a novel. It's based on Mama's recipes book.'

'Shit. Don't tell me you've been hearing voices again. I told you to get rid of that thing.'

'It's not like that. Reserve judgement until you've read it. Please?'

He sighed as Boz jumped off the couch and stared at me accusingly. Paul tossed me an exasperated glance, picked up the manuscript and began to read. 'Well don't just sit there watching me!'

I left Paul alone and after about an hour I returned. He was still reading. Boz was asleep.

'Wow, Kat. You have some imagination! It's really good.'

'You mean it?'

'Of course I do. The best thing you've ever written. You must have done a load of research.'

'See, that's the thing, I didn't do any. Please don't say anything. I know how crazy this sounds but Fotini told me the whole story. All I did was verify the facts, as I would for any interview. Paul, it all checked out. Every word, more or less—the important stuff anyhow—place names, dates, details. I couldn't have written any of this by myself and I knew that if what she told me checked out, then it had to be true. I'm not mad, Paul, I really can communicate with my dead ancestors.'

'Or maybe you studied it once at school and forgot about it.'

'The massacre at Chios? You must be joking! Why is it easier for you to accept that I have a mental illness rather than what I'm telling you might just be true?'

'Oh, I don't know—forty-five years of life experiences might have played a part. But why do you think?'

'Mama.'

It was then that it occurred to me that I was playing out Mama's marriage with Daddy all over again for myself. The voices were real for us but would never be real for them. I knew how this scene played out—argument, hostility, resentment, estrangement. Thank the universe Paul and I hadn't added any children to our personal version of hell. I had two options: deny the truth and keep the peace, or insist that I was right, that Fatima/Fotini was real, and run the risk of losing Paul. All instinct told me to stand firm. I was (almost) never wrong about things. Yet for the moment at least, I chose the former. I said nothing further to Paul about the book and we went along as if nothing had transpired. I now stowed Mama's cookbook in my car, safe in the knowledge that, one, I had both car keys in my possession and, two, given the state of my car, even if he looked there, Paul could never find it.

By the weekend, I had prepared myself psychologically to make my own *phyllo* pastry for the first time in my life when, quite unexpectedly, the whole notion of cooking anything for anybody seized me by the throat and threatened to shake the very life out of me. I sank to a new low. I looked at the recipe I had transcribed from Mama's book and it filled me with dread. Paul realised something was wrong when I went straight back to bed after breakfast.

'What's wrong, Kat? Don't you have to make cakes or something for the christening?'

'Not cakes, Turkish pies. Bourekia. But I can't do it.'

'Of course you can. What do you mean you can't do it?'

'I shouldn't have promised. Everyone knows I don't cook.'

'But you can cook. You cooked for me once.'

'Yes, but breakfast on Valentine's Day 2007 doesn't count.' Remorse bubbled up my throat like acid reflux. 'I am such a terrible wife! Of course I can cook and I should cook for you every night. Or maybe at least once in a while. What's wrong with me? I don't know why you put up with this shit. A wife who won't cook and doesn't want children—you should leave me. And now I'm going to let Nicole down. I am such a bad friend.'

'Are you finished?'

'What?'

'Self-deprecation. Running yourself down.'

'I'm sorry, Paul, I really am. But I can't cook the bourekia. I just don't know what to do…'

'No, Kat.'

'What?'

'I'm not going to save you this time.'

'Save me? Save me from what? When have you ever saved me?'

'I'm not going to make the bourekia for you. I'm not going to enable your culinary helplessness. You know it's all in your head.'

I was aghast. 'Did I ask you to?'

'You were about to.'

I was ready to launch into an argument, express my indignation at the very idea that I might be manipulating him into making the bourekia for me. Then I bit my tongue. Maybe that was exactly what I was doing. Was it possible that I was talking myself down, getting in the first blow just in case I cooked something and it sucked? Paul was right; he was always there. He constantly had my back. He saved me all the time but he'd just never called me on it before. I whimpered, 'I can't, Paul, I truly can't.'

'Then you have a problem, Kat.'

'I guess I have.' I rolled over onto my side and considered my options.

'Well?' Paul finally broke the silence.

'I suppose I could try to make the bourekia, if you would help me.'

Paul was quiet for a while. I held my breath.

'Okay. But no piking. The minute you quit, I quit. Agreed?'

'Agreed.'

Between them, Fotini, Nicole and Paul had got me into the kitchen and cooking for the first time in a long while. And for once in my life, I had to admit, the experience wasn't too bad. Two hours later, Paul and I finished baking Fotini's bourekia for Bailey's christening. We put them hot and still on their baking trays into large cardboard boxes (with holes punched for ventilation), into the car and we sped away in the direction of St Ignatius Church. Last pew, nearest the door, aisle seats. We waved at Nicole and her husband Alex cheerily and settled back for the show. After an all-too-brief ceremony, some sprinkling of water and posing for photographs, Bailey was christened and welcomed into the congregation with general applause. Despite our bargain, Simone had totally missed the main event. She arrived for the after-party at Nicole's unfashionably late and with a hangdog look, just as I was offering the little pies around.

'You're very, very late,' I hissed.

'Late? Lucky I'm here at all. Do you know these people?'

'Aside from you, Nicole's husband, her family and Paul? In a word, no. I have no idea who they are or how they know her.'

'Hmm. Nicole's a good networker. Do people still use that term?'

'I guess so,' I replied.

Together we gazed at the guests milling all around her. *Like moths to a flame.*

'Look at her. Nicole doles out her friendship as if she was rationing out the finest French truffles,' Simone said. 'You know why we put up with this shit?'

I shook my head. 'Not really.'

'She panders to our basic insecurities. Our primal need to be diminished.'

Whatever an indefinable attraction was, Nicole had it. She shone bright, like a new penny. Surrounded by people, she was in her element. Her greatest talent was the acquisition of friends in the way that some people collected stamps. She had the mysterious ability to make each one of them believe they were her BFF, for the time it took her to decide whether they were keepers or losers. Simone and I were among a select few she hadn't lost, frozen out or traded away over the years. We both knew this about Nicole and we loved her in spite, or possibly, if Simone was right, even because of it. I chewed on that thought for a moment as I offered Simone one of the bourekia.

'I can't believe that I came in exchange for your savouries. They'd better be fucking amazing, or I'm taking back my present and leaving.'

She gazed at the plate of cigar-shaped pastries in my hand, and took one half-heartedly. The *phyllo* crackled as she bit into it, offering up its filling of spiced meat. All she could manage was a muffled *really good!* between bites. With Paul's and Fotini's help, the bourekia had turned out better than good: they were fabulous.

'Thank heavens for that! I was wondering what use you would find for a romper suit,' I remarked, as Simone sank her teeth into another.

By the end of the party, the bourekia were long gone, my feet were aching and Bailey had fallen asleep in his father's arms. Nicole was having an animated conversation with the Argentinean wife of someone-or-other who once wrote a book and either worked with her husband, or possibly ran a small country single-handedly. Simone was exchanging email addresses with a woman I'd never met and hadn't been introduced to. Paul found me slowly vanishing into a white leather sofa (definitely bought BB—before Bailey) and sucking on a well-earned champagne cocktail.

'Shall we go?' he suggested. 'I can feel my brain atrophying and I'm about to fall asleep.'

'Good idea. Let's get out of here while I'm still sober enough to walk.'

'Don't forget to say goodbye to Fickle Spice and Intimidatrix,' Paul quipped.

'Shut up! One day someone will hear you.'

'And I'd care because…?'

I grunted at him and accepted his offer to help me off the couch. We approached Nicole, who was still surrounded by a crowd three people deep. She looked distracted as I thanked her and flung her a goodbye.

'You're leaving so soon? And we never even got a chance to talk.' She turned her full attention to me, pulled me through the throng and hugged me warmly. 'Thanks for the savouries, Kat. I hear they were delicious. I'm so upset that I missed out on trying them.'

'Never mind. I can make another batch,' I responded, as Paul pulled vomit-faces behind Nicole's back. Paul and Nicole exchanged waves and we made our way to the door.

'One day you'll get caught doing that.'

To which Paul faked a yawn.

22

There is something underhanded about keeping a secret from one's life partner, even if it is a benign one. I now began to understand how people must feel when they embark on an affair outside of their usual relationship—that rush of excitement, the anticipation of meeting their paramour, the stolen moments, the clandestine planning. It wasn't as if I was seeing anybody on the side, although I might as well have been for all the guilt I dragged around with me everywhere I went. I was having my own, secret, shameful relationship with Mama's recipe book. I did it compulsively, even though I knew Paul, or anyone else, would never understand or approve.

Whenever Paul announced that he would have to go out for work, my heart skipped a beat, especially if it meant that I would be alone for the best part of the day. Joy of joys if work kept him away overnight. I'd kiss him goodbye, tell him a hundred times how I'd miss him but, as soon as I saw him reverse onto the street, I'd be outside, digging the book out from under the passenger seat of my car. Only once was I sprung, pulling clutter out of my car in a frantic search for the book. Paul had returned to retrieve his forgotten wallet and pulled up undetected, alongside the house. He trotted up the driveway and stood behind me unnoticed, until he applauded my cleaning efforts.

'At last! Your car is disgusting, Kat. Make sure you throw all of that crap out.'

I straightened myself out. 'Of course I will, darling.'

He ran into the house as I hid the book in the folds of my dressing gown. As he was on his way back out to his car I called out, 'Now you make sure you have a great day! Love you! Call me! Miss you!'

His brow had furrowed.

Shut up, Kat, or he'll know something's up. I began hastily covering my tracks. 'Do you really have to go? Can't you stay home today?'

'I really can't. I've made a commitment and I'm already running late. But I'll try to get home early if I can.'

'Good,' in a kittenish voice. 'All right then, I guess you'd better go. Love you!'

'Love you too.'

And with that he was back in the car and gone before I could retrieve the book from between the pleats of my gown.

I was humming some silly song that had glued itself onto my mind, a tune about the desperation of unrequited love or something like that, as I fixed myself a second cup of coffee in preparation for settling down with the book for a few uninterrupted hours. I had written down a few questions I wanted answered—*What happens after you die? Does God exist?* You know, nothing special—and I let the leaves of the cookbook drop open at random.

Spanish doughnuts. And in my mother's handwriting, added much later in different ink, *Very Good.* I wondered at this. *Spanish? But no one in my family's Spanish, of that I'm absolutely certain.* The recipe was probably borrowed from elsewhere and incorporated into Mama's book somewhere along the line. I read on. *Take three cups of flour...*

'Hello?' I said hopefully. Nothing. *Two tablespoons fresh yeast...* Not a sound. Maybe I was right, there was no magic in this recipe. *Warm water...* A faint murmur? Perhaps I'd been wrong to leap so swiftly to assumptions. By the time I reached the honey, a voice chimed out behind me, loud and insistent.

'Kat?'

'Yes? And who are you?'

'My name is Aliki—I mean—Alegra. I am your fifteenth great-grandmother.'

I was puzzled by the name. To my English-speaking ears, Alegra sounded like musical terminology rather than a name. I picked up the questions I'd prepared earlier.

'Welcome, Alegra.' I took a sip from my cup and settled in for the morning. 'I have some questions I'd like you to answer.'

'Slow down there, girl. What's your hurry? How about we take a little time to get to know each other before I answer any questions.' I had the sense that she was summing me up. 'So you're going to make my *bunuelos*?'

'Your...?' I had no idea what she'd just said. 'No, I don't think so. I don't cook.'

'So then why are you bothering me?'

'Is that what I'm doing?' I said. 'I thought I was just reading recipes, in the hope you might appear and we could talk.'

'You hear her, Judah? She's eager to meet me, even though she doesn't know the first thing about me or my cooking. You know what they'd call you in my time? *Tonta*, a silly girl and pushy, very pushy. Just what I needed.'

I spluttered. Coffee splashed everywhere, only reinforcing her comment. *Silly? Pushy? Me?* I guessed that to deny it at this point would only convince her that she was right.

'How about we take a little time to get to know each other before you judge me?' She had been direct and so was I.

'Don't worry, I will.' I felt her scrutinise me head to toe, and not in a sympathetic way. 'So, according to the rules, I have to reveal to you everything about myself.'

My ears pricked up. 'Rules? What rules?'

'Never mind.'

'Whose rules?'

'I can't tell you. Stop asking or I'll leave.'

I wasn't pushy, so I cut her some slack. 'Well, well, you're my fifteenth great-grandmother. That's a long time ago.' As soon as the words passed my lips, I could feel her roll her eyes.

'Did it take you an eternity to work that out? What did I tell you—we've got a live one here, Judah!'

'What is it with you guys? Fotini came on all angry at first, but she was really a sweetheart. As for you, I don't have time for this. You can go right ahead and leave if you're only here to insult me,' I said.

'Very tempting, but no, I can't. If you want me gone, you have to shut the book.'

I left it open in my lap and smirked. I held the reins here. Since I had no idea where she was, I smirked both left and right.

Alegra carried on. 'Go on then, shut it.'

'No,' I said.

'Close the book. Slap it shut. You know how to do that, don't you?'

'No!'

'How dare you answer back to your great-grandmother! SHUT IT, I SAID!'

Her words hurtled me straight back to childhood and I closed the book with a snap. *How dare I? How dare she!* After a couple of minutes, remorse followed the silence. I leafed through the pages until I found the doughnuts again, and laid the book open on my knees.

A moment later, I heard: 'I can't believe you did that!'

'But you told me to. You yelled at me!'

'And you do whatever you're told, silly girl, like you have no mind of your own. The last four generations have been such a disappointment.'

The last time I had felt this irritated was the last time I'd seen Georgia.

'If we're such a disappointment, Alegra, then you and your cohorts there have only yourselves to blame.'

'Oh yes, and how do you figure that?'

'I am what you made me.'

'Not exactly true, but I'll let it pass. At least the girl has some guts! Go on, get it all out. You'll feel much better.'

As she spoke I did some mental arithmetic. If I had calculated correctly, fifteenth great-grandmother equated to seventeen generations times, say, somewhere between twenty and thirty years in a generation.

'You know you don't sound anything like someone who lived five hundred years ago.'

'Are you saying that from experience? Okay then, smarty-pants, how does someone who lived five hundred years ago sound?'

'I don't know. Humble. Polite. More thee and thou.'

'And just when it all was starting to look promising, she comes out with that! Listen. I've been dead for hundreds of years. That's a lot of time to revise one's education. Keep up with the times. Modernise or perish. But enough about that. My favourite topic of conversation just happens to be,' she paused for effect, 'me. Shall I continue?'

'I guess so. If you must.'

'Excellent. So, here's your first quiz question. What do you know about Spain?'

'So you are Spanish! I was right! That's why the Spanish doughnuts…'

'The bunuelos?'

'The doughnuts.'

'The bunuelos. You could say they were Spanish.'

'And you?'

'Okay, you want to know where I come from? Then let the history lesson begin.' Alegra cleared her throat. 'It just so happens that I was born in Valencia in Iberia, which is what we called Spain back then, in case you didn't know. I was given my grandmother's name of Alegra. I didn't know much about my family when I was a kid, because no one wanted to talk much about ancestors. In those days, you got the feeling that people were happiest when they were orphans and could forget all about them. But since I'm dead, I can tell you a whole lot about it.'

I leaned back and, for a moment, I imagined myself in a flounced dress, tap-tap-tapping to the rhythm of a flamenco guitar. Spanish sounded romantic. I could do Spanish.

Alegra interrupted my daydream. 'According to my grandmother Alegra (I called her *abuela* and sometimes when I was feeling really nostalgic *abuelita*), my mother's family had been in Iberia since Solomon. Late in his life, my father revealed to me that his ancestors had travelled to Iberia from Jerusalem centuries after Mama's, on a journey that turned out to be a bit like that of Moses leaving Egypt. By that, I mean it turned into an odyssey that took decades to complete. It seems they got a bit lost *en ruta*. If only someone had remembered to take a GPS, they might have got there sooner.

'Everybody is constantly in search of freedom and success, still, it's not easy to trade your homeland for another, doesn't matter how hard life has become. My father—and I still call him Papa—thought he was a scholar. He said—how did he say it? *Our ancestors had swapped oppression under the Byzantine Christians in Judea for self-sufficiency under the Muslims in Arabia. But self-sufficiency still isn't freedom…* I have no idea what he meant to this very day, but, anyway, Papa's ancestors eventually found their way to Seville, where they settled. For a while, at least. I don't know much, but sometimes I think our family was condemned to roam the earth by the curse of the faithless.'

I found myself frowning as I listened to Alegra talk. *Solomon? Jerusalem? The curse of the faithless?* How did any of that fit in with my clapping-and-tapping fantasy?

'Anyway,' she resumed, 'when I was born, Ferdinand was the king and things were always changing and there was such turmoil for everyone, just the same as it is today. At that time, it was extra hard for those of us whose heritage was Jewish.'

I put down my cup but before I could utter a syllable, Alegra added, 'Yes, you heard right, Kat, you are descended from Iberian Jews, also known as Sephardim, the Jews of Spain.'

'Jewish? Me?' I mumbled. Although the concept wasn't new, the thought that AncestorFinder DNA might have got it right was still too much for me to take in.

'Well, no, you're not really Jewish; although it scares me more than you know to admit this, but some of my blood does still flow through your veins, along with millions who have shared some of my DNA.'

'What? Millions? There are millions of people related to you and therefore to me? Out there?'

'No, Kat, they're not all alive right now. I'm talking millions of people over seventeen generations. But here's the thing: unlike you, only a handful of them have ever got to hear of Alegra Amato, much less meet her.'

'But your name—Alegra? That's not Jewish, is it? '

'Do you want to listen and learn, or do you want to keep talking nonsense?'

I said absolutely nothing.

'That's better. Now stay that way.'

23

ALEGRA

For Papa's family, after what they'd gone through, Seville looked like the land of milk and honey. Can you believe that the Jew was the equal of any other citizen there: they even had support of the king? At first, the men of our family went into the military, and if you had seen my great-grandfather, you would have understood why. Joseph Amato, son of Salomon, was no ordinary, everyday short-arse. He was as tall and as sturdy as a tree. You put him into a crowd of Spanish men and he stuck out like a giant redwood in a forest of small, dark Mediterranean olive bushes. And he was good-looking besides.

But time moves on, trees get cut down and kings die. The new kings see the world with different eyes and their ears are stuffed full of advice from men with fresh ideas. Over only a few generations, everything changed. Our family had to change too. Jewish men were thrown out of the military and so our family got itself into commerce. By commerce, I mean moneylending, of course.

Let me paint the scene for you. Back then, it was illegal to be a Christian banker. Christians couldn't charge interest on borrowed money, but we didn't have the same problem. A Jew was only prohibited from taking interest from another Jew, and if you read your Bible you'd know this already. So, say you're a Christian or Muslim and you need a little extra money to pay off a gambling debt, or to marry off a daughter with a moustache, where would you go for it? You couldn't go to another Christian or another Muslim. You would go straight to the Jewish quarter.

Turns out, the Amato men were great soldiers and they were pretty astute in business as well. They made a huge success of it, and without an ivy-league MBA, too. They were all self-made men. They taught themselves how to trade in debt. I can't tell you exactly how they did it, but they were very, very good at making sure every *maravedi* borrowed was repaid, plus some. No one ever dared to cheat an Amato—not if they wanted to see old age. Our family soon became rich, so rich that we could buy anything we wanted.

You might think that, with all that money, our family could buy some influence with the king. No, the king was happy to take the money, but he gave us nothing in return. Money bought our family plenty of food and clothes and paid the taxes, but it also bought suspicion, envy and hatred.

Now, as you know, I've been around a hell of a long time. It still makes me laugh when I hear someone say, 'I am one hundred per cent this' or 'We've always been that', as in, 'I'm totally British' or, 'We've never been anything but Lutheran'. I am itching to say to them, how do you know what you are? All I can say is Herr Hitler would've had some explaining to do if genetic testing had been around in his day. Arian, my arse!

You look hard enough and you'll find that everyone has something else in them. I've had five hundred years to work out that each of us is tied to one another through our ancestry, even when we don't know it. We are more alike than we are different. We all live, eat, shit and die, even when we deny it to ourselves every single day of our lives. Please! Angels weep at the crimes that fathers and brothers and cousins have committed against one another. And, worse still, committed in God's name.

You know what I've learned? No one comes out of Mama's v-jay-jay with any idea of who or what they are. Also, you don't pop out of the womb thinking that these people are good and those people are bad—those lessons are taught to you by others. But here's the thing—the more you discover the truth about yourself and everyone else, the less you are able to judge them. Unfortunately, most people know shit about themselves and their neighbours and worse still, they never bother to learn.

So, enough pearls of wisdom from Alegra. Back to our family. Where was I? Oh yes. Our family had been Jewish. I realised the shame of being a Jew almost as soon as I learned to talk, even if I could not understand why. I felt the humiliation of only speaking about Jewish things in a whisper, of prayers said quietly and in private, of a Menora hidden within folds of linen. Our family *had been* Jewish, but that's a story you must hear.

As I mentioned to you before, even though life had been particularly bad for Jews who lived in some parts of Spain, for a while no one in Seville appeared to care whether a person was a Jew or a Christian. Rumour had it that a long time ago, even the king's mistress had been a Jewess. She was a great beauty and very influential, if you understand my meaning. Then times changed and people learned to hate what they didn't understand. It all began with a tiny little spark. Then the spark was fanned by ignorance and became a firestorm, ready to burn us all.

It's a shame that film wasn't around in those times for you to see what we had to live through. Imagine for a moment that you're going about your business, doing the same thing you have done every day since you were born. Then someone unexpectedly points a finger at you and tells you that you are to blame for everything that's bad in the world. Suddenly you've stopped being an individual. You're no longer Alegra Amato or Kat Bower. No one calls you by your name, even when they have known it for decades. All of a sudden, you are defined by a thing over which you had no choice. Your birthright becomes your name—you become *The Jew* and you are hated, even by people you once called friend. Now hold that picture in your mind for a while and see how scary the thought becomes.

In the days of my great-great-grandfather, the queen started to speak publicly about her hate for the Jews. A bitch's son—and that's all I can call him—an archdeacon named Martinez took up her words, only his voice was louder and nothing and no one could shut him up. The queen died, but his words kept going. By his edict, they closed some of our synagogues and converted others to churches. They rounded us up as if we were lepers. They made laws to keep us away from Christians. We could not work, we had to live in a ghetto and wear clothes that distinguished us from everybody else.

But even that much evil wasn't enough for the bishops and their hate flowed right down to the very lowest of men. If a sailor or a soldier happened across a Jewish person, they spat at him. Spat at us? Spat at us, who had held the highest military positions in the land and who had made sure with our blood that the kings and queens of Spain kept their titles? Spat at us! Why did our family ever bother to fight the Moors and liberate the country from Islam? What a wonderful way for Spain to say thank you!

I wish people had just left it at that, but the Church had whipped everyone into a rage. We were filthy animals that needed to be exterminated. Too many people with too few brain cells heard this talk and spread it from one to the other, like the customers of a syphilitic whore. On the Sabbath, along with prayers, the synagogue filled with talk about how this family had their wealth confiscated, and how that family had disappeared. It was a crazy time. Some of my great-great-grandfather's friends were killed as they went about their business on the street or in their houses. Then the synagogues were closed, the talk was silenced and Jews were too frightened to go anywhere.

None of this is new. It has happened before—a very long time ago—and our family survived it then. We changed, we moved, we endured, but this time it seemed different. This time we knew we were all doomed to die, unless... What a choice to have to make! So what did my great-great-grandfather do? What would anyone do to save his family? He did exactly what thousands of others had done. He spoke to his sons. Together, they agreed. Then they went to a church and they were all baptised Catholics. They took on new names and moved to Valencia.

It was only later that my great-great-grandfather heard that hundreds of Jews had died in Seville and he thanked God that his choices had spared his family. Valencia was supposed to be a pit stop on the way to France or Italy or anywhere that didn't kill Jews, but once they were settled, they lost their drive to keep moving, for a while at least.

They had so many names for us: *Cristianos nuevos, marranos, conversos*. They weren't meant as a compliment and it didn't mean we were safe from persecution. It was just that our family had learned to keep quiet and live under-the-radar, as you say. Nothing had changed for our family, not really. We were Catholic now for sure. We went to church on a Sunday and dutifully learned our catechism. But we were like those candies you call M&Ms—our outside didn't betray what was hidden inside. In Valencia, my great-great-grandfather trusted that our family would survive. He hoped we could return to business and raise children in peace, and, for a generation or two, he was right.

I know it doesn't seem like much, but one of my happiest memories was that of my mother singing. I never heard my father sing a note, but Mama had a beautiful voice and she sang whenever she could. Some songs she sang loudly, not caring who heard, but others so quietly, that you could hardly make out the words. When I asked her what they were about, she said nothing and replaced the lyrics with a hum.

'Please don't ask me to teach you those songs,' she said. 'Not yet.'

Along with the *Our Father*, we learned to say our *other* prayers in hushed voices, those special prayers that my mother said we must never, ever repeat outside the house, or we'd immediately turn into cockroaches and end our days being stomped on by a boot. We still observed the Sabbath from Friday evening and we celebrated Passover as well as Easter, but we were sworn to tell nobody. Every Friday afternoon, Mama prepared a stew of chicken and rice spiced with cumin and studded with whole, unshelled eggs, and set it to cook slowly for the night, so that we would have a warm meal when we sat down together for Sabbath lunch. Mama and Papa taught all of us children to keep our own company and to mistrust everyone.

'Never draw suspicion on yourself. If someone offers you a piece of pork, eat it and say thank you,' Mama told us. 'It could be their way of checking if you are truly Catholic. And never, ever tell them anything of what we do on Fridays.'

'But, Mama,' I answered her. 'What am I then, if I am not truly Catholic?'

Mama had a beautiful smile. 'Yes, Alegra, we are Catholic, but we are a very special kind of Catholic. We remember the old ways. We have not forgotten God, and one day you'll see that

God has not forgotten us. Watch and learn everything I do so that, in time, you can pass this down to your children, too.'

Converso or not, my abuela, my grandmother Alegra, never ever considered herself anything other than a Jew and she wasn't that smart about keeping her mouth shut. I remember overhearing her say, 'So what if they took me to church and gave me a bath? I am still exactly who I was before they washed *mi kulo.'* Then Grandfather, my *abuelo,* told her to be quiet, it wasn't safe to say that sort of thing in these times.

Ah, Kat, they must have taught you something about the Spanish Inquisition while you were at school. So you're a little vague on the details? But how could that be? You did go to school, Kat, didn't you? Well, all I can say is that it was the unholy ghost that hung over our lives.

You've got the idea by now that the whole anti-Jewish thing had been going on in Iberia for centuries—sometimes it was better and sometimes worse. *El Tribunal del Santo Oficio de la Inquisición* marked the start of the definitely worse.

Since you learned so little from your teachers, I guess I'll have to teach you a thing or two. Inquisitions have been around Europe forever; the Catholic Church was always weeding out heretics and beheading them or burning them at the stake. It was a real crowd pleaser: the medieval equivalent to a reality show. This particular tribunal was only officially set up just before I was born because the Spanish king and his wife wanted to make sure that all conversos were truly Catholic one hundred per cent of the time, and not just on Sundays and holy days. The penalty was torture mostly followed by death, and, believe me, death was usually the best part of it. Hey, you have to wonder how good a product can be if you have to threaten people just to make sure they keep using it!

Anyway, this tribunal—this inquisition—was intended to sweep all the secret Jews out of Spain and to confiscate their wealth along the way. It may have begun in Seville (weren't we glad to have left there!), but it didn't end at the city limits. Its tentacles spread throughout Spain, even as far as Valencia. That's why Abuelo was so angry when Abuela Alegra said or did anything to suggest that we weren't really Christian.

It didn't take long for what Abuelo feared to become reality. At the time, we didn't know who overheard what, or maybe someone spoke out of turn, but somehow my grandfather's name was brought to the tribunal's attention. He was an old man by then and although I was still a child, I already understood that without his hard work and his sharpness, our lives would have never been what they were. He was as clever, cautious and focused as Abuela was scatterbrained, insensitive and difficult.

Abuelo had been taught bookkeeping by his father and sometimes, when he thought he could get away with it, he did a little moneylending on the side—not too much. He said he was just helping people out, but I can't help wondering if that was his undoing. Maybe poor Abuela, who ended up with most of the blame, was just the scapegoat. No matter why it happened, one day in June, Abuelo—my beloved *Abuelito*—was summoned to the tribunal and I never saw him again.

Our house was in chaos. I never heard Papa shout at Abuela before, but he yelled at her that day until she fell to her knees with her hands over her ears. I listened to Papa's words and I tried to understand them, but I was far too young. Mama told Papa to be quiet or the neighbours would hear him and he'd bring trouble on us all.

I found out much, much later on that my grandfather had been accused of being a crypto-Jew by an old friend, a converso who was exactly like us, and who had been forced to name names under torture, just to keep himself alive. Along the way to his trial, many other accusers joined in and the allegations against my grandfather got worse and worse. My father attended his father's trial for weeks on end. When he got home, he told Mama the evidence he had heard.

'One of Papa's best clients told the tribunal that he'd offered Papa *jamon* as payment and he refused it,' he told her.

'That man must have been jealous of what we have,' she replied, 'and that's why he said it.'

'Another client said that Papa kept a prayer book in his coat pocket and that he desecrated a crucifix.'

'What nonsense. They can't have believed him?'

'I don't know about that, but that wasn't the worst of it. A third gave witness that she'd once seen Papa drain the blood of a Christian child and drink it.' This final accuser was a woman who had borrowed money from my grandfather but had never repaid it. 'And that then she heard Papa give thanks to the devil!'

Mama's mouth dropped open. 'How could anyone even think such a thing possible!'

When he spoke about Abuelo's trial, Papa always said the inquisitor's name in a low voice, as if saying the word out loud might conjure up bad spirits. As ridiculous as the charges were, they were exactly the sort of thing the Inquisition thrived on.

'Calvo is not such a bad inquisitor,' I heard him say on several occasions. 'Papa may yet avoid the flames of the *auto-da-fe*.' Until the very end my father believed that the truth would be discovered and that Abuelo would be let go.

Despite the silliness of the accusations against Abuelito, despite my father's deep love for his own father and his faith in the inquisitor, Papa never once appeared before the tribunal as a witness. He was simply too afraid to say anything in Abuelito's defence. Papa said he was scared that if he endorsed his father, the inquisitor might turn his attention onto all of us. I thought he was weak back then, but now I understand silence can be the hardest, bravest thing. To act or not to act? In the face of almost certain death, choices like that are impossible.

So Abuelito denied his accusers, naturally, but he added nothing else to his own defence, probably because he feared the same thing as Papa. I can now tell you that he was given the *tortura del agua*—which was a bit like water-boarding is in your time. Then he was hung from the ceiling by his arms. It should have been enough to crack the determination of a man half his age. Despite the pain, Abuelito said nothing.

Children see everything in absolutes and, suddenly, Papa wasn't the great hero I'd imagined him to be. Am I angry with my neighbour and my father for what they did? I might have been a lot angrier if I'd understood what had happened and why, but I only caught a few short glimpses of the true horror. All I knew was that we had abandoned Abuelito. I have a different view of things these days. Who knows what you, or I, or anyone, might do in such circumstances?

All I can say to you is that my abuelito's suffering ended up as our salvation. As soon as he could make the arrangements, my father sold off almost everything we owned, converted it all into gold *dobla* and arranged passage for us all on a ship destined for Greece via Sicily, with the intention of going on to Constantinople—what you now call Istanbul. We were Jews headed back into an Islamic world, but from where we were standing, it seemed to be our only way to escape the persecution in this Christian one.

This was the only life I had known and I hardly slept the night before we left, my mind was filled with such sorrow and fear. In the morning we crammed the few possessions that remained into our bags. As we were leaving, I wriggled my hand from my mother's grasp to say goodbye to our house, and, last to depart, I slipped the key out of the lock and placed it in the pocket of my skirt.

'I will return. I promise,' I told the house, as I closed the door behind me.

24

When Alegra stopped talking, I shut the book gently. Where had I put the key? It had been such a curious, bulky thing to use as a bookmark and it had already stained so many of the pages that I had untied it and put it away. But where? I studied a year or two of psychology back in my undergraduate years and learned that memory was a bit like the warehouse scene at the end of *Raiders of the Lost Ark*. Everything was filed away neatly for later access, but the problem was knowing precisely where and how to retrieve things. *Forget trying to remember, there's nothing like a thorough manual search.* I rummaged around my desk. Nothing. Checked every drawer in the kitchen. Zilch. Turned out the toolbox. What had I been doing when I last saw the damn thing? Of course! I had been listening to Fotini. And after that, I had intended to bake…

There it was, sitting on the shelf in the pantry, right beside the flour. I picked up the key. Oxidation had gnawed through the better part of the shank and it rubbed off reddish-brown between my fingers as I touched it. It had to be hundreds of years old. *The key to Alegra's childhood home!* I was certain of it. I was struck by the thought that this key must have passed through the hands of dozens of my ancestors—and I had almost thrown it away. People were always wishing that their antiques could speak, and imagining the stories they would tell, yet here was I with a real connection to the past and wishing it silent. As I replaced the key in its position on the front cover, for the first time in my entire life I felt a tangible connection to my family and, more particularly, to my mother.

I tied the ribbon that kept the few loose pages from falling and I noticed that my hands were aching. Always looking for a shortcut, I'd had the magnificent idea of typing out Alegra's story as she spoke, as if she had been dictating it. I figured that would cut down on double handling but I hadn't figured that she'd say so much and speak so quickly. I looked down at what I had typed and realised that I'd greatly overestimated my abilities as a touch typist. If only I'd become a journalist twenty years sooner, I'd have learned shorthand. *Damn it!* It was going to take me longer to proof read and correct what I had written than it had taken to type it in the first place.

Then a second, more fantastic idea overwhelmed me. Since I'd already been certified one hundred per cent Jewish (plus or minus 0.01 per cent) and now that I was armed with much of Alegra's story, maybe I should connect up with a rabbi and find out more about marranos, conversos and Sephardim. I was certain of a warm welcome. A rabbi could put it all into context and help me understand Alegra's life. I knew that Simone had told me I wasn't Jewish and she was right, of course, I wasn't. But what exactly was I? I would lay it all out without pretence and try to make sense of who and what I was. *Simone. What better source of information and understanding?* I brought up *Simeon* on my phone's contacts and touched *call.*

'This is Simone Wilder. I'm sorry, I'm busy right now. Leave a message.'

Not what I had expected, I stabbed *end call* furiously with the tip of my index finger. I always sound stupid in messages so I refused to leave any. A moment later, my phone screeched and I shot out of my seat. I had to admit that Kinderkull could sound a bit harsh when Daley screamed to be heard. The screen flashed *Simeon.* I answered quickly, if only to silence the song.

'Hello, Kat speaking.'

'Did you just call me?'

'Yes.'

'So what did you want? Why didn't you leave a message?'

'I couldn't explain what I wanted in a message. Thanks for calling me back so quickly.' I thought I could hear Simone's foot tapping at the other end. I hurried straight to the point. 'Can you give me the name of a rabbi I could talk to?'

'Whatever for? You're not Jewish, Kat.'

'No, I know. I just want to talk to one.'

'Oh yeah, because the whole thing with the Edelbaums went so well. I'm done with recommending anyone to you. You know, Lena still won't talk to me.'

'That wasn't my fault.'

'I know. It never is. Sorry, Kat, if you want to talk to a rabbi you'll have to find one yourself.'

'But I wouldn't know where to look.'

'Try looking under "R" in the phonebook. Is that all?'

'I guess so.'

'Stop sulking. I can hear it in your voice. I'm sorry if I was abrupt—I have a thousand things to do today. We'll have lunch next week, okay?'

'Hmm. Do you really want to? Or are you just being polite?'

'Oh, jeez. I'm never polite, you know that. I'll text you. Besides, I couldn't help you even if I wanted to. I haven't spoken to a rabbi since I came out. All right?'

'All right.' It was touching that Simone actually cared that she'd hurt my feelings.

'I'd better go now. I'll see you next week. Bye, Kat.'

'Bye, Simone.'

I opened up my computer and Googled *rabbi*. Just as I suspected, there were lots of entries but none much help to me. Where would I start? If I wanted to speak to a priest I'd go to a church. Surely I could do the same with a synagogue. Then I wondered if they were all the same or if they specialised. Or if there was a born-again Jewish congregation that might embrace someone like me. I spotted an entry for a Jewish museum about an hour's drive away and decided that, even though it might not be entirely on point, it might be a good first port of call. A toe in the water, so to speak. First thing tomorrow morning I would go there and get some more information.

The next day was a perfect one for a visit to the museum. Paul was going to work from home, so any hope of getting the cookbook out was dashed. I had woken early, already posted my blog for the day (tips on making a living out of freelance writing) and put the finishing touches on a thousand words for the city daily's Sunday magazine about an up and coming politician, who also just happened to be an old school friend of Paul's. Since I was being paid by the word as a *name*, my think-piece pretty much validated everything I had just blogged about.

I told Paul that I was doing research for a 'thing' I was writing.

'Anything I'd be interested in reading?'

'You're never interested in reading anything I write unless it appears in the paper. Or in a magazine that just happens to be in a waiting room that you just happen to be in.'

'That's not fair and completely untrue. I like to read your stuff. I'm looking forward to reading the article you've just written about Steve after you leave. By the way, I thought that blog you wrote a while back about your mother talking to you "from the other side" was very funny.'

'You read that? But you never read my blogs.'

'I read everything. I just don't always tell you.'

I didn't know whether to be flattered or alarmed. Had Paul gone through my computer when I wasn't around? He'd know how to access it, password or no password. Surely that would be a breach of trust—he wouldn't do that.

'All right then smartypants, I'm taking my computer with me.' I smirked at Paul.

He looked mostly crestfallen and a little confused. 'I wouldn't hack into your computer when you're not around. Surely you know that by now.'

'But when you said… Never mind. I'm sorry, Paul.'

'I'm not sure if it's worse that you think I'd access your files behind your back or that you'd even have files that you wouldn't want me to see.'

'You're right, it was an awful thing to say.' Mama's book was making me paranoid. 'I was just being silly. There's nothing there I'd hide from you.'

'So where are you going today?'

'A museum. I really am doing research. For my novel.'

'Sorry, Kat. I don't know where this is all coming from. I don't want to feel like we're hiding things from each other.'

'And neither do I. I love you, Paul. Always have, always will.'

'And I love you too.'

'I'll be home for lunch. How about we go out for a bite when I get back?'

'Sounds good. We could go to that new deli. I have a sudden hankering for pastrami.'

I laughed at the timeliness of his remark while Paul still looked a touch confused. I picked up my keys and left my computer on as a supreme gesture of trust.

'Call me if you need me. I won't be very long.'

***

I don't quite know what I had imagined but, as an edifice, the Jewish Museum didn't live up to any of my expectations. It was simple, almost stark in design—an enormous glass door led into a vestibule that was dignified and contemplative. No glitzy, over-the-top gift shop here, just a quiet library adjacent to a tasteful museum store to the left and a directory to the right leading to more large glass doors. It was all perfectly harmonious. In contrast to the tumultuous history, or possibly because of it, the building, the staff, even the visitors, were all serene. I, with my untamed curls, my skin-tight pants and suede, lace-up, high-heeled ankle boots, was hopelessly frivolous by comparison. I bit my lip. If only I had worn something more sober.

Making myself as inconspicuous as possible, I crossed the foyer and went through the double doors leading to the first exhibition. Standing quietly alone just inside the door was a young woman, barely older than a girl really, headscarf tied at the nape, dressed in a calf-length skirt and a worsted jacket with a nametag: *Rachel*. I was playing Ziggy Stardust to her Bob Dylan. She looked up as I approached, not a hint of condemnation in her eyes.

'Hello. I wonder if you could help me?'

Rachel smiled faintly. 'I can try.'

I detected an accent, but it was too soon to tell her exact origins. Israeli, perhaps?

'I'm interested in finding out a bit more about Sephardic Jews.'

'We have an exhibition about Jewish history through the doors to your left. You might also like to visit the library afterwards.'

'Okay, that sounds good.' I was swept up in a sudden wave of potential kinship. 'You see, I'm descended from a Sephardic woman.' I found myself grinning at Rachel. Rachel seemed underwhelmed.

'Oh, how nice for you. So, have a look at the exhibition and if you have any questions, there are many volunteers.'

'Russian?' I said aloud.

'St Petersburg. How could you tell?' She became suddenly animated. 'Have you been there?'

'No. It's just your accent and a lucky guess.'

'Oh.'

As her face dropped, it occurred to me that perhaps I wasn't the only one looking out for a random connection. I thanked Rachel and left her behind as I drifted from exhibit to exhibit, uncertain of what I had expected to get out of the experience. By the time I had zigzagged my way around the entire museum, I had acquired a vague understanding of the salient principles of Judaism, the significance of oil lamps and where Sephardim fit into the major episodes of Jewish history. Was that enough for me to really connect with Alegra? Possibly, but I had one more stop to make before I left.

The museum's library was as tastefully restrained as the rest of the building. I asked a woman whose entire demeanour murmured *librarian* about conversos and Sephardim. She sat me at the end of a table surrounded by four empty chairs and began to pile books in front of me. Just as she turned her back to find me some more, my phone decided to ring. *Oh shit! I forgot to silence it!* The librarian's face turned inclement and an ancient man reading at an adjoining table went puce and seemed to be having a coronary in his seat. *Shit! Shit! Shit!* I mouthed an apology and scampered out of the library as fast as tight pants and high-heeled ankle boots would allow. *Damn Kinderkull!*

'Hello!' I spat down the airwaves the moment I reached the vestibule.

'Are you all right?'

'Of course I am. I was in a library and I forgot to switch off the phone.'

'Sorry.'

'Not your fault, Paul. What's wrong?'

'Nothing, except I thought you were coming home for lunch. I was wondering how much longer you were going to be.'

'Lunch? Why, what time is it?'

'Almost twelve-thirty.'

'Oh God, I'm so sorry, sweetie. I completely lost track of the time.'

'Do you want me to wait?'

'No. I'm going to be here a few hours longer. You go ahead and have lunch without me. I'm so sorry.' From Paul's end came silence. 'Paul?'

'I was just imagining Kinderkull playing loud and proud in a library. By the sound of it, you may have some apologising to do. Exactly how was Daley received by the other patrons?'

'Not well, I'm afraid. I think he may have been responsible for the demise of at least one elderly gentleman.' Paul thought it was a joke while I prayed I was wrong about that. 'If I didn't have so much research still to do, I'd be tempted to hightail it out of here and never return.'

Paul chuckled again. 'So you'll be back in time for dinner?'

'I'll be back in time for dinner. I promise I won't be late.'

'Okay then. Bye, Kat.'

'Bye, sweetie.'

I hung up, immediately changed the phone setting to silent and slid the phone into my pocket. And then I took it out again, checked it and rechecked it twice.

25

A touch after three I headed for home. On the seat next to me lay a folded piece of paper with the name, phone number and email address of a liberal rabbi who, I was assured, would be prepared to talk to me. In a paper bag on the floor were two books: one on the Jews of Spain and, only because I thought there had to be a twist in her tale (that whole Alegra/Aliki thing had set me thinking), I had also bought myself a copy of *The Jews of Greece* (with authentic recipes included).

My return to the library after the phone incident had been unashamedly sycophantic and apologetic. It turned out that Methuselah at the adjacent table was doorpost deaf and his reaction (which required the intervention of a co-librarian skilled in CPR as well as two paramedics), while well-timed, had nothing whatsoever to do with Kinderkull. Still, it all seemed too, too much when I turned on the CD player in the car. Daley's voice was somehow too shrill, his lyrics too scathing and the accompanying guitars too screechy. What was happening to me? I, who had always congratulated myself on enjoying the ear-splitting, was now reaching for the volume control. Even as low as it could go, Kinderkull jarred. Is this really what I had imposed on poor, long-suffering Paul, my family and my closest friends for all these years? With the push of a single button followed by a wrist-flick, I ejected Kinderkull. I left the CD where it fell in the passenger foot-well adjacent to my new books, and drove the rest of the road home conjuring up my childhood and listening to the velvety stylings of Barry White on the radio.

Paul was in the middle of making moussaka for our dinner by the time I arrived home. He had already made his *keema* out of minced lamb and tomatoes, and was weighing flour and butter for the béchamel sauce to anoint the top layer. Boz Scraggs lay next to the stove, looking hopeful. The glorious warmth of the cinnamon in the meat sauce teased my nostrils and set my mouth watering. I kissed Paul hello and made a beeline for the pan of *keema* to drink in the scent at its source.

'That smells fantastic.'

'Thanks. Your mother's recipe again.' Paul nudged Boz and me out of the way and resumed his spot at the stove.

'But how on earth did you get it? I don't have her book.' It was a truth of sorts—I had just neglected to add the *with me right now* at the end of the sentence.

'I copied out a few of her recipes before you got rid of it. It would have been a shame to lose her legacy entirely. And since you don't cook it's wasted on you.'

'Hang on a moment there—I helped make the bourekia, didn't I?'

Paul continued stirring the roux. 'I agree, but you know, Kat, a single frosty morning doesn't make it winter.'

'Hmm.'

I was beginning to tire of my own running joke. I could cook. I chose not to. Some people simply didn't feel the need to nourish others in order to make themselves indispensable, and I counted myself in that elite number. I wasn't an earth mother and I didn't care about familial duty, as Georgia did and my mother had. I had hidden talents by the shovelful, but cooking regularly for the unappreciative was mind-numbingly tedious.

That evening, Paul served his moussaka in shallow pasta bowls. It was good and we devoured it huddled together in front of the fireplace, washed down with a bottle or so of syrah. Although it wasn't winter yet, I was starting to worry that Paul's proverbial frost was already beginning to set in. After the embers had died down, we spent the rest of the evening eating chocolate and luxuriating in bed. I woke up the next morning furry-tongued and headachy. Paul woke up with an enormous grin.

Later that day I phoned the liberal rabbi, hoping he might have a free moment there and then. I had to settle for a teleconference the following morning. In the course of our ten-second conversation, I got the impression that he wasn't exactly thrilled about talking to me. I was anxious to get back to Alegra as soon as I could, and I tried to overlook the thought that now plagued me: that a day's delay meant the waste of yet another writing day. I was only vaguely comforted by the notion that I'd make more sense of her story with a context.

I hid myself away in the spare bedroom a few minutes before the prearranged time with my list of questions, telling Paul that I had a very important meeting with a rabbi. He naturally assumed that it was all connected to my DNA results. In a slightly different sense, my ancestry was exactly my motivation. Nervous anticipation was bubbling up my throat, even before I closed the door. I had interviewed people by telephone before, people far more formidable than Rabbi Caravita; this anxiety was absurd. I drew breath and dialled his number.

Our first attempt at a meaningful connection ended with a series of high-pitched squeaks but without a single word having been exchanged. Our second fared little better. I was about to put it all down to providence setting up barriers, when, on my third attempt, I finally connected.

'Rabbi?'

'Yes?'

'Rabbi Caravita?'

'Still yes.'

'Hi. This is Kat Bower. I called you yesterday.'

'Yes, Kat. I remember. You wanted to talk to me about Sephardim.'

'That's right.'

'So what was it you wanted to know?'

'Well, I've recently discovered I was descended from a Sephardic woman. I've read a couple of books about it and I understand the history but I don't get what the differences are from other Jewish people.'

'Are we talking theologically?'

'Yes. Theologically. Philosophically. Socially.'

'So, Kat, are you Jewish?'

'No, I'm nothing. Actually, technically speaking, I guess I'm Orthodox. Christian that is, not Jewish.'

'I'm going to put it to you straight. There are some differences in the way Sephardim and Ashkenazim observe holy days, but that you can find out from the internet. As you can probably tell from my name, my roots are Sephardic. I'm no philosopher and I'm not a sociologist, so I may not be the right person to talk to. Why don't you send me an email with your questions and I'll see if I can answer them? I might be able to put you onto someone.'

I didn't really need to know much more about Sephardim than I already did just to take down Alegra's story. I took another breath and asked the question I really wanted him to answer.

'Do you believe in ghosts? Can dead people speak to us?'

'Do you mean me personally or…'

'I mean both. You and the Jewish faith.'

'Maybe you can understand that I might not feel comfortable speaking about my personal opinions to a complete stranger. But I can tell you the answer to your question exists in the Bible.'

I had tried to read the Bible once. I stopped halfway through Genesis. I was grimacing at the notion of having to attempt it again.

'The short answer is that the Jewish faith accepts that souls without bodies can exist. Do you have a lifetime to spend on getting your long answer?'

'No, not really, Rabbi.'

'Then that's about all I can say. Have you heard of Kabbalah?'

'Jewish mysticism. Lots of celebrities practise it.'

'Not the nonsense the celebrities practise. You could spend the rest of your life getting the answer to your question, Kat.'

'So, Rabbi, if the Jewish faith accepts that ghosts can exist, can a ghost inhabit an object, such as a book?'

'Ah, no, that's Hollywood. Spirits don't inhabit objects. It is said that a spirit can attach itself to a person for a reason; let's say because that person has a lesson he or she needs to learn. But the spirit's not usually destructive.'

'Thank you, Rabbi.' I wanted to ask him if that mirrored his own beliefs but he had already made it clear he wasn't venturing into matters personal with me.

'Is that all you wanted?'

'I think that's all I needed.'

'If you want more you can email me. You have the address?'

'Thank you, Rabbi, I do. You've been more helpful than you could possibly know.'

'You're very welcome. I wish you all the best, Kat.'

I was about to put down the phone when it occurred to me that Alegra's spirit might agree to settle down in exchange for some divine intervention.

'Oh, there is just one more thing. Is there some prayer I can say for a dead Jewish relative?'

'There is, but it's a little complicated.' He paused and I didn't know if he expected me to fill the void. 'If you give me your relative's name, I can say *kaddish* for you.'

I told him Alegra's name and thanked him once more. I hung up and drifted back into the kitchen, notes in hand. Paul had gone outside without Boz, who had somehow got hold of one of my good purses and chewed right through it. I was thinking that he was probably possessed by a very different, malevolent spirit when he raised his eyes proudly to meet mine and waved his tail in my direction.

'You're a very bad dog.' I took the tattered remnants of my purse away from him, relieved that it had been empty of cash and credit cards. Just then, Paul came through the door.

'Here, these are for you.'

He thrust a homemade posy of roses and daisies towards me.

'Thanks.' I sniffed the roses. Beautiful but unscented. 'What's this for?'

'Do I need a reason to pick flowers for my girl?'

'Shit. Is it Valentine's Day already?'

I was met with silence. It couldn't be Valentine's Day, it wasn't even February. *My birthday? Nup. Anniversary? Same. So why the flowers?* And then I saw it in his eyes.

'What did you do?'

'Because I do something romantic you immediately think that I've done something wrong. Great.'

'Sorry. They're lovely.' Then I caught his eye. He was turning the tables on me. 'Wait a minute, I saw that! You did do something, didn't you?' I swear he'd given me the same look as Boz, and if he'd had one, Paul's tail would have been spinning in all directions. Here was proof positive that dogs and their owners do generally end up alike. Paul glanced down at his hands.

'I may have accidentally corrupted some of the files on your computer.'

'You what!' I immediately ran over to my computer, my most treasured possession, repository of my God-force and my innermost thoughts. It sat there, inert. I pushed its button and waited.

'The other day, when you were late coming home… We had that discussion and you left your computer on, remember?'

'Yes. Because I trusted you.'

'I may have looked at some of your documents.'

'Which ones? You read my story, didn't you?'

'I don't know what you did with it or what virus you've exposed it to, but suddenly it looked like it was being chewed up. I tried everything but it was impossible to fix. Please tell me that you've been listening to me and backed it up.'

'Hang on there, mister. You do something that disgraceful, and somehow you spin it on me?'

'The temptation was too great and it was a moment of weakness. I'm only a man, remember! Besides, this only happened because you lied to me.'

I rolled my eyes and logged onto the notebook. It was fixed with a single command.

'It's okay, Paul. I should be furious with you but I'm not. I didn't much like keeping things from you anyway. As for the computer, it's just a new security device one of my fellow bloggers got me onto. No harm done.'

'Must be a bloody good one. I couldn't crack it.'

I smiled. 'You're not the only one who knows a thing or two about computers.'

'I shouldn't have looked, I know, but I was worried about you. I thought you were having an affair or something. I tried to ask Fiona about it, but she thought I was just being paranoid.'

'Fiona? I'd never confide in your sister.' *Maybe Simone or Nicole, but never Fiona. And don't even bother to ask Georgia.* 'I guess I was having an affair in a way. I should have been open with you. Don't be angry, but I really, really want to continue this cookbook thing. I'm trying to keep an open mind this time and not get too obsessed. Of course, you realise that you could be married to a lunatic.'

'And maybe you are too.'

I smiled. It was a wonderful thing. No more deception, no more running around and hiding things. The freedom to commune with Fotini and Alegra and whoever else might turn up without worrying about detection. *What a relief!* I kissed Paul hard, which, to him, was the precursor of some afternoon loving. I nipped that in the bud with a single raised eyebrow.

'I'm going to get Mama's cookbook and make up for lost time.'

'Not now,' said Paul hopefully.

'Right now.'

His face sank. I wasn't about to reward Paul for what had clearly been some very bad behaviour. As I returned to my computer, I picked up a final shred of soft nappa leather (sodden with dog saliva) hidden under the table. *Who could resist that face?* I opened up the pantry and tossed Boz Scraggs a biscuit.

26

Ah, there you are again! Settled in or are you going to take all day? No, no, don't mind me, Kat, I'm just here for your convenience.

I was about to tell you what happened after my grandfather met his fate, when you cut me off without the simple courtesy of a warning. Do you think this is easy for me? Well, Miss Thing, I can make this story interesting or I can make it very, very dull. You snap that book shut once more and it'll be nothing but dull for you! Consider yourself warned! Now where was I? Oh, that's right.

I remember the emptiness I felt—we all felt—setting sail for a strange land without my abuelo. Children are the centre of their own little world, so for a while I thought that my grandfather's suffering must have been my fault and he had to stay behind in Valencia because of something I had done wrong. I didn't say anything at the time but I carried around that guilt for the rest of my life. It turned out that my poor, sweet abuelito never survived the torture.

I saw tears in Granny Alegra's eyes when the caravel in which we were sailing cast off. She looked in the direction of our old house and her gaze stayed there until Valencia disappeared over the horizon. She had been a young bride in that house and she raised all of her children there. As foul-mouthed and disrespectful as Abuela often was, and as rude to my grandfather as she had been throughout their marriage, she always had a genuine fondness for him, even if it could never have been classified as what you think of as love. Your kind of love is for romance novelists and celebrities. It's a bit like the spore of a dandelion blown away by the first puff of wind.

We sailed due east for a day and passed Ibiza to our south and later Mallorca and Menorca to our north. From there, the caravel tacked east-southeast to Cagliari, where we remained for a day while they unloaded some of its cargo of bolts of silk, which had been dyed brilliant scarlet. We stayed on board. From the deck of the boat and bathed in the sunshine, the city on the hill shone as bright as one of Mama's diamonds. The sight of its great limestone walls and magnificent white towers remained in my mind long after we had sailed away. That, and the taste of the sweet oranges Mama bought for us from a sailor. While the thought of never returning to Valencia filled me with huge sadness, the voyage had the possibility of turning into an extraordinary adventure.

Unlike our family's previous journeys, this time the world didn't try to stop our progress. The weather remained good, and so from Sardinia we made relatively quick time to Catania. It was there that my father announced we weren't going all the way to Anatolia after all, but we would be disembarking the caravel in Salonika. He had once been told that cousins of his lived there, but his decision was mostly made after speaking to the captain. The captain had also told my father that the sultan was eager to make sure his kind got a warm welcome there. To which my father asked, 'My kind? Who are my kind, as you say?'

'Jews, of course. Cristianos nuevos. You can make a home there. Many of your kind are prospering in Salonika without a problem. I should know, I brought most of them there.'

Experience had taught my father to be cautious at all times. 'We are all Catholic. I don't understand what you're saying.'

The captain's reply of 'Of course you don't' was emphasised by a snigger. My father said nothing, but you could see he was already deep in thought. Papa's uneasiness only seemed to lift when we left *Aslan Liman*—which you probably know as Piraeus—sailing north for our final destination.

Have you ever sailed on the Aegean Sea, Kat? Well, you have to one day, because only then can you really appreciate what I am about to tell you. I figured the Aegean out from the very first glance. I understood its mythology. It was glorious. I can't tell you why, but I suddenly felt as if I'd come home. I can't describe the beauty of the calm indigo under a sun-kissed sky nearly well enough, or the way the boat churned the water the colour of the finest aquamarines. The sea was so welcoming and I was so attracted to it, that my mother spent the remaining time on board worried that I would jump in and kill myself. Do you know that you have eyes the exact colour of the Aegean, Kat? If I had your eyes, I'd have been a huge hit with the men of Salonika. Now I've lost my direction again. Oh, that's right...

We finally reached the bay of Selanik—which was what the Ottomans called Salonika—at night, so we anchored there and waited until the next morning to disembark. My ears had had two weeks to get used to the sound of the Greek language by then. Courtesy of one of the sailors, my younger sisters and I had begun to learn the language and we had already collected a dozen or so words. I tried to teach Abuela a few of them, but she frowned and said that her old tongue could not perform the acrobatics needed to speak Greek. I told her that I was disappointed that she refused to even try.

We were rowed ashore by the same sailor who had sold Mama the oranges and Papa gave him a silver *real* to make sure everything we owned got to shore safely. We hadn't yet left the harbour when my father stumbled across a fellow converso and fell into deep conversation with him. It was all a bit boring, so my sisters and I dug channels into the dirt with the tips of our shoes, tired of the conversation, while Abuela fell asleep leaning against a post. I got the feeling that the man was offering my father a room for us to lodge in, but his accent was strange and it was hard for me to understand what he said. My father told me later that the man spoke Castilian rather than our version of Spanish, as did many of the Jewish people there. He said it might take us a while to get used to it.

'Does that mean I have to learn that as well as Greek, Papa?'

'Just be a good scholar and learn Greek. And promise me something.'

'What?'

'No matter what happens, hold true to your religion and always remember where you came from.'

'Of course I will.' I still believed myself to be a special kind of Catholic. I didn't really understand the importance of Papa's words until much later.

We left Mama and my sisters behind to keep an eye on Abuela, while Papa and I walked away from the waterfront and towards a road the converso called Egnatia. The paved road we were following was lined with strange little houses, some in the Venetian style, some Ottoman, but mostly with no style at all. They were made of anything and everything. Papa took a room for us all in a stone house with a balcony and crooked windows off a laneway, near the Aragon synagogue. The lodging was crowded with families just like ours. The six of us were sharing a space no bigger than the average bathroom of your day, Kat, but Papa said it wouldn't be for long and we believed him.

The strangest thing for us all to understand was that, in those days, the Ottoman Muslims had no problem with Jews. Picture that! Can you imagine what that feels like after four generations of continual fear that you will be found out for being something you are not? The Jews in Salonika were pretty much left to their own devices, so we were suddenly free to practise whatever religion we chose. Of course, Papa chose to return our family to Judaism.

The following week, he spoke to the rabbi about us doing *teshuvah*, and converting back. I overheard Papa tell Mama that the rabbi had been very encouraging, but he still wasn't sure how we would be received, having turned our back on our religion. He shouldn't have wasted his time worrying. Just about everyone in Salonika—with the exception of the very few Romaniotes who had lived in Greece for centuries—were conversos. A few weeks later, we all became fully-fledged members of the *kehila* of the Temple of Aragon, and Mama was no longer afraid to bake *roskas* and say the Sabbath blessing aloud. In all those years, we had kept our identity alive by passing down the traditions, the prayers, the songs and the recipes from mother to daughter. I was told I no longer had to say I was Catholic to all who asked. I was finally a Jew. And so our lives resumed pretty much where we had left off four generations earlier.

Everything we did was focused on our community, our *kehila*, and our lives weren't ruled by the Turks, as you might have expected, but by the leaders of the Temple of Aragon. Temple was where Mama quickly made friends and where she traded recipes. Temple was where Papa soon found commercial contacts and where he acquired the knowledge to start his new business. Temple was where I painfully learned my lessons and where I became acquainted with children who were exactly like me. Even Granny Alegra found companionship with widows almost as irreverent as she was! We were settled at last.

I told you before that I could either recite the long, dreary story of my life or the remarkable, snappy version. Since you've been attentive and your questions haven't been nearly as annoying as I thought they'd be, I'll do us both a favour and fast-forward a few years.

I had just turned fourteen and, courtesy of a pinch of good luck and a lot more hard work, Papa now owned the little stone house with the crooked windows. We had lodgers on the floor below us in a room next to where we kept the goats—the room we had all previously occupied—and we now slept in three rooms upstairs. Such luxury! Abuela was still alive, but her mind had gone missing for the last few years, and Mama spent much of her day either trying to prevent her disappearing or finding her when she had. It wasn't as if Mama had nothing to occupy her, since, aside from my sisters and me, she now had a son to raise. Papa had a thriving business right next to the port, where he sold foodstuffs and everything else any good Jewish housewife might need.

Papa was keen that I should marry soon, and he engaged the services of a *shadjente*, a matchmaker, to find me a suitable husband. Don't forget that, by now, we were stinking rich, and I was some match! Negotiations were begun with the middle son of the Boton family. He was descended from a line of weavers who had come to Salonika a few years after us. I knew him vaguely and we had exchanged greetings maybe once or twice, but I had noticed that his eyes always stayed on me longer than on anyone else whenever I passed by. Not that it mattered much, since marriages were forged on money and connections, but I was okay to look at; people sometimes even said I was pretty. I may not have been a ravishing beauty by any means, but he, on the other hand, was as ugly as my butt. Was I terrified by the prospect of marriage? You probably think you know the answer, but you could be wrong.

I thought about Judah Boton a bit like a traveller thinks of a distant transit port on the way to her ultimate destination. I knew I'd probably arrive there in the fullness of time, but for the minute I was more concerned with crossing the vast ocean. Judah Boton wasn't real for me, so I didn't care about him either way. It was the unending dullness of daily life that was driving me crazy. Unending, that is, until I met a blond boy with the palest grey eyes I had ever seen: an Ashkenazi named Yakov Weisstraub.

As you can see, I have a thing for eyes, and his were translucent. It was hard to tell where the irises ended and the whites began. I thought them hauntingly beautiful. Not only was I captivated by his appearance but, in a society where just about everyone was either Sephardi or Romaniote, Ashkenazim were rare. Rare for my father meant to be avoided at all cost. Rare for me meant highly desirable.

We had stumbled across each other at the port, by the boats of some Jewish fishermen, where I had gone to gaze out at my beautiful Aegean, as I did whenever I could escape from the grind of home. He had come for a similar reason and we exchanged a word or two. Since nearly everything about us differed, and even though we both spoke Ladino, a few words were all we were allowed to exchange. He told me that his family had left Germany for Salonika over a century earlier, chased out for being Jewish, much as we were, but with a bit less spectacle. They had settled further away from the port, in a poorer part of town, where his father had a business sewing clothes for the Ashkenazim and, when requested, for the Ottoman army. We arranged to catch up with each other at the same place in a week's time.

'I'll meet you but you can't tell anyone,' I told him. 'The elders of our community forbid girls to socialise with boys.'

'It is the same for us.'

I dreamed of the wolf-eyed boy that night.

Way beyond my fascination with Yakov was the attraction of having a secret, one which if discovered might cause no end of trouble, certainly for me and possibly even for my family. He and I were unfazed by that. It wasn't as if I had a thing for him—pale eyes or no, I felt nothing for him, really. It was more that I had fallen into a routine that I wanted to change but didn't know how. I guess Yakov was my way of mixing things up a bit, and it was a bonus that he was easy on the eyes. He and I met each other every so often, trading stories and maintaining an innocent friendship, until my younger sister saw us one afternoon and told my father.

'Do you realise the humiliation we would all suffer if the community learned of your indiscretion?' In my father's mind I was apparently a whore, even though I'd never even touched a boy who wasn't my brother. I watched my father's neck turn bright red and I really didn't care. 'You've forced my hand. You will be betrothed to Judah Boton as soon as it can be organised and married on the day of your fifteenth birthday. Count yourself lucky that it stopped here.'

'Yes, Papa.' That was my response. It all seemed a bit like being caught up in a vivid dream and not knowing what was going to happen next. I wasn't shattered by the thought of never seeing Yakov again—it turned out he wasn't that interesting after all—and I wasn't destroyed by my father's plans for me. I simply felt numb.

My father changed into high gear. He wasted no time in negotiating the *ketubah*, the terms of my marriage, and the date for my wedding was fixed. I just had to eat, sleep, breathe and work for another three hundred and fifty-three days, and I would be married to Judah Boton, a squat man-boy with a permanent pout and a squint. Deal done, all that remained was for Judah to sign on the dotted line and collect his purchase.

For a girl, it's all about the marriage. My trousseau had been assembled pretty much from the day I was born. My mother made lace and embroidered until her fingers bled—with three daughters, she had three chests to fill. Once I was betrothed, she began in earnest to train me for my future role as wife. She wasn't going to have Judah's mother telling the community that her daughter was ill-prepared, that she couldn't cook, or that she didn't know the traditions. Mama became a drill sergeant over-night. I read the *Siddur*. I cooked all the meals every other week. I sewed and mended. I washed and I cleaned. If I looked even for a minute as if I had nothing to do, my mother found work for me, so I learned the art of what I call active prevarication.

You have all types of shortcuts, mechanisation and assistance for everything you need to do these days. Need clean clothes? You pop them in a machine that washes them! No taking them to the washhouse, soaping and scrubbing them clean until your back aches and your hands blister. You want bread? Hey presto! It's already baked and in a thousand variations. You have got rid of toil and created stupid diversions to take your mind away from the passage of time, and yet you still bellyache. Can you imagine how it was for us? In those days there was nothing: no computers, no radios, not even a book to read, nothing but hard work from dawn to dusk, and what you did when the sun went down depended a lot on your marital status. Little wonder most people died young!

Our two families met up twice after the betrothal, on Pass-over and Succoth, and Judah and I were kept away from one another, so that we spoke little. When he did say something, it was always thoughtful. I gained the impression that Judah was an iceberg of a man—not because he was cold and desolate, but because his depths were unseen.

When it seemed to me that three hundred and fifty-three days would take forever to pass, all of a sudden there were only a handful of days left to go. On Sunday, Judah sent me a silk dress to wear for our wedding, and Mama and I spent the Monday making sweets of every kind you can imagine—baklava fingers dipped in honey syrup, bunuelos, roskas, marzipan sweets, pan d'espagna and so much more besides. She spread out every piece of linen we had prepared for my trousseau onto a bed that was destined to be delivered later that week to the Boton house to serve as our marriage bed.

The women of our community came by that afternoon, to exchange their gifts of perfumes and henna for a sweet drink made of ground melon seeds and rosewater, and to feast on our sweets. The following day was to be my *noche de alhenya,* when the same women returned to take me to the *hamam* and bathe me, paint my nails with henna, sing romantic songs and eat yet more sweets.

They sang about brides shining like jewels, of dark girls and of women loyal to their husbands. After my hair had been braided and they had all admired my trousseau, Papa and a handful of men picked up the lot and took it to the Boton house, while the women stayed behind and chatted.

'You must be happy with such a good match,' said one of the women to my mother, as her daughter listened.

'We are very happy, but truthfully, I will miss Alegra's company.'

'I would be very pleased if my daughter marries someone half as prosperous,' the woman continued.

The other women fell silent. We all looked at the girl cowering next to her mother like a frightened mouse, dark hair swept forward to hide remnants of a beard. You could tell that not one of us thought it remotely possible. Then Mama smiled at her.

'May the same happen to you!' said Mama to the girl by way of a blessing. She paused for a moment before adding, 'By the way, I can show you how to make sugar wax to get rid of that hair on your face.' The girl smiled shyly. She nodded at my mother. 'Yes? May as well be today!' Mama said, and led her away as the chatter recommenced.

I was up before dawn on my wedding day, eager to start a new life, with no idea what that meant. By the time I arrived at Judah's house early that afternoon for the *hupa,* I had been polished and primped and readied in every way. Judah Boton's mother had a nose long enough to rival her son's and an unattractive way of looking at people down its full length. She was nothing like Mama, who was by comparison a pretty songbird full of smiles. I stood between my two mothers as Judah came towards me. I remember thinking how unattractive he was and wondering how far I would get if I ran now. Granny Alegra kept alternating between sleep and calling out: 'What's happening? Why have you brought me here?'

Judah took my hand and walked me back to where the rabbi waited, and while I was too scared to look at Judah, his eyes never left me. A cloth was draped over both our heads, the rabbi recited blessing after blessing and our marriage contract was read aloud. When the glass was broken, we were truly married in God's eyes. Yet I was the same Alegra.

The throng hung around to celebrate with his family and mine, dancing and feasting and laughing. I snatched glances at my husband, terrified that if I looked at him properly I would find him repulsive. After what seemed like a hundred years, some of the guests made motion to leave. Two of the women sang a song they called *Dreams of Spain*, and Mama's eyes filled with tears. You see, it was a song about the key to a house in Spain brought here in pain and love by our ancestors. For my mother, it was a memory of where we had come from. The women stopped abruptly, saying they would not continue since she found it so distressing and the wedding had to be full of laughter, not tears.

After they had all gone home—the singing women, the pious men and my family last of all—Judah's parents led us away from the celebration and to our conjugal bed. I had never undressed in front of anyone other than Mama and my sisters. Even during my ritual bath, I had begged the other women to wait outside. I took off my clothes in the corner and we slept. We slept the following night too, but by the third, Judah had gathered enough confidence to kiss me. After that, you could say we did pretty much what most creatures do naturally. He wasn't very skilled at it and I guessed he was as new to the whole thing as I was. Why do you wrinkle up your nose like that? Sex is a fact of life. Your existence depended on it! You're just lucky I spared you the graphic detail.

We were left pretty much to ourselves for seven days. By the end of the week, I had been showered with gifts of gold, tested in my skill making the Sabbath bread, and jumped over a fish three times (in order to ensure my fertility; I later cooked the fish with tomatoes for dinner. It was delicious). Judah's Mama was nicer in temperament than she was in appearance, and I learned that she looked at everything down her nose because she was farsighted. The biggest surprise of all was Judah. He turned out to be a gentle, generous man and as funny as a stand-up comedian to boot.

Judah was a gifted mimic. He imitated everyone from his mother to the rabbi. He was clever and irreverent, and as I got to know him, I found myself noticing the squint less (he was also longsighted) and his character more. In my eyes, he became the handsomest man who ever lived and he treated me better than I could have ever hoped. I was the happiest of wives, Kat, I can say that without hesitating.

We had ten children during our twenty-four-year marriage. Six of our children died before they became adults, but that was the way it was. The last pregnancy turned out badly for the baby and me. I knew something was wrong when he had stopped kicking a few days before he was born, so I wasn't surprised when he didn't cry. The *comadre* took him away immediately, and I never even saw him. As company for my grief, I developed a high fever. Two days later, I drifted away from everything I had known and early the next morning, I died. You say it's tragic that I died in such a way, but I say to you that I would have happily given up my life a hundred times over, so that any one of my children might have lived. I understood the sacrifice Abuelito made so much better once I had a family of my own, so don't get too sentimental over it, Kat, we all have to go sometime! At least I wasn't around for the worst of it.

In lots of ways our life in Greece was as uneventful as any of us could have wished for, that day we sailed away from Valencia. The Greeks may have changed my name to Aliki, but that was such a small sacrifice for regaining my true identity. Of course, in my heart I always remained loyal to Spain and to Alegra. I finally learned to sing all of Mama's songs and I sang them as loudly as I wanted and nobody said a word.

So, after coming full circle from Jews to Christians and back to Jews, you can only imagine my pain when of my four surviving children, only two married within the Jewish faith. I'm sad to say that you are not descended from them. Their descendants still carry the name of Boton to this day and they still practise Judaism. Your ancestor, my only daughter, my precious Rebecca, broke my heart by converting and marrying a Greek. But you know what? She never forgot where she came from every time she sang or she cooked. I had already taught her the recipes of our heritage, which is how you come to have the recipe for bunuelos. When all else fails, food binds you to your roots.

Well, my sweet Kat, my *Gatita*, I guess that's all I can tell you. My only regret, if I had any at all, was that I never ever got to return to the little house in Valencia and use my key.

27

I didn't know what more I could say to Alegra, so I copied out her recipes for bunuelos and chicken stew, thanked her and closed the book as gently as I could. I was directly descended from a Fatima as well as a Rebecca. But for me, that only began to explain my personal genetic make-up.

It seemed that, so far, all roads led to Greece, via Israel, Spain and Turkey. I was still so puzzled by the result that labelled me totally Middle Eastern Jewish, that I wrote a pithy email to the proprietor of *AncestorFinder* accusing him of fudging the results. I got back the following:

> Dear Valued Client. Your query is important to us, but we do not respond personally where answers can be readily found on our website. Please refer to common Q and A.

I was certain he hadn't even read my question. As an act of rebellion, I didn't bother to look at the website.

That evening, Paul and I celebrated our twelfth wedding anniversary by going to a French restaurant and eating ourselves into oblivion. It all started well enough—lobster bisque with a medallion of lobster in the middle for me, fattened goose liver on toast for Paul, followed by matching filet mignons sitting in an unctuous puddle of bordelaise, crepes for desert and a plate of cheese. I had eaten enough to satisfy a large family for a week. In the wee morning hours I awoke with thunder in the pit of my stomach. How could I be hungry? The rumble turned into a growl. I rolled over and ignored it. When I woke up again, it was already past eight and Paul was still snoring off the previous night's excesses.

I swung my legs out from under the duvet and tried to stand up. The room tilted on its axis and back again as I held onto the bedhead. I must have had a lot more to drink than I had realised. A sour taste flooded my mouth and threatened to escape forcibly, whether I was ready or not. *Oh God, I'm going to be sick!* I barely had time to scurry to the bathroom than the contents of my stomach transferred themselves into the toilet.

Paul had stopped snoring. 'What's wrong? You okay?' He sounded groggy.

I was too busy puking to answer him.

'Are you vomiting?'

The boy was really slow to wake up this morning. I answered him with another almighty retch.

'Are you all right? Do you need anything?'

As if! Poor Paul was renowned for being a sympathetic vomiter. He couldn't abide the sound, let alone the sight and smell of it. I knew he would be tapping into all his resources to keep himself from being sick right then alongside me. I struggled a 'No, I'm good,' before heaving once more. After my fifth emission, I was done. There could be nothing left to bring up. I unclasped the toilet bowl, stood up, washed my mouth out and crawled back to bed.

'Errgh. Something I ate last night was definitely bad,' I announced as soon as I settled.

'But we ate pretty much the same meal.' Paul paused for contemplation. I couldn't even think of last night's meal without feeling nauseated. 'The lobster! It must have been the lobster.'

'Errgh. Don't remind me!'

'Well, at least I'm feeling okay.'

'I'm very happy for you.'

'I mean I could get you some water or a cup of tea, if you felt up to one.'

I turned towards Paul. 'Could you please make me a cup of tea? With lemon and two teaspoons of honey?' I implored in my best child-voice.

Paul padded off towards the kitchen, pleased to have something useful to do. I stayed in bed, sipping sweet tea and lemonade and chewing on crackers. By mid afternoon, my tummy had settled sufficiently for me to resume living, but I couldn't face opening the recipe book. Perhaps tomorrow, when I had expelled whatever beast had infiltrated my lobster and was running amok in my gut.

I was well enough to log on to my computer and I began to research Valencia. From everything I read, Alegra's story had the ring of truth, even if she'd been a bit scant on the detail. It was early evening when the crazy notion entered my mind. Why should I settle for reading about these places and my ancestry? Why couldn't we live it? Next time, I was going to ask Alegra where exactly she had lived, and Paul and I would go there and find her house. How cool would it be if the key still unlocked the door? It could be a pilgrimage in her honour. And since we would be in Spain, we could just as easily pop across to Greece. Fantastic research for my novel. But before we could contemplate such a journey in earnest, there would be two hurdles to overcome. Number one—we had no money to pay for the airfares, let alone cover the bills and the house repayments while we were away. Number two—and infinitely more challenging—Paul would never agree. I decided I would limit myself to subtly working on Paul for the minute and to simply dreaming about Spain and Greece. *If it's to be, we'll find a way.*

I consigned the rest of Alegra's story to my cloud drive, after adding my own embellishments, naturally. When I had finished I began to think seriously about my pilgrimage. I could probably work out where Fotini's house was located pretty easily. Alegra's would be far more challenging. Valencia was a city, not just a village, and she lived such a long time ago. From what she had already told me, her house was within the ancient city walls, somewhere near the old *Mercado*. I located it on the map and read on. I was heartened by how much of medieval Valencia was still standing. I probably should have stopped reading at that stage, because the paragraph that followed hit me like a bat to the head. *While the conversos played a major role in the development of Valencia* (blah blah blah), *none of the Jewish quarter of Valencia has survived.*

Could my plans be dashed in a sentence? All trace of Alegra would be gone. What was the point to her visitations if I couldn't put things right for her? The thought of being lumbered with the ghosts of my family's past for the rest of my life, as Mama had been, was nothing short of frightening. I put aside my computer and did what anyone would do in such an eventuality—I took Boz Scraggs for a walk.

We had gone barely a block when the buzz finally left my mind. In my blinkered state I had all but forgotten one thing—yes, the Amato family was Jewish, but they were crypto-Jews. They hadn't been Jewish when they lived in Valencia, or at least, they hadn't been openly Jewish. As conversos, surely they wouldn't have been daft enough to live in the Jewish quarter unless they wanted to provoke attention. Maybe there was a chance of finding her house and setting things right after all.

I took a shortcut home while Boz glared at me accusingly. He was so frequently neglected in the walks department that his face registered immediate disappointment when he realised that today would prove no exception. I ran the last dozen steps, grabbed Mama's book as I crossed the hallway and took it into our bedroom, while Paul cooked dinner. I opened it on the recipe for *Pan D'Espana*.

'I thought we'd finished already. What do you want now?' Unmistakably Alegra.

'I wanted to ask you about your home in Valencia.'

'What for?'

'I was interested in it, that's all.'

'But I've told you everything about it.'

'Not the address,' I ventured. 'You never told me the address.'

'What would you do with the address if I gave it to you? Write me a letter?'

'No...'

'Then of what possible use could it be?'

'I could visit your old house for you. Go on that journey you never got to go on. Return the key to its rightful place.'

'I was right, wasn't I? You are definitely a silly girl.'

'What? Why?'

'You still haven't worked anything out.'

'Then what is all of this about? Haven't you come to see me so I could return your key and you could get closure?'

'And you think it's all about that damned key?'

'Isn't it? Something that you didn't do in life that you need me to do?'

'If that's what you believe, then that's why I'm here and why you can hear me.'

'Okay, so what is it about, then?'

'Well, Kat, I'm not allowed to say. You'll just have to keep reading the recipe book to get the answer to that one. Listen to our stories and work it out.'

'But I have worked it out. Fotini needs me to go to Greece to find the family she left behind, and track down what became of her loved ones. You know, she never learned whether they lived or died. And you need me to return to Valencia. You both need closure so your souls can move out of the recipe book and on to heaven or wherever else you have to get to.'

'Maybe you're right and maybe you're wrong, but don't look to us to tell you. The answers are in the book.'

'What, it's against the rules to tell me? What else could it possibly be?'

'As I already said, that I can't tell you. It's different for everyone.'

'Keep reading?'

'Keep reading.'

'When do I stop?'

'You'll know when.'

I closed the book reverently although I was, to tell the truth, more than a little pissed off. *Thanks a bunch, Alegra!* I was being haunted by dead relatives for no appreciable reason. *Keep reading!* I had pretty much convinced myself by now that the visitations really weren't a figment of my own imagination, they were real. Now, if someone would just tell me why this was happening, I'd be happy.

My telephone rang in the kitchen, which was where I had last dropped it. Not Kinderkull, this time. Just a regular trr-ring, trr-ring. Paul came into the bedroom, holding it at arm's length. I sniggered at the sight of him wearing the frilly apron he had bought me years ago, and which he had always *admired* when I wore it. Preferably with nothing else but a pair of black stilettos. It didn't have quite the same allure on him.

'I'm so used to hearing Daley scream that, when it rang, I wasn't too sure what it was.' He tossed the still ringing phone on the bed.

'Thanks. I changed the ring tone.'

'I noticed. Better answer that, don't you think?'

I smirked at Paul and answered the phone. It was Tim Lawless's personal assistant. Could I please make a time to attend the office for a final distribution of the estate?

'Can I make the appointment with you now? When does Tim need to see me?'

'Any time this week. We just need a couple of signatures and you can nominate how you'd prefer your share of the estate paid to you. The rest of the family is keen to have matters settled once and for all.'

I bet Georgia was. 'How about Thursday? Yes, two-fifteen is fine.'

I hung up the phone. If I hadn't just had the little talk with Alegra, I probably would have taken the PA's call to be a sure sign that I was on the right path and that I should book our tickets there and then. My share of Mama's estate offered a neat solution to one of the impediments to travelling the world and, by doing so, putting all my ghosts to bed. But what if Alegra was right and I'd misunderstood the messages? Her words had been very clear. *Read on!* I guess I could delay my trip for a while, especially since Paul would be highly unlikely to agree without some solid persuasion, even if we had the money. I was willing to wait until I had finished reading the cookbook or had worked out whatever it was I had to do for my dead relations, whichever came first. In the meantime, I was caught up in another wave of lobster's revenge so I nibbled on dry toast while Paul ate the stew he had lovingly prepared for us. Then we snuggled in the comfy chair to watch television together, as Paul munched his way through a block of scorched almond chocolate and I felt well enough to let him.

The following day brought with it only the merest hint of lobster-be-sick, but it passed quickly and after that I was completely back to normal. To test myself I allowed my thoughts to drift to greasy hamburgers and fries dripping in oil. Not a trace of nausea ensued, so I determined that it would be okay to tackle more recipes and more of my relatives.

Paul was outside mowing the lawn. I opened the cookbook, and one of the loose pages slid into my lap. I pushed it back in place and flicked to the next page. The same recipe slipped out again and fluttered to the floor. From beneath the kitchen table, I heard the sound of cantors. It was the sound of a Sunday morning with Mama, memories of Chris and I being dragged along to a church with too few pews and too many people.

The memory brought with it childish tedium, unending ritual, and the piety of saints flattened into icons and glaring at me for sins I had yet to commit.

'How much longer, Mama? Can't we go home now? My feet hurt.'

'Stop whining, Katy. Can't I have a little bit of peace, even in church?'

And then the crowding around Mama after the service, the women's gossip, the pieces of dry bread we had to eat without dropping a single crumb, all the while clinging to Mama's skirt.

'These are your children, Mrs Elleni?'

'How big your son has become, God protect him.'

'What remarkable eyes your daughter has!'

'Kyrie eleison, Kyrie eleison, Kyrie eleison.'

Then the squeak of a mouse cut through my reminiscences. I picked up the sheet of paper, not all that old but badly stained, fraying and curled at the edges. The ink had faded and the recipe was hardly visible. I was terrified it would dissolve into dust even as I held it. I took out my computer and began to transcribe immediately: *Rabbit Stifado. Take at least a dozen small onions…*

And there it was again, barely audible. It was neither a squeak nor a mouse.

'Kat?'

'Yes?'

'Kat?'

'Yes.'

'Kat?'

This was getting stale. 'Yes, I'm Kat. Who are you?'

'My name is Ioanna Hatzifrangoulis.'

She said it so quickly that, to my ears, it was a rush of unfamiliar sounds. 'Who?'

'Ee-oh-an-na Hah-dzi-frahn-goo-lees.'

I recognised the surname of course, but I still struggled to pronounce it. *Damn those missed Greek lessons!* Clearly she could see the frustration on my face and added. 'If you find it easier, you may call me Jeanne, since that's what the nuns called me. I am your grandmother.'

I returned to the sheet of paper in front of me, only barely holding together. If I was to preserve it, I'd have to do something now.

'Grandma Jeanne, would you mind if I talked to you after I copy out your recipe onto my computer. It's so fragile, you see, I'm scared I might tear it and lose it altogether.'

'You want me to go away?'

'You don't have to do that. I'll only need a few minutes. I'm a very good typist, you know.'

'I don't know what you just said, but I've waited a long time to talk to you and I can wait a little longer.' Unlike Alegra, Jeanne was clearly not a ghost with an appetite for keeping up with the times.

'It's my new tablet. You know, a small, flat computer?'

Nothing.

'I have an idea. How about I scan the recipe and then I'll put it away and then we can talk? You probably didn't understand a single word I just said. I'll explain what it all means another time. Okay, so I'll be back in a few minutes. Hang on there, Grandma Jeanne.'

'All right.'

She sounded doubtful. I took away the single sheet and scanned it a handful of times, increasing the resolution until the entire recipe became legible. Never having been scanned myself, I trusted that the process wouldn't hurt Jeanne or her recipe. When I returned, I slid both the original and the copy back into the book and tied it up. There'd be no time to check on Jeanne until later. I knew Paul would be finished mowing shortly, our lawn being reminiscent of snooker table baize, only not quite as green, and he'd be back inside for more coffee in a few minutes. Mama's book was still problematic when Paul was around, no matter how discreet I tried to be, and no matter how tolerant he tried to remain. Even if he had gone a long way towards accepting that the cookbook was solely my research tool and that I had it all under control, sometimes it was just easier to wait until he was elsewhere before mingling with the ancestors.

I brewed another pot of coffee in anticipation of Paul's imminent arrival and began to read the newspaper on my tablet. *Economic Woes Hit China. Storm Cell Forms Over Caribbean. Earthquake hits Turkey—Thousands Homeless.* There was so much sorrow in the world that it threatened to become a bit ho-hum. Shit apparently was happening everywhere, yet hidden on the right-hand side column, about three-quarters of the way down the page, there it was: an otherworldly communication and exactly what I needed: *Jack Elliot Tickets Sell Out.* I read on. *World renowned medium Jack Elliot has added a third session to his tour after tickets for the first two sessions sold out within minutes… Tickets for the new session on Thursday night go on sale at ten today…*

A medium? Of course! *They speak to dead people, don't they?* Why had I wasted all that time and effort on doctors and psychologists, rabbis and museums when a medium was all I required? I looked at my watch. It was a little before eleven. Surely Jack Elliot hadn't sold out yet. I got onto the ticket seller's website. Should I get two tickets or one? Two might be harder to obtain and anyway Paul probably wouldn't want to go. I dropped down *Venue Pick up* and clicked *Buy Tickets*. I watched the little circle on my screen chase itself around for a full minute before my screen froze. I tried again. The second time was no better. Then the door creaked ajar.

'Hi, honey, what are you doing?'

Click. 'Hey, sweetheart. Coffee's all ready for you on the bench.'

'Thanks. What are you looking at?'

'Nothing much. Doing some online shopping.'

'Oh. Do you need a hand with anything?'

'No, I'm good.' Paul poured out two cups and handed one to me. 'Paul, what do you think about mediums?'

'Mediums? As in the size?'

'No. As in people who speak to the dead.'

'Not again, Kat.'

'No, not for me. For the book.'

'Uh huh.'

'Really. What if I spoke to a medium?'

'What if they tell you you're going to meet someone tall, dark and handsome…'

'That's a psychic, you fool. Besides I already have my perfect match.'

'So why do you need to go to a psychic?'

'A medium. Just for some research.'

'Why ask me? You don't need my approval. Go by all means, if that's what you want to do. But don't expect me to come with you.'

'I'll think about it.'

We sipped our coffee together and I tried once more. On my third attempt, the sold out sign had gone up and that was that. I was about to close the page when a tiny link caught my attention. *Missed out on tickets? Book a personal reading with Jack Elliot*. It was worth considering. I clicked the link and sailed across space into Jack Elliot's private cyber domain.

Two-fifteen Thursday arrived faster than I thought possible. I hadn't reconnected with Jeanne since our first short exchange and I felt a little guilty. I had been asked to write seven hundred words on *How to Keep Sex Alive in Your Marriage* for a major women's magazine, whose editor-in-chief had been an old workmate of mine in a former life. In my defence, all I can say is we had bills to pay. The piece had taken me the best part of half a day to trot out. The fun part had been making up various scenarios with Paul.

This time, Paul had agreed to drive me to the offices of Clark, Lawless and Clark but he had to cancel at the last minute when yet another client needed some software patches urgently. I was once again driving alone and this time without Daley. I didn't know why, but I was finding Kinderkull less palatable these days. Paul was a huge fan of the blues, so he lent me a Muddy Waters CD to educate my tastes. Nearly six hours' driving there and back, and only one CD for company. I had told Paul that, without him sharing the drive, I would probably stay the night in a hotel and I'd packed a bag just in case. I had also packed the recipe book. Just in case.

I arrived at the law office a minute or two late, which, considering the drive, was no mean feat. I was a little surprised to find Chris there, minus Georgia. I hadn't realised he'd be sitting in on the appointment. He raised his eyes from the book in his lap and looked at me uneasily as I entered.

'Hi, Chris.'

'Hello, Kat.'

'How are you?'

'Not bad.'

So far, so awkward. 'I heard your operation went well?'

'Can't complain.'

Fortunately we were saved from indulging in any further chitchat by Tim Lawless's PA. She led us into his office and then left to make coffee. Tim was just as creased and gangly as I remembered, but this time I hadn't dressed to impress and he looked frankly disappointed. He clenched his hands together and spoke.

'I'm pleased to tell you both that I am in a position to give you the final distribution of your mother's estate today. As you know, the sale of the house went through last week and I've received all the necessary paperwork. Katerina, I understand that you have collected your mother's jewellery. All we need are your two signatures, here, here and here. Initial here and here. As you can see, we have adjusted the amount by our fees, here.'

Chris and I signed on the dotted line, taking care not to brush each other as we passed the papers between us.

'Here are your three receipts, Christopher. Deposits have already gone into the accounts you nominated for yourself, Ethan and Poppy, just as we discussed. And here are your two cheques, Katerina.'

'Thanks.'

I folded them in half and slipped them into my purse. Even divided four ways, the estate was large enough to pay off our home loan, plus some. Strangely, I felt liberated and more than a little sad. I thanked Tim Lawless and said my goodbyes. Chris followed me out of the office. As we stepped outside, I turned side on.

'See you, Chris.' Short and sweet, there was nothing more to say.

'Bye, Kat.' And then he was gone.

After a lifetime of Chris, there would be no need to ever see him again. I imagined that this felt rather like a divorce. Ethan and Poppy could make up their own minds about me. They knew where I lived.

I was too numb to drive home that night and so I looked for a hotel. Coincidentally, there was one right next to the entertainment arena where Jack Elliot would be doing his readings that night. I slipped the car into the driveway, edging past tourists in line for an excursion and sidled up to reception. One young man was busy circling the sights on a fold-up map for a middle-aged couple in matching pedal pushers, Birkenstocks and T-shirts. The girl next to him dazzled in her new uniform, blonde hair and bleached teeth.

'May I help you?'

'Do you have a room for tonight?'

'Just the one night?'

'Yes.'

'Let me see… Just for yourself, madam?'

The word grated. She looked all of thirteen. Apparently, I had become a madam in my early forties. *Ah well.* 'Yes. Just me.'

'Hmm.' This was followed by a series of pointing and murmuring with the man next to her, while the middle-aged couple synchronised looks.

'You're in luck, we have had a cancellation.'

'That's great.' I pulled out my credit card and the transaction concluded. 'Is there a bank near here?'

'Yes.' The girl pulled out a fold-up map and began circling.

I glanced at the middle-aged couple. *Please don't let Paul and me ever look like that!* 'Never mind,' I said to the girl. 'I'll find it myself.' And with that I left.

Cashed up after my trip to the bank, I was drifting past the entertainment arena when, next minute, I somehow found myself standing front and centre at the ticket booth. The saleslady turned to face me after I had cleared my throat twice.

'Are there any tickets left for tonight?'

Boredom seeped out of every crease in her face. 'How many are you wanting?'

'Just one.'

The woman raised an eyebrow and stabbed furiously at the keyboard. Then she raised the other eyebrow. 'There's been a last minute cancellation. One premium ticket left. Do you want it?'

Apparently, today was my lucky day. 'Money is no object, my good woman.'

She raised both eyebrows simultaneously. 'You want it, yes or no?'

'Yes.'

My response was enough for her to cease her facial acrobatics and turn her full attention to her computer once more. The printer hummed and spat out what seemed like an enormous volume of paperwork for the business being transacted. I returned my credit card to its slot and crammed the ticket and receipt into my purse.

What a day it had been! Our home was finally our own. I had just secured the last room in the hotel and the last ticket to the show. It was a sign. *My destiny awaits.* Four hours to go until showtime. I returned to my room and unpacked. I placed Mama's book on the bedside table and pulled out a single, loose sheet folded in quarters, which I meant to replace later. Then I spreadeagled myself on the bed, turned on the television and ordered room service.

28

I must have fallen asleep after having eaten my meal. I woke up on top of the bed, alongside the room service tray. Something near me was buzzing. The curtains were still drawn and the streetlights were casting strange ochre halos onto the footpath below.

Oh shit! What time is it? The bedside clock said it was six thirty-eight, but was that am or pm? I wondered if I could have slept through the entire night. I looked at my phone, which I had switched to vibrate when I'd got to my room. Thank God for twenty-four-hour clocks and thank God for Paul having woken me! It said eighteen thirty-nine, and I had just under an hour to talk to Paul, get myself properly awake, dress and run next door for the show.

Paul was happy to be dispatched quickly and, once he realised I was still groggy from sleep, and making very little sense, he said he'd call me in the morning. I told him that I was going back to bed, which of course I was. I simply omitted the bit in between, where I was going to catch Jack Elliot. I grabbed the towelling gown from the wardrobe, buried my face in it and thought how much more inviting they looked on the hanger. It smelled vaguely chemically, which I considered was probably a good thing. A quick shower and a change of clothes and I'd be good to go.

I was ready and waiting for an elevator at a little after seven, made-up and curly hair tamed. By seven-fifteen I gave up waiting for the lift and was clunking down the fire stairs as quickly as I could in platforms and a tight skirt. Just as I was beginning to feel the vertigo that comes with turning the same way floor after floor, I reached the lobby. When the door swung open, I finally saw why I had been waiting for a lift that never came.

The lobby was crowded almost exclusively with women who, like me, had tickets for Jack Elliot. Unlike me, it seemed they travelled in packs—noisy, barely sober, chattering packs. I put on my best game face and charged through as if I had somewhere to go, and that somewhere was nowhere they'd be remotely interested in. Besides, even if we were headed for the same destination, I was there purely for research. I belonged to the elite press. I wasn't there because I believed in psychics and mediums, like these silly women, oh no, I was so much better than that.

Having taken the high moral ground, I soon left the cackling horde behind me. Unfortunately, I discovered another pack in the foyer of the entertainment arena, equally animated and equally loud. I glanced at my ticket and pushed my way around them until I reached entrance six. There I found myself waiting to be shown to my seat behind a small but lively line of seven women and a solitary, elderly man with whom I exchanged glances. If ever someone's eyes screamed *please save me*, his did. I arrived at my seat eight minutes before the buzzer that preceded the show sounded. That was the benefit of buying a premium ticket—as if I'd had any choice in the matter. The proletariat was still waiting in snaking lines to be seated.

I settled into my chair. I was so close to the stage that, if Jack Elliot had even a bead of sweat on his brow, I was certain to spot it. To the right of me were three twenty-something girls with one of the girls' boyfriend. I surmised that it must have still been early in their relationship for him to have agreed to come and to be so cheery about it. I listened in to the conversation for a moment before I realised he had only come so he could collect Brownie points that he'd later redeem for sex.

Just then, a middle-aged woman wearing a navy suit and a sequinned silver lame beret slipped into the single empty seat to my left. I had just enough time to register that her hat looked exactly like a pot scrubber, when the house lights dimmed. Glittering like a faceted diamond, the beret came into its own as a spotlight danced over it. It seemed to me that she was trying very hard to ensure she couldn't be ignored. I nodded in her direction.

'Isn't this exciting?' she said. 'I hope I get a message tonight. Are you here by yourself?'

'Yes,' I replied.

'So am I. No one wanted to come with me. They don't believe in it.'

I was thinking that they had shown better sense than anyone present, when she added, 'I'm Lil, by the way.'

'Ka…' I began. The rest of my name was drowned out by the noise.

As we exchanged greetings of sorts, a voice so deep that it sounded as if it was coming straight out of Hades, announced: 'Dandy Entertainment in conjunction with Elliot Enterprises are proud to present world renowned medium Jack Elliot.' The crowd erupted. For a full twenty seconds after he had arrived on stage in leather pants and a Nehru shirt, Jack Elliot had to wait out the frenetic handclapping, whoops and wolf whistles that had greeted him. He was a rock star from the tip of his golden ringlets right down to his unshod toes. When the room finally fell silent, the magic began. And by magic, I mean sleight of hand.

Jack glided across the stage and stopped suddenly on the far side. 'I sense that I'm being drawn to this side of the room.'

A woman halfway up the stand squeaked. Jack caught it in an instant and gestured in her general direction.

'Is someone here named Margie, or Marjorie?'

'I'm Mariah!' exclaimed the squeaking woman. *Amazing!*

'No, it's definitely something with an M and a J or G sound. That's what's coming through.'

'My mother was Marguerite.'

I was being drawn in. Could this man be the real deal?

'Then this must be for you.' He frowned momentarily, summoning his senses. 'Has she passed?'

'No.'

'Then this must be her mother. I see an older woman… You knew her?'

'No, she died before I was born.'

He went on to tell her how her grandmother was always with her. She'd been looking after her her whole life and grandma loved her. The message was a bit general, but I was still a believer. Lil with the Brillo pad on her head clapped furiously.

Next, Jack Elliot was drawn to a man in the bleachers, who looked as if he was trying very hard to morph into his wife's handbag. Apparently, he was getting a message via his mother's brother's keepsake—an old army-issue watch. The stunned man pulled it out of his pocket. Now this was nothing short of amazing, right down to Jack's revelation of the drawer in which it had been kept. And so it continued.

A little later in the show, Jack crossed stage right and arrived virtually under our noses.

'I have a message for a Lillian?'

The Brillo pad jumped. 'I'm Lillian.'

'Really?'

'Yes.'

'There's an older man here for you—no, two men.'

'That'd be my father and his brother.'

'Both passed?'

'Yes.'

'Unexpected?'

'Yes and no. My father had cancer. His brother had a stroke.'

'But their passing was at a time you weren't expecting it?'

'We didn't think Dad would die quite so soon, no. My uncle's death was a complete shock.'

I was thinking that she should stop volunteering so much information, and wait for Jack to reveal the message, rather than helping him.

'I'm getting the feeling that you were close to them.'

'Oh yes.'

'You were the apple of his eye?'

'Oh yes.'

'Only the father figure, he's got flowers for you. He's showing me love.'

Brillo Lil began to sob at this so violently that her hat threatened to topple off. I gave her a handkerchief. As I did so, Alegra's recipe for charoset, which had somehow found its way from the bedside table into my purse, tumbled out and settled at my feet. As I bent to pick up the page, it unfolded enough for me to see the writing.

'Thanks, Carla,' Lil muttered, wiping her eyes. She'd obviously heard me say the start of my name and then made up the rest.

As she spoke, Jack's face lit up.

'The woman next to you, Lillian,' he said indicating me. 'I'm feeling drawn to you.'

My heart thumped so loudly, I thought it would bounce out of my chest. The next moment I heard a familiar woman's voice whisper my name. Alegra was definitely in the room.

'I'm hearing a C or K name. Is that you?' Jack Elliot was waving in my direction.

He is the real deal! I nodded furiously.

Beside me, Alegra muttered. 'Whoa just a minute there, Kat. You don't buy a car without taking it for a drive first and seeing what it's made of.'

Jack Elliot was staring me straight in the face.

'Carla?' said Jack.

'Her name's Kat,' said Alegra loudly.

'I'm Kat,' said I.

'I have a young man here. You have a brother?'

'Yes.'

'Passed?'

I didn't react.

'No, he's not dead, you fraud,' screeched Alegra. From the sound of it, she was standing right next to Jack. 'I'm Alegra, her fifteenth great-grandmother. Repeat after me- Al-e-gra!'

'He's bringing chocolates for you. In a heart box. He says he's sorry he had to leave so soon.'

'My brother's not dead,' I said matter of factly.

'But there's a young man? I can see a young man... His name starts with K or S—as in Sam or Steve—or maybe it's Tom?'

'Alegra, you imposter, my name's Alegra. Now, why can't you hear that? There's no young man here—believe me, I'd know it if there was.' She was shouting so loudly, I was tempted to place my hands over my ears. I was watching my faith in Jack Elliot melt away and drift out of the arena.

'No. I don't know a Sam or a Steve or a Tom starting with a K or S. In fact, I don't know any young man who's died,' I said.

Jack seemed to be all at sea. He shook his head. 'Sometimes I get mixed messages.' He paused, head tilted. 'No, they're insisting. A friend who passed young, perhaps? A school friend possibly?' Jack was reaching out for a straw—any straw—that happened to float by.

'No.'

Jack remained silent for a few moments, looking at his feet. It seemed they didn't have an answer for him either. 'Then this must be for someone else.'

Just then, Brillo Lil tossed him a life jacket. She waved her hand.
'I had a brother named Stuart Thomas Carlsson who died young.'

'In an accident?'

'Yes.'

'Then I'm back with you. It was a message for you after all.'

'This is bullshit,' yelled Alegra. 'She's a plant. Wired for sound.
He's got a few of them working the crowd. Jack Elliot may be great
with his research and he can read people a treat, but medium my
arse.'

A plant! Of course. You never see what's staring you in the face.
Brillo Lil was so obvious, she wasn't obvious. Feeling a bit foolish, I
folded up Alegra's recipe and placed it in my jacket pocket. I tossed
a glance at the *like* girls and the boyfriend. The one with whom I'd
exchanged words was sitting on the edge of her seat. The others
looked only vaguely interested. *Good time to leave.* As soon as Jack
crossed over to stage left, I edged past Lil's knees, and walked back
to my hotel.

I fell into a deep sleep the moment my head hit the pillow and the
next thing I knew, my phone was vibrating under the sheets.

'Hello?'

'Don't tell me I woke you up again?'

'No, I was up,' I lied. I glimpsed at the bedside clock. It was a little after eight.

'You don't sound it. When are you coming home?'

'I'll leave as soon as I finish breakfast.'

'Okay, great. I'll see you soon. Drive slowly, okay? I love you.'

'I love you too, Paul.'

29

After a long shower and a croissant and coffee, I began the journey home. The Jack Elliot Experience had been a valuable lesson, but I still wondered if, like me, there were people out there who really, truly spoke to the dead. About three-quarters of the way home, I toyed with the thought of trying another medium. Perhaps not. I was still mentally debating the issue when the audio display read *Nicole* (one of the few names I'd entered into my phone correctly). I pressed the button on the steering wheel.

'Hi, Nicole.'

'Hi, Kat. Where are you?'

'Driving home.'

'You forgot, didn't you?'

'Forgot what? What did I forget?' I searched my mind. Her birthday? Bailey's?

'We were going to meet up for lunch.'

'Was that today? I thought it was next week.'

'Yes, it's today. Good thing I called you.'

'But it's not lunchtime yet.'

'But it will be in a half hour. Can you make it or not?'

'Of course I can make it.'

'Okay, good. See you in half an hour?'

'Okay. Although I could be a little late.'

'If a woman with a baby and a job can make it on time, you can make it on time.'

Probably not without getting a speeding ticket.

I let Paul know my return would be a bit delayed and pulled up a short walk from the café five minutes behind schedule. As long as I hadn't passed any hidden speed cameras within the last half hour, I would be fine.

Simone was already halfway through her Niçoise by the time I got there. Nicole was staring daggers at the door.

'You're late,' said Simone, even before I had the time to say hello and sit down.

'You're eating. What do you care?'

'I don't, but for some reason she does.' Simone pointed her fork at Nicole between mouthfuls.

'Is it too much to ask for you to remember our lunches and to come on time?' asked Nicole, signalling the waitress. 'Some of us have to go back to work.'

'But…' My protest was falling on deaf ears.

'We know, it wasn't your fault.' Nicole grimaced. The waitress was staring into space. 'I don't know why we bother to come here.'

'The food's good?' I suggested. 'As it turns out, it really wasn't my fault. You see I had to see Mama's lawyer yesterday and I stayed the night in town.'

'That was yesterday. And today?'

I slept in because I'd been up half the night watching Jack Elliot? It sounded pathetic, even to me. I settled for a conciliatory, 'I got a late start driving back. I have some good news, though: Mama's estate's been settled. Lunch, ladies, is on me.'

'Thanks, Kat. But don't think for a moment you're off the hook.' Simone put down her fork and sipped her double espresso.

The waitress finally found her way to our table and Nicole ordered minestrone. I was suddenly ravenous and no matter how hard I tried, I couldn't get past the homemade meatloaf on sourdough. Unlike the waitress, the meals arrived fast. I took a mouthful—it was the best thing I'd ever tasted.

'So, I have some news, too,' began Nicole, picking up her spoon. I summed it up in a single glance. I pondered for a second whether I should make a joke about being pregnant and steal her thunder, but I decided that would just be mean. 'Guess what, guys?' she continued, 'We're pregnant again!'

And now I'm psychic, as well as being a medium for the dead. Could be a career in it. Nicole was beaming and I was genuinely happy for her. 'Congratulations, that's fantastic news.'

'We've just had our twelve-week scan and everything's looking good.'

Simone put down her coffee cup. 'You seem very happy. What can I say? *Mazel tov.* What we need is another mini-Nicole in the world. How's Alex taking it?'

'Oh, he's fine,' Nicole replied, pushing her soup around in circles. 'We're both thrilled.' She may have been peddling it, but I wasn't buying it. *Never bullshit a bullshitter.* There was trouble in paradise.

'Sometimes it takes men a while to come around to the idea of having kids,' I ventured.

'How would you know? You've never been pregnant.'

Ouch! I'd struck a raw nerve. Simone looked at Nicole and then purposely caught my eye.

'I've got good news three,' Simone said, uncharacteristically happy. 'You know your friend Klaryse?' She looked at Nicole and I looked blank. Simone added for my benefit, 'Nicole's friend. The one that I met at the bris?'

'You mean at Bailey's christening,' Nicole corrected.

'Whatever. Well, the news is, we've been seeing each other. Actually, we've been seeing a lot of each other. I think she may be the one.'

'That's wonderful but I didn't know she was gay,' I commented.

'I didn't know she was Jewish,' Nicole commented.

'Not that it's any of your business but neither did she and she's not. In that order.'

'Wow. You converted her?' Kudos to Simone.

'Is that even possible?' Nicole looked troubled by the idea.

'I don't think she was particularly committed to the cause to begin with. Anyway, it's not about definitions or about being gay or straight. It's about who you fall in love with.'

'Well then, congratulations, sweetie. All I want is for you to be happy.'

'Thanks, Kat.'

'I guess I'm a bit shocked. What can I say?' Nicole placed her spoon on the table.

'How about, "I'm happy for you"? That would be a good start.'

'I just hope you know what you're doing and that you don't get hurt.'

'I'm a forty-two-year-old lawyer, Nicole. I think I have a thing or two figured out.'

'As long as you're sure.' Nicole could be so patronising. I was willing her to shut up.

'What the fuck?' Simone bit back. 'What's the deal here? Not that I need your approval, but you don't sound very pleased about this.'

'Well, neither of you sounded genuinely pleased about my news either,' Nicole retorted childishly. Attack being the best form of defence, she continued, 'And as for you, Kat, you waltz in late and never mind about an apology.'

'You're pissed about that?'

'Yes, I am actually. You should take a long, hard look at yourself some day. You might just find you're full of bullshit excuses about why nothing's ever your fault. You're always so angry about everything.'

'I should…' I was left mouth agape. 'Actually, seems to me that you're the angry one today.' I should have left it at that but, since she was being bitchy, I would repay her in kind. 'You treat Simone and me like we're part of your entourage. Toss us a bone every so often and pat us on the head. The rest of the time you're off making new, far more important friends.'

Nicole's face turned beetroot, which was probably not a good thing for a pregnant lady. She looked to Simone for signs of sympathy but, unsurprisingly, found none.

'You feel like this? Right then! That's a lunch you've ruined. But don't worry, I don't expect an apology, Kat.'

I felt the blood rushing to my head and was powerless to stop it. 'And you're not going to get one, Nicole. Here's the thing: this pregnancy's clearly got you rattled. In future, why don't you ask Alex how he feels about something before you go and do it anyway.'

'Not everyone is as anti-baby as you are. And for your information, I always ask Alex for his opinion.'

'Yeah, well that's great. You may ask him, but the fact is you never bother to listen to his answer.'

Nicole picked up her bag. 'I think I'd better leave.' She muttered something inaudible and tossed down a handful of notes to cover the cost of her lunch. I was expecting a dramatic exit, but she left as if she was just popping out to check on something and would be coming back. Except that I gained the impression that she wasn't coming back. Ever. Simone picked up her purse.

'At least let me buy your lunch,' I said. I was still staring at the door. 'I wasn't anticipating that.'

'Who was? Anyway, all of this was illuminating but I think I might go back to work now.' She stood up. 'Thanks for lunch. I'll see you, Kat.'

'See you, Simone.'

As Simone made her way to the door, I settled the bill. I left the café feeling deflated. That was the problem with actually vocalising the truth—once the genie had escaped the bottle, there was no way it was ever going back in.

I was home before two. Through the glass door, I could make out that Paul was taking a nap with Boz on the sofa. Boz's ears twitched and Paul's eyes fluttered and opened with the sound of the door unlocking.

'It's just me,' I said needlessly.

'Hey you.' I bent over him and he kissed me on the lips. 'I wasn't expecting you back so soon. How was lunch?'

'Urrgh.'

'That good? No wonder you look exhausted.'

'Well, I was only the tiniest bit late and Nicole made a song and dance out of it. Then she was angry with Simone because she's hooked up with her friend, Klaryse. You know, the one at the party. Oh, and by the way, she's pregnant.'

'Who? Simone?'

'No, Nicole.'

'And what does Alex think about that? If I remember right, he wasn't that thrilled the first time.'

'See? Thank you, that's exactly what I tried to tell her. And then she bit off my head and she left in a tizz.' I lay down alongside Paul. Boz sighed and scooted down to our feet. 'What's wrong with everyone these days?'

'Well, could it be that Nicole might have been a bit tired and emotional?'

'What?'

'Maybe she's just got a lot on her plate.'

'And I don't?' I sat bolt upright and stared at Paul accusingly. 'Is that an excuse for her to go on the attack? You weren't there; she was downright rude. To me and Simone.'

'Look, all I'm saying is if Alex isn't exactly thrilled about the new arrival, maybe she's having a hard time.'

'Oh great. So I'm wrong, I'm the bad guy here.'

Paul drew in breath. 'You're not the bad guy, Kat. It's just that you're not always the good guy, either.'

I frowned. Twice in one day?

'You know I love you, but sometimes you're not the easiest person to live with. You can be a bit headstrong.'

I didn't know what to say to that. Paul seemed uncomfortable with my silence.

'You see things in absolutes. Life's not like that. I think sometimes you don't realise that others are going through shit too,' he continued.

'I know that. You think I don't know that?'

'Okay, then maybe things aren't quite as black and white as you think.'

'I don't get it. How could I be at fault if Nicole's life is shit and she's decided to pay out on us?'

'That's the problem. Neither of you is at fault. It just is. You can't solve everything by blaming yourself or blaming others.'

I understood the words well enough, but the concept escaped me. Bad things were either your fault or someone else's. If they were someone else's, then you couldn't do anything about it. That's the way life had worked since the day I was born. When I was growing up, only occasionally were bad things my fault. Mostly, they were Mama's. And Chris and Georgia had taken up the slack since Mama's death. Of course, I didn't say any of this to Paul.

'So, do you get it now?' he asked, with an expression as hopeful as Boz's was before every meal.

'I think so, darling. I'll try to be better.'

Paul shook his head and went back to reclining with his eyes shut.

The following day was an at-home day for both of us. I told Paul that I had a lot of work to do and was not to be disturbed unless the house was on fire. I set myself up in the spare room we occasionally used as a study. Otherwise, it remained neat and tidy, to be used by overnight guests. Except that no one ever seemed to visit.

The truth was I had neglected my blog for a few days and I was worried I'd lose my few remaining followers if I didn't produce something pithy. I had started my cyberlife as a smart indie journalist and somehow morphed over time into a social commentator. Today's topic was the benefit of being right. It was designed to be polarising.

After I had posted my few hundred words, I turned to Mama's cookbook. I felt myself moving from curiosity to an obsessive desire to get to the point, whatever it was. I had to admit that probably wasn't the best way to look at the book. I was hoping it hadn't lost its allure.

I flipped the pages rapidly until I found the scan I had made of the rabbit stifado, not wanting to muddy the waters with any relative other than Jeanne. The duplicate sat on top of the original, which was by now way too fragile to handle. As I began to read the copy, a mellow voice rose out of the page and caressed my ears. I felt relief that, clearly, the spirit had transcended the scanner. It was Jeanne; I knew her by her soft, almost pious, modulation and I hoped I'd have the fortitude to stay awake as she spoke. It was odd that, calm as she was, I didn't have the slightest inclination to switch off. She was the aural equivalent of an inviting warm bath. Without giving it a second thought, I slid right in.

30

IOANNA

I inherited the name of Hatzifrangoulis when I was born and Ioanna when I was baptised. Like you, Kat, I descend from Fotini and Ilias, although I never knew them personally, either. Did your mama ever tell you about our origins or how we acquired our name?

I'm not boasting when I tell you that when I was at school, I won the prize for the best student of history. People think that travel is a modern activity, that no one moved around much before these times, but that's just not true. Our many times great-grandparents, the D'Estes, were the poor relations to a family of Venetian nobles. They had embarrassed their family by their talent for spending vast sums of money without having anything to show for it to the point that, with their last remaining ducats, they were put on a boat out of Venice heading east. Giulia D'Este was reputed to have been as beautiful as she was vapid, and Domenico D'Este was a wastrel and debauched. The D'Estes arrived in Greece four hundred years before I was born. After wandering the villages of the Ionian islands for a decade—and getting kicked out of most—they finally settled on Corfu.

One of their sons, Paolo, grew up there and eventually fell in love with a local girl, a Corfiot merchant's daughter named Vassiliki, who took Paolo in hand and changed him into Pavlos. Then she insisted that they marry in the Greek Orthodox church and so, along with his name, Pavlos left Catholicism behind. She distanced him from his family and together they made their fortune in shipping, starting with an old galley they bought from Malta with the sole purpose of importing goods her father could sell. In the matter of a decade, they owned a small fleet, criss-crossing the Mediterranean.

You see, Pavlos had the good fortune to inherit absolutely nothing from either of his parents. Then he had the good sense to marry a clever woman with determination and excellent connections. Vassiliki managed her business and her husband, as well as her enormous family. She bore him twenty-three children, many of which survived, and that was how the dynasty was born. But that's only half the story.

In those days, most people could barely write their own name and they certainly weren't scholars of history or geography. They rarely called anyone who came from the west by their surname, preferring to assign them a nickname, like 'Nose in the Air', or 'Short Pants', or 'The Frank'. Since he had come from the west (and everyone from the west were believed to be Frankish people), Pavlos's wife and everyone else developed the habit of calling her husband 'Pavlos the Frank' instead of Paolo D'Este, no matter that the D'Estes were Venetians, and Venetians were definitely not Franks. The practice continued until, eventually, they even forgot their name had ever been D'Este. The family came to be known as Frangoulis. Then a few of Pavlos's great-grandsons went to the Holy Land and had themselves baptised in the Jordan River. By doing that, they had become pilgrims, and had earned the right to add the prefix, *Hatzi*, to their name. It is this line, the Hatzifrangoulis, that you and I descend from.

They say it takes three generations to lose a fortune, but apparently we were slow learners, so it took us about five. Eventually, all the wealth had vanished and the vast Hatzifrangoulis family was scattered all over Greece and much of Europe. I'm told that one of them made it all the way to China. You already know that our line ended up in Chios, in the town of Thimiana. That was where I was born, the youngest of seven children, in the snowy winter of 1912.

By the time I was old enough to go to school, Chios was newly liberated from the Turks. Mama and Baba had left my twin brother, who was older than me by twenty minutes, and me with our grandmother in Chios, while they were away rebuilding the family fortune in Upper Egypt. It was there, in Luxor, that they reinvented themselves as distillers and merchants. In an obscenely short time, they recovered everything that had been squandered by previous generations and a little more besides. The family was so influential that your great-great-uncle was invited to join Howard Carter at the opening of Tutankhamen's tomb. It's true, he was there. But that's not really the point of my story.

For my parents, and many others besides, having children was a little like recruiting staff. Most of us were born in Greece and, just as our elder brothers and sisters had done, my brother and I continued to live with our *yiayia* in Greece until we were old enough to be useful. After that, we travelled back and forth, alternating between Greece and Egypt, importing and exporting, working and holidaying, and all the while enjoying a life that only serious wealth can buy. The boys of the family had it better than us girls—while they were out getting drunk and playing the field, we were destined for marriage to suitable men. There were only three characteristics that our potential husbands required: being Greek, rich and reputable. As the youngest of three girls, I had to wait until the others were matched and wedded before my time would come.

My eldest sister was baptised Sevasti, which means respectable. With her honey skin and deep azure eyes, Sevasti caught the attention of every eligible man in Cairo and as many again who were not. She was barely seventeen when she ran off and married a young, impoverished musician who wrote love songs by day and played piano accordion in a supper club band in Alexandria by night. Mama and Baba were both hurt and humiliated in equal parts. By all accounts, the musician was particularly handsome. I never met him and we very rarely spoke of her after that.

My middle sister, Eleftheria, whose name meant freedom and whom I adored, crushed my mother's hopes entirely by dying of typhoid fever a few months after we celebrated her eighteenth birthday. Before she fell ill, she had been betrothed to a balding man with a broad, gentle face who was more than twice her age. It was such bad luck. Mama began to think that we had been tainted with the evil eye. She said I needed to marry young, just to make sure that nothing bad happened to me as well.

After Eleftheria died, the balding man continued to visit us. I thought he was a little like a pup without a master. He was wealthy in his own right and from a good family, and such men were not to be discouraged when there was still an unmarried daughter in the house. His line ran a chain of groceries in Cairo and Upper Egypt, selling the exotic next to the mundane, from Russian caviar and Swiss chocolates in wooden boxes all the way down to Baba's awful brandy and the locally made wax candles, which were both handy when the electricity went out, which it frequently did. The man with the velvet eyes was called Theodoros, but everyone knew him as Theo. His shop in Luxor was known by everyone as Theo's Grocery. It was about a year later—a year spent celebrating life with my brothers and their many and varied girlfriends—that Theo finally began to show his hand.

I had only just turned seventeen. For the last five of those years, I had been closeted away in a French convent school, *Notre Dame De La Delivrande*, which was run by French nuns whose disposition was calm and generous, provided they never heard you speak English, Greek, Italian or Arabic—or anything other than French, really. How many times did I hear a disembodied voice from around a corner say to me, *En français, Mademoiselle Jeanne*, during the course of my school life. I loved learning and I was an excellent student. I desperately wanted to be a teacher or a nun, maybe because I knew it was something I would be good at, but probably because that had been the sum total of my life's experience.

My twin brother, on the other hand, managed to get himself tossed out of a succession of ever-worsening schools around Greece and Egypt. As a result, he found himself working for one of our father's businesses as a travelling salesman. He and I couldn't have been more different. He had inherited all the bravado and I was the mouse of the family. He nursed hangovers while I baked the liturgical bread and went to church.

When my mother came and asked me if I would consider marrying Theo if he proposed, my hopes of a position in either a religious order or education came crashing down around my ears.

'A nun? Have you gone mad? Only ugly women become nuns and teachers.' She may have been right about most of the nuns, but not sweet-faced Sister Dominique. 'Don't make me regret educating you. Your job is to get married and have a family.'

'But, Mama...'

'Fine. Since you're so hard-headed, you can do as you wish. But you had better tell your father yourself. After that, you can say goodbye to me and to everything you love, forever. You won't be welcome here any more than Sevasti.'

'But I would be honouring God.'

'You can honour God just as well by the way you live your life. If you want to teach, your children can be your students. Also, know that if you do this, your father will probably die of a broken heart. So enough of your nonsense. You're not a child any more, Ioanna. What do you say? Will you agree to marry Theo or not?'

I told her I would. It was the look of hope on her face that finally swayed me. Of course, there was a twenty-year age difference between me and Theo, and while that might sound a lot to you now, back then it wasn't that unusual. I'd watched Theo play the affable fool with my brothers and I'd seen him drunk, but I'd never seen him angry or unkind. If the path I wanted was blocked to me, why wouldn't I say yes if he asked me?

We were engaged in May and I spent the summer and autumn with my grandmother in Thimiana. The local dressmaker, a distant cousin of ours, made me a dress of ivory slipper satin. The finest Brussels lace encircled the boat-shaped neckline and ran down the centre of the bodice. I may have been bookish, but even I went to the cinema sometimes. My dress was copied from one I'd seen Greta Garbo wear in a movie—body skimming and with a train edged in even more lace. My cousin made me a fingertip tulle veil to wear, attached at the temple by two platinum and diamond clips in the shape of lightning bolts. My wedding was planned for the day after Christmas 1930, a few days after my birthday. It was the first day the church resumed celebrating weddings after its seasonal ban and after my religious fast ended.

I sailed back to Egypt with my dress, my grandmother, two of my aunts, their husbands and a gaggle of cousins a week before our special day. We were all crowded into four cabins all the way to Suez and crammed into only three train compartments after that. By the time Theo met me at the station in Luxor, I had had enough of them all. Thankfully, my father paid for them all to stay at the Winter Palace Hotel and Theo drove me home, just the two of us in his Packard convertible.

We had Christmas dinner together, all forty of us as well as Theo and his mother, in the enormous marble-floored dining room of our third floor apartment. After fasting for the last forty days, Mama and I had spent the preceding day cooking, not that I was particularly good at it. Sweet Eleftheria had both the disposition and all the talent, and she had spent most of her life either learning how to cook or devising new recipes while I exercised my mind. When I had gone to church and read holy books, she had baked gateaux. How much Mama and I both missed her at Christmas time!

Mama had already placed her tureen of egg and lemon soup on the table, ready to be dished out as a sign that the Christmas feast was beginning. First thing that morning, she had sent a whole suckling pig and an enormous turkey with potatoes to the bakery to be roasted, and then she accompanied me to Holy Liturgy. My eldest brother had collected the pork halfway through the morning, but the turkey roast wasn't done yet. Mama had tasked a servant to wait for it and bring it to us the moment it was ready, but she kept sending me out to the balcony every few minutes to see if it was coming, all the while threatening to go down to the bakery herself and give the baker a piece of her mind if it didn't turn up soon.

It finally arrived after midday in the arms of one of our servants, a long-limbed, dark Arab boy we had nicknamed Abu-Dax, meaning the son of a taxi. My father had given him the name because, when he ran, he was as swift as anything on wheels. Not only did the boy carry our turkey up three flights of stairs, but he balanced a loaf of bread on top of it besides, and his stick arms were red where the ridges of the pan had dug in.

I wondered how he managed it, since the meal in its enormous roasting pan must have weighed almost half as much as he did.

'*Hamdelella!*' said Mama, arms raised in the air. 'At last!' She slipped my brother a few piastres to give Abu-Dax as a Christmas gift and my brother relieved the boy of his load. Abu-Dax flashed us a smile of perfect white teeth.

'*Shokran, ya hawaga.*' He waved and darted through the still open door. His footsteps echoed as he retraced his way back down the marble staircase, whistling as he went.

Mama liberated the roasting pan from the paper and string that covered it and transferred the contents carefully onto a platter. We were all rendered speechless by the scent.

'Thank goodness the boy didn't touch the meat this year,' she remarked as she brought the platter to the table. 'He must have learned his lesson after last year's beating.'

As I tucked into the soup, it occurred to me that although he had worked for us his whole life, I never knew Abu-Dax's real name.

Education aside, I had lived half of my life there in that apartment, so elegant that we might have been in Paris instead of Luxor, and the other half in Greece in a tiny village house encircled by stone walls and the fields beyond. I had a foot in each world and was equally at home in both. Here, our apartment was situated in a quiet street adjacent to the corniche and from our salon, we could just see the feluccas sailing down the Nile. There, I helped my grandmother milk goats and went hunting for rabbits and pigeon with my twin brother. It was, I suppose, a schizophrenic existence.

We spent that Christmas eating vast quantities of food, playing games and joking at my expense. At the table, we drank champagne and toasted my nuptials and the wish that next year we might all gather together again, this time at my own house.

The following day, the rest of Theo's family and a few dozen friends joined my family to watch us get married. Naturally, it wouldn't have been appropriate for the rite to be performed by an ordinary priest, so at enormous expense the archbishop was flown up from Memphis by flying boat to officiate. Mama told me a thousand times during my childhood to be sure to stamp on my husband's foot during the wedding ceremony, so that I dominated in my marriage. When the time came, I could not. At that precise moment, Theo shifted his foot towards mine, and I slid it deftly out of reach. In the true spirit of Greece, I was determined that, if nothing else, our marriage was going to be a democracy.

After the wedding, we all celebrated the day by eating our own weight in oysters and beef imported from England at the Winter Palace Hotel's best restaurant. By the time we returned to Theo's apartment, I was tired and short-tempered. I looked at Theo, who was being exceptionally conciliatory and comforting, despite my irritation at everything he did. Who was this man with whom I had agreed to spend the rest of my life? I longed to go home to my own bed and to the familiarity of my family. He must have understood what I was thinking and we sat together quietly for a while, barely touching. Our wedding night may have begun in an argument, but it ended happily in a truce.

The following morning, we departed by flying boat for Alexandria, where we were planning to stay for the week. It is an odd thing to be married to somebody you really don't know, and for most of the long journey north, we said very little to each other. Last night, I had felt a connection to my husband. Today, we resumed as strangers. I didn't know how to make conversation with him, and whenever I tried, he looked bored. It was beginning to dawn on me that perhaps it wasn't enough to marry a funny, good-tempered man if you have absolutely nothing in common with him. I kept that thought to myself and told myself that we'd develop a relationship given enough time.

Theo had promised that, since he couldn't endure the cold of a European New Year, we would honeymoon in Paris later, perhaps in June, but for the time being, we might as well take advantage of the Egyptian winter's warmth. We were strolling along the corniche at Stanley Beach a few days later, when we spotted my eldest brother walking in the opposite direction, arm-in-arm with an American cabaret singer. He introduced her to us as Nancy, and told us that she performed Marion Harris's songs every evening at nine at the *L'auberge Bleu*, to an appreciative audience. I was surprised to see him, and Theo seemed positively elated.

'When Theo mentioned where you were going, it seemed like such a good idea that we decided last minute we'd all come,' he exclaimed, 'even Mama!'

Those few words signalled the end of our honeymoon. In the days that followed, Theo saw more of my brothers than he did of me. He was like a man destined for the gallows that had just been handed a reprieve. He visited the cabarets and bars with them, while I went to church with Mama and then waited endless hours for him alone in our room. When I begged to be included in his evening excursions, I was told that it wasn't a very wifely thing to do. In my eyes, his actions weren't particularly husbandly either. When I tried to say as much to my mother, she told me to be quiet. With so many brothers, how could I miss the point? That was men's business. Apparently, nobody likes a wife who whines.

We returned home the following Thursday. On Friday, my brothers brought over my trousseau and my clothes. By the time I had unpacked, Theo's apartment seemed far too small for the two of us, so he began looking for a larger one immediately. I began to wonder if he was going to deal with the tedium of married life by crowding it with a never-ending series of diversions.

Two months later, Theo had already paid a *bon de sortie* on a first-floor apartment that I hadn't seen, in a block adjacent to my parents. Of course, I was grateful to be close to them, but when I asked him why I hadn't been consulted before the decision was made, I was told that it was a man's job to provide for his family. Perhaps my father had been right all along and educated women had no place in marriage. But what could I do with this thought? The reality was that, in the world in which I'd been born, I couldn't do anything. Possibly the solution to my malaise might be to have many children. That was the one thing I could do something about.

We moved into the apartment within the month and I was happy to discover I was pregnant. You'd think that in a traditional household, I would have learned how to cook and perform domestic chores, but you'd be wrong. Growing up, Eleftheria had shown such promise in that area that I had been only too happy to leave the cooking to her and Mama, and the cleaning to the housemaid. Theo promised me he would employ a maid if I wanted one, so along with the new apartment I received help in the form of Soraya, an Arab girl who came with a recommendation from a friend of his at the sporting club. She was good-natured enough and she did everything tolerably well, but she did not cook European dishes. Theo never had acquired a taste for *molochia*, the garlic-chicken soup made with slippery greens the locals adored, or *kobepa*, their ghee-laden version of meatloaf. It was clear that I was going to have to learn to cook. Since Soraya had liberated me from all other chores, I spent most of the first few months of my pregnancy looking over my mother's shoulder as she cooked for my father and brothers. I was hoping that, if I watched her long enough, some of her skill might rub off onto me.

'I can show you the ingredients and the method, but cooking is all about love. I can't teach you that.'

I nodded as if I understood what she meant. She put down her wooden spoon and looked me straight in the eyes.

'This is how I express how much I care for you all,' she continued. 'Not only that, but I can tell who truly loves me without any need for words. When I cook for people who love me, then my food tastes wonderful. When they don't, my mayonnaise for my Russian salad curdles and the roux for the *pastitsio* burns. It is a disaster from the very start.'

I understood Mama's words to mean that, if a woman didn't cook, then she had no love to give and no channel by which to receive it. This wasn't anything I had ever been taught by the nuns but, if that's what it took, then I'd cook.

Most nights I went home from my mother's ready for the challenge of making just such a love-dish, and most nights I ate alone. How I came to loathe the sight of Abu-Dax running up the street, tripping up the stairs of our building two and three at a time, only to tell me that Hawaga Theo was either delayed in the shop, or he was entertaining important business associates or he was out with one or other of my brothers. At this rate, I would never be able to develop his love for me, since he would never be home to eat a single meal. In time, I discovered his Achilles' heel was his voracious sweet tooth, so every weekend I baked a syrupy walnut or semolina cake along with my liturgical bread for the Sunday morning service. On my baking days, Theo never went missing. He commented once that my pastries were even better than any he'd eaten at the *Petit Trianon* in Alexandria. I began to think that maybe there was wisdom in my mother's philosophy.

'You should open a café there,' he remarked as he chewed. 'I could lease you a shop in Alexandria on Saad Zaghloul Street.' And then again, maybe there wasn't.

I smiled, believing it to be a joke. 'But you'd miss me, wouldn't you, Alexandria being so far away from Luxor?' He shifted his gaze uncomfortably. 'Maybe I would accept your offer, if I wasn't in this state.' I rubbed the tight ball bulging below my ribs.

He took another mouthful. 'Well, maybe you should think about it after the baby is born.'

If all the desserts in the world couldn't make our life together sweeter, then I didn't know what would.

Our first child was born that autumn. How can I describe the joy I felt when the midwife handed him to me? He blew away all my fears with a single sweet breath. Such round, downy cheeks, such a furrowed, old man brow, such flawless cupid's bow lips—he was perfect. The second he wriggled into my arms and suckled, it was love beyond anything I'd ever known. When Theo arrived home from work that afternoon, he seemed pleased to be told that he had a son and told me that he loved us both, yet his words fluttered away in the breeze of the open window.

We named our son Eleftherios, in honour of my sister, and he was baptised before the winter. Another lavish party at the Winter Palace Hotel followed the baptism, another feast of caviar from the Caspian Sea and slow-roasted milk-fed lamb. This time my dress was Chanel and I was pure Gloria Swanson. I had never looked as radiant, and the more Theo failed to notice, the more audaciously I flirted. But nothing came of it and so I resumed my seat next to my mother while the men laughed and toasted our son with Napoleon cognac.

Theo and I never did resume our conversation about the café in Alexandria and I really don't know what I might have done if we had. You see, I was one of those fortunate women who got pregnant, stayed pregnant and delivered easily, so it was hardly a surprise when, early in the New Year, I found myself expecting once more. I didn't tell a soul at first, but when I couldn't hide it any longer, Theo seemed happy enough with the news. What do men care about babies anyway, other than to ensure that their name carries on? I'd already realised that babies don't anchor men and they certainly don't mend what's broken. When I was four months gone, I decided to take the next ship to Greece and stay with my grandmother for the remainder of my confinement. I raised this with Theo and he made no objection. I'm not as unemotional as you may believe, but you ask me how I felt about that, and I tell you, honestly, it didn't even make my ear sweat. Why should I waste my passion on something so fruitless?

The following morning, Teri (Eleftherios is far too cumbersome a name for a baby) and I were packed before dawn and getting ready to be driven to the station. It wasn't terribly far away and but for the trunks I probably could have walked. With this and that, time had run away from me, and Theo was yelling that if I delayed any longer, we'd be lucky to catch the train at all. The servants had stacked our luggage into the back seat of the Packard and, with my old-fashioned carpetbag, I had only just enough room to squeeze in beside Theo. Soraya placed Teri in my arms and waved us off. A few minutes later, we'd arrived and the train to Port Said was already boarding. A black porter came for the baggage as I stumbled out of the car.

'Take care of yourself and the child,' Theo said, brushing my lips with a kiss.

'You too.'

And with the merest of waves, he was back in the Packard and gone. When I boarded the train I discovered my mother already seated in our first-class compartment, reading a magazine. She looked up and smiled at my surprise.

'So he was able to keep a secret after all,' she said with a shake of the head.

'Mama, you don't know how happy I am that you're coming with us.'

'Do you think I would be crazy enough to let my little girl go through childbirth so far away without me? Besides, who would look after Eleftherios, once you're busy with the new one?'

'Yiayia wrote that she was happy to help out.'

'Yiayia is old and senile. You need me. No one else will miss me at home anyway.'

'They will the moment they get hungry.'

'Then, good. May it be so.'

Mama took the sleeping baby from my aching arms and he snuggled quietly in her lap. I unpacked the few things we'd need for the journey and bundled the carpetbag onto the shelf above the seat. The train lurched forward as soon as I sat down, then the engine sighed and the train shuddered to a stop.

'Oh ho!' exclaimed Mama, as Teri awoke with a start. She took a feeding bottle of boiled water from my bundle and crammed it into his mouth. He blinked and then let his eyes close.

A few minutes later, the whistle sounded and, with another jolt, the train began to move along the track. It was already unbearably hot and I was more than ready to say goodbye to Luxor for the summer. I rang the buzzer for the steward to bring us cups of tea and asked him to ensure that there would be soup and stewed fruit for Teri ready at lunchtime.

'*Bien sûr, Madame*,' he replied. 'I will notify the chef directly.'

'*Merci beaucoup*,' I replied.

We reached Port Said later the following day and boarded our ship for Greece that evening.

31

By week's end Mama, Teri and I were sitting in a mule cart together with our luggage, being transported up the hill to my grandmother's house.

'*Vre vre, ta pedia!*' Yiayia cried out in welcome, scuttling through the open door of her house the moment our cart stopped beside her gate. '*Kalo soristete!*'

I smiled at the sound of her Chian accent, so thick that it turned her words into seeds that had germinated for too long in the depths of her throat. There she was—my yiayia, my grandmother—all wild-haired and bandy-legged, still running about despite her ninety years. I hugged her, sniffing the familiar must of her woollen jacket and feeling the scratch of the shawl she wore all summer and winter long.

'*Yasou, Yiayia.* How are you?' I said.

'Let us say that I'm well,' she replied loudly. 'And the child? Where have you hidden him?'

'Which one?'

'Which one, which one… The son, of course, little Eleftherios.'

Mama had been holding him in her arms. Although he'd been crying, deaf as she was, Yiayia hadn't noticed him. She now danced about him, motioning for him to come to her.

The child took one look at Yiayia and clung to Mama. 'Let's go inside first. Then you can see him better.'

We followed her into the house, past the sweetly fragrant laurel and up the stone-paved path. I took off my coat as we entered and hung it on a hook by the door. Yiayia took one look at me and raised her palms to her cheeks in horror.

'But what happened to you? You're so fat!'

'No, Yiayia, I'm not fat. Remember, I wrote to you in my letter—I'm pregnant.'

'But so soon? Your husband must be an animal!'

I blushed. If she noticed, I would have never known, because she swiftly turned the conversation to her own pregnancies.

Mama raised her brow in my direction, as if to say *I told you so*, and left the room to settle Teri into bed. By the time she returned, Yiayia had brewed a pot of mountain tea. I drank in the perfume of the wild herbs as the pot hissed on the stove. It was the scent of home.

I hadn't realised quite how much tension I had gathered around me in my beautiful Luxor apartment until I tasted the freedom and hospitality of life in the village. Within the hour, three of Yiayia's neighbours dropped in with gifts of baby clothes that they had made themselves, to see us and meet Teri. Yiayia mentioned that my aunts and cousins were busy right now, but they were coming for lunch the following day. Once the neighbours had left, Yiayia set to work to slaughter a young goat, in preparation for the spit the next morning. While Mama made stuffed vine leaves, I fixed a *galactobouriko*, brushing the phyllo with Yiayia's hand-churned butter, all ready for tomorrow's oven.

You see, a person can have all the wealth and comfort in the world when what she really craves is community and purpose. For me, my Chian family, as humble it was, gave me that sense of belonging to a place. Unlike Luxor, from which we all came and went, my island was intransient. Added to that, my babies gave me my motivation. Young as I was, I had already grown to realise that we all need something to live for. How otherwise can we endure our lives? I gave birth to another boy without incident that autumn and we named him Anastassios in honour of the resurrection. By the time he was forty days old and blessed by the village priest, the weather had turned from the trailing end of a searing summer to the promise of a harsh winter. Mama, the children and I left Chios in early December, before the snow and the howling north wind made it too perilous to travel.

This then became the pattern of my life. It was church and family, absence and presence, in endless rotation. Things at home remained exactly as they had been, Theo providing for us all materially in exchange for his disappearances, but a shimmer in his eyes when he looked at the children made me think there was a hidden part of him that was proud of his ever-growing family.

Almost every other year, I found myself expecting another baby. I spent winters in Egypt and summers in Greece, sometimes with and sometimes without Mama, but almost never with my husband. That was my life's pattern; that is, until Adolf Hitler stepped in to intervene.

Let me put it into perspective. Before the war, those of us with money in Egypt lived life as if the rest of the world existed, but didn't matter. While America had prohibition, we drank the finest Scotch whiskey and French champagne. When America sank into depression, we threw away money on American cars. As Europe began to shiver, we basked in the warmth of a benevolent sun.

Of course, we'd all known about Hitler since he had become the chancellor of Germany, and those of us in Egypt who read newspapers became uneasy over his support of Italy's occupation of Abyssinia. If you don't want a woman to have an opinion, then why bother educating her? When I voiced my concerns about him to the women at church, they told me that I was worried about nothing. God always protected His own and we were counted in that number. Still, I had read about Hitler sniffing around Europe—first Austria and then the Sudetenland—and it was worrisome. Theo thought I was agonising about it far too much for my own good. He began tearing those articles out of the paper before I could read them. When I casually mentioned to my mother what he'd done, I expected her to tell me once again that I shouldn't complain. Instead, she said she hadn't sent me to school so that a man could dictate terms to me, and she simply handed me my father's paper the day after he'd read it. Nothing can be worse than ignorance, so while the news may have been a day or two stale, it was still relevant.

Despite things looking grim in Northern Europe and with East Africa only barely stable, the children and I still made our annual pilgrimage to Greece that summer of 1939. Mama had stayed behind in Egypt on this occasion, and for the first time in years, I was neither pregnant nor nursing. I immediately missed my daily dose of information, but nothing really mattered in Thimiana beyond the yield of a crop and the health of one's herd.

I heard about the start of the war from my aunt, who mentioned it in passing *(Oh, and by the way, Takis said something about a war. That Hitler's invaded Poland. He's a madman, don't you think?)*, just as one might mention a piece of gossip of no consequence. It was what I had feared the last four years.

'Remember me, O Lord, when You come into Your kingdom!' I said.

'You worry far too much.' My aunt left to milk her goats.

Anyone with any sense should have looked to the north and to the west and prayed that, no matter what happened there, Greece might be safe. War aside, we had been planning to leave Chios to return to Luxor in late autumn as always, when I received a letter from Theo telling me it would be safer for us to stay in Greece. He thought we should probably wait until we knew how this was all going to play out, and, besides, shipping in the Mediterranean had become problematic of late. He mentioned that three of the boys, including my twin brother, were planning to join the Greek army, but were still waiting to see what would happen next. They all sent their love and were worried about us. He said he loved us and wished we would be home soon. I folded up the letter and slipped it back into its envelope. We were stranded.

Yiayia had grown frail over the intervening years and ever more distracted, so that by the time I tried to tell her that war had been declared between Germany, and France and England, she thought I meant the Great War and that the Kaiser was alive and still striking his jackboot against Lloyd George's door. When I tried to explain that this wasn't the same war, she gazed at me blankly. Thank God, I thought, that she had such a convenient escape to her own reality.

Teri by now was eight, and he was both intuitive and intelligent. He had taken everything from my side of the family—straight, tall and resolute. He may have acted like a little despot when we were in Egypt, but in Greece he became more far malleable. Despite my best efforts, he saw the concern in my eyes when I told him we would be staying in Chios for a while. He kept the other four children in check for certain, but his orders now came directly from me, and he listened to no one else.

That winter seemed particularly bitter, probably because I hadn't spent one in Greece since I was ten or eleven. The children, who had never seen snow, thought it beautiful and magical as they played in it, only to run back inside at intervals, shivering and sodden. I already knew it was cold and wet. It felt like it had taken a long time for 1940 to arrive, and now it was taking forever for winter to leave. Towards the start of spring, Yiayia caught a cold with a hacking cough that made her poor, thin frame shudder. My aunt came over with potions and poultices and I asked the priest to pray for her health. Was it the reward of faith that, against all reason, she got over it? By the time the days became milder, Yiayia became invigorated. She soon seemed almost as perky as usual. Prayer, however, did nothing for her mind, which had been almost totally absent since Christmas.

If I had thought that the newspapers were stale in Luxor, by the time they made it to Thimiana they were good for little more than starting fires. My cousin Takis, fortunately, had a short-wave radio that he had used to listen to music from around the world, but since war was declared, he'd agreed that he would tune it into the BBC on the proviso that, since my English was far better than his, I'd perform a simultaneous translation for the benefit of the rest of the family. I could see from their eyes that they still considered me to be overly concerned about things that were happening so far away. But I had no faith in pacts and no trust in the promises of politicians.

Trouble came to our doorstep that summer. I felt sick the moment I heard Mussolini had advanced into the Sudan, and when, in September, the Italians invaded Egypt my thoughts drifted across to my family and stuck fast. How helpless you feel watching from a distance, even when you know your presence wouldn't make the slightest difference. A little over a month later it was their turn to worry about us. The Italian army had invaded northern Greece and we were at war, just as I had foreseen. A Greek garrison was soon stationed in Chora and no one ever questioned my judgement again.

In the meantime, war was raging between us and the Italians in the Pindus Mountains. Mussolini had evidently either hugely overestimated his own force's capabilities or greatly underestimated ours, and he found himself withdrawing back into Albania before Christmas. My aunt's husband was dancing with joy when he heard the news. When I told them that the war wasn't done with us yet, this time they nodded and fell silent.

You are so blessed to know little of these things, but at the time war is being played out, people only learn as much as they are permitted to know and what they can see for themselves. We never knew of the machinations between Hitler and our neighbours to overtake us, or of those between Churchill and the Greek government to keep us safe. We knew well enough that a second wave was approaching and that this time it wasn't made up of Italians with their silly plumes and their reputation for retreat. This was infinitely worse. You see, the Germans invaded through Yugoslavia at a time when the Greek and English armies were occupied elsewhere. A fortnight after we had celebrated Easter of 1941 with coloured eggs and *tsoureki*, the swastika flag was raised over the Acropolis. German planes began to fly routinely over the island, and we heard that Mytilene was under Nazi rule. A few days after that, German bombers flew over Chios, and a ship in the harbour was sunk. Like everyone else, I held my breath and waited.

We now had to prove that our revolutionary cry of freedom or death was not simply idle rhetoric. Although no one was going to allow the Germans to just stroll in and take over, that was precisely what seemed to be happening. Even with the best intentions, you can't hope to defeat the German *Wehrmacht* with old rifles and women with pitchforks. I had been a good student of history and geography, and I knew that lava consumes everything in its path and it doesn't stop until it finds a barrier equal to its own intensity. I assumed that the flow would reach Chios sooner or later and so I immediately began planning for that day.

For a little while at least, you kid yourself that life can continue exactly as usual. Every evening, we huddled together at my aunt's to listen to the radio and we knew that the British considered Greece all but lost. Still, every Sunday morning, I took my freshly baked *prosfero* bread to church to be blessed and turned into Christ's body, while I prayed for my family and for Greece before returning home to prepare Sunday dinner for us all. It was a few weeks after Easter that a notice was posted on the town hall that Chios was officially under German occupation, even though we hadn't seen any evidence of it ourselves.

On one particular Sunday evening, as I sat reading a battered old copy of *Les Misérables* for the fifth time, there was a beating on the door of such vigour that I leapt straight out of my seat. I put down my book and peered through the lace curtain. Outside was cousin Takis. Even in the twilight, I could tell that he was agitated.

'What's wrong?' His eyes were darting about as if he expected an attack from a savage animal.

'I came to tell you as soon as I heard. Hide your guns and any spare food you have. The Germans have arrived! There's a German ship and two destroyers in the harbour.'

'What?' But Takis had already rushed off to tell the neighbours.

That marked the end of any pretence of normality. By the following day, the presence of Major Winkler and the German army became an unwelcome feature of our existence. There were hundreds of German soldiers, a grey-green sea flooding off the troop ships, officers in jodhpurs that seemed better suited to a weekend horse ride than to serious warmongering. They claimed to come as friends, but, in the end, warmonger they did. In a heartbeat, they had taken over Chora, commandeered houses and placed fortified posts around the harbour. Then they ordered the Greek soldiers to give up their weapons.

Soon they took control of the mastic villages and the fruit and olive groves, and the few boats that hadn't been commandeered could only be used with permission. The Germans set up an outpost in Aghia Erimioni, not far from our village.

The Greek troops had been seriously outnumbered. Takis was so incensed when he heard we'd surrendered without a single shot, he threatened to kill any German who tried to steal from us. After a little thought, he decided he would take his rifle, head for the hills and live for the rest of the war as a bandit. My aunt was terrified that the only thing he would succeed in shooting was himself. The following day he made good on his plan and joined up with a small number of young men from the village, who were reputed to be communists on the prowl for Germans. His mother cried herself to sleep that night.

Our house had an advantage that few others had. Built during the time of the Turks, my great-grandfather had taken the precaution of installing a false cupboard that led to a set of stone steps down to a passage, which in turn led to an enormous cavern. It was never used and all but forgotten until the day my twin and I decided to play hide and seek. Clearly, he knew a trick or two, our ancestor, and it was pretty well ventilated and had a shaft lined with tin to illuminate it. When I heard about the Italian invasion, I stowed away our guns and ammunition, and began to stock the cavern with fuel, onions and potatoes, wine and oil, grain and tomatoes in tins, almonds and dried figs, preserved olives and cheese in brine, and sacks of beans. But I told no one. The immediate family knew about the cavern, of course, but as long as no one spoke of it openly and the war ended quickly, together we might all survive.

In the weeks that followed the invasion German soldiers took our goats, even though I begged to be allowed to keep one for the sake of my children, but there was nothing in their eyes. They took a barrel of oil and another of olives from our house and then went on to our neighbours. I could have immediately replaced almost everything that had been taken from the food hidden away in our secret store, but that would have caused suspicion, and this was a game of strategy. When the children complained that their tummies were growling I told them we had nothing but bread to eat that night. Do you think that was easy? What mother will deny their hungry child food? But we needed to be hungry to stay alive. The following day, I took Teri and Anesti into the hills and taught them how to catch birds and rabbits using simple wooden traps. I was never so grateful to have been raised with a brother. The boys' bounty was sufficient for me to make rabbit stifado, a stew studded with onions and braised in wine, every few days.

As spring turned into summer, we all lost weight, and by the height of summer, our stores were dwindling seriously. Yiayia had been ill for weeks on end, too weak to eat yet too strong to die. She watched with sunken eyes as the Germans' cars rolled down the narrow, stone-walled roads on their way from Chora to the mastic villages, and muttered that the Turks had returned. Then she fell silent again and asked to be fed a little soup. I suspected she probably understood far more than she let on.

It was when my boys couldn't trap any birds and the rabbits had disappeared that I realised that we might not survive the coming winter. I substituted beans and potatoes for the meat in our stifado. The streets of Chora were filled with walking skeletons of children, and desperation made people do things they would never dream of doing otherwise. Even though I had kept the family supplied with a little food, my cousin Dora betrayed our source to an *Unterscharführer*, with whom she had been having an affair in exchange for the right to black marketeer in food. While her brother lived in the mountains, attacking the tyres of the German cars and laying mines that barely caused any damage at all, she sold oil and grain at huge sums, and he and Dora shared the spoils. How long did they think this secret could be maintained?

She was a fine one. One day we all went to church leaving Yiayia at home in bed. When we returned, Yiayia seemed particularly agitated.

'What's wrong, Yiayia?'

'Don't ever leave me alone with that girl again. Promise me?'

'Who, Yiayia?'

'She brought the devil into our house. And look what he did.' She raised the sleeve of her nightgown past the elbow. Her fragile skin was already blackened with finger marks.

'Who did this to you?'

'Who? Why the Turk, the *Tourkos*, of course. The one who came with the girl with the blonde hair.'

'With Dora? Are you sure he wasn't a German, a *Yermanos*?'

'*Yermanos*, *Tourkos*, what's the difference. Then all hell broke loose, and just see what they did.'

How hadn't I noticed the trail of dried mud that trekked down the path as I'd approached. It was only when I went into the kitchen that I saw the door of the false cupboard torn off its hinges and the back panel destroyed. I followed the corridor down to the cavern. It was almost totally empty. A single sack of grain was left, propped against one wall. When I approached I realised someone had urinated over it. I put the damp sack on my shoulders and carried it out of the cavern, weeping silently. Urine or not, this solitary sack of grain might become all that kept us from starvation. I removed the contaminated grains, washed them in salted water and dried them on a sheet in the sun. What else could I do? We had a few litres of oil in a jug, a kilo or two of dried broad beans and a harvest of almonds, still on the trees. We may have been wealthy in Egypt but I never travelled with much. I had a few gold sovereigns in my purse and some of my jewellery, which I could exchange for food if I needed to.

Not satisfied with having taken our food, Dora, I presumed, had orchestrated the theft of our almond crop. By the time I arrived at the field at sunrise on Monday, the trees had been stripped bare. I collected the few husks that remained, a small sackful, and took it home to dry. It seemed that in Dora's book, blood counted for nothing.

The Germans had blockaded the island, and no supplies had entered Chios since the occupation. I will spare you the details of the horror of dying by starvation, except to say that the sight of swollen bellies had become commonplace and even the children had become accustomed to the sight of people fainting from hunger and the piles of dead bodies lying unburied in the cemetery. My dear Yiayia, who had survived nearly a hundred years on this earth, died from malnutrition before the Christmas of 1941. There was nothing to for us to celebrate that year, and Dora had divided the family so absolutely that there was a blood feud between cousins that endured the war. I warn you that hate between kin is deadly. I went to church to pray for my family and for Dora and the entire German population. My children went to church, not driven by their faith, but in hope of eating a little bread.

What did food mean to me? I, who had fasted every Wednesday and Friday since I was twelve, according to the church's laws? Oh yes, I fasted from meat and milk for fifty days before Easter, forty days before Christmas and fifteen days before the Dormition of Our Lady. I kept every holy day. Food, which had meant nothing to me, now meant everything. Whatever food we had, I divided among my children in order of age, but there was never enough to satisfy their hunger. In February, I sold my last sovereign for a sack of flour, a kilo of dried milk and a small bottle of oil. By March, my hair was breaking off at the roots, but along with the warmer weather there came hope of a harvest to come. By May, we had eaten everything we had and I hadn't eaten in a week. My head had throbbed for a while and I thought that perhaps I had somehow caught a cold. Anxious that my children remain healthy, I called Teri into my bedroom, took off what remained of my jewellery and placed it into his translucent hands. I noticed with shame how painfully thin he had become.

'Use this to take care of yourself and your brothers and sisters.'

'But, Mama!'

'Save yourselves. All my hope rests on you. Whatever happens to me, remember that God will always bless you and help you if you pray.'

'God has abandoned us. There is no God.'

'You must not say that, Teri. He loves us all and it is not for us to question. Promise me?'

He saw the agitation in my eyes. What is a body other than an earthly vessel for our souls? Beyond that, it has no purpose. Mine had suffered the agony of hunger and the awful cramps had only recently subsided. I couldn't raise my head, but my mind was clearer than it had been in weeks. I wasn't foolish enough to believe that I had found a way to live without food. It was just that my body was finished and my soul now longed to be free of it. I couldn't die knowing the last thing I'd heard Teri say was a blasphemy.

'Promise me you won't turn your back on God!' I repeated.

He remained quiet for a moment. Finally he took my hand. 'I promise.'

I never knew what became of my family in Egypt. From soirees and whiskey sodas, we had become destitute. I thought of those poor people we had passed dead or dying in the street and who had no money to be buried properly and no one to memorialise them. This then was to become my fate too. Teri and I never exchanged another word after that. I simply shut my eyes and allowed my soul the freedom it longed for.

32

'You starved to death?' I said to Jeanne, when I had finally recovered sufficient composure to speak. 'But my mother never told me.'

'Did you ever ask her?'

'What? Of course not.' Tell me about our family history, Mama. Oh, and by the way, did anyone in our family, a) get massacred in a monastery, b) only just survive the Spanish Inquisition or c) starve to death under Nazi occupation? 'But I would have thought it would be something you'd want to tell your kids.'

'Perhaps she never realised that's what happened to me. She was only five when I died. Maybe Teri never told her.'

I sat quietly for a moment. 'You never asked where God was when all of these things were happening to you?' It was unthinkable to me that this woman could maintain her faith so unshakably, despite her suffering.

'Do you always blame God for your choices, Kat?'

'My choices? Where does choice come into it? If God is as powerful as He claims, how isn't it His fault? How can dying of starvation be your fault?'

'It wasn't, but I made choices of my own free will leading up to that moment. If I had done just one thing differently, I might have survived. I might have even been around to meet you.'

'So you make one bad choice and you die before your time? Is that how it's supposed to work? You were a saint; surely God could have protected you.'

'But that isn't the plan and I wasn't a saint. You see, Kat, God is good and kind. He gave us free will, and we need to accept responsibility for that. The Nazis made choices and I made choices. I married a man I loved, but did not like. That was my choice. I had five children. My choice again. I left Egypt to go to Greece that year. I did all of it freely and without anyone compelling me in any way. I never said any of those choices were bad. The Nazis, well, that's another thing entirely. It's just that if I'd changed any one of my choices, the outcome would have been different.'

'I can't accept that it was your fault you died so young and so tragically.'

'It's not about fault or blame.' She sighed. 'I said the outcome would be different but I didn't say *better*, did I? Why do you assume that if you could go back in time and change one thing, then the planets would all align? Not everything that happens in life is such a tragedy. Say that I'd decided to marry someone else or to have one less child. *Poof*, I live, but I still never meet you, because suddenly, you, Kat Bower, don't exist and we never had this conversation.'

'And where was God when the Nazis were choosing to murder His children?'

'I'd imagine that He was weeping. This is a free world and we are free to do good or evil. It's our choice.'

'But you must have prayed. A woman like you must have prayed…'

'Yes, I prayed. I prayed for Greece and I prayed for my family.'

'So why didn't God answer you?'

'Of course God answered me. He always answers. He doesn't always answer your prayers in the way you want.'

'Oh, come on. Don't tell me you get what you need…'

'Yes.'

'I'm not sure I agree with any of this. Either way, I still can't forgive those bloody Nazi bastards! And if only your bitch of a cousin hadn't been such a conniving whore…'

'Oh, dear!' She was stunned silent. They probably didn't swear very often in the convent school.

'I'm sorry, Jeanne. I guess I'm just angry about it. I have to close the book now, if you don't mind.'

'All right. But be sure to reflect on what I've said.'

'I will.' I didn't mean it. 'Bye, Jeanne.'

I closed the book and put it aside. I didn't know if I felt angrier that she'd died as another victim of pointless malevolence, or that she'd adopted such a stupid philosophy to make herself feel better about it. *Feel better about it? Listen to me: now I'm turning them into sentient beings! Ghosts can't possibly feel anything.*

Exhausted, I had to lie down right there on the divan. For a moment, I felt overwhelmed by the tragedy that seemed to surround all of the women of my family. Faith, womanhood, war, evil—I needed to shut it all out.

The hardest thing for me was that, while my relatives had given me such powerful stories, aside from compiling them into a book and calling them fiction, I couldn't really share them with the people I loved the most. Of course, my ancestors' ghosts didn't stop me from telling others, it was just that no one would believe me. Heck, *I* only barely believed me. I likened it to having a girlfriend who tells you the best, juiciest piece of gossip meant for your ears only. You're bursting to tell the world even though (or just because) you know you mustn't. I so desperately wanted to reveal the truth to everyone I knew, and not just to strangers disguised as my imagination. But how? Almost everyone I cared about knew how I'd stumbled across the cookbook and how it had spoken to me. The problem was how they were beginning to perceive me.

By now, Simone was convinced I was crazy. Paul believed I was becoming my mother (and therefore crazy). Ethan was still open-minded about it: *Take two pills and call your psychiatrist in the morning.* Nicole wasn't speaking to me. Ditto Chris and everyone else I knew. Everyone I was acquainted with thought I was mad. Or sad.

I tried to close Jeanne off but something she had said replayed in my mind. I kept feeling that she was more than just another one of my family members who needed closure. Fotini, Alegra, Jeanne—I mentally added Luxor and Chios to my list of places I needed to visit, even though I had no idea what I would have to do once I got there.

I closed my eyes and lay there, hoping to float myself into a calmer, clearer place, even though my mind kept coming back to Jeanne. Then there was the bigger picture. *Dammit! I just don't want to think about it now!* If some omnipotent deity was able to make the world in under a week then, as far as I was concerned, he really had to accept some responsibility for the shit that happened in everyone's life. I had so missed the straightforward philosophy of Kinderkull lately. Take the lyrics of *The Devil Made Me Do It*, as an example. *If good things happen to bad people then bad is what I want to be—why waste my time on things divine when there's no one there to answer me.*

If everything was a simple matter of choice, how did that explain random events like illness and tsunamis, and all the disasters and horrors of the world? On the other hand, if absolutely everything is pre-ordained, why maintain the illusion of choice and perpetuate the myth that we are masters of our destiny? It was clear that my relatives were creatures of their time—Fotini's worldview was naive and Jeanne's faith made her blind.

So far, in pursuit of understanding and the certainty of my own normality, I'd chatted to a rabbi and to an imam, I'd listened to a couple psycho-babbling, and to a charlatan summoning up the undead. I'd had my brain photographed and my blood analysed. For completeness, I probably owed it to Jeanne to check out the Orthodox religion into which I had been born and, while I was there, I supposed I could have a memorial prayer read for her too, not that I believed in that kind of thing. Maybe that would be enough to settle the unquiet spirits. I wrote it down in my 'to do' column, finished typing up Jeanne's story, stretched out on the divan again and promptly fell asleep. When I awoke, Paul was standing over me and Boz was panting garbage breath straight into my face.

'Are you okay?'

'Of course I am. Why shouldn't I be?'

Eyes still shut, my voice sounded strange to my ears, as if it was coming from a cave and out of someone else's throat. I felt utterly exhausted and it was a struggle to wake up and not fall straight back to sleep again. I hadn't felt this tired since a very liberal summer twenty years ago, pre-Paul, when I had dated about ten different guys and ended up with a raging dose of glandular fever. Although my eyes were now open, my mind was definitely elsewhere. I pulled myself up, stretched and gazed out. Beyond the window, the streetlights were already glowing pools of ochre.

'What time is it?'

'It's a little after seven,' Paul replied.

'I guess I've been asleep for a while. Did you only just start to miss me?'

'Not really. I didn't want to disturb you so I cooked dinner. I've been trying to wake you for the last five minutes.'

'Sorry.' Mama's cookbook was still lying on the floor where I had left it. Paul caught me glancing across at it.

'Maybe once in a while you should stop reading recipes and try cooking something.'

'Don't be mean.' I hauled myself to my feet. Paul took me by the arm.

'Let's eat,' he said as he led me towards the kitchen. 'I'm starving.'

I was carried along partly by my husband but mostly by the scent of something delicious wafting down the hallway. I'd been so caught up in Jeanne's story that I'd totally missed eating lunch.

'So am I,' I said over the loudest of stomach growls.

After dinner we settled back, Paul sipping a cabernet sauvignon while I munched through half a block of dark chocolate and reflected on Jeanne. Paul poured himself a second glass of wine and told me that, as of tomorrow, he was swearing off alcohol, except on weekends, and going on a fitness regime. He didn't want to be fat and fifty. I reminded him he was a few years away from that.

'You could always do it with me,' he said.

'Are you saying I'm fat?'

'No,' he replied, but I wasn't convinced.

That night, Paul tried to make amends with kisses and cuddles. When he realised they weren't leading anywhere, he told me that he had never liked me too thin, anyway, and my new curves made me damn sexy.

'I can't keep my hands off you,' he confessed.

He looked so desperate and so appealing that I melted.

'Then don't,' I responded.

We fell asleep in each other's arms, but the cool air set me shivering and reaching for a nightgown. Meanwhile, Paul was lying on his face, legs splayed, and totally unconscious.

I glanced at the bedside clock. Four forty-two. Not even the birds were awake. I snuggled into Paul and he grunted and rolled over. I guess I must have slept, since next thing I remember was seeing myself at church, wearing nothing but underwear and trying to hide under a pew.

'You're having a nightmare.' Paul was shaking me awake.

'Huh? Hmm.' He was still jiggling my arm. 'Okay, I'm awake. You can stop that now.' The clock said it was eight-thirteen. 'I'm getting up.'

As I made coffee, I reflected on my dream and the fact that it had been a very long time since I'd last been to church, Mama's funeral excepted. That didn't count, since the whole affair had been so tightly orchestrated that it could have been conducted anywhere. I hadn't connected to the spiritual part of it at all, and I was beginning to think maybe that was exactly what I needed.

I wasn't sure of how to approach a priest, or what precisely to say. I could have asked Georgia, she'd have known for sure, but that would necessitate talking to her. All I knew of church protocol was that I needed to cover up and look suitably pious. I pushed it all out of my mind and made some of Mama's french toast.

That afternoon, I looked on the internet for the closest Orthodox church. St Barbara's was a mere twenty-minute drive and one mouse click away. *Like us on Facebook!* When had things changed so radically? My mind turned to the thought of priests posting jokes on social media sites: *A priest, a rabbi and an imam walk into a bar. The rabbi asks the priest, 'How's business?'* Then again, no, that was never going to happen.

In a moment of weakness, I told Paul that I was thinking of seeing a priest, to talk about Mama and to settle my feelings towards her. I added that there was a service underway, meaning that someone would be there right now. He said he thought that might be a very good idea.

'Nothing else has worked so far. You need to do something to get over your anger,' he remarked.

'What do you mean by that?' I caught him looking at me cautiously, choosing his words.

'You get a bit upset sometimes. You know, towards your mother… It's your grief, I guess.'

Hmm. 'Nice try but that's not what you said. Do you really think I'm an angry person?' Was this the second time he'd brought it up? Paul wasn't one for needless repetition.

Searching for something diplomatic to say, he ventured a non-committal, 'Well, you have to admit you can get pretty worked up over things.'

'Go on. I'm interested in what you think,' I countered.

Paul was sweating. He was scratching at words like a hen in a coop. 'I think you haven't gotten over your mother's issues. Now don't get hurt when I say that you're not the only person in the world with a strange family or who has had a difficult upbringing.' He was scrutinising me for a reaction. Usually I would have leapt to my own defence but this time I chose to hear him out in silence. No grimace, no guffaw. He raised an eyebrow and it made me stop and think. *Am I really such an angry person?*

Paul continued. 'By the time most people get to forty, they do one of two things—get over it or get help for it. You can't keep blaming your mother's mental problem for everything that's wrong in your life and you can't stay angry with everyone. You and Chris need to figure yourselves out. This isn't how family behaves.'

'And you just lost me. You had me eating out of your hand until you said that. You really think that you and Fiona are poster siblings for family harmony? Face it, the real reason you and your sister get along is because you almost never see each other.' I could see him bristling for an argument and I wasn't in the mood. 'But you're right, I do need to sort my shit out. Don't look so shocked, I agree with you.'

'So what are you going to do? After you see this priest of yours?'

'I'm not sure, really.' I had been hoping all along that someone might have all the answers. I had tried everything else, so why not a priest? I just didn't want to get into a religious argument right then and there with a man as profoundly atheistic as Paul. 'We can talk about it when I get back. I'd better go. No point in keeping God waiting.'

Paul frowned. I picked up the keys to the car, kissed him and headed for church.

33

I arrived at church at the tail end of the service. Lapsed Orthodox that I was, I still knew enough to cross myself as I entered—two fingers pinched tightly together with the thumb, *Father Son and Holy Ghost*, then light a candle and kiss the icon—all the while feeling totally disingenuous. It was as obvious as if it were emblazoned on my forehead: *Here comes the imposter.* The eyes of a few of the faithful were looking around as I entered, settled on me and determined, exactly as I'd feared, that I was indeed a fraud. At the front of the nave, the priest had already reached the point of blessing the crowd and dismissing them with the exhortation that they pass the remainder of the day without sin. *Ha! As if!* After he finished, I approached him and stood patiently in line, while he turned his attention to the needs of the sinners who had arrived first.

The remainder of the congregation, who seemed to be the same old ladies I remembered as a child, had left the church and were milling about outside. Through the open doors I watched them exchanging stories, gossiping about this person and that. They were squabbling, opinionated, clucking hens of women. As I moved forward in the line I returned my mind to the matter at hand. What was I going to say? Still deep in thought, I discovered I was next.

'Pater,' I said.

He replied in a flood of Greek, while I blinked rapidly and mouthed something demonstrating my complete ignorance.

'What is it that you want, my daughter?' Finally, something I could understand.

I expected him to have a strong Greek accent. He didn't— clearly not a recent arrival.

'May I speak to you privately, Father?'

He looked about and, finding no one else needing his attention other than his deacon, invited me into his office. We settled into a small room off the narthex with an old desk and a few mismatched chairs. It was decorated, quite predictably, with more icons. Unpredictably, this time, instead of fearing them, I found them quite engaging. As the priest shuffled papers and stuffed them into drawers, I studied their faces and decided that I'd been wrong; they weren't judging me at all. They were all busy contemplating paradise. The passage of time had made them quite compassionate.

I selected the least rickety of the chairs and sat down. Father Andrew and I traded names and settled down to business. He was clearly a no-nonsense Pater.

'Now, what is it that you wanted?'

'Well, that's a good question,' I remarked. Father Andrew raised an eyebrow.

What did I want to say? I tossed his question around my brain for a moment, searching for a better answer. He watched me vacillate between responses, weighing up which would result in the least painful encounter. I could spin him the usual story about researching a book, and leave the meeting with some guidance, but little help. Or I could be honest and let the chips fall where they may.

'Well, Father, I'm not sure how to put this.' I glanced at him for inspiration, but drew a blank. I sucked in a breath. *Here goes nothing.* I dipped a toe in.

'I was wondering what the Church's view on ghosts was.'

'Ghosts?'

'You know. Phantasms. Dead spirits.'

'Yes.' He knew what ghosts were. 'Why?'

Time to plunge in headfirst.

'My mother used to hear and see people who weren't there.' I probably should have stopped there but my mouth and my brain weren't synchronised. 'Please don't judge me, but I hear voices too sometimes. I guess they're ghosts.' I was armed with a verbal scattergun and I'd released the safety catch. 'Or then again, maybe they're not,' I giggled, wishing I'd sent him an email instead of coming in person. 'My dead ancestors speak to me, you see.' My brain had, by now, completely disowned my mouth. 'Oh, it doesn't happen all the time, only when I open a certain book. My dead mother's recipe book.' *Dammit, I'm a writer not an orator!*

He raised the other eyebrow while I shut my mouth tightly and resisted the urge to fire off another random volley. Then he asked all the usual questions of the when, where, who and why variety. I tried to look serene and composed as I struggled to answer him as honestly as I dared. Truthfully, I was exposed and vulnerable and it was uncomfortable. I remembered having that exact same feeling elsewhere—*I know, I'm undergoing a spiritual pap smear!* I had the good sense to keep that observation to myself.

Father Andrew scratched his beard for a while. Finally he spoke. 'So, you believe that you've encountered some ghosts. I'll tell you what I think of that in a moment. But first tell me, did you do something to summon them?'

'No, all I did was open the book and read from it. I never did anything to summon them. Why would I? In fact, mostly, I wish they'd go away.'

'Interesting.' Another scratch. 'Even among the clergy there are divided views on such things. You may find a few who believe that the dead can and do contact the living. Some see their dead relatives in a dream, asking for prayers or offering guidance.'

'And you, Father? What do you believe?'

'Demons can masquerade as ghosts. Not just people but objects, too, can be possessed. Please don't be alarmed by this, but have you considered this may all be the result of demonic possession?'

Considered it? I frowned at him while I chose my words. That my visitations were spectres—probably. That I was delusional—possibly. But demonic possession? Never. Absolutely not. My head had never spun around, as far as I knew. I didn't speak with weird voices or spew forth pea soup. For the sake of clarity, I told him as much, restricting myself to as few words as possible.

'That's Hollywood,' he replied. 'Although I did witness a woman speaking in a man's voice once myself. You asked me and I tell you that this is what I believe. Demonic possession isn't all that unusual, and it can be cured. There are prayers I can say over you to expel the demons.'

'Are you suggesting exorcism?' I was hoping to hear a resounding negative response.

'Yes.'

He had gone straight to the point. Meanwhile, I rummaged around for a suitable comeback while simultaneously allowing my mind to imagine the worst. It had come down to a good old-fashioned exorcism. I hadn't even been able to watch the movie from beginning to end, so I was fairly certain I wouldn't survive the experience.

'Can I think about it? I have a very busy week ahead, you see, what with family obligations and all that. Also, I'm going away too. And you, you're probably booked solid with things to do—other exorcisms, funerals and the like.' Evade and switch subjects—it was my tried-and-true, best response under extreme pressure. Added to which, I wasn't above lying to a priest. Which made me think that maybe he was right. Maybe I really did need to be exorcised.

'I could do it now if you wish.' He was apparently a mind reader.

'No, I'm not ready for that. I'd sooner think about it for a while.'

'It's your choice, but things will not improve until you deal with it.'

'I understand. Thank you, Father.'

'It won't take long.' Evidently 'no' did not appear in his vocabulary.

'Will it hurt?' I felt myself swaying.

'Not if I do it correctly.' He smiled.

A sense of humour. Who knew? It wasn't enough. I was going to stick to my convictions. 'I don't feel prepared right now but how about I bring the book with me next week and you can bless us both?' I tossed in a sweetener. 'And maybe a prayer for some of those dead ancestors?'

He opened his diary and flipped pages. 'Next Tuesday at six?'

'Next Tuesday at six.'

He wrote the appointment down while I attempted to enter it into my smartphone. I left feeling apprehensive, and who wouldn't, given the circumstances. I had done some interesting things in pursuit of an answer, but exorcism?

It was only when I arrived home and caught sight of Mama's book on the kitchen shelf that I realised that, if this exorcism worked, I might never again hear the voices of my ancestors. A couple of months or so ago, I might have greeted that prospect with joy, but I had since grown accustomed to having a conduit into other lives and, honestly, the thought of closing that off forever was bittersweet. I felt surprisingly tearful, so I sat down until the urge to cry passed.

Just then, Paul, in too-tight shorts and worn running shoes, burst in through the back door in a lather. Boz Scraggs followed him at a trot, his lolling tongue drooling saliva threads onto the clean floor. They were both struggling for air.

'What have you done?' Paul was bent double, in an effort to catch his breath. If they'd both died there and then, I wouldn't have been the least surprised. Boz was lying on the tiles, head barely raised, eyes fixed on me, imploring me to help him. 'Poor Boz.'

Between gulps, Paul said, 'I told you I was getting myself fit.'

'But you've gone from zero to a hundred. What's wrong with starting slowly?'

'Slow is for wimps.'

'Slow is for middle-aged men who want to see forty-six.'

He poured himself a glass of water and took a sip. 'You should come with me. You looked good in bike shorts.'

'Thanks, but I don't think so. And FYI, I still look good in bike shorts. Anyway, you didn't seem to mind my curves much last night.'

Paul dived towards me, now fairly much recovered. I dodged his grasp and pushed him away as Boz struggled to his feet, trotted across the room and drained his water bowl in a single slurp.

That evening, we'd arranged to catch up with an old university friend of Paul's named Dominic, whom I'd met once before and who just happened to be passing our way en route to a Sci Fi convention. He'd told us to meet him at the Singing Lark at seven, with a view to going somewhere for dinner. Paul hadn't had the courage to tell him it was a gay pub, although we were both fairly certain he wasn't. Knowing the importance of favourable second impressions, I dressed as stylishly as possible. Also, I didn't wish to be outdone by anyone else who might have been there.

We arrived a few minutes early and sat at the bar. As far as bars went, in my limited experience, this seemed like a particularly quiet one. Three men stood by the bar and another four were scattered over a dozen or so tables, and not one of them was competing with me. I was starting to think that the new ensemble and full make-up had been a complete waste of time. Paul, however, was getting some attention from a middle-aged bear in full leather, leaning on his elbow at the bar. Paul asked me if I thought it might be because of his new exercise regime. I told him it was probably a bit too soon to tell. Maybe next time he should wear his running shorts to the pub and I could take a straw poll.

We glanced at the drinks menu to pass time. The cocktails were a blast. At seven-fifteen, we ordered a watermelon mai tai each. At seven-seventeen, two vibrantly fuchsia concoctions arrived with rainbow umbrellas. At seven-eighteen, Paul's phone lit up with a message from his friend, asking where we were. Paul responded that we were in the pub waiting for him, and where was he? He replied he was in the pub waiting for us. Three messages and no resolution later, Paul called him. Turned out, someone had told him the Singing Lark was a gay pub after all and he'd changed venues, hadn't we got his message? I told Paul that life was far less complicated when people simply used to pick up the phone to talk to each other.

Just as we rose to leave the attentive bear, the wildly iridescent cocktails and the Singing Lark far behind us, Simone and her new girlfriend Klaryse popped through the entrance. Simone tried to pretend that she hadn't noticed us at first, but since we were already halfway between the bar and the door, she had no choice but to acknowledge us. She said they were commemorating their second month anniversary as a couple by having a drink. Since the Singing Lark was the closest bar to their new place, they had just happened by. They had eyes only for each other and when Paul explained our previous commitment, I swear I saw relief on their faces. I told them we'd catch up another time, airkissed them both on the cheek and left them alone to celebrate. After three pizzas and a night full of strained conversation with avowed bachelor Dominic, Paul and I finally arrived home.

'Why do we do this to ourselves?' I remarked as I pulled off my heels and rubbed my toes. 'If you haven't seen someone for a decade, there's usually a good reason for it.'

'That's true.'

'Let's make a pact. Next time anyone calls us to catch up on the way to somewhere else, let's say we're busy. I'm not interested in seeing anyone who considers us the stopover, rather than the destination.'

Paul grunted. He'd stripped down to his trunks and t-shirt, fallen into bed and was half asleep, courtesy of the watermelon mai tai and four beers. I slid in next to him, completely sober, and warmed my feet on his legs. He didn't budge an inch and I knew he was out cold. A moment or two later, he began to snore. Good wife that I was, and knowing that he had an early appointment the following morning, I let him. Until Tuesday arrived, I planned to spend every day with Mama's book.

Although Paul had set the alarm for five—he was going to fit in an early morning run before starting work—I was afoot and blogging an hour before his head even left the pillow. Oh, I'd tried to rouse him at five, and then fifteen minutes later, and another fifteen minutes after that, and so on until seven-fifteen.

'Shit,' he said when he finally woke up. 'Why didn't you wake me?'

'I tried to nine times.'

'Oh, sure you did. You're probably trying to sabotage my new exercise regime.'

'Yup, that'd be right.' My mind flitted to the man at the bar last night. 'I'm jealous. I want you fat and flabby and all to myself.'

With that he got up, showered and took a couple of aspirin before muttering something about feeling exhausted and never having to worry about hangovers when he was young. Paul, my easy-going, well-intentioned, kind-hearted, teddy of a husband was becoming decidedly cantankerous. Then it dawned on me: Paul was in the middle of a mid-life crisis. As a gesture of love and reconciliation, I packed him a lunch and a travel mug full of coffee, and hoped he wouldn't consider it to be reinforcement of his unpalatable behaviour.

After he left, I put the finishing touches to my blog. Since I had begun reproducing my ancestors' recipes in my blogs (with some backstories included), my devotees had proliferated into the high hundreds. I wasn't hiding the cookbook from Paul any more, but I had stopped telling him any details about the girls. He had become a Bower-Buddy, as my blog followers called themselves. I may have been an abject failure alone, but with my dead relatives as inspiration, we were proving to be a huge hit. Who knew?

I had developed a bit of a ritual around Mama's book of late, which involved hot chocolate and shortbread. I had noticed that maybe I'd put on the teeniest bit of weight—and hence Paul's comments—but

I was a long way from overweight. *Nothing wrong with a bit of boob and booty.* I was approaching *un certain âge* after all, as much as I hated to admit it; maybe a chubby middle age was looming.

I settled down with my cup, sniffing the delicious fumes of Belgian chocolate caressing my face and opened the cookbook at random. It fell open to *Rosie's Sponge Sandwich.* I nibbled my shortbread as I read. *Rosie?* For a moment I was searching the far recesses of my brain for a Rosie in my mother's family. Odd name for a Greek, but then, so many of my ancestors hadn't turned out anything like what I'd expected. *Rosie.* Then it dawned. *But of course.* Rosalind Bower had been my paternal grandmother, whom I'd never met. I'd never heard her referred to as anything but Granny Bower. So, this recipe must have been hers. No ingredients listed at the top, just straight in. *Separate the whites from the yolks of four fresh eggs…*

I craned my ears for the slightest sound of a voice. Nothing. Maybe the magic only worked with women from Mama's bloodline. I took another bite and read on. *Beat the yolks and sugar until foamy…* And then…

'Oi, there!'

'What?'

'Oi, I'm talking to you! What are you doing scattering crumbs all over my nice, clean recipe? Haven't you ever heard of a plate?'

Here we go again. Weren't any of my ancestors going to be lovable right off the bat?

'Sorry!' I put down my cup and crammed the rest of the shortbread into my mouth. I'd either hugely underestimated how much of the shortbread was left or I'd overestimated the size of my oral cavity. It was a tight fit but there were no crumbs. *Happy now?*

'Like your sweets, do you, my dear? Very ladylike that is, I must say. So you're my granddaughter Kat…'

I wasn't too sure if it was meant as a question or an expression of her disappointment. Either way, my mouth was too full to answer. I struggled to emit a single, nasal grunt.

'Now, now, don't choke yourself, girl.' She tut-tutted. 'I always suspected that anyone silly enough to marry my Charlie wouldn't have the good sense to teach her child manners, and now I see I was right.'

I wanted to defend my parents, but the shortbread had stuck to the roof of my mouth like super glue and I had been rendered absolutely speechless.

'I was a very good baker,' she continued. 'You'll find some lovely recipes in the book. Have you tried any of them?'

I took a small sip of the hot chocolate, wiggled my tongue around my palate, and managed to disengage some of the mass. I was now somewhere between certain choking or further ridicule. I turned away from the book (as if it had eyes to see), slipped a finger into my mouth, prised the sticky, choco-shortbread goo off with my nail, chewed it and swallowed. Not my finest moment. I detected a non-verbal, ghostly eyebrow raise, but at least I could finally speak.

'No, I haven't tried any of your recipes. I don't cook.'

'What do you mean, you can't cook?'

'Oh no, I can cook all right. I just don't.'

'But how could a granddaughter of mine…?' She stopped short. 'I love to cook. Especially cakes and sweets—food that makes people happy. Cooking's about happiness and home.' She paused. 'So you say you don't cook—now, I don't understand that at all.'

'That's right, I don't cook. It's not confusing, it's a choice. I don't cook. And for the record, although it probably doesn't look like it, Mama and Dad did teach me manners.' I crossed my arms and seriously considered putting away the book for good.

'Oh, sweetheart, don't get upset! Don't break your heart over a silly comment! I'm winding you up, darling, that's all I'm doing. Let's start over again, shall we? Dear little Kat, my name is Rosalind Bliss Bower, otherwise known as Granny Bower. And I'm very, very pleased to meet you at last!'

I couldn't help but smile. Her voice was all ripe strawberries and clotted cream. I could have sworn that, if she could, she would have manifested in a puff of baby powder.

'I'm sorry for getting shortbread all over your recipe, Granny Bower. I should have been more respectful. I suppose you're here for a reason?'

'Oh yes, my dear, I am.'

'Of course. You tell me your tale and I'll try to ascertain what it is you need me to do for you.'

'Need you to do for me, Kat? Why, daa-arl-ling,' she chuckled, 'you have got hold of the wrong end of the stick!'

Wrong end of the stick? What did she mean by that? Why couldn't my ghostly relatives just come out with what they wanted? I imagined it must have taken a lot out of them to leave the spirit world for my benefit. What was wrong with expressing exactly what had dragged them back? *Clarity is so vastly underrated.*

'All right, then,' I said. 'So you're all here to do something for me.'

'Yes, of course. That's exactly why we're here. Didn't any of the others tell you?'

'Not in so many words. And none of you can tell me about the Big-G or what happens to us after we die.'

'No, dear, I'm afraid we can't. We're only here because something in your life needs to change.'

'And what's that?'

'I don't know. You'll have to work that out for yourself.'

'Is that why my mother saw you guys too? She had something she needed to change?'

'I really couldn't say. Now you just sit back and let Granny Bower tell you a story, my love.'

34

ROSIE

Where to begin, where to begin? I guess the beginning's a pretty good place to start, right, darling? You ever been to London, Kat? Of course you have, hasn't everyone these days? When I say Bow Bells, do you have the slightest idea what I'm talking about? No? What a shame. It's all Westminster and Bloomsbury with your lot, but I'll tell you there was more living and dying happening east of the City than there was anywhere else in London. That's right, darling, I was born within a few hundred yards of the London Hospital, in the most dreadful place in the whole of England.

My mum and dad grew up next door to each other, in a street just off the Commercial Road in the middle of Whitechapel. And what a life that must have been! There was six of 'em in Mum's family and another eight in my dad's, all sharing the same privy with five other families. At the end of their street was a synagogue, and most of their neighbours were Jews, although they themselves were Protestant. They kept pretty much to themselves, which was, I suppose, how they ended up married to each other.

Mum's family, the Aubers, had been Spitalfields weavers, and my granny had told Mum that their lot come from France, a very, very long time ago. They were doing all right at the beginning, but once the industrial revolution happened, there was no need for hardworking craftsmen like them no more. All of a sudden, nobody cared about the quality of the cloth, you see, but everybody worried about the price. They fell into some very hard times, the Aubers did. Anyhow, after the weaving trade died, my granny took in work as a laundress and my grandad did whatever he could—he was a night soil man one day, rag and bone the next, and everything in between. There was never enough money to buy food as well as pay the rent, so Mum's family often went hungry. One way or another, everyone worked back in them days, even the kids. Mum grew up next to a washbasin and a mangle, with lines of other people's linen drying in front of the fire, so she couldn't even get near it to warm herself. The minute she was tall enough to reach into the tub, she began washing alongside my grandmother. They were a lot poorer than the Blisses, and, even when they were only small children, Dad used to sneak food for Mum. Always taking care of her, he was. I suppose you could say that when she married my Dad, she married up.

By the time I was born, the twentieth century was a couple of years old. We were all Edwardians now, and the world around us was better than it had ever been. Whoever believed that clearly had never travelled east of Tower Bridge! Oh yes, life may have been better for Lord and Lady Muck in Mayfair, but let me tell you it wasn't much chop for the rest of us. The Whitechapel I was born into was a right old slum. We were surrounded by women selling themselves on the street and gangs of Jews and Gentiles warring against themselves and each other with guns. Seemed like everything around us was either dead or dying. I remember Mum saying it was no safer in her day, what with the Whitechapel murders and all. Mum was a big storyteller—must be where you get your talent for writing from. She used to say she saw the Ripper himself the night Elizabeth Stride was killed. She said he was small and dark and she thought he was a boot-maker. That, or possibly a butcher. I thought she made it all up, myself.

That's right, Kat: Rosie Bliss was a Cockney. Oh, your father never said? Well, why would he? It's glamorous to be a Cockney these days, but don't you think for a minute I was proud of being Cockney. Not a bit of it. All I could think about was going somewhere that didn't stink of unwashed bodies and sewerage and wet clothes and gin. But for all that, I can tell you we was one of the luckiest families in Whitechapel. You know why? Because our dad was a lighterman, just like his dad and his grandad before him. Which meant he had a job. Which meant we had boots on our feet, a roof over our heads and food on the table. If you have a spare moment, you really should try my light-as-air sponge cake.

By the time I was five, there was Mum, Dad and seven of us children—four older ones and two younger than me—living in two rooms, which was one room more than most families I knew. But don't imagine we was comfortable; the rooms were scarcely bigger than cupboards and all us kids shared two beds. It wasn't as if you could just find yourself a nice house to rent, even if you had a little bit of extra cash. Lodgings were hard to get and people did all sorts of things so they wouldn't have to sleep in the street. The family in the next room rented out their beds to strangers and sometimes they even rented the space under their beds! Can you imagine it? They slept in shifts. At least we never had to share our beds with strangers. And our beds had the chance to go cold.

There would have been twelve of us kids, except that Mum lost three as babies and another two later on. I don't remember any of them dying until I turned four, and then I remember Mum holding one of my older sisters one day and crying. I remember she was like a rag doll, all floppy and twisted. Then my dad took her away from Mum and we never saw our sister again. Yes, it was a different world back then.

Mum always wore black, but it wasn't as you might think for the children she lost. She said she was in mourning for Queen Victoria, the mother of our nation. I doubt she mourned the loss of her own mother for as long. These days, you change your clothes without a second thought, but Mum only ever had the one dress as long as I can remember, and she wore it with a little suffragette brooch made of amethysts, green garnets and moon-stones, which Dad said he'd found on the road one day on his way to work. It was funny that she wore it, since Mum didn't care whether women were allowed to vote or not. In our circles, you see, nobody had the right to vote.

Even if you spent most of the time elbow deep in other people's washing, you were never clean yourself. You should have seen me as a child! With all the filth on my face, if you'd popped a turban on my head I'd have looked more Indian than English. Baths? Oh, there was bathhouses all right charging tuppence a pop, and we all went once a month, whether we needed it or not. The towels were as hard as tree bark and almost as scratchy. I was nearly twenty before I had a proper bath in a proper bathroom with hot water and soap and a real tub! Bath or not, it was impossible to stay clean in them days. Black didn't show the dirt and when Mum paired her dress with a white lace collar, all clean and starched, she may have still smelled like a workman's armpit in summer, but at least she didn't look half bad.

And then there was Dad. You know, my dad was quite a decent man when he wasn't elephant's. You don't understand what I mean do you? I said he was a good man when he wasn't, you know…when he wasn't elephant's trunk—drunk. Dad kept odd hours rowing up and down the river on his barge, shifting cargo, and sometimes, when the docks were busy, we didn't see him for days at a time. But Dad was never drunk at work. Can you imagine? One step left or right and he'd have ended up in old father Thames. Or, if the barge was empty, they'd have found him dead at the bottom of the hold. Once a week, he'd come home pissed and cashed up, shuffling along Buross Street in his peculiar, lighterman way, all pigeon toed and bent forward, and loaded up with silly, pointless gifts for us all—ancient clay pipes and old pots and jugs with bearded faces, which he had bought from the mudlarks for a ha'penny. I'd have much preferred a bar of Fry's chocolate cream myself personally, but I never had the heart to tell him.

I'm not upsetting you with all this doom and gloom, am I, Kat? You mustn't fret, my dear, really. Life may have started off sad, but we have the chance to change our destiny, don't we—I mean, if we really want to. We can all make silk purses out of sows' ears, if we're shown how. It's important to see the happy side of life, isn't it, dear? Do you think I was going to live in a slum any longer than necessary? My parents and their parents may have been locked in all right, but for us there was a way out. When the other kids in our neighbourhood was out stealing, or working in factories, or selling lumps of coal on the street just to survive, we was marching ourselves past the London Hospital and over Whitechapel Road to the Durward Street School. How lucky were we? We may not have been the best-educated children in London, but we all learned to read and write and do sums. Which was how I ended up getting a job in a teashop. Knowledge, Kat, now that's the key to any door.

Even now my childhood flashes through my mind like it was all a silent picture show. When I was five, I remember Mum taking me and two of my brothers to the London Hospital to see Queen Alexandra and her sister Empress Maria. We was holding flags made out of pieces of paper with the Union Jack painted on and stuck on sticks, standing for what felt like hours. Then my brother Dick slipped away from Mum and ran off home. Always a bad'un, was Dick. After that, Mum held me so tightly that my little wrist ached for days.

I remember we was standing below and to the left of the stairs that led up to the entrance of the hospital, behind a row of nurses who were hopping from foot to foot as they waited in line. The moment the royal entourage began descending the steps, I somehow wiggled free of Mum's grasp and pushed between the skirts of the nurses, who were now clapping and curtseying. For all my efforts, I never really did see the Queen, although I did for a moment glimpse her ankles. Mum darted forward to pull me back, and it paid off for her. Just as she caught me, the Queen and her sister stopped their descent and Mum caught a glimpse of them. To the day she died, Mum spoke about how the Russian Empress, seeing her predicament, had smiled and nodded at her. What I remember most is how sore my little feet was by the time we had walked home.

Now I see myself at school, sitting next to my dear friend Dulcie Ward. We was thick as thieves, me and Dulcie, and we did everything together. We were almost the same build and so similar in looks that one of the teachers could never tell us apart. You can imagine how much fun that was! I remember us playing Ring a Ring a Rosie and falling on top of each other, rolling around until the dust clung to our dresses. We got into so much trouble, we did. Then Dulcie suddenly stopped coming to school and I never knew why. I tried to find her. Oh, how I missed her!

I was twelve when the Great War began. I left school the year after, and at first I stayed at home to help Mum. Dad was too old to be conscripted at the start of the war and too sick by the time it ended. My brother Bill was called up in 1916, Dick the year after, and then John got his marching orders in March of 1918. I thought they looked handsome in their uniforms, but Mum said I was young and I didn't know very much about war. Each time one of the boys left, Mum cried her heart out and Dad went to the pub for the whole day. He did the same when he found out that Bill died in the Battle of the Somme, his head blown apart by artillery fire.

When I turned sixteen, I got myself a position as a kitchen hand in the ABC Teashop in Ludgate Hill, not far from St Paul's. I'd never seen so many people drinking tea and chattering like flocks of birds, while our waitresses fluttered around them. People came in waves. Breakfast early, then elevenses, then lunch, and again at four. By the end of the day, my head and hands were aching—and my feet! My poor feet! I never knew they could hurt so badly.

I could have taken the underground there from Aldgate, but most times I walked. It took me a bit over a half an hour, but I loved my stroll, even in the middle of winter. It was so nice to leave the smell of poverty behind that sometimes it took everything I had just to walk back to Whitechapel of an evening. From dawn to dusk, I washed cups and plates until my hands was red and cracked, filled more teapots than I could count, sliced scores of cakes and buttered a mountain of scones. And I loved every minute of it. There was little Rosie Bliss from the slums in the City of London, preparing food for ladies who didn't have a care in the world. I kept my mouth shut and my eyes open. It was there at the ABC that I discovered my talent for making cakes.

I soon fell into a tight company with one of the waitresses, a girl named Gladys, who was a year or two older than me. She had travelled down to London from Birmingham to find an occupation, although much later she confided in me that she did it to get away from her dad, although I never knew precisely why until later. She was beautiful in my eyes, all tall and slender like a gazelle. I like to I think she thought me the same, only shorter. For a while there, we did everything together, me and Glad.

By the time the war ended, I had saved up enough of my wages to think about leaving the East End and taking a room in a lodging house. I was earning nearly a pound a week at the ABC and giving most of it to Mum. Dad wasn't working by then, you see. He'd been pinched a while back for taking a barrel of rum off a ship and keeping it for himself. Between you and me, when I think about it, I reckon it wasn't the first time. To this day, I put it down to luck that he avoided the Old Bill all those years. As soon as he was fingered, he give the rum right back, but he was still sacked for it. Lost his lighterman's ticket and all. Mum was beside herself with grief, but what was I to do about it? The boys were coming home from the war soon and they could get jobs and help out.

I had nothing in the world but a bag of clothes and a spare pair of shoes. When I kissed Mum goodbye and shut the door behind me, it was the best feeling in the whole world. I remember my sisters were crying as I left, but I couldn't hide my smile. I found lodgings in a house near Blackfriar's Bridge and paid six shillings for it. It wasn't much, but it had a bed, a heater and a chair. What more could I want? I told Glad that we could share the room if she liked, but she said her fiancé would be coming back from France soon and then they'd be married. I never even knew she had a young man, let alone that she was spoken for. I thought I knew her pretty well, but she kept a few secrets, did Glad. I thought I should be happy for her and I told her I was, but I wasn't.

Ah, well, it's no matter. A wedding's a joyous occasion, isn't it, dear? I bet you looked beautiful at yours. You know, I baked my first wedding cake especially for Glad. Made up the recipe myself I did, from what I'd seen in the shop. I'd saved up to buy a flask of real Jamaican rum to put in it—shame I couldn't have got some off Dad, innit—and it was rich and dark and I covered it with marzipan and royal icing. All the girls thought I was very clever but I thought it was all a bit of luck, really, that it turned out as nice as it did. Glad left the ABC early April and she got married just before Easter. I never did get my invitation to the wedding and I imagine that the silly girl must have forgotten to send it. Never mind! I still went to the All Saints church in Haggerston, and slipped into a pew in the back corner, just to watch. She looked so striking it took my very breath away. I was happy to think they'd be eating my cake after the ceremony, even if I wasn't going to be there to enjoy it myself. Of course, I never did see Glad after that. Last I heard, her husband had got himself a job in an aircraft factory and they'd moved all the way to Hounslow.

I settled into life away from Whitechapel pretty well. I hardly saw my family once I'd put down roots and the lodging house proved to be a real godsend for a girl like me. Mrs Best, the landlady, kept a tidy house and let me tell you she kept all us girls in order. I can't say that I've ever been very ambitious and I was happy enough scrubbing dishes at the ABC. Then it turns out that I have a natural talent for baking, and Gladys's cake hadn't been a happy accident after all. The girls were always asking me to bake them a sponge cake or a tray of gingernuts in Mrs Best's kitchen. When friends were about to come round for afternoon tea, Mrs Best always asked me, 'Rosie, do you think you could whip up a batch of your fluffy scones?' And I did. You know, Kat, I was never happier than when I was cooking.

After a while, careful with money as I was and since I never had to buy my own dinner as there were always bits left over at work, I'd saved enough money to think about opening my own teashop. I knew I was a far better baker than anyone working for the ABC. Mrs Best was right behind me and I told her I was looking for somewhere cheap, near a station and as far away from Whitechapel as I could afford. I found exactly what I was looking for an easy stroll from Waterloo station, right on York Road, and the landlady was Mrs Best's former bridge partner. The shop was long and narrow, only barely two tables across, but it was enough for me. And did I ever feel proud signing that lease! The son of another friend of Mrs Best's, a lad named Ned with spots on his face who was learning the carpentry trade, divided my little shop into two. He fitted an old wood stove as well as a charcoal stove in the back half, which he'd salvaged from God-knows-where. I never asked and he never told. There was already a sink in one corner. I began to think of Mrs Best as my benefactor, especially after she give me a dresser and a long wooden table. I bought sets of second-hand plates, bowls and pans, five round tables with their chairs and a long display counter. I was set. With the ABC far behind me and my future laid out ahead, I like to think that 1924 marked a turning point of my life.

35

I spent the next week painting everything that could be painted in my little shop, and scrubbing everything what couldn't. Mrs Best's friend's son turned out to be a bit of a godsend, and he hung about to help me fix the place up. Even did a bit of art on the window, drawing a big cabbage rose in shades of pink. Nothing was too much trouble for him and, between ourselves, I think he might have even fancied me a little bit. More fool him, don't you think? A week after that, the doors of The Rose Tearoom opened.

The day before the grand opening, I baked my little heart out, and the shelves of the display cabinet were loaded with all kinds of cakes and biscuits. I'd been standing up so long that my poor toes were raw with blisters where my stockings rubbed, even before I opened the door. Ned came in for breakfast as soon as I unlocked the door, and it was nice to have the company. We had a cup of tea together and then he ate his way through three rounds of toast and dripping, two fried eggs with bacon, a slice of black pudding and a dish of beans. I was left wondering where he put it all. Ned had been so obliging, I didn't have the heart to let him pay that one time. But I made it very clear this wasn't to become a habit. He left at half seven for a job on the other side of the bridge.

By nine, not another single soul had come inside. By midday I'd boiled the urn three times, only to make myself cups of tea. Then Mrs Best and two of her friends came in to see how I was travelling. I made them three teas, but I couldn't exactly charge them either, could I? After all what she'd done for me? At three, my first paying customer wandered in, took a look around, and was about to wander right out again, except that I stopped him and offered to make him tea and sandwiches for tuppence. He agreed, except that he only had a penny ha'penny in his pocket. At that rate, my shop would close down in under a fortnight.

Right, I thought, *if no one's coming inside, then I may as well go outside.* I sliced up my best tea cake, popped it on a platter, shut the door and walked up and down York Street, giving it all away. *Here's what you're missing out on. Brought to you by The Rose Tearoom,* I told 'em. And you know what, Kat? Blimey if it didn't work! By week's end, I'd broken even. Another month and I could pay myself a wage. But didn't I work hard those first few weeks! It wasn't exactly the clientele I'd expected, but soon I began making a roaring trade feeding the mourners on their way to and from the necropolis. Burying the dead is such a hungry job! By year's end, I had employed my own nippy in a black dress and white apron serving the customers, as well as a girl to help me in the kitchen. I was so happy there with my two girls, working all the hours God gave me and glad to do it.

One afternoon in May, about a year later, who should come walking into my shop but my brother Dick. He came in just as I was reloading the window display, so I couldn't pretend I didn't see him. He was dressed in a suit, not new, mind, but nice enough for me to notice. On his arm was a girl a bit younger than him with curly red hair, fairly busting out of a dress with forget-me-nots all over it.

'Rosie?' he said, 'Is that you?'

'It's me.' I hadn't seen my family since before I opened the shop. Last time I'd visited, Mum had stung me for money, so I never bothered going back.

'What are you doing in Lambeth?' he asked.

'Working,' I said.

'I can see that. Shop yours?'

I didn't know which answer would save my bacon, so I kind of nodded.

'I've just moved in round the corner, myself,' he said. 'Been there a week. By the way, this is my fiancée, Kitty. Kitty, my sister Rosie.'

'Sure as I'm delighted to meet you,' she said. She sounded foreign.

'Likewise,' I replied. 'Look,' I told Dick straight, 'this is my place, but if you're going to sit down and have something you're going to have to pay for it, all right? The only thing that's free in here is the air. Otherwise you can leave the same way you came.'

'Now don't talk like that, Rosie. I know you and Mum had a falling out, but we've always been the best of friends, haven't we? I've still got the letters you wrote me when I was in Ypres.' He pronounced it 'Wipers'.

'Hmm,' I answered, like I was trying to blow something out of my nose. 'Family is family, I suppose, but business is business all the same.'

Dick and Kitty sat down. 'You're a right businesswoman now, aren't you, Rose? Be a pet and serve us up two teas and some of them scones and cream.'

I went into the kitchen to prepare his order, but I got Bess the nippy to serve it. When time came to clear the plates, he asked Bess to fetch me. I was none too pleased, let me tell you.

'What do you want, Dick?' I said to him.

'Just wanted to make sure you got fair payment. Here.' He shoved a pound note into my hand.

'What's this for, then? Two teas and scones are sixpence. I can't give you change from this,' I told him.

'You don't have to. Let's call it part of Mum's debt repaid,' he said to me, and then they both stood up to go. 'If you ever have any trouble or if you ever need anything, just tell me, all right?' He gave me a note with his address on. 'I know some very helpful lads.'

'Trouble come through my door the moment you walked in.' As I opened the door to let them out, the bell at the top of the door rang and Kitty looked startled. Poor girl didn't know what she was getting herself into. 'Nice to have met you, Kitty. Don't bother yourself on my account, Dick.'

'That's what family's for,' he said. Then he give me this strange smile as he left and I had a feeling that this wouldn't be the last time I'd see him.

A few weeks later, I'd all but forgotten Dick's visit and life was going along very nicely, thank you very much, without any help whatsoever, what with the funeral teas and the ladies having tea and the workers dropping by for breakfast and supper. I saw him a handful of times over the next year, skulking along the street in his greatcoat with the collar turned up, or talking with someone or other. He was as dodgy an individual as you'd ever want to meet. I always made out I hadn't seen him, in case he decided to happen by. Kitty sometimes came in for tea by herself when she had the opportunity, and I couldn't help but notice that as the date for her wedding came closer, she looked more and more worried. I got up the courage to ask her what was wrong once, but she didn't say.

Don't let me give you the impression that I never had time to play, my darling. It really wasn't all hard work. When I finished cleaning the shop up of an evening, I sometimes passed by Mrs Best's parlour soirees, for which she was famous throughout Lambeth. She held them once a week and she played music on her gramophone and all the ladies dressed up and smoked and drank like they was men. What a sight, ahhahahaha! Why, I even picked myself up a trouser suit second-hand, just so I could play the part! It was a riot, dancing and laughing with the others, I can't tell you. Sometimes when I look back, I think of them days as my happiest.

During one of her visits to the teashop, Kitty sat me down and opened herself right up. Even though Dick had said nothing to me about it, Kitty asked if I would come to the church on her wedding day, because she said she wanted to be able to look out and see at least one kind face in the crowd. I asked her why she was getting married, since she felt that way. She said she was so far away from her family in Ireland, and it was near impossible for a girl like her to earn enough to keep herself, and that Dick really was the best thing that had come her way. I didn't know if she was trying to convince me or herself. I didn't really want to see my family again but I told her she could count on me. She said she was happy and she give me a hug, right there in front of everyone.

Dick and Kitty was married in the spring of 1925, and a sorrier sight you never saw!

One day in April 1926, Mum come past to tell me that Dad had died. It was a shock to see her outside of Whitechapel first, and an even bigger shock to see how grey and thin she'd got in just a year. I told her that and she said I'd grown big and fat from eating all them leftovers. Then she broke down and said they had no money to bury Dad, so I said I'd take care of it.

'Don't you worry, Mum,' I told her. 'We'll do right by him.' She was ever so grateful.

I arranged to have him transported to the London Necropolis by train—third class, of course—and I paid for all ten mourners besides. For the first time since I'd opened, I took the whole morning off and left my girls in charge. We come back for the wake at The Rose Tearoom and Mum and me put our differences behind us. That's the thing about family, isn't it, Kat? No matter how bad it gets sometimes, at day's end you'll find you're still stuck with each other. Something inside me was at peace after that, because I knew I done the right thing by Dad.

As the years ticked along, what with motorcars and all, the mourners taking the train got less and less. Strikes and unemployment meant that life got harder everywhere, and business started to go downhill. Mum said that girls weren't meant to be in business and they shouldn't live alone. It wasn't natural. She never warmed to Mrs Best when she met her, and she said she thought Mrs Best was a queer old soul. 'That woman,' she said to me once, 'wants to be a man.'

Mum had been telling me that I should get married since the day we first met up again at my brother Dick's wedding. I kept telling her I wasn't ready yet. She said that even Sally had got engaged and I was her only daughter still on the shelf, and I ought to be ashamed of myself. The thing was, Kat, if I can be perfectly honest with you, I never did fancy getting married much. Until one day, who should happen past but Ned, you remember, the son of Mrs Best's friend, the lad who'd helped me set up my shop?

I hadn't seen Ned in nearly six years. He told me that he got married the year after I'd opened my shop and that's why he hadn't come for a visit in all that time. He said he was a widower now, but at first he wouldn't say anything more about it. I found out later from Mrs Best that his wife had run off with some Tom Tit a couple of years after the wedding, and he'd only recently got wind of where she'd gone. He'd been planning to see her and get her back. By the time he caught up with her, it seems she'd married her boyfriend in a town up north, without bothering to divorce Ned first. He would've gone to the police about it, but she'd gone and got herself pregnant, so he left 'em alone. Then a few months after that, he found out that she died in childbirth. So poor Ned was a widower, living by himself in a single room in Brixton.

Now his spots had all but disappeared and he looked a lot older and wiser. He was such a nice, gentle man, I liked him straight away. He said he'd never forgotten about me, and did I want to go out with him one day? Gladys, Kitty and everyone else I cared about was settled down and having babies. When I talked to Mrs Best about Ned and what I should do, she said that women like us marry men for security.

I must've felt sorry for Ned or something, and so the next day, I said I would go to the pictures with him, if he asked. He asked and we went to see *Blackmail* at the Ideal Cinema. You're looking a bit peaky, Kat. Are you all right, my love? Was it something I said? Let's take a break, shall we?

36

Granny Bower was correct. I hadn't been feeling well so I closed the recipe book. From the little Mama had told me about her, I had always imagined Granny Bower to be a happy, kind-hearted soul, who was constantly away from Dad and Grandpa Bower, 'on holidays'. Mama never met her in person, but Dad had spoken about her occasionally. His photographs of her showed her to be as plump as her jam roly-poly and almost as rosy. Her story so far had proved a bit surprising, but it had given me little cause to change my opinion of her.

I placed the recipe book on the shelf and went off to brew myself a pot of tea—something I rarely did. It just seemed right, somehow. By the time I got back to the recipe book, my phone showed I'd had three missed calls from 'Simeon' and a new email from *Ancestor-Finder DNA*. I checked the missed calls first.

Simone hadn't left a message, which was probably a bad thing. It signified that whatever she'd called about must have been very important, hence the two successive attempts, and apparently too sensitive to condense into a few words. A break-up perhaps? I hoped not. Simone was so rarely in a relationship and so bitchy when she was getting out of one, I didn't relish the thought of a long, anger-soaked, shriek-infused conversation about how awful/wonderful Klaryse was/wasn't/had been. I dialled Simone's number begrudgingly, knowing I had so little time to finish the recipe book before the exorcism that I really needed to return to it asap. Simone's phone rang. *Trring-trring.* She answered on the third trring.

'Where the fuck were you? How come you didn't answer me just now?' A fine hello. Simone was ever the diplomat.

'Hi, Simone. I was taking a dump,' I lied. 'What's wrong?'

'Has Nicole or Alex called you?'

'No, we're not talking, remember. Why?'

'Why? She lost the baby, that's why.'

'Oh no. When?'

'She started cramping or bleeding or something yesterday morning. They rushed to the hospital but it was all over by four.'

'Where is she now?'

'Home.' Simone hesitated. 'I don't know how to say this,' she stammered. Simone was never lost for words. Never. 'She was pretty upset after that argument at lunch. Alex called me instead of you because she'd been saying how she thought you'd be happy if she miscarried.'

'Why would I be happy she miscarried? I might not have thought the second baby thing was her greatest achievement, knowing how Alex felt and all, but I never hoped she'd miscarry.'

'Well, I don't think you should call her right now. Her hormones are doing strange things and I don't know how you'd be received.'

'Isn't it at precisely these times friends need to band together?' Nicole and I had had our differences before. We cooled off and then resumed where we left off.

'Friends, yes. But I think this time she crossed you off that list.'

I was probably falling off the end of it anyway, to be replaced by someone more relevant. 'Okay then. If you speak to Alex, tell him I'm really, really sorry. And let him know I never wanted any of this.'

'I will. I just thought you needed to know.'

'Of course, Simone. Thanks for the call.'

I put down my phone and began to think. I started to consider the previously un-considerable. *Could there be something wrong with me?* If I had faults, in my mind they were explained away by my upbringing—after all, I had a crazy mother and all that. I thought I knew exactly who and what I was and I'd generally assumed the world saw me as I did: smart, sassy, occasionally funny and straight-forward. Not perfect, no. I was too quick to anger, sometimes selfish and often impulsive. But fundamentally honest. Loveable. I had to admit, though, lately I wasn't feeling the love.

That Nicole could believe I wanted her to lose her baby was hor-ribly upsetting. I felt instantly compelled to spring a surprise visit on her, but stopped myself long enough to ask myself why. Would I be going for her benefit or mine? Was I that egocentric that I needed to defend myself, justify my actions at any cost? *No, it's not about you, Kat. Nicole needs to grieve.* It wasn't the time to patch up our friend-ship. I thought of how estranged from her I'd felt lately. A virtual stranger at Bailey's christening. Maybe it was too far gone already and there was no friendship to salvage anyway. Still, I felt an uneasiness in my stomach, as if I'd eaten something that wasn't quite right.

I was capable of obsession *(I should add that to my list)*, so to keep my mind from fixating on Nicole, I checked my emails. It was there among the hundred or so emails I hadn't yet read but kept, just in case I felt the urge to read them someday. *AncestorFinder DNA: You have a new match!* Aside from telling me that I was pretty much one hundred per cent Middle Eastern Jewish (apparently Dad had contributed almost nothing to my personal make up), *AncestorFinder DNA* had hooked me up with cousins I never knew I had. Most of them were in the fifth and greater category of cousin, so I hardly even bothered to look at their names. Today I would make an exception. Along with taking charge of my own feelings, I'd tidy up that inbox and hook up with some living relatives, for a change.

I logged into my account and clicked on my matches. I took a sip of my now lukewarm tea. A few seconds later, a series of names popped up, with details about the degree of our relationship. Usually, it was meaningless and ho-hum, but not today. Leading the list today was a new third cousin. Fearing I'd drop my cup, I positioned it on the far side of the desk. The name stunned me. There it was, in navy blue and white: *Georgia Bower. What the fluke? It's probably a common name. Maybe there's more than one.* I clicked on the smiley-face icon beside her name and waited. A moment later a grimacing Georgia and her brief bio popped up. *No doubt about it, that's Chris's Georgia, all right.* Georgia was indeed my new third cousin.

I logged out of *AncestorFinder DNA* and back in again, just to see if anything changed. Nothing did. I was desperate to tell someone. I wondered if Georgia knew and what she was going to do with this unexpected knowledge. I was too agitated by this information to return to Granny Bower, and I began pacing impatiently, willing Paul to return home. I stopped long enough to perform some basic calculations. Third cousins meant that Georgia and I must have had a common great-great-grandparent. Which also meant that Georgia and Chris must have had a common great-great-grandparent. Which, to me, seemed an uncomfortably close kinship for husband and wife.

My mind swung from Georgia to Nicole. It might have swung back again if I hadn't stopped it in mid-swing and kept it on Nicole.

I mulled over our evaporating friendship and where it had gone wrong. I knew it wasn't always, or ever, equal, especially now that Nicole had married and moved on to a world populated with other, new, more relevant friends with children. I was willing to wait out this latest fling, knowing she'd come back—eventually. Our friendship had history. It had endured bad hair, boyfriends and break-ups but it now seemed that what it couldn't endure was a simple difference of opinion. I was right and Nicole was wrong, but in the end what did that matter? *She really thinks I wanted her to miscarry. What kind of psychopath does she think I am?* I was faced with two choices: try to work myself out or continue pacing until Paul returned. Luckily, I didn't have to wait very long.

'I have some important developments to tell you about,' I said the moment he came in.

'But I've only been gone a few hours.'

'The first one's very sad. Remember how I told you that Alex and Nicole were expecting again? Well, Nicole's lost the baby.'

'That's awful.' Paul genuinely looked upset. 'What are you going to do?'

'Me? What can I do? Simone said that Nicole blames me for it. Remember how she reacted that day at lunch? Well, apparently she thinks I'd be happy about the miscarriage, so I'm giving her some time to get over her loss before I contact her.'

'That's sounds like a good idea. Is that it?'

'No, there's more. Take a look.' I pointed to my computer on the table. He plodded over, sat himself down and glanced at the screen.

'Woo hoo!' he exclaimed.

'Woo hoo what?' I said. 'How can you woo hoo that news?'

'But it puts you well and truly back in your place.' I felt a shadow pass over my face as he spoke, and he must have spotted it. Back-pedalling now, he added, 'I mean, you'll have to sort out your relationship with Georgia, now that you're cousins.'

'Nonsense. We don't have to do any such thing. But I can't help thinking about Chris and Georgia. That has to be no more than a couple of degrees of separation. I mean, it's a little bit sick, isn't it?'

'It's not sick. How do you know we're not related? I bet there are cousins—siblings even—who have married each other, or killed each other in a war, and never even known it.'

'I'm fairly certain we're not siblings,' I said.

Paul laughed and caught me in an embrace. 'What do you say, sis?'

'You're fully sick.'

We ended that conversation in the bedroom. After an early dinner of ham, cheese and spinach tarts from the bakery and a cup of coffee, I told Paul that I'd be transcribing Granny Bower's recipes for the rest of the evening.

'She been telling you tales, too?'

'Why do you ask? You don't really want to know.'

'It's just that you haven't said anything about them for a while.'

'I'm solving the problem. I have an appointment with a priest for the book and me to be exorcised next Tuesday. Which means I have four days left to get everything down, because I really don't know what might happen after that.'

'Okay, so she has been talking to you.'

'Yes, Paul, she has. But I really don't think I have a psychiatric disorder, and if you hear me out I'll tell you why.' He didn't say a word. 'I only hear the voices when I read the book. I assume that if I was certifiable I'd see and hear things all the time, but I have no other hallucinations, ever. That is, other than the one in which you're a supportive husband.'

Paul bristled. 'How haven't I been supportive? Have I said anything lately?'

'No, but I always feel like you're watching me, judging me, in case I lose it and start threatening strangers with carving knives or something.'

'That's called paranoia.'

'Uh huh. And what you just did now? Do you have a label for that, too?' Paul looked suitably admonished. 'At first I thought Mama's recipe book was a curse. You know what I've learned from all of this? So what if I did have the same problems that Mum had? It's not a bad thing, is it?'

Paul choked on his coffee. 'That's a turn around.'

'It is, isn't it, though? I've been working my way through a few things lately and I've had an epiphany.' Paul looked alarmed. 'I'm thinking that Mama didn't ask for her affliction any more than I asked to be given a talking recipe book. I'm starting to believe she probably did the best she could bringing us up. Under the circumstances. Not a great childhood, not even a good one, but the best she could manage.'

'And?'

'I feel lighter somehow. Relieved. I just wish Mama was still alive, so I could tell her that.'

Paul hugged me in a way that only Ethan (the world's best hugger) had ever hugged me. Paul enveloped me in his arms and held me tight. It felt like swaddling must feel to a baby. I was warm and safe and strangely euphoric.

Ten minutes later, I returned to Granny Bower. I lay on the couch with the recipe book propped against my knees and let it fall open at her fluffy scones. Granny Bower's voice started up exactly where she'd left off without missing a beat.

37

Ned and I stepped out together for a month before I let him kiss me and another three before he asked if I'd think about marrying him. On the Friday, I said I wanted a bit of time to decide, and you should have seen his face. He knew better than to say anything, other than that he'd wait for me for as long as I needed. I didn't know what to think. What did I want marrying Ned Bower? Wasn't I happy enough with my shop and my friends? Why would Rosie Bliss want to spoil all of that by getting married?

Mrs Best said that her children were her finest achievement—not that I ever saw them visit her. She said that there was no reason why I couldn't get married and still see my friends when I wanted. Mum wanted me to get married more than she wanted anything else in the world. Ned wanted to marry me and he'd had such a bloody awful time with his last wife, my heart ached for him. Everybody knows that weddings are the happiest of times and getting married was the sensible thing to do. It was the right thing to do. A nice, kind man like Ned would see me right. That's what I told myself. On the Monday, I said to Ned I'd marry him and stick by him. Ned and I tied the knot just a month after Lawrence Olivier married Jill Esmond. Except that my dress was twice as big but only half as grand as hers.

We didn't start off married life nearly as fast as most newly-weds. I was a chubby girl by then, you see, and I never felt comfortable cuddling up with him, if you know what I mean. Somehow, it never felt right for me. Anyway, Ned wanted me to sell the teashop and he said not to worry, he'd take care of me and our babies when they came. He had enough work as a carpenter to see us all right. Trade at the teashop had got so slow of late, I didn't know if I had a business to sell. Still, if you don't ask you don't get, so I put out the word that The Rose Tearoom was seeking a new proprietor. Blow me down if I didn't get an offer a week later! That night we had a slap up meal and I got a bit tipsy at the Black Horse, hahaha. Ned and I moved off the starting line that night.

With what money I'd saved and what I got from the sale of my teashop and what Ned had scraped together, we had just enough to buy ourselves a small flat in Brixton. Most of Ned's work was in South London anyway, so it made sense for us to stay in the same neighbourhood. It wasn't much but it was clean, it had four proper rooms, it had electricity and it meant I didn't have to share a toilet anymore. I celebrated the day we moved in by baking Ned a cake. Was I happy? Of course I was, Kat, my love. Why would you ask?

Our Charlie was born in 1933—yes, that's right, your dad, Kat—right there at home in Brixton. I thought on Mrs Best's words that first time I clapped eyes on my boy. He was all wrinkly pink and white and chubby, just like one of my iced cupcakes. She was right; he was our crowning achievement and wasn't Ned chuffed to finally have a son. I got a fright after the birth, when I tried to fit into my old clothes. I'd eaten for two when I was expecting and no matter what I did, the weight never did shift itself. Not that Ned ever complained. He said I should buy myself a set of new clothes, but for a time there, I could hardly get myself out of bed, let alone go out shopping.

Ned must've been concerned because he sent word to my mum, and she come over for tea one day, all of a sudden. She said she understood how I was feeling and that, for a while after she had each one of her babies—but me especially—she didn't know what was wrong with her, neither. It was like someone had drained all the life out of her. She said not to tell anyone else, lest they call me a cruel mother or some such, and lock me up in an asylum. She said I'd come right sooner or later and I should make sure Ned never catches me running about in my smalls ever again. As bad as I was feeling, she didn't half make me laugh that day. Can you imagine? With all that jiggling about!

When Charlie was four months old, Dick come back into my life. One day, when Mum come over to visit our Charlie with my younger sister Annie and her boy, as we was talking, she let slip that Dick had been nabbed for selling stolen goods in the Black Horse pub around the corner from us. She said that him and Kitty had been living about a hundred yards away in a boarding house for quite a long time. I never saw either one of them in the neighbourhood. She said that was probably because Dick was in the Scrubs these last few years and, since I was asking about him, would I go to visit him with her? Me, visit Dick in prison? Was she mad? But your great-granny was ever a bit of a nag. A half hour later I said I would. Ned was none too happy about it, let me tell you.

The next week, Mum and I took the tube to East Acton station and walked to Wormwood Scrubs prison from there. Dick was looking as scrawny as ever, and sporting a black eye, courtesy of one of the other prisoners. They'd quarrelled over something or other and Mum told him to be sure to watch his mouth in future. If he'd been at home, she'd have clipped him behind the ear for good measure. Anyhow, he asked if we'd drop in on Kitty sometimes and see how she was going, since she hadn't come in to see him for a while and he was worried sick about her. I told Mum on the way home that, if she liked, I'd visit Kitty for her, since we'd got along so well before, and she said that would suit her fine.

A week or two later, I made good on my promise. Kitty was living with her little girl in a single room what she rented off a man from South Africa. To say it was horrible just didn't do it justice. She was working in the Railway Hotel and scared silly that one day someone would find out she was leaving her girl all alone in the room while she worked. I told her not to worry, she could drop her with me and I'd look after her, at which Kitty cried. Anyway, I watched her Sally while Kitty worked and we got even closer.

The one thing about being dead is you don't need to lie about anything no more. I wanted to tell it to you straight. You probably guessed I wasn't like most girls. Me and Kitty, well, after a bit we fell in love. I was always too embarrassed to say it until now—we fell in love. It just seemed right to us. I knew I liked girls much better than boys since I was young, but when I was

a kid, I thought everyone did. I expected to grow out of it someday, but I never did. It turned out that I liked them in a different
way, but you couldn't say anything in them days. They said it
was unnatural. Oh, how I prayed and prayed just to be normal!
It was only when I met Mrs Best and her friends that I realised
there were women like me everywhere.

Anyway, Kitty said she hated Dick. She felt the same about
me as I did for her, and we saw each other as often as we could.
It never occurred to me that I wasn't just cheating on my husband, but on my brother as well. If I went to see Dick and he
asked about Kitty, how my heart pounded. I thought he'd see it
written on my face. We kept it between ourselves, me and Kitty,
and our love blossomed in a run-down, single room in the worst
street of Brixton. That was until Dick walked in one day and
caught us.

I knew Dick must've been due for release, but he never said
exactly when, or if, he was coming home. That day, as luck would
have it, me and Kitty was in bed together when he walked in. At
first he looked confused, but then his face went all red and the
veins in his neck stuck out. 'You sodding bitch!' he yelled, and
grabbed me by the hair and pulled me off the bed.

While Dick lay into me with his fists, Kitty threw herself on
his back screaming.

'Stop it, Dick, you'll kill her.'

'I should kill both of you!' He was lashing out at us like a wild
animal. He slapped Kitty across the face and she fell backwards.
'So this is what you do while I'm doin' bird? You're a pair of sick,
perverted bitches!'

He kept throwing punches at us, some of which found their
mark and some of which missed by a mile, until he lost his bal-
ance and fell over. His head hit the floor hard and he was out
cold. Kitty was crying hysterically that he was dead, and her
neighbour was pounding on the door. I put on a dressing gown
and I opened it a crack.

I must've looked a sight, all battered and bruised.

'We're sorry for the noise. My brother came home drunk,' I
said. 'He's bad when he's drunk.'

'I should call the police,' she said. She was a bloody busybody, that one.

'No, no need for that. He's knocked himself out. There won't be no more trouble, I promise.'

She was trying to see in, but my foot was right up against the door, so she couldn't push it open. 'Another peep out of any of you, and I'll get the police,' she said.

'All right, yes. There won't be.'

I shut the door. The room looked like I'd slaughtered a pig. Kitty was holding a hankie up to her nose to stop the blood. She was making a sound a bit like a dog when it's had its rear end kicked. Her left eye was already swollen shut and she looked like she'd gone ten rounds with Jack Bloomfield.

'We have to do something now before he wakes up,' I said.

Kitty stopped whimpering and she started shaking. I got her dressed as best I could, while she sat there on the floor. Her clothes looked a bit cock-eyed but at least she wasn't naked. I took a look at my face in the mirror. Really, I wasn't too bad. His fists had landed mostly on my body. I was thinking it was a good thing that I was fat enough to take the punches. I was also thinking, thank God we'd left Sally with Ned.

'Come on, girl,' I said, cleaning her face up with a bit of old towel. 'We can't stay here. Pack your things and we'll find you somewhere else.'

I was already thinking of Mrs Best, my port in a storm. Kitty packed a case and we left just as Dick began groaning and rolling over. She took the key and locked him in. It was when the cold air hit me that I felt the pain. Kitty pulled her hat down as far as she could to cover her face, but no one was looking at us. I don't quite remember how, but we got to Mrs Best's before dark. She said she was sorry, the house was full up, and then she made a few phone calls and eventually found Kitty a room with a friend of hers. With Kitty settled, I just had to go home and face Ned, glad that I'd never given Dick our address and hoping that Mum wouldn't.

By the time I got home, Sally and Charlie had had their supper and were asleep. Ned took a look at me and shook his head.

'Where the hell've you been?' he asked. 'I've been worried sick.'

'Has Mum been round? Or Dick?'

'No, no one's been. Why?'

'Dick's out of jail. He come round Kitty's and gave us both a right walloping.' I took off my coat. My neck had bruises where Dick had tried to strangle me—I forgot to tell you about that bit—and the rest of me was black and blue.

'Where's Dick now? I'll kill the bastard.'

'No, don't do that.'

'Why? Why did he do that to you?'

'He had his reasons,' I said hoping he wouldn't ask but knowing he would.

'Rosie? What were you up to, girl?'

'I'm so sorry, Ned. You're such a good husband. You don't deserve this, especially after the last…'

'Rosie?'

Best tell the truth. He was bound to find out sooner or later and there was no chance that Dick would keep his trap shut. 'I was with Kitty. In bed.'

'What? Was she sick?'

I told Ned what we were up to and I thought he was going to keel over. His mouth dropped open and he couldn't look at me for a long time. Then he got up and slapped me across the face.

'What's wrong with you, girl? And what about Charlie? Did you even think of him?' I hadn't really. 'Wasn't I good enough for you?'

'It's not that, Ned. I couldn't help it.'

'That's exactly what she said when she left me.' I knew he meant his ex-wife.

'I'm sorry, Ned. I'll change. I'll never do it again. I promise.'

'I loved you, Rosie, and then you go and do this. What do you want me to say?'

I thought about it for a bit, then I saw the tears in his eyes. 'Say you'll forgive me.'

He sat down quietly with his head in his hands. Eventually, he looked up.

'Will you see a doctor?' he asked me.

'Yes, of course.'

'If you see a doctor and get yourself treated, I'll think about it. You sleep with the kids tonight, Rose.'

I slept with Charlie and Sally for three nights, then Kitty come over to collect Sally when I was out. Mum dropped in later that same day to tell me how much I'd shamed her and how she always knew there was something wrong with me. She said Dick was furious with me and Kitty, and I should make certain not to give him any further cause to look for me. Unless I stopped all this nonsense, she said, I wouldn't be her daughter no more.

I kept my word to Ned and I went to see Dr Smith the next day. He said he had a friend named Dr Lewis, working at the Maudsley Hospital not far away, and he'd set up an appointment for me at Dr Lewis's outpatient clinic. He did and I went. He was a nice man, Dr Lewis was, and he said it would be hard, but some German doctor called Fraud—I said he should have been a lawyer with a name like that—said that if I was determined enough, I could develop proper feelings for Ned. He said I'd learn to control my feelings for women, but they mightn't go away completely.

I got myself right back into baking cakes for a café down the road. Dr Lewis said it was my therapy. What joy it was to be surrounded by flour and eggs and butter and sugar! What happiness to watch a sponge swell up and go golden brown! And then the decoration turned it into a bit of happiness on a plate! Ah, I'd missed that.

I was doing all right for a while there, until I got a letter from Kitty saying she was going back to Dublin with Sally. She said Dick had been sniffing around, saying that she was an unfit mother and that he was going to take Sally away. She said she was sorry for what had happened and it was all her fault. It was better that we never see each other again. I tore up the letter and then I felt sad I'd done it. I tried to glue it together, but it wasn't any good. Now I had nothing left of Kitty.

I don't know what happened to me that day, but it was like someone turned off the light. I hadn't felt that bad since just after

Charlie was born and I didn't know what to do. I stayed in bed for days and I didn't want to see nothing or hear nothing. Ned became a dab hand at cooking and cleaning, and he kept us both right enough, I suppose. I just didn't want to *be*, if you know what I mean. I got so bad one day that Ned got scared. He stuck me in a taxi and took me back to the Maudsley Hospital. They kept me there for a while until I began feeling better and then I went home.

I was in and out of hospital more times than Charlie could count. Ned told him I'd gone away on holidays each time and sometimes Charlie begged and begged for me to take him with me. Of course I never could. First they give me pills that made me sleepy, then they give me electric shocks. They give me all sorts of treatments meant to make me better. At the end of it all, there I was, not knowing who I was no more or what I wanted. Oh, I laughed all right for as long as I could manage it when I was home, just to keep Ned and Charlie happy, but the bliss had gone right out of poor old Rosie.

Charlie was six when the war with Germany began. A few weeks later, the children was being evacuated out of London and Ned said that Charlie should go too. I was crying that day as I packed his little case, and still crying as I put him on the train and waved him goodbye. He asked me to come, but I told him I couldn't. This holiday was just for children. Then he said it was funny, wasn't it, Mum, that this time he was the one going on holidays and I was the one staying behind. How my heart broke! They let us know that he was safe with a nice family in Sussex. Charlie sent us a letter, which I kept, in which he'd written his name and drawn us a cow.

By the end of the year, they was rationing meat and, when I was well, I became an expert at going off on the tube to the country, and looking for nettles and berries and mushrooms and turning them into something delicious. By then, I really could make silk purses out of sows' ears—not that we had too many of them about, more's the pity. Not long after that, Ned was called up. I only went out foraging occasionally after that. I didn't see much point to cooking for one.

I don't remember exactly where I'd been the day I heard that Ned had been wounded in action. They said that they had confirmed he was in a military hospital. Time stood still after that and I thought, rather than being idle, I'd do something positive. The next day I went out mushrooming by myself, and I found some lovely mushrooms. I thought, right, I'm going home now to make myself a mock-meat pie out of them mushrooms and I did. It was nothing short of delicious and, greedy pig that I was, I gobbled it all up. I mustn't have been as good a forager as I'd thought, because blow me down if I didn't start cramping in the stomach something shocking. Sick as a dog I was. Turns out those mushrooms had been toadstools. I never did hear that Ned'd died in that military hospital that day, because I got there first. Can you believe it? I'd gone and poisoned myself! What a silly, silly me!

38

Granny Bower's story left me open-mouthed. Poor Rosie! I could never imagine Simone marrying a man and having to deny her sexuality. Tears welled in the corners of my eyes and spilled down my cheeks. I, who hadn't cried since childhood; I, who hadn't even cried when either her father or her mother died. I had been so busy judging everybody, I had forgotten to remember that people came with backstories. Everyone was fallible, even me.

'Oh, darling,' said Granny Bower. 'There I've gone and made you sad again. Don't cry, my little Kitty-Kat!'

'But Dad? What happened to Dad?'

'My mum brought up your dad, Kat. Surely you knew that?'

'He never said.' I dabbed at my eyes with my sleeves but it soon became obvious I'd need to get something more substantial. 'It all makes sense now. Dad was marrying you when he married my mother. You both had problems—different ones, of course—but he was trying to fix them! Poor Dad! I've been such a bitch to everyone! I feel so sorry for all of you! You didn't do anything wrong, none of you, it was just the way you were! And there I was hating poor Mama!'

'Oh no, darling Kat, don't break your heart over us. It's all been a bit of a shock for you, hasn't it, love?'

'I suppose it has. I am so glad to have met you all,' I wept. 'Would you mind if I put the book away now?'

'Mind? Me? Of course not. You have a little rest, my love, and I'll be here when you need me.'

'Thanks. I love you, Granny Bower.' There. I said it. It didn't hurt and I meant it. I put away the book, picked up some tissues and wiped my eyes and nose. All the emotion of the day had exhausted me. That, and I still wasn't feeling completely myself. I made a mental note to make an appointment with my doctor in the morning.

Paul had already been asleep in bed for an hour by the time I climbed in next to him. He stirred for a moment and then went straight back to snoring. As I listened to him, I realised that he had a gift. Like Jimi Hendrix, he was able to do the snoring equivalent to simultaneously playing both lead and rhythm on the same guitar. While his throat kept up a gurgling drone, his nose and mouth whistled with each breath in and out, a bit like a harmonica. Other nights, it would have made me angry. Tonight, I kissed his stubbly cheek and cuddled into him. He had been far more patient with me than any normal man would have been. *Thank God he isn't normal.* I sniffed his neck. He smelled warm and sweet and, well, Paully. From the foot of the bed, I heard a doggy sigh. Boz Scraggs had settled in for the night and all was well.

I fell asleep with my arm draped over Paul's chest and dreamed of my mother. In my dream, she was middle-aged again, vibrant and happy, which in life she had so seldom been. When I awoke from it, I remembered two things about the dream: the first was that Mama had said that she loved me over and over again. The second was that she had asked me to cook a meal for my dead relatives.

'Set the table and cook food from my book, Kat, and five of your relatives will come.'

'What, Mama?'

'Promise me, Kat. You must cook for them. It is the only way.' She was insistent. 'Do not forget; cook this meal for them.'

'All right, Mama. I promise,' and then I was conscious.

The clock said it was a little after three and Paul was now sleeping peacefully on his back. Cook for five of my relatives? I began to mull it over. Of course, she must have meant Fotini, Alegra, Jeanne, Rosie. *That's four. And Mama—five.* I knew from past experience that I could have a brilliant idea halfway through the night which, having assured myself I would remember, was all but forgotten by morning. For that reason, I always kept paper and pencil by the bed. I felt for it and scrawled myself a brief message in the dark. And then I rolled over and fell into a deep sleep.

Just before breakfast, I called the doctor and made an appointment for the following Monday. I made coffee. Only then did I tell Paul about my dream.

'Okay,' he responded, 'so you think that she meant the dead will be turning up to our house for a free chow down? I didn't think they did that sort of thing.'

'I don't know. Maybe it's all about the recipes. Or me cooking. Maybe they'll turn up but not eat. I can only tell you what she told me.' Paul's eyebrows were raised higher than those of an aging Hollywood star after a Botox treatment. 'Sounds weird, I know, but I promised her.'

'All right. And when is this thing going to happen?'

'It's Saturday today, so I was thinking Sunday lunch. The exorcism's Tuesday, therefore it's probably best to do it as soon as possible, just in case it works.'

'Do you think that's enough notice?' he wisecracked. 'Don't get your hopes up, Kat.'

I smothered Paul with my breasts as I hugged him. 'They're getting bigger. I like it,' he commented.

Bigger and sore. Oh, wait a minute, I know! I'm pre-menstrual. I began to make mental calculations. *When was my last period?* With Mama's stroke and then her dying, the arguments with everyone, the lawyers and the cookbook, I had totally forgotten about my period. I counted out days on my fingers. *That couldn't be right, could it?* I counted again. *Seventy-nine days?* I hadn't had one in nearly three months. I wasn't the most regular of gals, but I couldn't ever remember being that late.

I teetered about, chewing over this revelation until Paul asked me what was wrong. 'Oh, nothing. Just thinking about the lunch,' I lied. 'I'm making up a shopping list.' I picked up my phone, found my shopping app and typed in the first item of what would undoubtedly be a very long list. *Pregnancy test.* Now I would be able to focus my attention once again on the recipes.

39

After we cleaned up the breakfast dishes, I returned to my notes rather than the cookbook, to figure out which of the many recipes to choose for my lunch and which to leave out. I started by choosing sixteen of my favourites. That done, I shortened the list to ten. I hadn't cooked anything much since the christening bourekia, and even then I had needed Paul's help. Ten dishes were far too many. I decided I would pick just one recipe from each of my four relatives plus Mama, without whom I wouldn't be. Five courses to celebrate their amazing lives. It didn't seem nearly enough commemoration, but it would have to suffice. Not having cooked for lunch guests (dead or alive) in a long time, if ever, really, I figured it'd be best to keep it relatively simple.

I chose Jeanne's egg and lemon soup followed by Mama's spinach and leek pitta, Fotini's bandit's lamb and, to finish, Alegra's bunuelos and Granny Bower's light-as-air sponge with coffee. Two sweets seemed decadent, but this was a celebration feast and I'd had a hard time choosing between them. I ran the menu past Paul, who looked disinterested.

'Seems an awful lot for us and five dead people,' he commented.

'Well, you can never have too much food. Don't forget, some of my relatives haven't eaten in centuries. They're probably starving.' Then I thought of Jeanne and felt ashamed of my flippancy.

'Okay, whatever. Just don't whine about it.'

The old me would have leapt at Paul's throat and to my own defence, but he was right: I whined a lot and the new me was woman enough to admit it. 'I won't. If I get into any trouble, I'll ask pleasantly for your help.'

I made out the rest of my list and left Paul, who was going to take Boz for a long walk. I drove to the shopping centre and found everything I needed and it all seemed pretty straightforward. Except the pregnancy test. I hadn't used one for nearly a decade and things had clearly changed. There were blue ones, pink ones, ones that had early detection, others that told you how many days since conception—

who knew there would be so many choices? A decade or so ago, the only result I'd prayed for was negative, but I had to admit that I'd experienced a subtle shift since then. I examined my feelings. I wasn't so certain what I wanted now. Suddenly, the possibility of life didn't seem quite as daunting. My immediate problem was just which stick I should pee on. Uncertainty in my case always led to profligacy, and so I bought one of each. Just to be sure.

I had become so adept at sneaking the recipe book in and out of the house that Paul, who always helped me bring in the shopping, knew nothing about the tests. I thought it was best not to say anything to him yet, in case I was just going through an early menopause. I probably wasn't pregnant so why worry him about something that might never eventuate?

I read and re-read the recipes. Sunday lunch was now less than a day away. *You can do this, Kat, you know you can.* I was worried on a number of levels. Would I be able to cook the dishes and do them justice? Were my dead relatives all going to turn up, and if so, what form would they take? What would I do if I was pregnant?

I decided against taking the test before our Sunday lunch—I didn't want the added distraction if I was, or the heartache that I had to confess I'd probably feel if I wasn't. If I didn't know either way, then I'd be free to enjoy the moment. I resolved I'd do the test on Sunday evening.

I began lunch preparations immediately, washing the leeks and the spinach three times, just as Mama always instructed, slicing them and sweating them off in a frypan. Once cooled, I mixed in the feta, sprinkled it with nutmeg and tasted it. It was unbelievably good. I covered the bowl and put it in the fridge. *Look at me, guys, I'm in the zone!* Under my direction, chicken carcasses were transfiguring themselves into an unctuous broth. Lamb was marinating, paper parcels ready for layering, vegetables washed and dried. I whipped cream in a bowl and set it aside. I decided I'd make the bunuelos and sponge cake in the morning.

Meanwhile, Boz Scraggs sat diligently under the kitchen table, hopeful that something—anything—would fall off the bench, so he could tidy up the mess and then mop the floor clean. Paul came and went, asking if I needed anything and nodding with approval when I said no, I had everything in hand. He washed up as I prepared, made us teas and coffees, doled out crackers and cheese, all without saying a word. For once, everything was in harmony.

By twilight, with preparations complete, I was totally worn out. We ate out that evening, in a little Italian restaurant we used to visit when we first moved into our house, but had since forgotten about. There was a new sign outside but inside, time had stood still. Nothing had changed in the intervening years, not even the rickety, bentwood chairs, which were probably the most uncomfortable I'd sat on in recent memory. But the scent of tomatoes and garlic wafting from the kitchen was heavenly. With a plate of *pasta con pesce e vongole* steaming my pores open, I was in heaven.

When we were done, the owner approached, a quizzical look on his face.

'I remember you,' he said, '*ma*, you no come here in years.'

'We went away for a while. We only just came back.' There was no good way to say *we got sick of your limited and unvarying menu*, so Paul, bless him, devised a little white lie, designed to protect the owner's feelings.

'Oh. So where you go?'

It would be foolish for Paul to over-complicate his lie, so I stepped in and did as I always do: I deployed my masterstroke, taking up the conversation. 'Yes, but you've been here a long time.' Judging from the decor, it could have been half a century. 'Twenty years? But your food is even better than I remember.'

'*Molto grazie.* We been here thirty-eight years. *E* you? You have a *famiglia* now? Any *bambini*?'

'Perhaps,' I replied. Paul stared at me. In my defence, it was the exhaustion speaking. I hadn't had time to properly form the answer in my mind.

We exchanged a few more platitudes with the owner, paid the bill and Paul ushered me through the door.

'Perhaps?' he asked as soon as we'd cleared the entrance. 'He asks, do you have kids and you answer, perhaps? What on frigging earth does that mean?'

'Oh, is that what he meant? I thought he was asking if we were staying here for good…' Even I wasn't convinced by my explanation.

'No, you didn't. You know exactly what he said.'

I didn't respond until we'd reached the car. As soon as Paul shut his door I began. 'There's a chance—a very, very small chance—we might be pregnant.'

'What?' Paul returned, followed closely by, 'Wow!'

'I didn't want to get your hopes up 'til I knew one way or the other, but it just slipped out. I haven't had a period in a while. But there could be other reasons for that.'

'So, why don't you get a test kit and see?'

'I already bought one today.' No need to tell him the full horror of my indecisiveness.

'And?'

'And I'll take the test tomorrow. After lunch is over.'

'Why not now?'

'Tomorrow, Paul. We've waited this long, a few more hours won't make any difference.'

'I guess so. I mean, I'd want to know straight away but I suppose I can't make you do it.'

'Tomorrow, Paul.'

Paul started up the car. Having said it aloud had somehow made it more real. I began to think that, if we were—although we probably weren't—but, if we were, and only for simplicity's sake, it would probably be easier if I shared the same surname as my child. Kat Cage was definitely still out, although Katerina Cage sounded quite melodious. It was a great writing name. *Katerina Cage.* I put it down on my long list of things to consider.

40

Sunday, it rained. It was drumming on the roof even before sunrise, and it just didn't stop. Fat, pregnant drops were tumbling like coins from heavens the colour of slate. If I had been expecting real-world guests, I might have been concerned for their welfare, but as it was, I imagined a bit of water would hardly prove an impediment to Sunday lunch. I showered and dressed, hair tied up in ribbons.

'Ooh, sexy mama,' quipped Paul.

'Shut up.' *Not really in the mood, today.* 'It's purely utilitarian. I'd prefer not to shed hairs in my cooking.'

'I doubt our guests would care,' he replied. 'You, on the other hand, look good enough to eat.'

'Paul!'

I shimmied past his outstretched arms and into the kitchen. Beaters at the ready, I began the dough for the bunuelos first, so they'd have plenty of time to prove. I turned to the sponge cake next. *No fat on the beaters or the bowl, please, madam.* I could hear Granny Bower's voice ringing in my ears, even though she hadn't yet arrived. I made an amazing fluff mountain out of egg whites, cutting the flour into the yolks gently and slowly, not to upset the magic in progress. *Joy.* I was in my element. The batter ribboned out of my bowl and settled into the tins. A sharp tap, and I pushed them into my preheated oven. Through the glass, I watched them puff and colour. When they'd developed a midsummer tan, I took them out gently.

By eleven, the sun had finally broken through. The sponges had cooled on their racks, ready for assembly. The lamb had already been baking for a few hours and the pitta was awaiting its turn. I'd start heating the stock just before one and add the finishing touches that turn it into soup. I expected my guests would have arrived by then.

The scents of the meal combined in the kitchen and then drifted off into their separate corners, each one a paradise in itself. Paul came and went, looking pleased with himself, even though he had hardly lifted a finger. By one-fifteen, we were waiting for our guests to arrive. I figured that was close enough to lunchtime in any realm.

Five minutes later, the doorbell rang. *Strange, that they should choose to come through the front door.* From the kitchen, I heard voices in the hallway: Paul's *I'm so glad you could make it at such short notice,* followed by an inaudible response. I pulled the ribbons out of my hair and scurried towards the dining room.

'Ethan!' I glanced at Paul who had tactfully turned away.

'Hi, Kat,' said Ethan, kissing me on both cheeks and giving me one of his trademark hugs. 'I guess I beat my parents here.'

'It's so good to see you!' I said, leading him into the kitchen. 'You might as well help me take this in.'

'My parents were so surprised to hear from Paul yesterday, and so happy that you wanted to mend your relationship,' he continued as he followed me.

'I'm glad to hear it,' I replied. 'It's crazy for family to break apart this way.' What was Paul thinking? This could prove to be a very interesting lunch. Paul made himself scarce, rustling up a nice *nebbiolo* to serve with the meal.

'I couldn't agree more.'

The doorbell rang again. Paul rushed past me in a blur, arriving at the door first. It was Chris (much thinner now) with Georgia and Poppy in the rear. Poppy looked tanned and fabulous.

'Come in,' chimed Paul. 'So glad to see you all.'

We might have exchanged air kisses but the sentiments were real. I put my arm around Georgia and led her to the dining room.

'When Paul said you were cooking,' said Chris, 'I told him we wouldn't miss it for the world.' As he sat, he added, 'You were such a good cook when you were young, Kat. I always wondered why you stopped.'

I thought for a moment. 'I guess I just didn't want to be like Mama.' *Four of them and two of us.* I moved the seventh chair away from the table and back into the corner. 'Before we begin, I just want to apologise to you all for having been so angry all these years.'

'And I want to apologise for always being so correct and judgemental,' returned Chris.

Paul poured out the wine. 'Here's to family. To those we are born with and to those we collect along the way. To those present today and to those passed. Let's always remember to celebrate our differences as well as our similarities.'

'To family.'

It occurred to me as we sat and talked and ate, that this must have been what Mama had intended for us all along. Maybe no one else was coming for lunch today.

'You know, Chris, these dishes are all made from recipes out of Mama's cookbook. You remember, the one Georgia almost threw away.'

'They're delicious,' he replied, helping himself to another piece of pitta and a chunk of lamb.

'I'm sorry about that, Kat,' said Georgia. 'I don't know what came over me. Can you forgive me?'

'Actually, I believe I can.'

At the end of the meal, just before dessert, Chris darted back to the car and returned with an enormous, misshapen parcel, tied up in brown paper and string.

'Mama left me all of Dad's tools. I don't know why, I was never any good with my hands. Anyhow, I made you this.' He thrust the package in my direction. I unwrapped it and looked at it for a while. It was a large, hinged cuboid made out of oak. It weighed a ton.

'Why it's a… It's a…' I was lost for a description.

'It's a manuscript box. For when you finally get around to writing that book you've been talking about for years. That, or you can just store odds and ends in it.'

'That's so thoughtful! It's really beautiful, Chris.'

Chris frowned as he resumed, 'You probably won't believe this, but I have to tell you about this weird thing that happened every time I got out any of Dad's tools…' Georgia flashed him one of her shut-up-immediately-or-you'll-pay-for-it-later looks. After my recent experiences and, now that she and I were cousins, I knew exactly what she meant. Chris stopped abruptly without finishing what he was about to reveal, and never again returned to the topic.

We chewed and chatted for the rest of the afternoon and it was already dark by the time Paul and I waved them goodbye.

'Now that's what they'd call a seismic change in attitude all round,' he said.

'Yes,' I agreed. 'They must have been the relatives Mama was telling me about in my dream. It feels good to have cleared the air. I missed them, you know.'

'I know. I guess I should call my sister too.' Paul was evidently feeling sentimental.

'Why don't we invite her over for a meal,' I suggested.

'Okay, I'll ask her.'

We started clearing up the vestiges of a meal well enjoyed. As we did, my mind drifted back to Mama's message in my dream.

'The thing I don't understand is why Mama said that *five* of my relatives would be present.'

'Maybe she meant me?' Paul suggested.

'No, no I don't think so. I think she was definitely referring to the guests being five blood relatives, not including either of us. It makes no sense to me, otherwise.'

We washed up whatever didn't fit into the dishwasher, straightened the dining room and I made a pot of camomile tea. We sat on the sofa, sipping the tea and eating the rest of the bunuelos. Then Paul brightened.

'So, you're sure your mother said there'd be five of your relatives at lunch?'

'Yes.'

'Well, maybe she was right.' I opened my mouth to protest as Paul continued. 'Work it out, Kat: Chris, Georgia, Poppy and Ethan. But what if there was a fifth all along?' He grinned at what seemed to be a private joke. 'What if we just couldn't see them?'

'Are you saying Mama's spirit came along to watch?'

'No, not really, but here's an idea.' I strained my ears to hear Paul's spin on this one. *This better be good.*

'What if you brought the fifth guest along with you?'

'It's okay, I'm being exorcised on Tuesday, remember?'

'No, that's not what I mean.' I willed Paul to get to the point. 'I'm thinking number five's somewhere in there.' He pointed to my belly. 'I'm thinking that maybe you'd better hurry up and do that pregnancy test.'

The pregnancy test! After an afternoon of conversation, warm company and wonderful food, I'd completely forgotten about the pregnancy test. I trotted back to the bathroom and pulled out all four boxes and returned to the kitchen. Unabashed, I spread them out on the table.

'Which do you think I should do?'

'Don't they all do the same thing?' Paul was as clueless as I was.

'Probably. Maybe I'll do the simplest one first, the one with the quickest response. Then I can slowly work my way through all of them.'

'Sounds like a plan. Do you need some help?'

My dear ever-obliging husband. Did I really need his help to pee on a stick? I told him I thought I could do that by myself, no problem and without a worry in the world. So then I gave Paul a kiss, went straight to the bathroom, tore apart the packaging and I did.

The End

THE RECIPES

Jeanne's Egg and Lemon Soup

1 whole 1.8 kg chicken, or equivalent weight chicken
    pieces or chicken carcasses

cold water

1 onion, peeled

1 carrot

1 stick celery

1 bay leaf

handful of parsley

2 tsps salt

pepper

⅓ cup short grain rice

1 tbsp cornflour dissolved in a little water

3 eggs

juice of two lemons

Place chicken or carcasses into a large saucepan and cover with water (about 2 to 2 ½ litres). Add (whole) vegetables, herbs and salt. Bring slowly to the boil, skim off any scum and simmer gently for about 45 minutes, till the chicken is well cooked and almost falls apart. Strain out the vegetables, herbs and chicken and pour the stock into a large saucepan. Discard the herbs and any bones. If you want a traditional soup, use the chicken meat and vegetables elsewhere. If you prefer a hearty version, chop them roughly, keep warm and reintroduce into the soup just before serving.

Reheat the stock and when it reaches boiling point, add the rice. Simmer gently for 20 minutes or until the rice is cooked, stirring occasionally. Take the stock and rice mix off the heat while you stir in the cornflour and water mixture, then replace on the heat and bring back to a simmer for a few seconds.

In a large bowl or heatproof jug, beat together the eggs and the juice of one of the lemons. Take the stock mix off the heat, allow it to cool slightly and trickle five or more ladlefuls of the stock slowly into the egg and lemon mixture as you stir it. Then very slowly dribble that mixture back into the remaining stock as you stir the soup, taking care not to let it curdle. You can reheat it very gently, provided you stir and do not cover the saucepan. Never bring the soup back to the boil after eggs are introduced, as it will curdle. Season and add additional lemon juice, to taste.

Mama's Spinach and Leek Pie

1 packet commercial or 1 quantity homemade phyllo

150 g unsalted butter, melted

2 tbsps breadcrumbs

2 tbsps olive oil

1 leek

3 bunches of spinach or 500 g spinach leaves

500 g good Greek feta

1 beaten egg

¼ tsp ground nutmeg or a large handful of fresh parsley
or fresh dill

Trim off any coarse green outer leaves and the ends of the leek and any stems off the spinach. Wash the leek and spinach very thoroughly (at least two or three times) to remove all dirt. Drain well and slice the leek finely. Slice the spinach if the leaves are very large.

Heat the oil slightly in a large frypan, add leek slices and sauté gently. Soften but do not brown. Add the spinach in batches and cook over a low heat until completely wilted. Allow any juices to evaporate or alternatively take off heat and drain any juices away in a sieve. Place the leek and spinach mixture in a bowl.

Chop either parsley or dill finely (but not both) and add to the bowl. If using nutmeg instead of the herbs, sprinkle it over the mixture. Drain and crumble the feta into the bowl. Add the egg and mix thoroughly. Season with pepper but not salt, as the feta has enough salt to season the mix.

Brush the baking dish with a little butter and layer with about 8 sheets of commercial phyllo (or 3 homemade sheets), brushing a little butter between each sheet. Allow the edges to overlap the dish slightly. Scatter the bottom with breadcrumbs, spoon in the filling and top with another 8 sheets of phyllo, brushing well between each sheet with the butter. Tuck in the edges, brush the top and score into squares or triangles. Bake at 180 degrees C moderate oven until golden (about 45 mins).

Fotini's Bandit's Lamb

1.5 kg lamb leg, cut into large pieces, on or off the bone,
    or lamb chops

3 onions, sliced

4 large potatoes peeled and cut into large pieces (optional)

2 tsp salt (or to taste)

1 tsp pepper (or to taste)

2-3 cloves garlic, sliced

juice of 1 small lemon

2 tsps dried oregano (preferably Greek rigani)

2 bay leaves

¼ cup olive oil

a large sheet of baking or greaseproof paper (about 40 cm
    x 70 cm), and another of heavy brown paper and
    string to tie, or foil

Take the sheet of greaseproof or baking paper and fold it in three widthways, so the two end thirds overlap slightly. Open the paper out again. Lay it on top of a sheet of heavy brown paper or foil, slightly bigger than the baking paper.

Place all the ingredients except the onions into a bowl and mix together. Put aside. Spread half the sliced onions in a layer, covering the centre third of the paper, leaving a border of about 5 cm top and bottom. Season lightly. Mound the lamb (and, if using, the potato) mix on top of the onions. Top with remaining onions and season lightly again, if desired. Fold the baking paper over the lamb mix and onions and seal the top and side edges by folding them together twice, to make a pouch. Then wrap the pouch well in the paper or foil to create a parcel and secure either with string, or by folding and crimping the foil. If the foil is thin, wrap the parcel in a second layer of foil. The parcel must be well sealed, so it keeps in the steam as much as possible. Place it on a baking tray. Bake in the oven at 160 degrees C for at least 3 or 3½ hours. Turn off the oven and let the parcel rest for about 15 minutes. Cut parcel open to serve.

(Although not traditional, I often open the parcel, peel the paper back and return it to the oven for 15 minutes at 190 degrees C before resting it, to add some caramelisation. The juices and onions make a delicious sauce when thickened.)

Alegra's Bunuelos with Honey

1 sachet (2¼ tsps) dry yeast

2⅓ cups warm water

½ tsp salt

1½ tsps sugar

1 tbsp oil

3 cups plain (all-purpose) flour

oil for deep frying

honey or powdered sugar and cinnamon to sprinkle,
    if desired

In a large bowl, stir the yeast into 1 cup of the warm water and allow to prove a few minutes. When bubbly, mix in the remaining water, salt, sugar and tablespoon of oil. Slowly stir in the flour, and keep stirring until you have a smooth, wet dough. Cover and allow to rise in a warm spot for at least 1 hour.

In a saucepan or frypan suitable for deep frying, heat several centimetres (at least 5 cm) of oil to between 190 and 200 degrees C.

Either drop spoonfuls of the dough in the oil or moisten hands in a bowl of water, take a small handful of the dough, form it into a rough ball and poke a hole through the centre. Drop carefully into the oil. Repeat for as many as will fit comfortably in the saucepan without touching, but do not crowd. Fry until golden brown on both sides, flipping them once. Remove them with a slotted spoon and drain them on paper towels. Drizzle with honey or dust with powdered sugar and serve immediately. They will soften and are not suitable to keep.

Rosie's Light as Air Sponge Cake

⅔ cup (100 g) cornflour

⅓ cup (50 g) self-raising flour

4 large eggs, at room temperature

⅔ cup caster sugar

1 tsp cream of tartar

½ tsp bicarb soda

pinch salt

½ tsp vanilla extract

Grease 2 x 18 cm (7 inch) round cake tins and line bases with baking paper. Preheat oven to 180 degrees C moderate.

Sift dry ingredients (except salt) three times. Separate eggs. Beat egg whites and salt until stiff. In a separate large mixing bowl, beat egg yolks, sugar and vanilla till thick. Sift the flour mixture over egg yolk mixture and fold in with a large metal spoon until just combined. Mix in about a third of the whites to loosen the yolk mix and then gently fold in remaining whites. Divide the mixture between the prepared tins. Bake for approximately 20 to 25 minutes or until cakes are golden, have shrunk away from the sides slightly and spring back to the touch. Turn out onto wire racks, carefully peel away baking paper and allow to cool completely. Sandwich sponges together with jam and whipped cream (or anything you wish) and sieve powdered sugar over the top, or spread with icing.

ACKNOWLEDGEMENTS

I'd like to thank my precious goddaughter Natasha Sullivan, whose beautiful face illuminates the cover of this book, for her patience, generosity and kindness, and to Simon Woodcock for the photography. I am also immensely grateful to Linda Nix of Golden Orb Creative for her invaluable help and guidance through the final editing and publishing process.